I SAW WILLY W
THE AIRPORT MEN'S ROOM.

In hot pursuit I shoved my way inside, where I was immediately confronted by a guy making good use of the urinal.

"Hey, babe. Something I can help you with?" he asked, turning slightly to show off his wares.

"Police business," I growled, keeping my eyes straight ahead. Somehow, I didn't think "Fish and Wildlife" would have the desired effect.

My bathroom Lothario quickly tucked himself in, zipped up his fly and fled.

Whoosh! A toilet roared. I checked under the row of doors and saw a pair of snakeskin boots in the end stall. Dropping to all fours, I saw Willy, intent as a bombardier on a mission, poised to drop five illegal parrot eggs into the toilet.

Plonk! The eggs plopped one by one into the water as I squirmed under the stall door, cursing the staff for not cleaning more often. I reached the toilet just as it gulped all five eggs in a victorious flush.

Willy smirked like a half-witted hyena. "Hey there, Agent Porter. What's the matter? Don't they allow you in the ladies' room no more?"

Other Avon Books by
Jessica Speart

BORDER PREY
GATOR AIDE
TORTOISE SOUP

JESSICA SPEART

BIRD BRAINED

A RACHEL PORTER MYSTERY

AVON BOOKS
An Imprint of HarperCollins*Publishers*

AVON BOOKS
An Imprint of HarperCollins*Publishers*
10 East 53rd Street
New York, New York 10022-5299

Inside cover author photo by George Brenner
Library of Congress Catalog Card Number: 98-91012
ISBN: 0-380-79290-7
www.avonbooks.com

First Avon Books printing: November 2000
First Avon Twilight printing: April 1999

Printed in the U.S.A.

10 9 8 7 6 5 4 3 2

For my mother:
If you don't like it, don't tell me!

Many thanks to Jennifer English, a top notch special agent with the USFWS; Lennie Jones, whose passion for protecting wildlife is inspiring; Regina Cussell for sharing her knowledge of parrots; and Connie Hansen and Russell Peacock for their hospitality during my trips to Miami.

And to George, who not only reads my manuscripts but puts up with the insanity.

One

The shine that emanated from Tony Carrera's white patent leather shoes ricocheted off the walls of the dingy warehouse. I hadn't planned on being at the cargo area of Miami International Airport on a Sunday night. Obviously Tony hadn't counted on my presence, either.

But I'd received a hot tip about a flight coming in from Brazil, and found myself with some time to kill. Besides, weekends at MIA are notorious. The U.S. Fish and Wildlife office is closed, so it's the perfect occasion to smuggle unlucky members of the animal kingdom in and out of Miami.

"For chrissakes, Porter! The shipment's already been cleared. What the hell else do you want?" Carrera fumed.

An exotic-animal dealer famous for trying to beat the system, Carrera had somehow finagled clearance on the paperwork for his reptile shipment sight unseen, days before it even arrived. His plan had been to sneak out of the warehouse after collecting his cargo. My surprise appearance had effectively screwed up his scheme.

"What I want is to open the boxes so that I can check what's inside," I calmly informed him.

"I don't got time for this crap," Carrera grumbled, chewing on the soggy remnants of a stogie. "Take a look at me, will ya?" He pushed out his chest as he gestured toward his apparel. "I'm not all dressed up for my health, ya know. I got a hot date right after I drop off these goods. Nice, huh?"

Carrera was the proud owner of a bad toupee which clung to his head like a poodle trying to keep its balance atop a bowling ball. Tonight he was decked out to kill in a pair of white polyester pants that highighted his huge belly. A short-sleeved paisley shirt of 100 percent nylon lay wide open, revealing a heavy gold chain nestled against a dark mat of fur, with additional chunks of jewelry adorning his wrists and his fingers. It was apparent that Tom Jones had little to worry about.

"After she catches a glimpse of you, I'm sure your date won't mind waiting the few extra minutes," I assured him.

Tony threw up his hands in frustration as I studied the documentation on the box before me. The paperwork listed its contents as "venomous snakes." Great—now I understood why it had been given clearance. Nobody liked to risk life and limb to examine a bunch of writhing, poisonous reptiles. Least of all, me. But I also knew that was exactly what dealers like Carrera counted on, which made it the perfect scam for sneaking wildlife and even drugs into the country. It's also one of the reasons why fewer than 10 percent of smuggled critters are ever caught. I was looking to up the ante.

I pried a crowbar under the wooden lip of the first crate, and the lid gave way with a creak. Then I picked up a snake hook and gloves. But Tony beat me to the punch, pulling a short-handled pair of tongs from inside his case.

"Oh, for chrissakes, Porter. These things are in bags. What the hell are you afraid of?" He pushed open the top and shoved his hand deep inside the crate, where he grabbed hold of a blue cloth bag.

A movement beneath the fabric caught my eye. "Tony, watch out! I think there's something loose on the bottom!"

Carrera twisted his head up toward me with a lewd grin. "All you chicks have the same problem with snakes—and I've finally figured out what it is. They're long and they're hard . . . but they won't buy you dinner."

As Tony broke into raucous laughter, I saw a pair of lidless eyes that gazed coldly up toward the light from deep within the dark wooden confines. A shiver sped through me, but faster than I could speak, a king cobra sprang up, revitalized by the rush of fresh air, the skin on its neck flaring out in a regal hood. Carrera's laugh abruptly caught in his throat as he zoomed in on my expression, his brain already guessing what had risen behind him. The snake's bronze eyes focused on its prey as a thin layer of sweat broke out on Carrera's skin.

"Oh, God," he whispered, his eyes beseechingly locked onto mine.

"Listen to me, Tony. I'll angle around and grab the snake with the hook. Just don't turn and look," I cautioned in a soft, even tone.

"No! Don't go anywhere. It'll strike!" Tony's voice was high and tight and his face was paler than his pants.

"Okay, Tony," I tried to calm him. "I'm going to very slowly get my gun. This will all be over in less than a minute."

"Don't you dare!" Carrera hissed, a drop of sweat slipping between his lips. "This thing cost me big time. Besides, I already got it sold. Shoot it and I'll sue you."

I stared at the man, wondering what other deadly goodies he had hidden in his crates and what he felt they were worth.

"All right," I said, working to keep my cool. "Then just move away slowly. Don't jerk and you'll be fine."

But Carrera could no longer restrain himself and swiveled around to confront the snake, which swayed in mesmerizing fashion.

"Oh, shit!" he shrieked.

My hand raced for my gun, but the cobra was faster. Lunging forward, it sank its fangs into Tony's forearm as he screamed. Just as quickly, the snake relinquished its hold with a quiver of victory. Tony jerked away and I slammed down the lid, locking the cobra back in its lair.

The critter must have packed quite a wallop. Within sixty seconds Carrera was down on the floor, jerking like a fish pulled out of water. Cobras are neurotoxic, so it was only a matter of time before Carrera's central nervous system began to shut down. He was already losing muscle coordination and his breathing had turned ragged and slow. I had to get him to Jackson Memorial as quickly as possible.

A cargo worker made me swear on my life, my mother's, and those of my unborn children, that the snake couldn't get out of its crate before he could be persuaded to come down off his forklift to help. That ate up precious minutes. By the time we'd half-carried, half-dragged Carrera into the back of my Ford Tempo, swelling had already begun to set in. I quickly pulled off his rings and bracelets before it was too late.

"Yuur nuffin' budda thif," Carrera moaned.

Slurred speech. Bad sign.

"You'll get it all back, Tony," I consoled him. "I just don't want you rupturing any body parts in my car."

I tore out of the cargo area, grateful that traffic was relatively light on Sunday nights. Any other time and Tony would have been down for the count. Swinging onto the Dolphin Expressway, I dragged out my cell phone and punched in the number for Dr. Bob Samuels.

I'd met Dr. Bob soon after I'd landed in Miami. Recurring headaches and nausea had sent me galloping to Jackson Memorial Hospital. I figured it was either side effects from my last assignment in southern Nevada, or I was pregnant. Neither prospect was thrilling. Dr. Bob ran a battery of tests, cost me a minor fortune, and told me to stay away from places that cause you to glow in the dark. We'd been friends ever since.

I filled Dr. Bob in on his latest patient. I only hoped the hospital was stocked with the appropriate antivenin.

"What's your estimated time of arrival?" he asked.

I surveyed the growing traffic that had mysteriously congregated before me and then glanced in my rearview mirror. Tony had begun to drool like a slap-happy Saint Bernard.

"That depends on how much my driving scares everyone else off the road."

Dr. Bob chuckled. "That should be no problem for you, Rachel. I'll expect to see you shortly."

Miami traffic is a melting pot of the craziest drivers in the world, from confused tourists to geriatric seniors to immigrants with their own rules of the road. I veered onto the shoulder, slammed my hand on the horn in lieu of a siren, and pressed down hard on the pedal until we were flying at warp speed, counting on convincing the other drivers that the lunatic barreling along the side of the expressway was too demented for them to even attempt to challenge. A few hardy souls went so far as to cheer me on. When I pulled up in front of the emergency room, Dr. Bob was ready and waiting.

By the time we slid him out of my car and onto a stretcher, Carrera's arm was the size of a championship watermelon. His uneven breathing had stopped, as had his drooling—though a memorial pool lay on the floor of my car.

I ran ahead with Dr. Bob, leaving Tony's bloated carcass to be rolled inside by strangers.

"Is he still alive?" I asked, wondering if I'd risked life and limb only for Tony to die thinking I'd stolen his jewelry.

Dr. Bob scratched the wispy whiskers on his chin that he insisted were a beard. "It may seem he's not breathing, but your guy is alive, all right. He can hear everything that's being said. He just can't respond."

Tony lay stiff as a day-old corpse, his eyes wide open. "Are you certain he isn't dead?"

"If someone's received a bad bite and I'm not totally sure they're still alive, I ask them to move their eyes. But trust me, this guy is fine." Dr. Bob's rail-thin body moved briskly down the hall like a greyhound in training, and ushered the stretcher into a small room where he readied an IV. "If you want, you can wait in here with your friend while I get the necessary supplies."

"What! I thought you'd have the antivenin ready and waiting!"

"Don't worry. I'll be back in plenty of time," Dr. Bob assured me.

I walked over to the stretcher and looked down at Carrera. Not a muscle moved. I felt for his pulse—it was barely there.

"God, Tony! Why didn't you just let me inspect the shipment properly? If you weren't always trying to smuggle things in, you wouldn't be in this mess."

I'd been after Carrera for the past six months, since I'd arrived in Miami. But Tony knew how to play the game too well, and had eluded me every time. This wasn't the way I'd have chosen to catch him. Then again, perhaps this brush with death would make him mend his ways.

"You know, Tony," I told him, "maybe you should give some thought to what you've been doing and start showing more respect for wildlife and the law. Otherwise, tonight's surprise inspection was just the beginning of what you can expect. I'm going to make certain that from now on, your shipments are never cleared ahead of time. I swear, Tony, I'll do whatever I have to, to nail you."

His face was now ashen and drawn. I touched his pulse for reassurance, and panic bells went off in my head as my fingers left his wrist and then rushed to his neck. Tony's pulse had gone from barely there to absolutely nothing.

Oh, no! "Please don't tell me you're dead! Come on, Tony, you can make it. Hang in there!" I grabbed his hand. "Move your eyes, Tony—even a little bit, to let me know you're still here."

If Carrera had been auditioning for the role of a zombie, he'd have won the part hands down.

"Oh, my God—he's dead! If only there'd been no traffic—if only I'd driven faster!" Then I started to get mad. "How could you be such a damn idiot? What the hell were you thinking, with your macho games with poisonous snakes? Was it worth it, Carrera? You made me crazy, but I didn't want you to die!"

Dr. Bob chose this moment to reappear with vials of antivenin in his arms.

"It's too late. I finished him off!" I wailed.

"What are you talking about, Porter? He was fine just a minute ago. Exactly what did you do?" he questioned.

"I was only talking to him, trying to show him the error of his ways. But I think I may have given him a heart attack!"

Dr. Bob rolled his eyes. "Remind me to keep you away from my other patients."

"His pulse is gone—and your sure-fire method of checking a victim's eyes? Carrera can't move them," I said frantically.

"Then what would you call that?" he asked calmly.

In amazement, I followed his finger to where a tear was creeping out of the corner of Carrera's right eye.

I watched as Dr. Bob readied the antivenin and stuck the needle in Carrera's arm. My pulse pounded hard enough to revive a corpse as I waited in silence, barely daring to breath until Tony began to come to. He opened his eyes and slowly rolled his head, stopping when I came into view. His tongue snaked out from between his lips, and he carefully worked his jaw. Finally he opened his mouth, doubtless to share some pearls of wisdom from his near brush with death.

"Goddamn you, Porter," he croaked.

A bubble of relief traveled up from my toes and settled in

my chest, and I could feel a giddy grin spread across my face like butter hitting a piece of toast.

At least this job is never dull.

I wriggled my way back into the conga line of traffic heading toward the airport. Rush hour in Las Vegas, my previous posting, had been a breeze compared to this. I hadn't asked to leave Nevada. The "powers that be" had decided I'd gone beyond making waves to a full tsunami, and my assignment to the "black hole" of Miami was considered the ultimate punishment.

"You'll see plenty of action," were my former boss's parting words. "Miami's a hotbed. There are not only more legal wildlife dealers per square mile in Miami than anywhere else in the world, it's also the center of the illegal live-animal trade in the entire U.S."

When you consider that the illegal-wildlife trade runs second only to drug smuggling, and that much of the merchandise for both comes from Latin America, you can see why Miami had become the smugglers' port of choice. Miami had the added distinction of having the worst wildlife law-enforcement record in the country. Careers weren't made here; they were destroyed.

There had been whispers that in the past, Fish and Wildlife agents and inspectors had been paid off by dealers to look the other way as shipments came in. It wouldn't have been hard to do. In a perfect world, every box and crate would have been opened and thoroughly checked. But more than 300 shipments of wildlife come in here every week, each shipment running anywhere up to 200 boxes. Stack that against six measly inspectors and you begin to get an idea of the odds. If you liked being a Fish and Wildlife inspector, every day could be considered Christmas in Miami.

I got into the airport just as the flight from Brazil finally landed. Miami International goes through a remarkable transformation with the setting of the subtropical sun. During the day, the terminal bustles with wholesome-looking families intent on enjoying a fun-filled vacation. With nightfall, Mom and Dad and the brood are replaced by a cast of characters straight out of a Fellini flick. It's Disneyland one minute and then *Satyricon* until dawn.

I waited for the Brazil flight to disembark, and soon saw my quarry, Willy Weed, limping toward me up the hall. A small-time breeder of cougars, Willy sold them to those longing to own a pet that could rip you in two. But Willy's love for wildlife didn't stop there. He was an equal-opportunity exploiter, selling whatever form of wildlife he could get his grimy hands on.

I routinely caught him smuggling in one or two reptiles at a time. Willy would simply pay his pittance of a fine, promise never to do it again, then go right back to business as usual. Our most recent encounter had taken place just a month ago, when Willy had gotten off a plane only to fall to the floor of the terminal screaming in pain. It seemed that the one-and-a-half-foot boa constrictor he'd hidden inside his boxer shorts hadn't been fed in a while. Not surprisingly, it proceeded to wrap itself tightly around the closest thing it could find.

Willy's ex-wife had passed on today's tip. He had foolishly let his alimony payments slide. In return, Bambi had decided to dish out some payback—and true to her word, here he was. Willy made a unique fashion statement, wearing a long winter coat that looked like something out of a bad spaghetti western, complete with a cowboy hat slapped on top of his head. Not exactly seasonal wear for your typical flesh-melting Miami summer.

Just then Willy caught my eye and took off, hobbling like an out-of-control Chester from an ancient episode of *Gunsmoke*. For a man with a limp, Willy slipped in and out of the crowd with remarkable ease. Every time I thought I had him cornered, he disappeared, until I again caught sight of his long greasy hair flying in a different direction. The crowd seemed to work like a wave, breaking apart to let Willy through and then closing ranks as soon as I came near. I called upon my old New York habit of jabbing to the left and pushing hard to the right. While it wasn't making me any new friends, it worked.

The cowboy hat was a recent affectation for Weed, in deference to a local sport. Willy was infamous for running down deer in the Everglades with his airboat. After that, he'd jump onto the frantic animal's back, grab its head, and slit its throat. The event had been dubbed the Homestead Rodeo, in homage to his hometown. Weed had proudly taken to calling himself "The Swamp Cowboy."

I preferred to refer to him as "Swamp Thing." If there was ever a walking, talking definition for the term "cracker," Willy had to be it.

It was due to such high-flying antics that Willy was saddled with a limp. He'd recently been balanced on the front of his airboat, preparing to leap for the kill, when his craft hit a rock. Weed was thrown head over heels and landed straight in the mud along with his rifle, which went off, shooting him clear through the knee.

I caught a whiff of Willy now—the smell half wet dog, half dead snake—and turned to see him entangled within a group of tourists. He bumped up against a hefty blonde sporting a head full of Bo Derek cornrows, who turned on Willy with a snarl and pummeled him to the ground. I seized the moment, but the airport gods weren't flying with me. As I sprinted forward, I knocked over a suitcase as I tripped on someone's foot, and came perilously close to being run down by a luggage cart, only to lose sight of Weed. I finally caught a glimpse of his cowboy hat and made a beeline for it, but the body beneath the hat no longer belonged to Weed. In its place was a geezer who gleefully cackled, pleased with the trick. He flashed me a rack of empty gums where his teeth should have been.

"Dat boy ain't here," he giggled. "He done disappeared."

Damn! Then I saw the sign for the men's room. I shoved my way inside, where I was confronted by a guy making good use of the urinal.

"Hey, babe. Something I can help you with?" he asked, turning slightly to show off his wares.

"Police business," I growled, keeping my eyes straight ahead. Somehow, I didn't think that "Fish and Wildlife" would have had the desired effect.

Presto! My bathroom Lothario quickly tucked himself in, zipped up his fly and fled.

Whoosh! A toilet roared as it flushed. I quickly checked

under the row of stalls, pounding on each one that sported a pair of feet.

"Willy?" I called, knocking on one of the doors. "Let me in!"

"Get away from here, you crazy bitch," came the reply. Unfortunately, it wasn't Weed's voice.

The flush of another toilet brought my attention to the stall at the end of the row. A pair of snakeskin boots clearly screamed, "Willy."

"I know you're in there, Weed. Come out now!" I ordered, ramming my shoulder hard against the metal barrier. I shoved once more against the door, then dropped to all fours. Sure enough, there was Willy, intent as a bombardier on a mission, poised to drop five eggs into the toilet. Any eggs coming out of Brazil were most likely those of parrots, which were as illegal as a smuggler could get.

Plonk! The eggs plopped one by one into the water as I squirmed under the stall door, cursing the hired help for not cleaning more often. I reached the toilet just as it gulped all five eggs in a victorious flush.

Willy stood smirking like a half-witted hyena. "Hey there, Porter. What's the matter? Don't they allow you in the ladies' room no more?"

His coat was lying next to the toilet, along with his T-shirt and a vest. As if the bathroom floor hadn't been disgusting enough, I was now confronted with the sight of Willy's naked flesh at very close quarters. A chest tattoo proudly proclaimed, 100% REDNECK. His rack of ribs gave him the appearance of a skeleton, and every inch of his skin was coated in sweat.

Willy dunked his hands into the toilet and slapped the bona fide eau de toilet under his arms and over his chest. Then, holding his breath, he immersed his entire head in the bowl. He came up for air shaking his wet hair like a coon dog after a hard chase, and droplets of liquid grease splattered against the tile wall. Weed was the living, breathing poster boy of what not to bring home to mother.

"Done freshening up?" I asked.

Willy grabbed his T-shirt off the floor and rammed it over his head, where its neck caught on the cougar's-tooth earring that dangled from his lobe. The black T-shirt was unfurled to reveal a white skull along with the motto, BAD TO THE BONE.

I gingerly picked his wet vest up off the floor, and held it at arm's length as I examined it. Made of spandex, it resembled a large Ace bandage except that rows of pockets had been sewn into its interior. They were just the right size for carrying eggs. Worn close to his body, the vest had functioned as a portable incubator.

"How long have you been dealing in birds, Willy?" I wondered which endangered species had just been flushed down the toilet.

"What you talking about, Porter?" he sneered. "I don't see no birds in here. You see birds in here? Course, if you like, I'll be glad to show you my cockatoo."

Willy flashed me a grin, exposing a gold tooth with a ruby lodged in its center. I wondered if he'd sprung for the bucks to have it implanted, or if he'd just superglued it himself. His fingers tickled the metal teeth of his fly. I'd already seen more of Weed than I ever wanted; one more inch of exposed flesh and I'd scream.

"Save it, Willy, or you'll spend the night in jail," I warned.

Weed didn't have the funds for a trip to Brazil, which meant that he was working as a mule for someone else—someone with enough money and smarts not to get caught smuggling parrot eggs himself. Pinpricks of anticipation raced through my veins. So far, my time in Miami had been filled with too many Willy Weeds and Tony Carreras. I was itching to hit something big.

I carefully probed each pocket of the vest, searching for a piece of eggshell. What I came up with was a minuscule dab of yolk. While it wasn't much, I played the speck for all it was worth.

"I don't need the eggs, Willy. I've got all the necessary proof right here." I pointed to the yolk, giving him a "gotcha" look, hoping to con him through the sheer force of my will. "You know what DNA is, Willy?"

Weed caressed the stubble that covered his chin and washed down his throat. "Hmm. Let's see. That must stand for Dumb New York Asshole." Willy cupped his hand to his ear. "What? No winning bell? So, where's my *Jeopardy* prize?"

"Very cute, Willy. But if it turns out that you were carrying endangered parrot eggs, you'll be watching *Jeopardy* from behind bars for a long time to come.''

Weed wasn't intimidated by the threat—but then, there was no reason to be. The majority of wildlife crimes are hard to prove, which explains why endangered critters have exploded into the latest rage in the criminal world. Trade in illegal wildlife is nearly as lucrative as dealing in drugs. But that's where the similarity ends. Get caught with a kilo of coke and it's off to jail you go. Get caught with a hot bird and you get a slap on the wrist and a $500 fine, at worst.

Weed held his wrists out toward me. ''Go ahead, Porter. Cuff me. Take me to the big house, why doncha?'' He laughed maniacally.

I tried my best to act like I had some leverage. ''Listen, Willy. I know you're working for someone, so why take the fall? Just tell me who it is and it'll be as if I never caught you.''

''That's a good one, Porter,'' Willy said. ''Right now all I'd need is a *half*-assed lawyer to prove that you haven't got me. I believe what I have here is a win-win situation.'' A smirk plastered itself across his face.

But I refused to give in. ''I hear you haven't been to see Bambi in a while. What say we take a trip over to her place right now and let the two of you have an intimate little tête-à-tête?''

Willy's smirk instantly vanished. According to a police report, his last visit home hadn't been exceptionally cozy. What had begun as a dispute over alimony payments had ended up with Willy on the floor and Bambi straddling him, threatening to ''Bobbittize'' him, adding substance to her vow by waving a large, sharp butcher's knife in her right hand. Fortunately for Willy, his screams had alerted a neighbor who had called the police.

His hands strayed toward his groin now. ''For chrissakes, all right! If I puke up the information, you promise to keep that bitch away from me?''

''Sure, Willy.'' I'd already given Bambi the name of a lawyer who had a reputation as a homicidal psychopath armed with a law degree. With two kids, a stack of bills, and a mortgage, Bambi needed all the help she could get.

"So, who were you supposed to deliver the eggs to Willy?"

"Alberto Dominguez," he hissed from between clenched teeth.

The name caught me by surprise. "Is that also who hired you?" I pressed.

"For chrissakes, lady," swore a gruff voice from the neighboring stall. "You wanna tell me where a guy has to go in order to crap in peace around here?"

"Try the ladies' room," I snapped. "All right, Willy. Give it up."

Weed's eyes were hard. "I don't know who I was hired by."

I shook my head. "How could you have no idea who's paying you to do the job? You'll have to do better than that."

"Yeah? Well, how is it that you were hired by Fish and Wildlife to slow down the trade, but have yet to make a good case?" Willy retorted.

The guy was beginning to get on my nerves.

Weed sneered at me. "Fuck you, Porter. I've told you what I know. I'm outta here."

"Whatever you say, Willy. Want to pick up some flowers for Bambi here, or should we stop on the way to her place?" I reminded him.

A vein began to throb in Willy's forehead like a metronome keeping time to a silent beat. "I ain't going to Bambi's," he sulked.

I rattled the handcuffs clipped to my belt suggestively.

Willy scratched under both armpits. "Listen, Porter. All I know is I got a call from some guy telling me there'd be a plane ticket in my name at the Avianca counter. The only other information I cared about was who'd be shelling out the bucks once the job was done."

Weed's hands left his armpits to ferociously scratch at his back and his sides. I took a step away.

"And that was?" I began to feel itchy myself as I watched Willy rub his back against the tile wall.

"Dominguez." Willy's fingertips were now on a search and destroy mission along the top of his head. "Cash on delivery."

I figured there was a good chance that Weed was leaving out some vital information, but I also knew that was all I'd get from him for now. I let myself out of the stall before Willy's vermin could spread.

Two

I squeezed my Ford back onto the Dolphin Expressway and headed south for the Palmetto. My pulse was racing faster than the speedometer on my car, which was stuck at an infuriating thirty-five miles per hour.

Alberto Dominguez. Damn him! Alberto was supposed to be one of my main informants. A local bird breeder whom I'd nailed a few months ago by chance, he had disembarked at Miami International carrying more than just his luggage: He also had a parrot stuffed inside each pocket of his coat.

Alberto had dosed the birds with a shot of tequila before boarding the plane in Mexico City, and all went as planned while the parrots lay in a deep, dreamless sleep. But as luck would have it, he crossed my path just as the parrots awoke, nursing a hangover and pissed off as hell. Alberto's pockets suddenly sprang to life, screeching and flapping. I'd threatened to make his life everlasting misery unless he consented to turn informant. Alberto quickly agreed.

Like much else in this world, a former TV show had contributed to the sudden surge in exotic birds. Robert Blake's career had tanked after the series BARETTA, but his costar, a wisecracking cockatoo mouthing mucho macho attitude, inspired a demand for parrots and macaws that skyrocketed straight through the roof.

That's when the carnage began.

Peasants were paid to snatch chicks from their nests inside hollow limbs. Soon, 200-year-old trees were being chopped, hacked, and chainsawed to get to the nestlings, but eight out of ten babies never survived the process. Of those that did, another 90 percent ended up dying in transit. And since the adult parrots had been left without nests to breed in, the bird population plummeted. In the grand American tradition of supply and demand, prices soared, making parrots and macaws the most sought after of all endangered species. Then in 1992 Uncle Sam stepped in, outlawing the importation of all wild-caught birds. And bingo! A booming legit business was born. The domestic breeding of parrots and macaws quickly became a multimillion-dollar industry, with the land of citrus and sun its hub.

That's where Alberto came in. Bird breeders in southern Florida had recently become the newest target for thieves. At large breeding compounds, up to $250,000 worth of birds could be snatched in a single heist. Word had it that the thefts were the work of a Cuban gang with a pipeline into the black market. I'd given Alberto the mission of discovering the mastermind behind the plot. What I hadn't counted on was being double-crossed.

I turned off the Palmetto and onto Dixie Highway. Wall-to-wall strip malls guided my way. I sped past condos which melted into trailer parks which in turn bumped up against used-car lots, their banners screeching of bargains. Fast-food bodegas beckoned for me to pull in and stop, but I was too angry at Alberto to give fried plantains more than a fleeting thought. An infinite series of traffic lights further added to my bad mood. By the time I swerved onto Southwest 248th Street, I could have propelled the Tempo on my head of steam.

I headed toward the Redlands as row after row of tall, ghostly palms appeared and then vanished, momentarily illuminated by a sly moon playing hide-and-seek behind a bank of foreboding clouds. I pressed down hard on the gas pedal, speeding up to match the pounding of my pulse as the night streaked by.

As the moon darted out once more, Dominguez's compound came into view, its front wall of concrete crowned with gleaming barbed wire. An electrified fence added further protection, stretching back to cover the rear. Alberto's house and aviary lay nestled inside. Dominguez had sworn to me on his mother's grave that all of his 250 feathered occupants were completely legal, born and bred within these compound walls. Now I questioned that.

I pulled up and pushed against the car door, which creaked and groaned in protest, refusing to open more than halfway. This had become a battle of wills, which so far, the Ford was winning. I shimmied out of the car and walked up to the gate, looking around. The block was deserted except for a utility van parked down the street, though no workmen were in sight. A flurry of thunderstorms had rolled through the other night, keeping the power company busier than usual.

I pressed the bell and waited, the gathering silence as heavy as the humidity. Either Alberto wasn't home, or Weed had already called and warned him of my impending visit. I leaned against the security gate as I considered the best way to sneak in. Fortunately, I didn't have to battle barbed wire; the gate swung open beneath my weight.

I squeezed back inside my car and drove up to the house, not daring to step outside without first calling to Cariba, the compound's trained killer dog. Surprisingly, no warning snarls or gnashing teeth came hurtling my way. I cautiously left the Ford, on guard for a sneak attack as I walked up to the front door. On previous visits, the buzzer could scarcely be heard above the raucous squawks and screeches of hundreds of birds. This time the bell rang crystal clear. I was beginning to suspect Alberto had packed up his parrots and hotfooted it out of town.

I gathered my courage and headed toward the back of the compound. If Cariba was going to attack, I figured she would have done so by now. I passed by Alberto's black Ferrari, snoozing in his open-shed garage. And then I saw a large, gaping hole cut in the fence, breaching the compound's security. The ominous silence grew heavier as it drew in tightly around me.

The back door opened at my touch, as if I'd been expected. Alberto kept all his birds inside the house, taking every precaution to guard against robbery. On a good day, bird shit and feathers lightly coated the floor. Apparently, this had been a bad one.

It was as if a down comforter had been sliced open, its contents tossed wildly about the room. Feathers clung to my sneakers as I passed cage after cage, each standing as empty as a desecrated coffin. The trail of scattered plumage looked like a fan dance gone berserk. I followed it into the breeding room. Normally filled with the raucous cries of mating, now not even the ghost of a peep could be heard. Phantom wings next herded me into the nursery, where not a single hatchling was to be found.

A tiny feather worked its way up inside my nose to tickle my nostrils, the torment continuing until I sneezed, stirring up a storm of down which gently settled on my shirt and in my hair. I stared in disbelief around me. Every single bird had disappeared, down to the eggs that usually lay fast asleep, safe in their incubators. Like breadcrumbs, the feathers continued their trail, luring me still deeper inside the house.

Room after room merged, all one jumbled mess of furniture that had been slashed and torn. Piles of papers lay scattered, occasionally caught up in a medley of stuffing and springs.

I was of two minds. I was eager to corner Alberto and tear into him for his dealings with Willy Weed. But if he hadn't flown the coop, I was afraid of what I might find.

I received my answer as I stood rooted at the bedroom doorway. Alberto lay on his back, his limbs flung against the hard wooden floor, his face a Kabuki mask of red streaks and long, jagged gashes. The pattern of rough slices continued down his throat and ripped through his chest, where strips of his shirt clung in long, lifeless tatters. Alberto's once ruddy complexion was now ghostly white, as if the blood had been drained from his flesh. The majority of it had been, and was now splattered against the walls.

I took a deep breath, struggling to regain my equilibrium, which was spinning faster than a carnival ride. I leaned my hand against the entry to steady myself, only to pull away, my palm suddenly sticky and wet. The room began to close in, cutting off my supply of air. I realized that the blood was still fresh. Pinpricks of moisture broke out over my face and neck, erupted on my chest, and slithered down my back. I rummaged for a tissue in my purse, but as hard as I wiped, Alberto's blood clung stubbornly to my skin, then sank beneath flesh and bone, pounding in rhythm with my own.

Get a grip! You've done this before!

But confronting death still wasn't easy. Alberto had died

with his mouth and eyes open wide in terror, emitting a silent scream that swept around the room. Dots of moisture froze in place on my flesh, tiny ice sculptures held prisoner thanks to the magic of air-conditioning. A wave of nausea engulfed me.

I concentrated on taking slow, steady breaths until the room began to recede, reverting to its normal scale. It was then that a torn swatch of fabric caught my eye. As I walked over and picked it up, Alberto's eyes followed me like those in a dime-store painting of Jesus; refusing to let go, insisting I unlock their secret. The scrap was a piece of his shirt, wet and slimy to the touch.

I quickly stood up and went in search of a phone. It wasn't until I walked back through the clutter of the living room that I noticed the large muslin sack that sat on the floor. I bent over the bag, my fingers working to loosen the drawstring that held the top closed. The fabric rustled against my skin, chiding my clumsiness even as it urged me to move faster. Finally the knot came undone.

Inside lay six colorful parrots in a drugged sleep, unaware of what had taken place around them. But there was no time to register much else—I suddenly knew I wasn't alone. Nothing definite had tipped me off to the threat; just a tightening of my stomach, the moisture turning clammy again on my flesh. As the hair rose on the back of my neck, I heard a sound—a low, throaty cough that came from directly behind me.

I dipped into my purse for my gun, but I didn't move fast enough. An arm swung from behind, clamping around my neck. I struggled to wedge my fingers under it but the harder I fought, the tighter the arm pressed down on my windpipe, cutting off the air until I was gasping for breath. My heart kicked into high gear, sprouting hundreds of wings that beat all at once, but there was nowhere for me to fly.

The grip constricted still tighter and my mind began to shut down. I made a last ditch effort, frantically ramming my elbow back as hard as I could. A throb of pain shot through my forearm, sending sparks of electricity skittering into my fingers as my attacker let loose a low grunt. Then a hand whipped round in front of my face, a handkerchief in its grip. I took one last gasp as a familiar odor raced straight for my brain, the cloth molding itself to my nose and mouth as I fell into the gaping darkness that stretched out before me.

I was aware of the steady pounding in my head before I realized I lay sprawled on the floor. No hangover had ever been like this before. I brushed aside the cobwebs in my mind as a raging fire kicked in, burning the back of my throat in a fury. Then I remembered. I hadn't been drinking. I closed my eyes and listened. No guttural cough could be heard; only Alberto's silent scream which slithered around me, as constricting as any choke hold.

I inched my way up, resting on my butt before attempting to rise to my feet. My eyes throbbed as they struggled to focus; my fingertips gingerly probed my neck. I scanned the room, but my attacker was nowhere to be seen. Also missing was the muslin sack with its valuable cargo. In its place was a white handkerchief. I picked it up and took a whiff, only to have the drum in my head pound harder. Chloroform still clung to the fabric.

Goose bumps covered me like a second skin. The murder could have been the work of the Cuban bird ring. Even worse, I might have been responsible: it was at my insistence that Alberto had set out to infiltrate the group. Perhaps his ruse had been uncovered and this was his punishment for planning to squeal. Up till now, the gang had stuck to robbery. Alberto might have been their turning point.

I hauled myself up and dug through the mess, finally locating Alberto's phone. But the effort proved to be worthless—I couldn't get a dial tone. Either Alberto hadn't paid his bill, or last night's storm had knocked out the line.

I headed outside to the Tempo and dug through my black hole of a glove compartment, finally excavated my cell phone, then placed a call to Metro Dade to report Alberto's death. I'd still have plenty of time to poke around on my own. When it came to dealing with dead bodies, Metro Dade police were thoroughly buried up to their necks. They would be in no rush to get to another.

I wrestled my way back into my car, where I grabbed a flashlight and a pair of white cotton gloves before walking down the driveway and out the front gate. Sure enough, a wire hung dangling from the telephone pole that led to Alberto's domain. It didn't take much examination to reveal that the damage wasn't due to any storm, though. The wire had clearly been cut.

I hightailed it back inside the house, anticipation sharpening my curiosity. The best way to get to know someone is to have free rein to prowl through that person's things. Unfortunately, this isn't considered socially acceptable in most cultures. Unless, of course, that person is dead. I donned the gloves and let my fingers do the walking as I poked through Alberto's closets and drawers, resolutely ignoring his corpse.

I soon found the four coolers stashed beneath Dominguez's bed. Why do people always think that's the last place a robber will look? The tune "Getting to Know You" began to play in my mind as I flipped open the first lid. The cooler was chock full of illegal cigars—pedigree Cubans, straight from Havana. The other containers held exactly the same. Altogether, 120 boxes of Cubans lay neatly wrapped in plastic, nestled inside their makeshift humidors. Either Alberto had quit the smoking habit, or he'd been busy raking in mucho dinero. Each individual smoke could sell for up to fifty dollars on the black market.

It's been illegal to import and sell such cigars since 1962, when JFK slapped a trade embargo on Cuba. Punishment for violating that is severe. Alberto could have received a $250,000 fine and ten years in jail for his crime—a far harsher penalty than he would have paid for hawking endangered species. Looked like Alberto had found himself a sideline. I closed the lids and moved on, certain he must have something I'd find of more interest.

In the living room, Alberto's desk offered fertile snooping ground. Poking through drawers has always come as second nature to me, and my fingers danced through the minutiae of Alberto's life. A stack of bills included one from a local feed company for bags of bird seed, along with another from a lingerie store for a number of girdles and bras. The thought that Alberto might have been a cross-dresser was quickly dismissed. A mistress with a weakness for lingerie seemed more likely.

I moved on to the next drawer, which contained an assortment of anti-Castro propaganda. An array of bumper stickers proclaimed CUBA SÍ, CASTRO NO, while another variation touted, NO CASTRO = NO PROBLEM. It was unusual in Miami not to find a car without at least one such sticker plastered onto its rear.

The bottom drawer served as Dominguez's file cabinet, where hanging folders held receipts for assorted bills. While it was nice to know that Alberto had paid regular visits to his doctor and dentist, I skipped past those files, being privy to his current state of poor health. My fingers kept going until they reached a folder marked BREEDS, with a complete inventory of Alberto's birds. Recorded were the usual blue-and-gold, scarlet, and military macaws, along with yellow-naped Amazons and African greys. Other charts noted purchases, births, and sales. But nowhere was there a listing of what I could have sworn I'd seen lying inside the muslin sack: a pair of hyacinth macaws.

Rare and highly protected, hyacinths are hard to mistake. They're giant birds with distinct cobalt-blue plumage, golden eye rings, and sickle-shaped beaks that can easily sever a finger. Only 3,000 still fly free in their jungle home of Brazil, making the birds worth their weight in gold. A single hyacinth sells for a cool $12,000, while a breeding pair can easily fetch $30,000 or more.

But that wasn't all that had been in the bag. I'd spotted bright green feathers with splashes of red at the throat: four Cuban Amazons had rounded out the booty. Found only on the island of Cuba, the birds' numbers have dwindled thanks to hunting and habitat loss.

In 1492, Christopher Columbus took forty Cuban Amazons back to Spain as gifts for the king and queen. It appears he started a trend. These days, the birds are smuggled out of the country in suitcases, bras, and coats. As illegal as Cuban cigars, Amazons come with a hefty price tag, snagging up to $5,000 apiece. I knew that Alberto hadn't been breeding Amazons.

The fact that he had no records of the six birds' existence meant only one thing: they'd been smuggled into the country.

My attention became riveted back on Alberto's bedroom. I'd consciously ignored the low whistle when it had first begun, certain my mind was playing tricks. I'm not always good in strange houses late at night, with dead bodies lying around. But the noise continued, growing progressively louder. I flashed back to the low, throaty cough with its chloroform kick and my skin instantly turned cold.

I shot a glance through the doorway, checking to make sure that Alberto's corpse hadn't moved, my antennae finely tuned to poltergeist alert.

There's no such thing as ghosts! I reminded myself.

Who was I kidding? My knees were shaking at the mere thought.

Just as mysteriously, the sound stopped. I stood and listened for a moment, cursing my overactive imagination.

Wuss! I scolded, planting a mental swift kick.

Then the sound cranked back up, nearly shooting me right out of my skin. I could either make a run for the door and cower outside while I waited for backup, or, putting my rusty acting skills to use, pretend I was Peter Falk and *Columbo* it as best I could.

I slowly approached the bedroom, keeping an eye out for any unusual signs—say, a large corpse hurtling by. But Alberto was still in his place. I tiptoed around the body and headed toward the bed, and the sound instantly stopped.

"Hello?" I whispered, every nerve in my body on end.

"Hello!" hurtled back the reply.

A startled cry escaped me. In response came an uncanny imitation, accompanied by movement beneath the covers of the unmade bed. I warily grasped the top sheet and quickly pulled it back, unmasking the culprit below.

A large, glossy white cockatoo stared up at me, the deep pink feathers of its crest standing erect in salute. I'd heard that Alberto had a special bird he'd been close to, one that even slept with him. My money was on the avian mimic that now waddled toward me like a bad Charlie Chaplin routine. The bird teetered back and forth, balancing on short legs and oversized feet, its wings spread to keep from toppling over. Without so much as a how-de-do, it hopped onto my arm and proceeded to climb up my shoulder. By the time I remembered my earrings, it was too late.

''Stop that!'' I ordered, caught in a tug of war to remove the gold hoop from its beak.

Fortunately, my feathered friend seemed to prefer conversation to chomping on jewelry. ''Stop, thief! Stop!'' the bird responded.

I deftly removed both earrings before he could make another swipe at them. ''A little late for that, isn't it?'' I reminded him.

The bird wrapped its beak around my curls and gave a good jerk, which helped jump-start my brain. I realized that the creature that had hold of my red mop was the only eyewitness to Alberto's murder. It had been cunning enough to escape being caught. Who knew what he might eventually decide to screech and tell?

A car door slammed, announcing the crew from Metro Dade had arrived. I spied a perch in the corner of the room and placed my secret weapon on it, telling him to sit tight. Then I headed outside to find Vern Reardon and Mervyn Tubbs walking the grounds. That was enough to tell me that the chief didn't consider the case to be worthy of star billing.

Reardon was on the fast track to retirement, with only six months to go before he turned in his badge and gun. He'd never been one to burn up shoe leather when it came to an investigation, and he saw even less sense in doing so now. These days, Reardon spent his time daydreaming about his version of paradise: a shack on the Keys with a rod and a reel and an endless supply of cheap beer.

The biggest clue into Mervyn Tubbs' character was that he considered Vern the paragon of what a cop should be.

Alberto must never have given a dime toward any local Metro Dade funds. Otherwise, a different duo would have certainly been assigned.

Vern was checking around the place with about as much interest as ticks on a yard dog. ''You're looking in the wrong area, Vern. Try over here,'' I advised, pointing out the gaping hole in the security fence.

Vern did a slo-mo take, first staring at the breach before raising his flashlight to shine it on me. ''Hey, there, Porter. I had a funny feeling you'd be around.''

Hmm. I wondered if that was because I'd discovered the

body, and called it in. "You might want to check the telephone pole just in front of the gate. The wire's been cut," I added.

But Vern wasn't about to be rushed. "Slow down, Porter. It ain't like Alberto's going nowhere."

He ran a hand across the salt-and-pepper hair he cut to resemble a Fuller brush, and lifted his chin as if he were about to bay at the moon. Instead, he pulled a couple of Twix bars out of his pocket and threw one in my direction. I reached out and caught it, calling it dinner. "What are you doing here, anyway?" he asked.

I went for the easy explanation in between bites of chocolate and caramel. "Whoever killed Alberto made off with his birds."

Vern stuffed the entire bar into his mouth and began taking slow, deliberate chomps. "Pwob da cube gan," he responded, cookie crumbs flying like projectiles in every direction.

"What's that?" I tried to sidestep the airborne debris.

"He said it was probably the Cuban gang," Mervyn interpreted.

Weighing a good 300 pounds, Tubbs took small, delicate bites out of a king-size Hershey bar, hoping to make it last the whole night. I often wondered how Mervyn managed to stay on the force, certain that one good chase after a perp would do him in.

"You go take a look at that phone wire, Mervyn," Reardon directed. "I'm gonna check out the house with Annie Oakley here."

"Yeah, John Wayne and I have got it covered," I added, flashing a grin.

Tubbs frantically shook his head, his eyes bulging wide. He'd once let it slip that Wayne was Reardon's idol. Ever since, that's what Vern had been dubbed by the younger cops.

"What's that you said?" Vern glared.

Apparently, Tubbs had forgotten to mention just how sensitive Vern was about being ribbed. Great. What I didn't need tonight was any enemies on the police force.

I scrambled for cover. "You know—Annie Oakley—Westerns—John Wayne. It's free association."

Vern gave me a suspicious glance before he turned around

and walked off in perfect John Wayne fashion, his hand hovering above his revolver. I followed my Metro Dade gunslinger inside the house.

Reardon sneezed as a cloud of feathers rose up to greet him. "Yep. Seems the Cubans got all the birds. Must have been one hell of a haul." He reached inside his nose and pulled out a small pinfeather.

"I'm not so sure it was the Cuban gang," I ventured. "This isn't their usual MO."

"MO, huh?" Reardon kicked at a pile of down. "That's a good one. Where'd you pick that up, Porter? From watching *Miami Vice*?"

I didn't bother to inform him that *Miami Vice* had gone off the air ages ago. "That gang is into stealing birds. They're not looking to do hard time. I don't believe they'd raise the stakes by killing someone."

Vern reached up and tugged at the phantom brim of an invisible cowboy hat, in silent tribute to the Duke. "There ya go. That just shows me how much you don't know. Hell, those Cubans are a vicious bunch that are capable of doing most anything. They've changed the goddamn face of Miami almost overnight."

He was right about that. Now there was good food and music in town.

I led the way through the rubble to Dominguez's bedroom, where Vern shook his head as he scanned the body, his tongue clucking like a manic hen. "Now, there's a real Cuban rubout if ever I saw one."

He had me on that one. "What exactly makes this a Cuban rubout?" I wondered if I'd missed some vital clue, like a runaway plate of rice and beans, or a poster of Che Guevara that had been left behind.

"It just is." Vern scowled, refusing to give away any trade secrets. "I got a sixth sense when it comes to these things." He knelt down by Alberto's mangled form. "See how those boys have gone and knifed the hell out of one of their own? There aren't too many Caucasians would do something this vicious."

"Yeah, you're right. Jeffrey Dahmer would have done a much neater job," I replied.

The knot in my stomach was coiled tight as a spring, the Twix bar as heavy as lead. The only other time I'd witnessed a slice job this close had been in New Orleans, when a stripper had been murdered. That, and when a razor had danced across my own throat, scarring me in more ways than I cared to admit.

I bent down and focused on the cuts, working to block out Alberto's insistent eyes. I stared at the deep puncture wounds that circled his neck. My heart pounded like a Caribbean steel drum.

Focus. Focus and concentrate.

I studied the trail of jagged, angry gashes that ripped through Alberto's flesh. The thin sliver of lines that had covered the stripper were as fine and distinct as those on a road map; a murderous work of art. Alberto's savage slashes screamed out in rage, every tear an obscene violation.

"Maybe he wasn't killed with a knife at all," I thought out loud.

Vern's chin dropped to his chest, as if an invisible force had sucked all the strength from his neck. Then he shook his head in mock resignation. Taking a deep breath, he exhaled in a loud sigh, letting me know he'd been expecting me to make trouble.

"Okay. I'm game. What did him in then?" Vern instantly raised his hand to hold back my answer. "Don't tell me; let me guess. Musta been a weed whacker. Right?"

I ignored the sarcasm. The sound I'd heard before being attacked washed over me again. "It might have been some kind of animal."

Vern chuckled, apparently feeling mighty high in the saddle. "Yeah, that's it. Maybe he didn't feed his birdies the kind of seed they like, so they all got together and pecked him to death."

He slapped the outside of his holster, sharing a good laugh with the Duke. "You got critters on the brain, Porter."

Mervyn had finished outside and now waddled toward us, transporting enough feathers to resemble an overfed, partially plucked turkey.

"Hey, Vern, you're right—it coulda been just like in the movie that fat guy made. Where a bunch of birds swoop down and attack all the people in town?'' Tubbs stuck a finger in his mouth, dislodging a hunk of leftover chocolate. ''It didn't matter a dang that the townsfolk closed all their windows and bolted their doors. Those darn birds still managed to get in. They nearly poked one guy's brains clean out of his head. Heck, they also pecked straight through some poor woman's eyes. Folks found her upstairs dead as a doorknob, right there in her own attic, with two big holes where her blinkers shoulda been.'' Mervyn's chins wobbled as he warmed to the topic. ''The damn birds beat a few people up just by slapping 'em around with their wings. They scared the hell out of that poor Tippi gal, real bad. She got stuck in this phone booth, see, and all these big birds began ramming real hard on the glass. You remember her, Vern? She grew up to be that Melanie Griffith's mom.''

Vern had his shoulders hunched up around his neck, a shiver working its way from the base of his spine to the top of his head. ''Will you cut it out with the damn birds already?'' He glared at Tubbs. ''You're giving me a case of the heebie-jeebies.''

''What's the matter there, Vern? Dead bodies finally beginning to get to you?''

The unexpected voice took me by surprise. I bolted up and turned to see Hal Cooper, a medical examiner with Metro Dade. He strolled through the doorway, the bounce in his walk making it look as if he'd swallowed a jumping bean. A muffled clap of thunder roared off in the distance.

''My calling card,'' he grinned, and then gave me a wink.

He was what my grandmother would have called a dandy. Whenever I saw Cooper, I came away feeling like Secondhand Rose. He was always impeccably dressed; every white hair in his jaunty mustache lay neatly in place; and his manicured nails gleamed like ten tiny headlights set on high beam. It was enough to make a girl give up before she even got started.

He sauntered over, careful not to step in Alberto's blood. ''So, what do you say, Rachel? Have you changed your mind yet? Ready to give an older, experienced man a try?''

Besides being impeccable and jaunty, the man was also notoriously horny, hitting on any woman in sight.

''For chrissakes, Coop! Can't you rein in those raging hormones of yours for one goddamn minute?'' Vern asked, exasperated. ''What the hell kind of vitamins are you taking, anyway?''

For the past three months, Cooper had steadily bombarded me in an all-out blitz to go on a date. It seemed the more I refused, the more determined he became.

''I'm afraid you'd be too much for me, Hal,'' I'd told him, knowing I was right. He'd caught me alone in his office just once. By the time I made it out, I'd had the best aerobic workout of my life. Running from him made my NordicTrac feel like child's play.

''I'm not going to give up,'' he told me with a determined smile.

How lucky could a gal get? One dead man at my feet and one live suitor champing at the bit. It was enough to send me running for the nearest bar.

Vern brought Hal's attention back to the issue at hand. ''Porter's trying to horn in on this investigation by claiming it was a critter did in ol' Alberto. What do you make of that, Coop?'' Reardon grinned, waiting to see me shot down.

Hal Cooper momentarily held his missile in abeyance, as he pulled out a pair of wire-rimmed spectacles and slipped them on, taking plenty of time to gaze up and down my denim-clad form. Only then did he kneel next to Dominguez and study the pattern of gashes.

''So, what do ya, think?'' Vern prodded.

''I don't know,'' Hal murmured, sneaking another look in my direction. ''Not ready to say just yet. But those puncture wounds on the body look like they could have been made by some mighty sharp teeth.''

I'd been vindicated! ''And I'm pretty sure Hannibal Lecter didn't stop by,'' I gloated.

I knelt next to Hal to see the puncture wounds that I'd missed on my first go-around. He scooted over until our thighs were nearly touching, then pointed out a series of two distinct perforation marks.

''Of course, you're forgetting one thing,'' Coop added, capturing my hand between his. ''If it *had* been some sort of animal, Alberto would have been torn apart. Visualize the enormous upper and lower canines that most large critters have. You know your predators, Rachel.''

I knew enough to recognize there was one hovering right next to me. Hal lightly tickled my palm with the tip of his finger, infecting me with Vern's heebie-jeebies. I pulled my hand out of his grip and moved away from his side.

''Don't be angry, sweetheart,'' Coop continued. ''Just think about it for a minute. Most likely, Alberto's scalp would have been ripped off. The critter's claws would also have eviscerated the poor son of a gun. Being a natural-born hunter, our predator would probably have gutted him next, and then made a meal out of his liver.''

Hal's eyes performed a seductive tango, his mustache twitching to the tune. ''Add a little Chianti to that and it doesn't sound half bad. What say we discuss this over a bottle of vino tomorrow night?''

''I've got plans,'' I hissed, furious with Cooper for flirting while grinding my theory into dust. ''And don't call me sweetheart.''

But I couldn't fault him on his reasoning. I felt like a total fool, allowing my eagerness to overcome my objective judgment. Then again, this wasn't the first time. I knew it also wouldn't be the last. I could almost hear Vern snicker under his breath.

Hal joined the other two men as I continued to concentrate on the scars. I studied the gashes up the chest to where Alberto's throat had been slashed, and then followed them down his arms. Though his left arm was badly torn apart and the shirtsleeve was ripped to shreds, a flash of green and red stood out on the remaining skin of the bicep. On closer examination, I realized the colors were a tattoo. The trio of men were deep in discussion of a pay raise, so I quickly lifted what was left of Alberto's sleeve to snatch a better view. The tattoo was partially obscured by blood, but enough remained so there was no mistaking the symbol drawn on his arm. It was a parrot with a rifle clutched tight in its talons.

I released the fabric as the men brought their discussion back around to the corpse at hand.

''I'll autopsy the body and have more information on his death in a few days,'' Cooper said, returning to my side.

"Why don't you come by my office on Tuesday, Rachel? I'll fill you in on what I have then—say at the end of the day? We can brush up on bite marks together."

I just bet we could. "I'll call for the information," I replied.

Mervyn moved in to take his first good look at the body. "Jeez, he looks pretty bad. If you ask me, I think it's that damn Skunk Ape done him in. That's why Alberto died lookin' so scared."

Skunk Ape was the latest rage throughout the Everglades, having been sighted as far west as Big Cypress Swamp and the Ten Thousand Islands. Touted as the Southern cousin to Bigfoot, Skunk Ape was portrayed as six to eight feet tall, covered in long shaggy fur, with incredibly bad body odor and decked out in worn-out overalls. So far, that description covered at least a dozen people I'd come across during my six months in Florida.

Skunk Ape had sparked a surge in the tourist trade that translated into big bucks. Organized tours had wasted no time in offering visitors a trip into the swamps with the lure of sighting the "one and only, legendary creature." And if you were unable to spot Skunk Ape, you could still take a memento home—say, an authentic Skunk Ape T-shirt. It just so happened that Vern and his brother-in-law had a concession set up on the side, devoted solely to promoting the smelly ape.

"Don't be going and showing off your ignorance to this Yankee here, Mervyn," Vern scolded. "You know Skunk Ape don't travel outside the swamp. Besides, what the hell would he want with two hundred and fifty damn squawking birds?"

Knowing Vern, this was probably his version of damage control. The last thing he wanted was for word to get out that Skunk Ape might be a vicious killer. He was looking to keep the creature more in line with the lovable giant in the children's film, *Harry and the Hendersons*. It was easier to sell souvenirs depicting a shy, sensitive yeti than a bloodthirsty primate.

"I think this is one of those nutso Santeria cases. They probably took the birds for some of their sex rituals." Vern pointed to a series of particularly nasty gashes. "You see those jagged cuts there? I'll bet you that Coop here finds they were made with one of those serrated knives their worshippers use for special ceremonies.''

When all else failed, it was standard practice to blame an unsolved murder on Santeria. Its voodoo overtones of blood, sex, and black magic made even the toughest police officer wary of digging too deep. Just the mention of the word caused all four of us to stare at Alberto's corpse with trepidation.

''Dirty bird!'' screeched a disembodied voice behind us.

Vern nearly jumped straight into Mervyn's arms, while Hal Cooper flew to my side, where he took advantage of the moment to brush his arm against my chest. I pushed the offending tentacle away, far more leery of Coop than I was of any ghost.

It took Vern a moment before he recovered his wits and whirled around to face the demon. ''Holy shit! That damn thing's alive!''

The cockatoo was now hanging upside down from its perch, clutching the wooden pole with one claw.

''I thought that goddamn bird was some kind of stuffed ornament,'' Vern sputtered, his face flushed with embarrassment.

''We got so involved with Alberto that I forgot. I found the bird right before you showed up,'' I said by way of explanation.

''You mean you knew that thing was there all along?'' Vern asked, giving me the evil eye.

Uh, oh. I was going to pay for this oversight, big time.

''The bird did the same thing to me,'' I tried to soften the blow. ''I found it under the bedcovers. I think it was Alberto's favorite pet, and used to sleep with him.''

I walked over to the perch and the cockatoo hopped onto my arm, scurrying up my shoulder in search of my missing earrings.

Vern made a face, shaking his head in disgust. ''I knew Alberto was kind of a wacko, but sleeping with a bird? That's plain perverse and downright disgusting.''

I started to head in Vern's direction, only to have him throw up both hands, warding off my approach.

''Stay where you are! You keep that flying rodent away from me!'' he threatened.

Then I remembered that Reardon was afraid of things that

fly. Or crawl. Or walk on four legs. He'd had a chunk of his leg removed by a pit bull a few years ago, and it seemed he wasn't taking any more chances. Especially with something sporting a beak the size of a miniature sickle.

That helped me decide what had to be done. "In that case, I'll take the bird and house it for now. If no one has any objection, that is." I knew there wasn't an animal lover among the lot.

"Yeah, sure." Vern waved me off, glad to be rid of the problem. "That winged rat is yours. Just keep in mind that the bird is key evidence in a murder case, which means you're legally responsible for its welfare."

It would be hard for me to forget, with a screeching cockatoo around. I grabbed the perch and headed out with the smart-mouthed bird balanced on my shoulder.

"Be seeing you, Rachel!" Cooper called after me.

"In your dreams," I muttered under my breath. Actually, I wasn't all too crazy about that, either. I could guess the kind of dreams Coop probably had.

I spotted a bird carrier as I passed through the breeding area and coaxed my feathered companion inside. When I reached the car, I artfully rearranged the junk that filled my trunk, finessing the perch in next to my officially issued .870 pump shotgun. I realized I'd also need a cage, and remembered that my landlady used to have a parrot. Upon the bird's death, its cage had been reincarnated into a planter. I was certain I could convince her to let me borrow it.

I placed the carrying kennel on the backseat, then wedged myself in behind the wheel of my car. As I pulled out of the gate, I glanced in my rearview mirror and caught Vern and Mervyn scurrying outside, four boxes of Cuban cigars tucked under each of their arms. I had the sneaky suspicion that the contraband wasn't headed for the station. Instead, the evidence would be taken to their homes, where it would slowly be burned. One cigar at a time.

Three

With my transfer to Miami came the task of finding a place to live. I had given a moment's fleeting thought to renting in a quiet, safe suburb, but knew I would lose my mind there. Instead, I headed due south for the tip of Miami Beach, chasing memories of a vacation I'd spent playing tag with the waves as a child.

I remembered glitzy hotels, like the Fontainebleau and the Eden Roc, where glamo-kitsch was defined by women sporting lavender hair while decked out in mink coats and gold mules. The bubbas and grandpas hibernated at the row upon row of dowdier hotels. Their main activity was lying in beach chairs, soaking up every last ray of sun before hitting the early bird special. I used to think of them as birds heading south for winter, except for the senior citizens, moving to Miami was shorthand for checking into God's waiting room.

Now, I swung onto the MacArthur Causeway and joined the caravan of cars headed for the mecca of South Beach. Something happens as soon as I leave the mainland and am suspended on the bridge high above Biscayne Bay. The smell of the ocean gathers strength with each revolution of my tires. The port comes to life, with its cruise ships bobbing like mutated marshmallows ready to head out to sea. But that's just an intro for the carnival that waits up ahead. Gone are the days of Jackie Gleason, the June Taylor dancers, and my grandparents' Miami.

These days, Miami Beach can be summed up as buffed, blonde, and burnished. Especially South Beach, the southernmost tip of the island, where looking good is the primary activity, rollerblading the national pastime, a cell phone is a must, and *Baywatch* babes are a dime a dozen. Even guys in thong bikinis put my butt to shame. It wasn't the best ego boost for a perpetually sunburned redhead who daily faces the battle of trying to fit into last year's jeans. Naturally, this was where I chose to call home.

I turned off the air conditioner, rolled down my window, and was smacked in the face by the sultry night air as my tires touched earth to be swept up in the frenzy of South Beach. A red signal brought me to a stop next to a Chevy Impala whose chassis had been raised high off the ground. The driver glanced at me over his shades and cranked the radio up a decibel above earshattering. Then the Impala gunned its motor and took off, the neon running lights on its undercarriage reflecting against the pavement like psychedelic snakes on speed.

My budget didn't permit me to live in the oh-so-cool heart of the action on Ocean Drive. Instead, my neighborhood was enough off the beaten path to have a slightly run-down, seedy feel, complete with bodegas, bottles of Gallo wine at four bucks a pop, and the occasional abandoned building waiting to be discovered as Art Deco. A light layer of grime seemed to coat the entire neighborhood, seeping into its very bones.

The place where I lived was the exception, standing apart like a gaudy costume jewel. Hidden behind a dense wall of foliage, my house stood in a postage-stamp tropical jungle. Passion vines intertwined with sweet-smelling night-blooming jasmine, and garlic vines climbed up the thick stucco walls in a jumble. A wild profusion of hibiscus and bougainvillea jockeyed for space in a sensuous floral tango, clotting the air with their heady perfume. Elegant palms provided a discreet canopy for the orgiastic frenzy below.

My cottage looked like something that had been chewed up and spat out by a Caribbean disco club, with its hot canary-yellow exterior and iridescent tangerine door. While it might have been short on charm, it attracted every lizard and chameleon for miles around.

This was fronted by a concrete wall the color of pink cotton candy, inset with a row of sea horses determinedly standing guard. Access into wonderland was gained by passing through a turquoise gate topped off by a bright red arch laden with sea shells and pieces of colored glass. But this just set the stage for the real showstopper: the main house in which my two landladies resided. There was no other way to describe it than as a work of modern art gone awry. The dwelling was painted an intense periwinkle blue, adorned with salmon-and-green shutters. But that tended to change from week to week, according to my landladies' whim.

I struggled through the gate, the perch in one hand and the kennel in the other. Lulu, the resident cat, lay asleep outside my house atop an ancient air conditioner that wheezed a decrepit tune. The feline's eyes magically sprang open the instant I walked by, locking onto the ball of feathers.

''Forget about it,'' I warned the cat.

I set the perch up in a corner of my bedroom and then released the bird, giving him a view of his new abode.

''What a dump!'' screeched my new roommate.

I turned and stared at the cockatoo, its crest raised as if to warn me that that was its final word. Just what I needed—a critic. The bird's head bounced up and down with silent laughter, taking delight in its keen appraisal.

''Hey, this is as good as it gets, buster—unless you have some house-cleaning skills I don't know about yet,'' I said, laying down the law from the start.

I left the cockatoo to cool his feathers. Pouring myself a glass of wine, I headed into the bathroom, where I stripped off the grunge of the day. Off came the shirt, with its layers of dirt and sweat. My jeans, doused in the aroma of Miami International's bathroom floor, were rolled up and thrown in the hamper. I stepped into the bath and took a sip of wine, luxuriating in the warmth of the cabernet until I tingled right down to my toes. I had opened a good bottle, figuring I deserved it after the night I'd been through.

Closing my eyes, I rested my head back against the porcelain rim, only to discover that Alberto had followed me home. His eyes bore into me with an unspoken demand. I shivered, the bath water suddenly feeling cold. Leaning forward, I twisted the knob and a gush of hot water surged out, streaming down over my hands and fingers until my skin glowed pink. Oddly, it made little difference. My body continued to quiver.

I took a larger sip of wine, determined to rid myself of any lingering bugaboos. But there was no stopping the replay in my mind. I fast-forwarded to where the sack lay on Alberto's living room floor, heard the rustle of the fabric with its mocking whisper, the feel of rough cotton pulling against my skin, as my fingers hurried to uncover its contents. Next came the flash of sleeping parrots with their vibrant whirl of deep blue feathers bedded down next to a shimmering green.

I turned the hot water back on, the warmth curling up past my stomach, to circle my chest and comfortably encompass my chin. But I couldn't drown out memories of the heavy arm that had clamped around my neck, pressing harder and harder until I could no longer breathe. And there was no escaping Alberto's eyes, which refused to stop haunting me.

Water dripped off my body as I stepped out and grabbed a towel. I had just begun to dry off when, in a horrifying replay, a pair of strong arms flew around me from behind, locking my body in place. My adrenaline soared, fueling my strength as I broke free and whirled around to confront my attacker, only to have the towel torn from my grip, its cover ripped off my body.

Then, before I could scream in rage, Jake Santou's mouth firmly silenced my own. The world blurred and my blood pounded with the urge to fight, still furious at being caught off guard. But Santou's fingers determinedly explored my body, transforming my fury into desire. I wrapped my legs around him and drew him down against me, where he paid for his transgression by ever so slowly putting out the fire.

I nestled against Santou's shoulder, satiated and content. Heavy relaxation seeped through my limbs until a shriek sent both of us flying out of bed.

"I'm a horny boy!" screeched my neglected roommate.

"What the hell is that?" Santou demanded, pouncing for his gun.

I turned on the light and walked over to the perch. "Meet my newest acquisition," I said, giving the bird a sour look. "Actually, I'm housing him as evidence."

"To hell with the commander!" the cockatoo squawked.

"You want to tell me about it, Porter?" Santou asked, nodding in the bird's direction. "On second thought, I'll grab the wine and you can fill me in outside."

I threw on a shirt and headed out to join him. Santou was settled on a makeshift bench, which in a former life had been the front seat of a '68 Catalina. He held a glass of wine in each hand. I relieved him of one and sat down beside him, our legs comfortably entwined.

My transfer to Miami had turned into a compromise of sorts for us. A Louisiana Cajun, born and bred, Jake was a detective with the New Orleans Police Department. I'd already put in my time with Fish and Wildlife there, and wasn't anxious to head back yet. The fact that Jake liked Miami meant that we could now spend weekends together without my having to fly out of state. Santou considered the arrangement a warm-up for the main event. To me, commitment was the fact that I'd given him a key. The thought of anything further threw me into a cold sweat.

I'd nearly lost Jake due to a breakup while I was stationed in Las Vegas. Now I couldn't imagine my life without him, even if it was one weekend at a time. A few more silver strands were threaded in among his tousled black curls, and the creases lining his face had grown a bit deeper. But Santou could still make my pulse race more than any man I'd ever known.

"I found an informer of mine murdered this evening," I told Jake. "All his birds had been taken except for the one in there."

"The perp probably knew what he was doing when he passed that bird by," Jake wryly noted as a series of squawks, screeches, and shrieks issued from inside the bedroom.

"Actually, the bird was smart enough to hide. He'd scooted under the bedsheets," I revealed. "That's where I found him."

"Lucky you." Santou flashed a lopsided grin that warmed my skin nearly as much as the wine. "Any idea who murdered your informant?"

"Metro Dade has narrowed down the possibility to either a Cuban bird theft ring, the Skunk Ape, or followers of Santeria," I said scornfully.

"Santeria?" His hooded eyes penetrated straight through

me, even in the dark of night. "Why Santeria?"

I began to squirm and instinctively resented the intrusion. "Birds are sometimes sacrificed in Santeria rituals," I replied calmly.

But Santou's eyes continued to burn, demanding more of an answer.

"Jagged cuts were found on the body that might have been made with a serrated blade. Evidently that type of knife is used in certain Santeria ceremonies." I kept my tone nonchalant.

Nonchalant wasn't an adjective to be found in Santou's vocabulary; his moods swung between intense lite and intense dark. His moodometer now veered toward the dark mode. "I hope you don't plan on getting involved any further in this, *chère*."

I didn't answer but kept my eyes on my wine glass, studying the curve of the rim. The abundant foliage in the garden cast shadows that ranged from ebony black to ashen gray, as a breeze rustled the fronds of a coconut palm, setting off a flurry of whispers.

"What are you, crazy, Porter?" he asked, his tone tinged with disbelief. "Do you have any idea what it is that you're possibly getting involved in?"

"A three-hundred-year-old Afro-Cuban religion which is big on animal sacrifice for marking the passage of such events as births, deaths, and initiations into the faith." I hoped my meager knowledge on the subject was scoring some points. "There are close to seventy-thousand followers here in south Florida."

I'd already seen the aftermath of Santeria ceremonies left lying beside the Miami River. The most memorable had been a goat's head I'd stumbled upon, its white muzzle stained where it lay in a pool of brown blood. Next to it, a Santeria vessel had been overturned. But I was damned if I was going to cave in to yet another boogeyman in the dark.

"What their gods are big on is blood—and not just from animals, either." Santou's voice seared through me. "A hell of a lot of their ceremonies go way beyond a blessing or two at marriages and births. I'm talking black magic, and playing with people's minds. This stuff is as powerful as voodoo—

maybe even more so. And they don't take kindly to strangers butting in."

"I never realized that Cajun superstition of yours ran so deep, Jake. Besides, mind games don't work unless someone is a true believer. You're overreacting. I'll be fine," I remarked impatiently.

Santou stood up and went inside without a word, returning a few moments later. "I want you to carry this with you at all times," he said, thrusting a small spray can into my hand.

I didn't need a ray of moonlight to read the label. I already knew what it was, and I hated pepper spray. It had been used as part of my education at Glynco, a U.S. Fish and Wildlife training center, where an instructor had taken great pleasure in making sure that each and every one of us got hit with a dose in the face. It didn't matter that coolers of ice water had been placed directly at our feet; I still couldn't get the fire out of my eyes and lungs fast enough. The only consolation had been that even the most macho guys were brought to their knees for a good twenty minutes.

"No way, Santou. This stuff is death in a can." I set it on the bench between us.

"For Christ's sake, look at where you live, *chère*. There's enough crime on this street alone to make New Orleans look safe. Now you're telling me that you might be running around getting involved with practitioners of black arts?"

"Why is it that I never give you the fifth degree about cases you're working on?" I shot back. "Yet you constantly feel it necessary to question and prod everything I do and say?"

"Because you work alone, Rachel; I always have backup. I see you walking by yourself into situations and taking stupid chances. You never bother to consider the consequences."

I shot him a warning glance but Santou ignored it, determined to drive his point home.

"Since the day we met, I've spent way too much time worrying about you and the foolhardy choices you make," he said, a harsh edge to his voice. His finger traced the faded red scar on my neck that had been made by the kiss of a razor. "That's a permanent reminder of one of your run-ins. And let's not forget the housewarming bomb you received in Vegas."

Santou played with the Saint Christopher medal that dangled from a chain around my neck. A gift from its previous owner, it had been meant as a memento to keep me safe. So far it had.

"This won't be enough to protect you next time. I love you, Rachel. Don't make me regret that." Jake picked up the pepper spray and dropped the can inside my shirt pocket.

"Danger comes in all different forms," I sharply reminded him. "Sometimes it's a razor. Sometimes it's white powder that people snort up their nose." I instantly regretted the remark, as Jake nailed me with a look that chilled me to the bone.

"That was my past, Rachel. What we're talking about is your present and our future." Santou picked up the wine bottle and refilled both our glasses. "This is something we've been needing to discuss for a while anyway. It might as well be now."

My stomach twisted into a tight knot, already aware of where the conversation was leading. "Backup or not, your job is just as dangerous as mine," I pounced, taking the offensive. "The only difference is that I manage to live with what you do. Why can't you accept me for who I am, and realize that my work is as important to me as yours is to you?"

Santou sighed deeply. "Because I have enough stress just dealing with my own career. And I don't think I can stomach downing any more Mylanta."

"Whoever asked you to deal with mine?" I quickly retorted.

Jake stared at me for a long moment, as if weighing what he was about to say. "There's no way I can help it, *chère*." Then, taking hold of my finger, he dipped it into his wine glass and slipped the tip into his mouth, gently sucking on it until my soul clung to the edge of my skin. "Remember, I said there'd be no games between us?" His voice was as deep as a tom-tom beating a warning.

Those were the words Santou had used back in Las Vegas, when he'd first asked me to marry him. My finger fell from between his lips, and I suddenly felt cold.

"We can't put this off any longer, Rachel. It's way too important, and you've been dodging the issue for months. I'm ready to settle down. I want a real home, with a wife and children. I'm not talking about some time in the foreseeable future. I mean here and now.''

''Don't tell me: You've got a justice of the peace hidden around the corner, just waiting for you to give him a sign,'' I teased, trying to ignore the lump in my throat.

''Say the word, and I'll have one over here faster than you can whip up a wedding garter,'' Santou challenged.

''I don't even know if I can get a transfer back to New Orleans,'' I replied, playing for time. ''Unless you're thinking of applying for a job with Metro Dade. In which case, I'll have to check and see if Fish and Wildlife would be willing to let me stay on in Miami indefinitely.''

Santou's expression put a stop to my rambling. ''That's what we need to talk about, Rachel.'' He hesitated and my heart teetered on the edge of a bottomless precipice. ''The more I think about it, the more I realize I can't deal with a part-time wife and mother who fits me and our kids in between working on cases and shrugging off death threats.''

I began to laugh, only to realize that Jake was serious. ''You're joking. You expect me to give up my job?'' I asked incredulously. ''All for kids that we don't even have yet?''

Santou veered away from my gaze, but only for a moment. Then his eyes met mine, their intensity settled into stubborn resolve. ''That's part of it. I also need someone who's there for me, 100 percent of the time.''

''Don't you think I am?'' I asked, the words dry as sawdust in my throat.

''Only when it fits into your schedule,'' he replied. ''From what I can tell, you're interested in a relationship that takes place in installments, depending on where you're transferred next. That's not something that I can live with.''

I couldn't be certain which was pounding harder—the beat of my heart, or the throb of my growing anger. ''You've known from the start that I'm not the domestic type. Since when did you become such an old-fashioned guy?''

Santou's jaw visibly tightened. ''Call it what you want, Rachel. But I need to be number one in your life, and our children number two. You can't deny the fact that your job takes precedence over everything else, at the moment.''

''I didn't realize my work posed such a threat,'' I responded with forced coolness. "But if those are your demands, then maybe I'm not the right woman for you." I held my breath, waiting for him to vow that there was no other woman in the world for him.

A nerve twitched beneath Jake's right eye, as if in reaction to an invisible slap. "Should I take that as your final word on the subject?" he quietly asked.

I nodded, unable to speak.

"Then maybe you're right, Rachel. Maybe you're not the woman for me, after all," he replied, equally cool. And then he stood up.

"Where are you going?" I asked numbly, too stunned by the speed of events to believe what was happening.

Jake leveled me with a look. "I'm going back to New Orleans," he said, his voice betraying the slightest tremble. "We're headed in two separate directions, Rachel. It's best we realize that now, before it's too late."

How could he give up so easily?

In a fit of white-hot rage, I snapped, "You're absolutely right. Any man who truly loved me would never feel threatened by what I do. And he certainly wouldn't demand I give up something that's so important to me. I'm glad I found out how you feel before I made a terrible mistake."

Santou didn't answer. Instead, he turned and walked away, his footsteps echoing as he headed down the path, through the arch, and out to his car. Then I began to cry too hard to hear anything more.

When I woke up, my bed felt empty. I caught a whiff of Jake's scent on his pillow and put my head against it, fighting back tears. I thought of the promises Santou had made in the past. At one time, he vowed I would learn to trust him. He'd been right about that. I had allowed myself to believe that true love was real and we were meant for each other. One more fairy tale shot to high hell. *Damn* the man anyway!

I showered and dressed, moving on automatic pilot to a cockatoo serenade. Then I headed into the kitchen, determined not to let thoughts of Santou rule my day. I found my landlady, Sophie Gertz, waiting with two steaming cups of *café con leche,* an unlit cigar stuck in her mouth. Sidestepping into her midsixties, Sophie could have been your typical Jewish grandmother—but with a definite twist.

Sophie had unceremoniously dumped her husband of twenty-two years and moved from New York to Miami a decade ago. That's when she'd come roaring out of the closet. She claimed to have spent the majority of her life toiling as a designer in the garment district, though to look at her, I had my doubts. Along with a weakness for turbans, Sophie dressed as if she'd been peeled off a pop art canvas. In addition, her taste in sunglasses was as varied and changeable as the colors she painted the house.

This morning she was decked out in a nod to the fifties, wearing a hot fuchsia top and white capri pants that had pink poodles running up and down both legs. A kelly green turban sat like a beehive on top of her head. The only modern item was her deck shoes. I walked in with Baretta Jr. perched on my shoulder, but I had the feeling Sophie already knew what to expect. She'd have to have been stone deaf not to have heard last night's antics.

''Like the specs,'' I said, hoping to defuse the situation with some flattery. Her sunglasses were encrusted with a sea of tiny rhinestones, their frames flaring out larger than the fins on a late-fifties Caddy. Her penciled-in eyebrows hovered above, looking like two bats in flight.

''These are the glasses I wear when I haven't been able to sleep,'' Sophie rumbled, her voice half Mixmaster, half Lauren Bacall. She locked onto the twenty inches of white feathers that stared back at her. ''Don't I have a rule about no birds somewhere in my rental clause?'' she queried, handing me a cup of brew.

I took a sip. The thick espresso and steamed milk was loaded with enough sugar to rattle my teeth. Mmm . . . just right.

''Not that I know of.'' I girded myself for the inevitable jolt of high octane that rushed through my body.

''Remind me to stick it in next time,'' she flatly replied.

''Have a nice weekend?'' I asked.

''Trying to get me off the subject?'' she parried without a blink.

Sophie and her Cuban lover, Lucinda, took off on weekend

jaunts whenever there was a hot-to-trot rally taking place along the East Coast. The only requirement was that the battle be pro-gay, pro-woman, pro-choice, antiviolence, or anti-Castro.

"What was the rally and where was it held this time?" I grabbed a banana and an orange, figuring they'd pass as breakfast for the bird until I stocked up on its proper feed.

Sophie handed me part of her *Miami Herald*, and we headed into the garden with our coffee.

"Columbia, South Carolina. Gay and lesbian rally." She balanced her cup on the bench and struck a match, holding the flame to the tip of her cigar.

"You're not supposed to smoke that, you know," I reminded her.

Sophie was trying to quit cigarettes for the umpteenth time. Her new theory was that cigars helped dull her craving for them, along with the Nicoderm patch that she wore.

"Smoking means inhaling. Do you see me inhaling?" She adjusted her turban, which had begun to lean at the same angle as the Tower of Pisa.

"Puffin', puffin'!" interjected my feathered companion.

Sophie removed her glasses and studied the cockatoo. "That's exactly right, what I'm doing is puffing. You've got yourself a smart bird. All right, you can keep him."

My fingers dug through the orange rind and a geyser of juice hit a small green lizard that lay on the ground, enjoying the sun. It raised its head and glared at me through the bright yellow circles orbiting its eyes, before skittering off on fragile toes into the underbrush.

"Who's that for, anyway? You or the bird?" Sophie asked.

"The bird," I answered, squirting myself in the eye.

"Figures he'd eat better than you." She took the orange out of my hand, and the cockatoo immediately hopped onto her arm. "Just give him the whole thing."

The bird sank his beak into the rind and tipped his head back, extracting the juice with his tongue. Then, holding the orange in his claw, he tore the fruit apart.

I figured now was as good a time as any to hit Sophie with the news. "By the way, you know the cage that you keep your houseplants in?"

She grimaced at me, her Mixmaster voice set on grind.

''Don't tell me. The cage comes as part of your lease?''

I grinned and took a sip of coffee, turning to the paper she'd given me. The news was filled with the usual deluge of dirt: fiscal mismanagement, a commissioner being sent off to jail for digging into the city's till, and election fraud in which absentee ballots were signed by long-dead voters. All in all, nothing unusual.

I scanned the rest of the paper while the bird continued to whoop it up with the orange. Microsoft was battling it out again in court, some militia group in the West was high-fiving it in a government standoff, and another invisible electric-fence company—also referred to as pet containment—had been blown up, this time in central Florida. Invisible electric-fence companies were recent targets in a series of bombings that had started in Georgia and were working their way down through the South. So far, no employees had been hurt.

Just then, Lucinda walked out and joined us. A short, compact woman with closely cropped jet black hair, she was garbed in a wildly colorful robe that was a Sophie Gertz creation and a pure Peter Max rip-off.

''Whatcha got there?'' Lucinda asked. The bird had finished with the orange, and was preening my tresses.

''We've got ourselves another tenant. What do you think? Should we raise the rent?'' Sophie quipped.

A light, silvery laugh trickled from Lucinda as she stepped out of her robe, displaying an original Gertz bikini along with the body I had wanted since I was twenty years old.

Lucinda was a born-again bodybuilder who'd begun lifting weights on the day she turned fifty. She made it a practice to religiously oil her skin every morning, while still wet from the shower. The result was that rays of sun dappled her form like a beautiful work of art, highlighting each well-developed muscle.

She raised a cup of coffee to her lips, unconsciously flexing a bicep that Arnold would have been proud of. Not an ounce of flab reared its head on a stomach so tight it would have reduced Jane Fonda to tears. The latissimus dorsi muscles in her back rippled like miniature dolphins at play under skin as sleek as a cat's. As for her buns, they were solid as Mount Rushmore, but better sculpted. Hers was the kind of butt men wanted to reach out and touch, just to see if it was truly real. Woe had befallen the few males crazy enough to try. All this came wrapped up in one amazingly feminine package.

Lucinda eased her feet into a pair of Rollerblades, preparing for her morning spin. God, I envied the woman.

"Sugar, you can have this body, too," she'd once told me in authentic Jack LaLanne fashion. "But I can't lie. You're gonna have to work hard to get it."

I'd decided to forego the bikini, instead. I put the paper aside and filled Sophie and Lucinda in on how I'd wound up with the bird.

"So, what do you think?" I asked Lucinda. "Does the murder sound like it could have something to do with Santeria?" She was open about the fact that many of her Cuban relatives were followers of the faith.

"Listen, darling. I know there are stories floating around about graves being robbed for body parts to be used in black-magic rituals. But I've never heard of any followers resorting to murder for their religious beliefs. Of course, that doesn't mean they won't kill you for some other reason." She grinned.

"I'll keep that in mind," I replied.

Lucinda's attention migrated to the cockatoo on my shoulder. "Aren't you worried, letting that bird sit out here in the open? It might decide to just spread its wings and fly away."

The cockatoo rubbed his head under my chin as I scratched along the side of his neck. "He can't. His wing feathers have been clipped. That makes him too unbalanced to fly."

Lucinda wrinkled up her nose at the thought. "Sounds just as barbaric as Santeria to me."

I put my arm out and the bird ran down it, hopping onto the bench, his head boinging up and down like a plastic figurine in the rear window of a car.

"There are people who believe that birds become better pets that way. They're more docile when their wings are clipped," I explained.

"Sure. Why not? If someone were to break my arms and legs, I'd be more dependent on them, too," Sophie dryly replied. "Of course, that doesn't mean I'd have to like it."

Her response caught me off guard. "Why, Sophie—I didn't

think that would bother you. After all, you used to have a bird.''

''That's exactly why I never got another,'' she responded. ''Doesn't matter if it's animal, vegetable, or mineral. I've learned that everything needs to be free.''

We sat quietly for a moment, watching the bird attack my coffee cup. Finally Sophie broke the silence.

''So, what are you going to call this thing, anyway?''

The bird waddled over, fell onto his back, and kicked his feet against my hand. Great. Instead of kids, I was saddled with an unruly bird. I pushed the cockatoo away, propelling him along the upholstered bench like a disc in a game of shuffleboard. Instead of being irate, the bird erupted into the uproarious laughter of a lunatic on the loose. He immediately bolted back over, demanding that I repeat the action again and again and again. I looked up and caught Sophie's eye, knowing there was only one thing he could be called.

''Bonkers,'' I said. ''He's definitely Bonkers.''

Four

I helped Sophie remove the menagerie of houseplants from inside her birdcage. After that, Lucinda hauled it to my place while I pretended to assist. The contraption was nearly as large as my apartment in New York had been.

By the time I was ready to head out, Sophie walked in, a bowl of fruit in her hand. She foisted an apple on me.

"If I'm gonna feed your bird, I might as well try to keep you healthy, too. Just be sure and eat it!" she commanded.

I took a big bite of the apple to please her, and received a pinch on the cheek as reward.

"Don't worry about your bird," Sophie advised. "He'll spend the day outside with me while I do some touch-up painting on the house. I'm feeling magenta and lime today."

I'd given up on the idea of privacy soon after moving in, when I discovered Sophie painting outside my bedroom window, bright and early, at five o'clock one morning. At first, I'd been startled. But Sophie had cheerfully waved and invited me outside to inspect her latest flash of inspiration. That's when I realized why the rent was so low—my landlady had a hard time holding on to tenants.

I'd come to appreciate Sophie's company during my routine bouts of insomnia. It was during those wee hours that she'd finagle me into a game of canasta, deftly cleaning me out of liquid funds. On the other hand, the woman made a mean late-night margarita, nicely accompanied by a dish of Lucinda's black beans and rice.

I'd asked Sophie once why she was so compelled to continually paint the house such outrageous colors.

"I'm like a performing artist. I gotta constantly create," she'd said. "This is my living canvas. This way my art never ends."

I walked past her ever-evolving creation and under Neptune's arch to squeeze behind the wheel of my car. Destination, points south. I crossed over the MacArthur Causeway, leaving behind my Miami Beach state of mind. I was going to pay Willy Weed a visit.

I brazenly propelled my way into the bumper-to-bumper traffic on Route 1, knowing that the guy in the Beemer was a lot more worried about dents than I was. Homestead's claim to fame was that it had been ground zero back in 1992 for that tree-smashing, trailer-bashing storm of the decade, Hurricane Andrew. Years later, not a whole lot had changed. I exited onto a small two-lane road that skirted Homestead and led straight for the boonies.

Row upon row of stripped live oaks flashed by, their trunks bedraggled but proud, like old women who wake one morning to discover the night has stolen away with their youth and beauty. A boarded-up Baptist church stood melancholy and forlorn in a grove of Dade County pine, its battered sign promising to reopen soon. I pulled behind a blue pickup that shuffled maddeningly along at the speed limit, my mind wandering as a bald eagle soared lazily in the sky. I could have thrown a stone in any direction and hit a bird-breeder's facility right about now. Forty seven hundred of them are registered in this state, each and every one of whom had plopped down twenty-five bucks to the Florida Game and Freshwater Fish Commission to obtain a license to legally ply their trade. That's all it took.

I knew that Homestead and its environs were especially loaded with bird breeders not only because of the number of thefts that had taken place in the area, but also because of a handy-dandy little book that listed every breeder's name and facility, along with their address and telephone number. The book was made available by the Game and Freshwater Fish Commission to anyone willing to fork over five dollars. Unless you were high-tech and modern, that is. Then seventeen smackeroos got you a floppy from which you could download all the necessary information. It made for a convenient shopping list, one that the Cuban bird gang surely had the brains to have gotten hold of.

As I turned off the asphalt onto a narrow dirt road that led through a forest of scrub palmetto and pine, an explosion of black starlings erupted overhead, annoyed at my unannounced presence. A gang of black-headed vultures remained languidly indifferent, content to hitch a ride on a thermal while scanning the ground for their next meal. The dirt path curved to the right and opened up to reveal a large clearing with three broken-down house trailers and two dozen decrepit cages, each containing one or two listless critters inside.

I pulled up next to Willy's Dodge Ram, its roof mounted with four big headlights that Weed used for jacklighting deer. A vanity tag bore the logo *HELL'S BELLS*, while slapped on the vehicle was a worn-out bumper sticker that pretty much summed up Willy's take on life. WILL THE LAST AMERICAN TO LEAVE PLEASE BRING THE FLAG? It was a popular sentiment with most of the area's crackers, or ''lizard eaters,'' as some of the locals are called, who worried that an influx of Cubans was insidiously working its way toward them from out of Miami.

I opened my car door to a surge of heat so humid it was almost liquid. Ninety-five degrees of sticky hot air rolled over my body like the swell of a wave to turn my skin into an irresistibly moist calling card for every tiny deer fly around. They banded together in miniature squadrons, attacking my body with the expertise of a panzer unit programmed to kill. My efforts at swatting them away only provided the insects with a much welcome breeze as they munched at my flesh in uninterrupted bliss.

A hand-painted sign was nailed onto one of the trees. It announced that I was about to enter THE ENDANGERED CREATURES OF GOD FOUNDATION, for which all donations were gladly accepted. That was a scam Willy had come up with a few months ago, when he'd decided to try and pass off his place as a sanctuary. In reality, Weed's hovel was a dump living in hope of conniving its way into a tax write-off.

I kicked through the cans and debris that littered the ground to a cage holding a dejected cougar. The animal paced back and forth across the floor of its small pen with neurotic precision, its deadened eyes scarcely acknowledging my presence, its six-foot-long tawny body a scraggly mass of bones and fur. Next door, a 450-pound Siberian tiger could barely stretch out in its pigeonhole of a cage. Other enclosures held bobcats and leopards and servals; all thin and neglected, and all for sale. In Florida it was deemed a right to own whatever animal one desired, be it a lion, an elephant, or a zebra—any or all of which could be purchased right here in the exotic wildlife capital of the world.

A vulture landed nearby to pick at a rotting chicken carcass that one of the mangy cougars had refused to eat. I turned away from the pathetic menagerie and checked out the squalid mobile homes that lay spread out before me. The music of Guns N' Roses was cranked up and pumping through the thin, metal walls of the first trailer, making it a sure bet to contain Willy. I climbed the cinder-block steps and wrenched open the aluminum door.

The stench nearly rocked me off my feet: a reeking brew of heat, body odor, rotten food, and mildew. Empty beer bottles littered the floor next to a cardboard box that contained remnants of fossilized pizza. A pile of laundry, midway through the process of fermenting, sat in a corner with a discolored jockstrap perched on top. Heaps of garbage overflowed from overturned paper bags, smoldering in an experimental indoor compost heap. Just one quick glance made the cages outside look pretty good.

Willy Weed stood dead center in among the debris, his greasy strands of hair half in and half out of a half-assed ponytail, a joint hanging from his lips. The tattoo on his bare chest swam in a pool of sweat as he went through the motions of completing a bicep curl, a twenty-five-pound weight barely gripped in his hand. His jeans hung well below a pair of bony hips, making it obvious he didn't bother with the usual formality of underwear.

Willy mumbled something that I couldn't understand, his eyes glazed over in a stoned-out state of nirvana. I didn't bother trying to yell above the deafening wail of music. I just beelined to the nearest electrical socket, where I euthanized Guns N' Roses.

"Now, what was it that you said?" I asked, enjoying the sweet sound of silence.

Willy guffawed, nearly swallowing his joint. "I said, hey, Porter. Wanna join me in a toke?"

Down-home hospitality, crackerjack style.

"No, thanks, Willy. I think I'll pass."

Weed gazed at me through half-closed lids, his bicep twitching as the twenty-five-pound weight struggled to make liftoff. "That's the trouble with you uptight Northern girls. You don't know how to have yourselves a good time and relax."

"You do enough of that for both of us," I assured him.

A ray of sunlight managed to bypass the dirt on one of the dingy windows. The gleam caught my eye as it streamed in, glistening off what appeared to be military medals that had been mounted in a frame and hung on the wall. Weed didn't strike me as a man who would risk his neck without big bucks egging him on.

"Who did you steal the medals from, Willy?" I asked, motioning toward the display.

Weed took a deep toke before removing the joint from his lips. "I did my time in the service," he exhaled.

"Yeah? What military prison would that have been?" I prodded.

"That's real cute, Porter. Poking fun at a disabled vet," Willy feigned hurt.

I didn't bother reminding him that I knew just how he'd received his limp, but let him ramble on.

"I happened to get those for serving my country—bravely, too, I might add, during the mother of all battles in Desert Storm. I'm a Top Gun," Willy drawled.

He swayed to his left and hooked onto a Bud, ramming a finger deep inside the open bottle. As Willy chugged the Bud, beer sloshed down his chin and onto his chest, the liquid running straight inside his jeans.

"Damn! I hate when that happens," he grumbled. "Good thing I didn't get around to doing my laundry just yet."

I looked away in distaste, and noticed an enormous mound of writhing flesh that had begun to rearrange itself in a darkened corner of the trailer.

Top Gun looked over, curious as to what was vying for my

attention. ''Why, that's Big Mama.'' He grinned. ''Wanna make nice and say hi?''

Big Mama slowly lifted her head from where she lay coiled, and flicked out a tongue. An eighteen-foot Burmese python, the snake had the girth of a telephone pole and must have weighed close to two hundred pounds. Her muscles rippled beneath a shiny skin that would have delighted any fashion maven in search of a high-priced handbag and matching shoes. Gorgeous reddish brown splotches were delicately outlined in a luxurious cream, set against a subtle background of cocoa. Burmese pythons have no use for venom. All they need do is wind themselves around their prey and slowly constrict, steadily suffocating their quarry in an excruciating dance of death.

''What do you feed that thing?'' I asked. It had to consume at least a chicken or two a day.

''I like to vary her diet with pain-in-the-ass wildlife agents,'' Willy cracked with relish.

The stench and the heat were beginning to get to me. ''I guess you haven't bothered getting around to paying your electric bill.''

Willy put down the dumbbell and threw me a beer. ''Big Mama likes it hot in here.''

I twisted off the cap and took a gulp, grateful for the liquid. ''Maybe you ought to consider keeping her in a different trailer, then.''

''No way!'' He grabbed a greasy deep-fried nugget of gator tail from an equally greasy plate, and held it toward me. I passed up the offering.

''Big Mama and I are like one,'' he said, shoving the chunk into his mouth. ''If she ain't with me, she gets mighty cranky. And trust me, you don't want eighteen feet of snake pissed off at ya. But she's still the best woman I've ever had.''

I was beginning to wonder just how close Willy and Big Mama actually were, when my eyes were drawn to his snakeskin boots. I pondered whether that had been a former pet as well.

Willy followed my gaze and chuckled. ''Got a yen for a pair?'' he asked. ''That's what I'm getting Hector ready for.''

Weed disappeared into the back of his trailer, and returned a moment later carrying an aquarium in his hands. Inside was an eight-foot python with the smallest head I'd ever seen. Now I realized how Weed managed to kick a profit out of his snakes so quickly. He overfed the pythons he planned to skin, forcing their bodies to grow faster than their actual age would have allowed. The result, known as "pinhead syndrome," was that their heads remained the proper size for their chronological age, while their bodies grew too fast and too big. I had reached my limit with Willy.

"I went to Alberto's last night straight from the airport."

Willy turned sullen. "Oh, yeah? You two must have had a real nice, friendly chat. Did you make sure to rat me out, Porter?"

I watched as he relit the joint and then picked up the weight again in his right hand. "You're home free on this one, Willy. By the time I got there, Alberto was already dead."

But Weed wasn't pleased with the news. "Goddammit to hell! That lowlife mope owed me big time for the last two hauls!"

"And what exactly might those have been?" I promptly asked.

Weed's lip curled up, displaying his gold tooth and ruby, which glistened like a drop of blood. "Some special bird seed I was delivering to him," he sneered.

My fingers itched to wring his scrawny neck, but I gave the art of patience another stab. Besides, Big Mama was silently watching. "What kind was that?"

Willy wasn't appreciative of my tact. "The expensive kind," he snarled. He threw back his head and tossed a gator-tail nugget down his throat.

I tried my best to keep from wishing that he'd choke on it, but gosh darn it to heck—that pesky thought just kept wriggling into my mind.

"I found some hyacinth macaws and Cuban Amazons at Dominguez's place. Do you know anything about that?" I was wasting my time, unless I hung around long enough for Willy to get so stoned that he let something slip.

"Yeah, he had 'em. So what? You still gotta prove they're illegal," Willy flippantly replied.

I bit the inside of my cheek to hold back the smile. Weed

had unknowingly just confirmed the fact that the birds hadn't been captive-bred.

The muscle in his bicep began to twitch uncontrollably, as if it were in spasm. Weed took another deep toke on the joint. "Bet you're feeling mighty good right about now," he leered. "Getting yourself a haul of those expensive birds. The boss man musta given you a big ol' gold star."

"Well, that's the other interesting thing," I revealed. "It seems I surprised whoever murdered Dominguez. I was knocked out, and when I came to, the birds were gone."

Willy howled, a trickle of drool falling onto his bony chest. "That's a good one! Boy, would I have loooved to seen that!" He rearranged the sweat on his face with the back of his hand. "In that case, I don't know nothing about no birds. You musta been hallucinating when you thought you'd seen 'em. You got yourself some good drugs I should know about, Porter?"

"Cut the crap, Willy," I snapped. "You already admitted that you were muling for Alberto."

But Weed was riding high, puffing on the joint as if it were his last breath. "That musta been one helluva fall you took at ol' Alberto's, cause I don't remember ever sayin' nothing like that. Guess you knocked that noggin of yours somethin' good." Weed giggled and gave me a wink. "There goes another case down the drain. Ain't that right, Miss Fed?"

I wondered if I could get away with giving Weed a whopping dose of pepper spray. Damn—it was in my other shirt.

"Course you could stop buggin' me with all these questions and just go right to the source. Old Alberto, himself." Willy slapped a hand to his forehead. "Whoops! That's right. Dead men don't talk, do they?"

Willy's giggle suddenly turned into an ear-shattering shriek as a dull thud shook the trailer floor. The twenty-five-pound dumbbell had rolled out of Weed's hand to land squarely on top of his right foot. Willy screamed, hopping around like a Holy Roller in the midst of his sermon.

"Oh, Lordy! Jesus save me!" he babbled, tears springing from his eyes. "I broke my foot! Oh, my God! I'm a cripple!"

I had a hard time dredging up very much sympathy. I folded my arms and simply moved out of his way. "That's too bad,

Willy. Seeing how it could cut into your rodeo stunts and other extracurricular activities,'' I observed.

Weed flashed me a dirty look, but held back the snarl. ''You gotta get me to a hospital, Porter. My foot feels like it's hangin' on by a thread!''

''I could do that. But I'm going to need some information from you first.''

''I'll give them all that mother's maiden name crap when we get there. Let's just go, Porter!'' Willy insisted, wincing in pain.

''Mmm. No. That's not the kind of information I'm talking about,'' I told him.

Weed stopped hopping long enough to give me an open-mouthed stare. ''You gotta be kidding, bitch. You're hitting me up for dirt now?'' he wailed.

''That's right. Either you talk or I'm out of here.'' I hesitated for a moment. ''Of course, that shouldn't be a problem. You can always drive to the hospital by yourself.''

''Goddammit, Porter! You know I can't do that! It's my right foot that's broke!'' Willy sputtered.

''Whoops!'' I slapped my hand against my forehead. ''I forgot about that!''

Weed gnashed his teeth. ''What the hell do you want to know?''

Ah, power! It made me feel all warm and gooey inside. ''How long have you been muling for Alberto?''

''Just that once, when you caught me last night,'' Weed whined.

''The truth, Willy!'' I demanded.

He emitted a high-pitched yowl. ''I swear on Big Mama's life!''

Weed hopped over to a cabinet, pulled out a bottle of Southern Comfort, tore off the cap, and upended it into his mouth.

''How many eggs did you bring in?'' I wondered if Willy would stop chug-a-lugging long enough to answer the question before he passed out.

''Five,'' Willy panted, quickly raising the bottle back up to his lips. A trickle of bourbon ran down his chin and onto his chest, heading inside his jeans where it mixed with the beer.

But I was beyond caring about his lack of etiquette. Weed

had just handed me another important nugget of information: He'd definitely brought the eggs in from Brazil.

"Were they hyacinth eggs?" I asked.

"You're gonna burn in hell for this, Porter," Weed yelped, stalling.

"Then I guess I'll have you there to keep me company," I replied. "This is your last chance, Willy. Were those hyacinth eggs that you flushed?"

Weed let loose a low growl, his bloodshot eyes boring straight through me. "Hyacinth eggs are illegal, Porter. Remember? I know your goddamn stupid laws."

"Obviously not well enough. Bringing in undeclared eggs of any kind is illegal," I reminded him.

"Yeah," Willy snarled in a mixture of anger and pain. "But you could shred my ass good if they were hyacinths."

I stared at him. "Alright, then. At least tell me where Alberto got the Cuban Amazons from."

"For chrissakes, Porter! From Cuba! Where the hell else do you think?" Willy roared.

I smiled as I threw Weed a shirt from off the top of his laundry heap. "Congratulations, Willy. You just won yourself an all-expenses-paid trip to the emergency room. Those were the first honest words to come out of your mouth."

I dropped Willy off, then headed over to Alberto's to take another look around. Battered trees gave way to nurseries producing oranges and ornamental palms as I headed southwest, leaving Homestead and Willy behind. Driving into the Redlands was like cruising through a produce wonderland, since it's here that the majority of Florida's fruits and vegetables are grown. Each field that I passed was a lush patchwork of greenery in kaleidoscopic shades of kelly, pea, chartreuse, and emerald. I rolled down the car window and took a deep whiff as I passed a farm with crops of kiwi, lychee, and guava, their dusky fragrance permeating the air.

Off to my right lay an okra field, dense with tiny white flowers. The serene scene was abruptly disrupted when hundreds of diminutive swallows took flight, catapulting into the sky like feathered rockets. I held my breath, my grandmother having told me that a flock of birds could steal away your soul.

I turned onto Alberto's street, opened his unlocked gate, and pulled up the drive. His black Jaguar sat impatiently in the shed, its motor silently pleading to be revved. I could sense Alberto's presence even as I sat outside. I waited until the feeling had passed, then dug out my cell phone and punched in a call to Vern.

"Hey, there, Porter. What you doin' back out this way again?" Reardon asked between slurps of his coffee.

"I was visiting Willy Weed and thought I'd stop by Dominguez's, place," I replied.

"You got some interesting taste in friends, Porter. I gotta hand you that," Vern chuckled. "Maybe you oughta give ol' Hal Cooper a tumble, after all."

I let the remark slide. "So, is it all right if I take a quick look around inside Alberto's?"

"What's with you, girl? Can't get your fill of hanging around with the dead? Or ain't there enough to keep you busy without you poking your nose into my investigation, too?"

I took the opportunity to jump in with both feet. "Speaking of that, have you come up with any more plausible theory as to who might have had a motive for killing Alberto?"

Vern bit into what I imagined was a cinnamon bun. "I already told you. All evidence points to it being another one of those wacky Santeria murders."

Since he had one foot firmly planted in the retirement pasture, I suspected Vern's workload was clogged with any number of "Santeria" cases.

"So, what do you say, Vern? Can I take a walk through since I'm already here?" I asked once again.

Vern continued to munch on his calorie-ridden treat, making my stomach rumble. "Everything's been dusted, so I guess it's all right. But don't go removing anything inside that house, ya hear?" he warned.

"Loud and clear. Thanks, Duke." I quickly hung up before he could blast me.

I shimmied from behind the wheel and stepped outside, where a slab of heat pressed slow and steady on top of my head. Entering through the back door again, I found that mounds of dingy feathers had been kicked around the floor, sullied by a parade of feet trampling in and out as they went about the task of collecting evidence to substantiate a murder.

I checked around the nesting boxes, where bits of broken shells lay like chips of fine china. The breeding room held even fewer clues. Only the rustle from the fallen rainbow of plumage offered a hint of the nightmare that had occurred.

I walked past the nursery and then came to a dead halt, certain that Alberto was by my side. Standing still, I listened as the silence slowly slithered around me, cutting off my breath as effectively as a shroud.

There's no such thing as ghosts.

But my teeth had begun to chatter. I tried to make myself laugh by thinking of Vern and Mervyn with their Skunk Ape, but my thoughts gravitated toward Santeria and the goat's head I'd found.

I wanted to move, but the space around me had become dense as molasses, and my limbs useless as empty balloons. Reverting to an old childhood trick, I closed my eyes tightly and yelled as loud as I could to scare my own fear—along with any ghosts—far away. Then I opened my eyes and moved on.

Everything was just as I had left it last night; no ghostly cleanup crew had materialized to straighten up the mishmash of papers, or the slit innards of sofas and chairs. I began to rummage through Alberto's desk drawers, defiantly turning my back toward the open bedroom door.

The stack of bills was the same; the bumper stickers remained untouched. Only the bottom drawer had been tampered with. The thick bird-inventory folder was now gone. I made a mental note to ask Vern for a copy of the records and then thoroughly searched the kitchen, the bathroom, and the living room once again, in a futile attempt to delay the inevitable task of walking through Alberto's bedroom door.

Finally having run out of places to explore, I forced myself to stare at the space where Alberto had lain. There was no dodging Dominguez's blood, its splatters hardened and dry on the walls and the floor. I took a deep breath and attempted to swallow my fear, but it remained firmly lodged in my throat as I stepped over the threshold.

I tiptoed around the outline, taking well-placed steps to avoid as much of Alberto's dried blood as I could, wondering when I would ever outgrow my irrational fear. Alberto's voice whispered in my ear, confirming what I already knew to be true. *Never.*

A creak skittered across the floor behind me and I jumped, my pulse rate soaring into the stratosphere.

"There's no contest. You win; I'm afraid," I called out to whatever spirit might be there. "But I'm not leaving until my work is done. So let's just call a truce. What do you say?"

I waited to hear a sound, feel a cold wind, watch furniture fly past. But all remained quiet. I took it as a sign that we had reached a meeting of the minds and turned back to see what I could discover.

A search through Alberto's closet produced an array of colorful guayaberas, traditional short-sleeved, loose cotton shirts. Also pressed and neatly hanging were a tangerine jacket and pants that must have made Alberto look like walking sherbet. I left the closet and headed over to his bureau. Each drawer appeared to have been thoroughly raided; nothing of interest was left lurking inside. With nowhere else to turn, I dragged the four coolers out from under Alberto's bed. Sure enough, every single cigar was gone, without so much as a band or a wrapper to betray their former presence.

I ran my hands between Alberto's mattress and springs, knowing full well that everyone before me had surely done the same. Finally I dropped down to the floor and sent my fingers to work, intent on examining the metal bed frame inch by inch.

Nothing was hidden along the frame on that side of the mattress. Then I stretched my arm to examine the center support bar. As my hand strained to reach its middle, I was rewarded with the rustle of paper between my forefinger and thumb.

I grasped the rough material, but it refused to budge. It took a few hard tugs to dislodge the secret from its hiding place. Out came an eight-by-ten white envelope, its flap sealed tight. If I were to play by the rules, I was required to hand the secured package over to Vern. I held my breath and listened, straining to hear if Alberto would disapprove. There wasn't a whisper to be heard.

I reached into my pants, removed a pocket knife and flicked it open, brushing away any thoughts of impropriety. I'd decide what to do once I viewed the contents. The blade smoothly sliced its way into Alberto's private life.

I pulled out the contents, surprised by what was revealed. A series of photographs portrayed different beach studs of the month. But these were no amateur photos, and the men were no ordinary nine-to-five hunks. All were well-polished Adonises, with gold Rolexes on their wrists and deltoids to die for. I knew the species. Buff young men able to speak a couple of languages, well versed in the pleats and tucks of Gucci and Armani, with abs off which you could bounce formal dinnerware.

Some of the photos appeared to have been shot for modeling portfolios, while others were more casual. One finely sculpted blond had been captured in a slim sliver of a Speedo, strawberry daiquiri in hand, designer shades carefully veiling his thoughts. Not a speck of body hair interfered with his tan.

I wondered if Alberto might have been running some sort of escort ring: men posing as actors, models, and personal trainers, for hire—preferably long-term, salary to be paid on the first of the month, plus the usual perks and goodies. But I shelved that idea. I also doubted that he'd taken the photos, since no camera equipment was lying around. I received my answer as I reached the bottom of the pile. Scribbled on a piece of paper was the word, ENJOY. It was signed, ELENA.

I placed the photos back inside the envelope, and carefully tucked Alberto's secret back into its hiding place. I didn't need Vern coming to the conclusion that Dominguez had met his demise at the hands of a gay Santeria killer.

There was nowhere else I could think of for something to have been hidden. Still, feeling unsatisfied, I couldn't bring myself to leave. Alberto restlessly hovered beside me as I thoroughly rechecked the kitchen cabinets, the drawers, and the freezer. By the time I got back to the living room I was ready to give up, whether Alberto's ghost was happy or not. Then my eyes came to rest on a large, ornate birdcage.

This was the only cage in Alberto's area of the house, which led me to believe it had been Bonker's quarters. I eyed the contraption. Either I'd gone round the bend or Alberto had been pretty clever, after all. There was only one way to find out. I walked over to the stainless-steel cage and popped the latch on the door. Empty shells of sunflower seeds lay scattered in one food dish, while a shallow pool of water stagnated in another. Dried bird droppings littered the sheets of newspaper that lined its removable tray. I grabbed hold of the knob and tried to slide it out, but the layers of paper were built up too high, jamming it in place. I reached inside and started removing one layer of paper after another.

Out came sections of the *Miami Herald* from Friday, Saturday, and Sunday. I was beginning to feel like the bag lady I'd always feared I'd become, when I finally hit pay dirt. Lying on the very bottom of the cage were two thin sheets of stationery. I quickly scanned their contents.

The letter was from one Maria Santiago in Cuba, who asked that Alberto make sure his friend bring along a girdle—"size medium, please"—on his next trip.

"I need one if I'm ever to catch a man," she confided.

My hand reflexively crept over my stomach and down my hips, to feel if my own body had expanded since I'd checked early this morning. It was consoling to know that the problem was universal.

Maria had other requests. "A few Victoria's Secret bras would also be nice. Something shiny that pushes up to make good cleavage. Please be sure to get size 34 B."

Now I knew what Alberto was doing with receipts for lingerie in his desk drawer.

"And don't forget to have him bring some makeup, as well. I would like Max Factor since it is what the movie stars wear," she continued. "Also, Consuela asks that you be kind enough to include some vitamins. She still isn't feeling well. And please, please send any videocassettes that you can of Tom Cruise movies. In return, I will have ten green coins ready."

Apparently Alberto had been running some sort of courier service. While it was common for exiles to send money to relatives who lived there, an illegal messenger service supplying the island with American goods was brand new to me. I also wasn't familiar with the term "green coins," unless it was Maria's slang for currency.

I honored my promise not to remove anything from the house by slipping the correspondence back where I'd found it. I took one final look around, then headed out. I'd learned only of Alberto's apparent weakness for handsome young men, and that he'd had good taste in picking lingerie. All in all, not anything that was especially helpful for tracking down endangered birds.

I was heading back to the Tempo when a flash of color caught my eye. There on the ground lay a deep cobalt-blue feather. I picked it up and twirled the first piece of hard evidence I'd found. The luminous violet-blue feather could only belong to one species of bird.

I carefully wiped off bits of dirt and tucked the feather in my bag without the least bit of compunction. After all, I had made no promises about what I found outside.

Five

My stomach decided it was time for lunch. Since I'd promised Sophie to broaden my culinary horizons beyond McDonald's, I stopped at a local barbecue dive appropriately called Porky's Last Stand, though I suspected it wasn't quite what she had in mind. Red-and-white checkerboard oilcloths were flung across the flimsy metal tables, and wagon-wheel chandeliers completed the slapdash Wild West mood.

I walked past a group of local yokels hefting long-neck Dixies and gnawing on ribs, the twangy strains of "Dueling Banjos" running through my brain. Their eyes followed me as if I were on a list of critters to be nailed, until a twenty-two-year-old waitress pranced by. Then the eyes swiveled like magnets irresistibly drawn to a much stronger force field: a midriff top and tight short-shorts that rode halfway up our server's buns.

I sat down nearby, fully convinced that I possessed all the allure of road kill. I proceeded to drown my sorrow in a Mason jar of iced tea. What the heck—I even threw in an extra packet of Equal. My waitress smiled sweetly, blissfully unaware that in ten years time, her outfit would be a plaything for her kids as she struggled to do just one more sit-up.

A sign on a nearby wall declared OUR BAR-B-Q IS MADE FROM PIGS THAT MADE PERFECT HOGS OF THEMSELVES. It was enough to make me order the catfish sandwich, though I couldn't turn down a side of fries. I ate lunch serenaded by the strains of Aerosmith, as my beer-drinking buddies discussed the merits of silicone implants and when Skunk Ape had last been seen. A glance at an even younger and more shapely waitress persuaded me to forego any thought of ordering a slice of Key lime pie. Instead, I headed back toward Homestead. It was time to check in with Willy's ex, Bambi Weed.

I flew by the rich red soil of the Redlands with its groves of mango, avocado, and orange trees, and the landscape reverted once again to boarded-up buildings and amputated coconut palms, announcing I had arrived in Homestead. Along with blowing houses and landscape away, Hurricane Andrew had ripped cages containing wildlife off their very foundations. The result was one enormous jailbreak. More than 3,000 monkeys and baboons escaped from primate breeding facilities to form marauding bands that still roam the area today. Fugitive African lions lumbered through the Everglades, while construction workers chased three-foot-long green iguanas off the Rickenbacker Causeway in downtown Miami. In Homestead, nine-foot-long monitor lizards attacked people's dogs, then wrapped themselves around the engines of Grand Ams for an afternoon nap. It was Noah's Ark run amok.

Eighty percent of the wildlife running loose in Dade County are exotics gone native in their new subtropical home. Some of the blame could be pinned on Andrew, and some on critters escaping from cargo shipments at the airport. The rest is due to people's realizing that thirty-foot snakes make lousy pets, and kicking them out the door.

Now overgrown cobras and pythons have taken up lodging in choice neighborhoods, while capybaras—giant South American rodents—doggy paddle in local canals, and Jesus Christ lizards slap their tootsies across the water's surface at Everglade National Park. "Watch your dogs, your cats, and all small children," has become South Florida's clarion call.

I pulled up to Bambi Weed's abode. A run-down shack that had barely survived Hurricane Andrew, its shingles hung off the roof in slapdash fashion, the tar paper undercoat ragged and torn. Blown-out windows were still boarded up, and large patches of paint peeled off its plywood walls.

I got out of the Tempo to be greeted by a dog so tattered and bone thin that even a ravaging boa would have passed him by. The mutt backed away from me, its snarl little more than a whimper as I walked toward the door. Before I could make it up the steps, two young boys came bounding around from the back of the house. Both looked as if they'd been rolling around in a pig sty, covered with more dirt than clothes. I guessed them to be around seven and eight from their size. There was little doubt that the two belonged to Willy: Each sported a cougar's tooth dangling from an ear, and had a Super Soaker water gun clutched in his hands. The boys eyeballed me nearly as closely as the gang back at Porky's, sizing me up for a wet T-shirt showdown. I convinced them otherwise with my own warning growl, backed up by two Hershey bars as a last-ditch bribe. The kids ripped the chocolate from my hands in record time.

I moved toward the door to find that the dog had also changed its mind. The critter was latched onto me, its paws wrapped around my leg. I dug through my purse in a desperate effort to find something to give him and found a health bran muffin that Sophie had foisted on me a few days ago. I offered it to the mutt and gave a loud knock on the door, hoping it would open before the muffin was devoured. My prayers were answered as Bambi appeared.

Ever the modern-day mom, Bambi's version of a housedress consisted of a red bustier and a black plastic miniskirt, dark blue eyeliner and white lipstick, giving her just the right touch of heroin chic. Her short platinum tresses had been carefully gelled into a helmet of spikes. Except for being barefoot, she could have been headed straight for a guest appearance on *Jerry Springer*.

''Get outta here, you mangy mutt!'' she screamed at the dog.

The critter fell to the ground and onto its back in a show of subservience, as Bambi quickly pulled me inside.

''God, I hate that thing.'' She gave the door a swift kick as the dog clawed at the other side, attempting to break in. ''It's always trying to hump my leg, ya know? You oughta see him when I'm nude. I mean, that dog stares at me like he's gonna rape me or something.'' She gave a little shiver that ended in a shimmy, a habit from having been a dancer in a topless joint a few years ago.

''I used to have a life, ya know what I mean?'' Bambi had once confided. ''I gave up my career to have Willy's two kids.

Now what am I supposed to do with these?'' she'd asked, holding up a pair of 38 Ds. ''You know what kinda damage breast feeding does to them? You bet your sweet ass that snake owes me alimony.''

The raucous screech of a parrot filled the air, informing me that something new had been added to Bambi's menagerie.

''When did you get a bird, Bambi?'' I asked. There was no way the woman would ever have paid a red cent for any kind of pet.

''That's another thing Willy unloaded on me,'' she snorted. Bambi pointed in to the kitchen with midnight-blue nails that had been manicured into sharply honed rapiers.

A parrot paced methodically back and forth on the perch in its cage. The bird was predominately green, with rose-red feathers covering its cheeks and throat. I heard a sharp intake of breath and realized it was my own. Sitting in Bambi's kitchen was a highly prized Cuban Amazon.

''Willy tried to convince me this thing is worth a coupla months' alimony. Can you believe it?'' She shook her head in disgust as she pulled two mugs out of a dented metal cabinet, and filled them from a coffeemaker that looked as if its contents had been sitting around for days. I found a spot on the rim of my cup that wasn't yet chipped and took a sip, the cold, bitter brew launching my body into its own caffeinated shimmy. I walked over to the cage and gazed at the Amazon, which instantly screeched and lurched threateningly toward me. What do you know? It was a mini-Willy with wings.

''Oh, yeah. Don't stick a finger or anything in there,'' Bambi warned as she flipped the parrot the bird.

''I guess its not too social,'' I said, wondering where Willy had gotten an Amazon from.

''Social? That's a good one. The damn thing's demented!'' Bambi stuck a finger in her mouth, sucked on it, and then held it out in front of me. A red scar was deeply etched into the flesh. ''You see what that no-good bag of feathers did to me? That miserable bird bites anything that moves. I gotta hold it off with a frying pan lid in one hand while I try to fill its damn food dish with the other. Is that crazy or what?''

''You're a bitch! You're a bitch!'' the bird happily prattled.

''Cute, huh? Guess who taught it to say that?'' Bambi stuck

her tongue out at the bird. "I keep threatening to feed it to the lousy dog, but those kids of mine won't let me."

"You don't want to do that, Bambi. This is a very valuable bird," I informed her.

"Yeah? So what good does that do me? I'll tell you what good it does: none. Nobody's gonna buy the damn thing; it's too frigging nasty. I ain't taking no more animals from that creep. From now on, it's cash only." Bambi stomped a bare foot on the dingy linoleum floor to emphasize her point as she walked away.

"So, did you catch him last night with the goods?" She approached again with the coffeemaker in hand.

I motioned that I was still working on the first undrinkable cup. "I found him. But it was too late."

Bambi raised a tweezed eyebrow.

"He was carrying parrot eggs. He managed to flush them down a toilet before I could get to him," I explained.

"You see? The man's a genius! That's what I'm up against." Bambi pulled at the spikes of her hair in frustration.

I chose not to comment on Willy's intellectual prowess. "Do you know if he's been dealing in birds lately?"

"Nah. It's mostly the usual thing—you know, selling a few of his cougars and snakes to bikers, and maybe a coupla drug dealers who're looking to guard their stash."

What sounded like a burst of gunfire shook the one intact window in the kitchen. Bambi screamed and hit the ground. The coffee in my cup went flying in the air.

"Big Mama! Big Mama!" the bird screeched hysterically, adding to the chaos.

Laughter erupted outside the kitchen door.

"I'm gonna kill those little bastards!" Bambi vowed.

The boys hit the window with another round from their Super Soakers. But by the time Bambi flung the back door open, the two minidelinquents were already gone. She slammed the door shut, causing the window to rattle.

"You got any kids?" she demanded, the spikes on her head standing on end.

"Nope," I said, dabbing at the oily residue of spilt coffee.

"Well, do yourself a favor and don't." She readjusted her chest inside the bustier.

If I'd needed any convincing, five minutes alone with her offspring would have done the trick. I brought the conversation back to where we'd left off.

"So as far as you know, Willy is still just selling his own stock of reptiles and cats?" I asked.

"Yeah," Bambi said, examining a nail. "Though I'm not even sure how much of that goes on, with him gone so much of the time."

That bit of news caught my attention. "Just how much is he gone?"

Bambi wrinkled her nose. "I'd say he's usually out of town one or two days a week."

"Any idea where he's going?" I kept my tone casual.

"Who knows?" she shrugged. Bambi hooked a nail between two of her molars and dislodged a shred of beef, examining it before flicking it onto the floor. "You wouldn't happen to have the lowdown on what it costs to hire a hit man these days, would you?"

I stared at her. Talk about a change of topic.

"Hypothetically, of course," Bambi added.

"I haven't priced it out lately," I told her. "Why? Are you planning to have Willy knocked off?"

Bambi gave a smile that curdled my blood. "Yeah, if he doesn't start coughing up some of these payments he owes me. You be sure and tell him that."

I wondered just how far Bambi would go to collect the money. "Funny you should bring up the subject of murder. Alberto Dominguez was killed last night."

Bambi looked at me in alarm. "Hey! Wait a minute! Whadda ya think, that *I* had something to do with it?"

"No," I assured her. "But since Willy was working with him, I thought you might have heard something."

"Then you think *Willy* knocked him off." Bambi drummed her fingers along the curve of her hip.

"I don't think he did it, either." I tried another approach. "Did you ever meet Alberto?"

"Yeah. I met him once over at Willy's place. He was walking around like he was afraid something might bite him in the ass. Not only that, but he didn't even try to hit on me and I was looking real good that day." Bambi's eyes began to mist up. ''I remember 'cause I thought that me and Willy might be getting back together. Which is why I went and got this.''

Bambi turned around and hiked the miniskirt up above her rear end, revealing a bottom attired in microscopic black thong panties. I followed the path of her midnight-blue nail across her skin to the middle of one exposed cheek. In the center of her flesh was a tattoo of a heart bearing Willy's name. This was far more than I needed to know.

Bambi glanced at me over her shoulder. ''Now what am I supposed to do with this thing? You tell me that!''

I had to admit she had me on that one.

''Do you know if Willy got your bird from Alberto?''

Bambi pulled her skirt down, one tight quarter inch at a time. ''Nah. That nasty pile of feathers didn't come from Alberto. Willy got it as part of a payoff from some broad by the name of Elena. Hell, she probably gave it to him as a bribe to sleep with her. That's why we broke up, you know.''

''Why was that?'' I hadn't heard this part of the story before.

''Because he'll sleep with any cheap piece of ass that asks him to. The man has no willpower. Hell, he'd screw a loaf of rye bread if it wasn't stale,'' Bambi moaned. ''Sometimes I think it isn't really his fault. It's just that women find Willy irresistible.''

Were we talking about the same man?

''That's the other way he made money when we were together,'' she confided.

''You mean Willy was a gigolo?'' I wondered what delusional woman would have paid for his services.

''Nah, not that. He rented those big cats of his out for *Penthouse* and *Playboy* photo shoots. He was in tight with Hef and that Guccione guy. Willy even promised that he could make me a centerfold. Then I found out the bastard was sleeping with all of the models! He told me he had to do it to keep the girls happy. Otherwise, they'd refuse to pose with his pets and we'd starve.''

Could the woman who'd given Weed the Cuban Amazon be the very same Elena who'd sent the photos I'd found at Alberto's? Bambi continued to pace angrily, her bare feet slapping against the grimy floor.

''What do you know about this Elena?'' I asked.

Bambi stared blankly at me, preoccupied with chewing on her broken nail. ''Who?'' she asked.

''The woman who gave Willy that bird.''

Bambi leaned back against the Formica countertop, balancing on one foot, as the other performed figure eights in the air.

''She's some rich Cuban bitch that calls herself a photographer. I've seen her work and trust me—it sucks. She's just a fag hag.''

''What do you mean?'' I asked.

Bambi rolled her eyes and sighed. ''She specializes in taking photos of beefcake. But the guys are all pansies, ya know? You tell me what she gets outta that, huh?''

Bambi raised her foot higher and I saw that the sole was encrusted with dirt.

''Now to me, *that's* sick. You oughta see some of the pictures she takes. Those guys pose with their equipment just about hanging out like it was flagpoles.'' Bambi hoisted herself onto the counter, her skirt riding up past her thighs. ''I'm telling ya, that Elena's just an example of what's going on. The damn Cubans have taken over Florida, and you know how they did it?''

She stared at me sullenly, demanding a response.

''Working hard and starting businesses?'' I ventured.

''Hah!'' Bambi's mouth pulled into a tight, straight line. ''That's exactly what they want you to believe. But the truth is, the good ol' US of A hands them a pile of money just for coming over here and getting off their boats. It's all a plot to make Castro look bad so that the Cubans back home will revolt. Meanwhile, good Americans like me are stuck in shit holes like this, and runaway Cubans are living high on the hog.''

The back door suddenly slammed open as Bambi's two boys tore through the kitchen and then sped out the front door, allowing the dog to slip in. The critter immediately homed in on Bambi.

''I dare you to tell me that life's fair!'' Bambi complained as she tried to pry the dog off her leg.

The subject of government handouts brought me back

around to Willy. "By the way, I saw some medals hanging up in Willy's trailer. I didn't know that he'd been in the military."

Bambi shoved the dog out the back door, bribing it with a biscuit. "Yeah. He was training to be in the air force. I think he was in for about four months before he got kicked out. It near broke his heart. All due to some captain's wife hitting on him, wouldn't ya know. But he still stays in touch with an old buddy of his from the base."

"He told me that he got those medals for serving in Desert Storm."

The dog yelped as it tried to claw its way back in.

Bambi gave a harsh laugh. "Desert Storm, my ass. Don't you believe a word he tells you. Hell, he told me that he was a one-woman man."

"Then where do you think he got the medals from?" I prodded.

"Where do *you* think?" She stared, clearly finding it hard to believe I could be so dumb. "Where he gets everything else from, of course—some truckload of hot goodies." She looked at the bird in its cage. "You think this thing would taste any good if it was cooked?"

The bird squawked as if it understood.

"You don't want to do that, Bambi. I'd have to report it and you'd just get in trouble."

"Boiled, baked, or broiled, whadda ya say? How about I just fricassee this noisy pile of feathers?" Bambi grinned. "Relax, Porter. I'm not gonna touch the thing. Besides, who knows? Maybe I'll go back to dancing and use the damn bird in my act. If I fry anything, it's gonna be Willy's ass. You tell him from me to start coughing up some bucks before I begin to turn the heat up on him."

I left Bambi's, the remnants of my chloroform headache beginning to kick into high gear. Calling it a day, I veered onto the Palmetto and joined the rest of the flock heading north.

I tried taking deep breaths, driving the speed limit, and pretending I didn't care as car after car passed me by. After five minutes, I was sure the relaxation would kill me. I changed gears, cut into the fast lane, and floored the Tempo for all it was worth. By the time I turned off onto Bird Road, my tension headache was gone.

I stopped in at a pet store, determined to make Bonkers a happy bird. I was easy pickings for the saleswoman who swooped down upon me, making sure I bought a book on caring for cockatoos, as well as Krazy Krunch sticks in four exciting flavors: Real Fruit, Real Nut, Real Veggi and Double Cookie. I also bought a bag of bird seed and a swing so that Bonkers could "experience a natural swinging sensation just as if he were perched on a swaying bough." I didn't know if Bonkers would be happy, but I certainly felt fulfilled.

I left and swung onto the Rickenbacker Causeway, heading for Key Biscayne to hang out at my favorite hideaway. *Ba-bump, ba-bump, ba-bump.* The cadence of the Tempo's wheels cruising across the causeway was as mesmerizing as a hypnotist swinging his watch, each revolution of my tires helping to soothe my soul.

I turned onto an unmarked dirt road where lanky Australian pines majestically cooled the air, slowly thinning out until they disappeared altogether. After that the road quickly deteriorated into an obstacle course of potholes and ruts. Along with no sign, no telephone, and no directions to the place, it was a surefire way to keep tourists, as well as most locals, from venturing any farther.

I drove slowly, easing the Tempo in and out of one hole after another as I passed a down-and-dirty group of shacks, their once-electric Caribbean colors now as faded as my grandmother's housecoat. Rumor had it that the TV show *Flipper* had been filmed here in the sixties. If so, the road's brush with fame was long gone; what was left of the set forgotten and neglected.

The dirt path curved and a cove came into view, surrounded by a thicket of mangroves whose spreading branches intricately interlaced to form an aerial canopy. In the middle of a clearing at the water's edge was an open-air chickee stand. Its thatched roof covered a ramshackle bar where a few drunken fishermen sat listing on stools. Off to the side stood a wooden shack that housed what was loosely referred to as the kitchen.

I spotted Tommy in his uniform of ragged shorts and faded

luau shirt, with flip-flops protecting his feet, and a sailor's cap slapped on his head. His skin was as brown as the bark of the mangrove trees and nearly as rough, having become permatanned over the years. Tommy was owner and proprietor of the establishment, but there were never any guests on the premises. Only those he considered to be part of his drifting family. Come once and if you didn't pass muster, you never came back again.

I parked the Tempo next to a few broken-down pickups and took a seat on an empty stool. There was no need to request a drink. All that was served was beer—a homemade white lightning out of a cooler that Tommy kept behind the bar. I picked up the tin cup that was set before me and took a sip, the liquid working its magic.

I also didn't need to place an order for the soft shell blue crab sandwich that appeared, accompanied by a small bag of chips. There was never any menu at Tommy's. There was also no choice as to what was served. The catch of the day was prepared in whatever manner Tommy wanted to make it. A former military man, turned fisherman, transformed into restaurateur, Tommy figured the place was his and it was run his way. If you didn't like it, he'd point you toward the Rusty Pelican, a tourist trap back on the strip.

I bit into the sautéed crab, so tender and sweet it nearly brought tears to my eyes. Off in the distance the skyscrapers of downtown Miami glimmered, silver monoliths set ablaze by the waning sun, their reflection caught in Biscayne Bay. Coming to Tommy's was the most relaxing thing I could do. Especially at this time of day. A muted palette of colors painted each ripple that lapped at the cove. Its message: There was nothing that couldn't wait till tomorrow.

A steaming cup of coffee was placed in my hands, shaking the somnolence that threatened to overtake me. I looked up to see Tommy's sea-blue eyes twinkling. One evening after several beers, Tommy had revealed that he'd lost a daughter to leukemia years ago. Oddly enough, my father had died of the same disease on the day I'd turned eleven. Ever since then a silent bond had formed between us, as if we somehow helped to fill each other's void.

"Hey, Tommy. What do you know about the illicit

exchange of goods back and forth between Cuba and here?" I asked.

"That it goes on," he replied. A smile tugged at the corners of his mouth.

"Is there much activity in the way of Cuban cigars?" I queried.

His laughter embraced me in its warmth. "Shit, yes. That's big business around here."

I followed Tommy as he left the bar and walked over to a rusty old oil drum. He lit a fire inside its belly and then fed the flames with the leftover garbage of the day. I took a seat on the ground, where I watched the dark body of a little blue heron skim the surface of the water, and a white ibis delicately tiptoe between the gnarled roots of a nearby mangrove. Miami was just a shell toss away, yet from Tommy's, it seemed like a billion miles. I hugged my knees to my chest and closed my eyes, all the better to hear the fire crackle. When I opened them again I found Tommy sitting next to me, his eyes glued to the horizon, studying something only he could see.

"What about Cuban Amazons?" I watched the shiny black body of a cormorant make its last dive of the dying day. A moment later the bird broke the stillness of the water's surface, his orange throat pouch bulging with a meal.

"What about 'em?"

I looked down at the man's hands, as knotted and hard as the mangrove roots.

"How are they brought over?" I asked quietly, not wanting to disturb the sounds of twilight.

"That's easy," Tommy answered. "There are any number of ways. Usually they come by cigar boat from Cuba into the Keys, maybe unloading around Matecumbe. Or a crew will sail into the Bahamas with a stash, and from there, someone will mule them by plane into Miami International. Sometimes they'll skip using a boat altogether, and just fly the birds straight out of Cuba."

"I had no idea." My words drifted out over the bay, carried on invisible wings.

"There's a lot you have no idea of, little girl." Tommy grinned, his eyes now indigo as they sparkled with merriment. "I bet you also don't know about the anti-Castro paramilitary groups that still practice their maneuvers out in the Glades.''

''You're right; I don't,'' I admitted. ''Who are they? A bunch of old men playing at being soldiers?''

''That's what most people think, and some of them are. But the original Cuban exiles don't make up the bulk of the volunteers anymore. Now it's their sons and grandsons. The dream of invading and taking over the homeland has been passed on to the next generation.''

''What do they do out in the Everglades?''

''They do their share of blowing up silhouettes of old Fidel.'' Tommy pulled a small cigar out of his pocket, bit off the end and struck a match against the side of the drum. He waved the flame along the tip of the cigar like a magic wand, taking deep, steady puffs. A smell like sweet cedar, with a hint of nutmeg, wafted toward me. ''But they have other artillery, too.''

''What kind are you talking about? Automatic weapons?'' I probed.

Tommy blew a smoke ring that slowly merged with the still evening air. ''The sky's the limit. Anything and everything that you could ever imagine.''

I'd seen enough action films to imagine plenty. ''You're kidding. Where are they getting all this stuff?''

Tommy was caught up in a silent communion with the roll of tobacco stuck in his mouth. The ritual of cigar smoking continued to mystify me. I had yet to figure out what was so damned enjoyable about puffing on a wad of burning leaves.

Tommy grunted and stood up. ''Hang on a minute. If I'm gonna walk you through history, I'm gonna need a little help.''

He disappeared briefly, to return with a bottle of cognac and two snifters in hand. Tommy poured us each a generous dollop and then raised his glass high in a toast against a background of orange flames. The flames crackled and hissed as they licked the night air like an angry nest of vipers. I watched, entranced, as their reflection became ensnared within the snifter, appearing to set his cognac on fire.

''To the land of Ponce de León. May we all find our fountains of youth.''

I was with him on that one. I took a sip and savored the liqueur as it rushed like liquid sun through my veins. If only staying young could be this easy. I took another taste, silently clicked my heels three times, and made a wish.

Tommy settled himself back down on the ground. ''Once upon a time, in 1961, Cuban exiles in Florida, who had been trained and armed by the CIA, attempted to overthrow Castro with our government's help and blessing. They landed at Playa Girón or, as we gringos know it, the Bay of Pigs. But when it came down to the nitty-gritty, our government reneged on its promise to supply air and naval support, so that most of those poor bastards ended up either getting shot or thrown in prison. JFK slapped an embargo on Cuba in retaliation and since then, no trade has been allowed with the island.''

Between books and Oliver Stone, this was history I already knew.

Tommy paused for a moment. ''Of course, that didn't stop the hanky-panky. The CIA quietly continued their secret war with Cuba throughout the sixties. The big boys amused themselves with cloak-and-dagger antics, hatching harebrained schemes to try to knock off Fidel using exploding cigars and poisoned scuba suits. They also kept the exiles armed. By the seventies, all that had pretty much petered out. Except for the Cuban footsoldiers, that is—some of whom happened to be former CIA agents themselves.''

Tommy swished his cognac, exhaled a cloud of smoke, and took a deep drink. ''During that time, over a million and a half Cubans sought asylum in this country—most of them right here in southern Florida. What that means is they're an economic and political power to be reckoned with. When they speak, believe me, Washington listens. There are also still those in our government who remain loyal to the exiles and their cause. So our friends in the Glades continue to sneak in and out of Cuba, where they quietly carry out their attacks and raids. As to where they get their backing and armament from?'' Tommy shrugged. ''Who knows? But I can tell you that our government never talks openly about their existence.''

''And the embargo still goes on, no matter how much American business kicks and screams,'' I added.

''That's right.'' Tommy smiled. ''Which makes it good pickings for entrepreneurs who have the cojones to risk smuggling Cuban cigars into this country. They're making a frigging fortune doing it. More than they'd ever make if the damn things were legal."

"Just how much money are these guys raking in?"

Tommy rolled his cigar back and forth between his fingers. "Well, last I heard, illegal imports were running about five to ten million cigars a year. In terms of revenue, that would mean they're producing anywhere from seventy-five to one hundred million dollars in cold cash. Which, pound for pound, makes Cuban cigars as lucrative as dealing in marijuana. A hell of a lot safer, too, I might add."

Tommy laid back and stared up at the sky, having said his say on the topic.

"I notice that your cigar doesn't have any band to identify what kind it is," I remarked.

"That's right. But I don't wear some designer's name slapped on my ass, either," he replied, leaving me no wiser.

Any further questions I had were put on hold as Tommy pointed to a flock of brightly colored Quaker parrots performing an avian ballet. Descended from escaped pets, a feral population of the birds now called southern Florida home. We watched until they were no longer in sight, only the echo of their raucous cries serving as a ghostly reminder of their performance.

"Now that's what I call beautiful. A group of parrots spreading their wings as they fly across the sky." Tommy raised his glass in homage. "They're no different from the rest of us. Birds were meant to be free."

I raised my glass and silently agreed.

By the time I arrived home it was dark, but Sophie had turned on the lights in my cottage, along with the TV, so that Bonkers would have company.

"Hi ya, sweetie!" he screeched.

I approved of the greeting. The remains of sunflower seeds, mango, and banana littered his dish. I counted my blessings that Sophie was both a friend and a landlady.

"Boy, are you one lucky bird," I told Bonkers, letting him out of his cage. He crawled onto my shoulder and rode into the kitchen, hopping onto the counter where he helped me unpack groceries. Out came cabbage, watercress, carrots, green pepper and peas, corncobs, papayas, and grapes, filling up my normally empty refrigerator, all for one wisecracking bird. Then I poured myself a glass of red wine and handed Bonkers a carrot as we headed into the garden to watch the stars.

The tangy smell of the sea entwined with the sweet fragrance of frangipani to wrap around me in a savory bouquet. I felt something scamper over my bare feet, as light as a whisper, and knew it was the green lizard that had been sunning himself earlier in the day.

As Bonkers chewed on the carrot, crunching close to my ear, my mind drifted to Bambi. It was obvious that life hadn't turned out the way she had planned when she'd first gotten married. I was caught off-guard as thoughts of Santou swept over me, as powerful as salt in a still-open wound.

Bonkers brought me back to the present as he gently pulled on my ear, testing how far he could go. I brushed him down onto my arm, where he amused himself by chewing on my watch before climbing back up to nuzzle his head under my chin. That's what I was afraid of: being like Bonkers, my wings clipped just enough to make me dependent.

Then Sophie and Lucinda's laughter trickled from their bungalow, tantalizing me with what life with someone else could offer. Bonkers nestled close, his beak nudging my hand until I finally got the message and began to pet him. The bird squawked in protest each time I stopped, as if cursing his luck for being saddled with such a dense human.

I went to sleep with Sophie's laughter still ringing in my ears, only to dream of being locked out in the cold, all alone.

Six

The next morning found me jamming with the rest of the traffic heading west on the Dolphin Expressway. It was time to show my face at work. The U.S. Fish and Wildlife office is tucked away in the duty-free zone just past the airport, an area rife with industry. Its charms include trucks belching exhaust and enough convenience stores to keep me from running low on caffeine.

I walked in to find my boss, Carlos Cardenas, in his usual pose: staring at a computer screen while sniffing the barrel of his unloaded gun. I had the feeling he wasn't all that happy with his promotion. The title and pay were good, but now he was stuck behind a desk in charge of more paperwork than one man could handle, responsible for an office that battled an unusually high number of scandals.

I'd heard various rumors of what he'd done to cause the gods of Fish and Wildlife to strap him with Miami. They ranged from carrying on investigations without prior approval to telling the top brass just what he thought of them. He'd been branded a crazy man, making him sound like my kind of guy. I'd arrived in Miami hoping we'd hit it off. After all, neither of us were on the Service's A-list, but were token minorities in a whitebread, old-boy world. Instead, Carlos had viewed me as his version of the Cuban man's burden from the first morning I'd walked through the door.

"I want you to know that you're here against my will," he'd told me. "I've got enough to deal with. What I don't need in Miami is having a white female who doesn't speak a word of Spanish foisted upon me because of some affirmative-action hooey.''

''*Hola* to you, too,'' I'd responded, making good use of my one Spanish word.

He hadn't been amused. ''They're really out to shaft me this time, aren't they?''

See, that was another thing we had in common. I felt exactly the same.

Maybe it was this sense of unwarranted bad luck that caused him to have such a foul temper. Or maybe it was just Carlos's way. But his moods were a lot like the prize at the bottom of Cracker Jacks: I always pretty much knew what to expect, and it was never what I wanted.

I'd just settled down at what I presumed was my desk, disguised as a blizzard of paperwork, when Carlos beckoned me into his office in his own gentle way.

''Porter! Now!''

We'd quickly developed a shorthand that takes other couples years to perfect. I looked upon it as an updated Lucy-Desi routine. I walked in, prepared for my latest Cracker Jack prize.

''*Oy vay.* You're one royal pain in the ass.'' His head was resting heavily in his hands.

''Is that a gun over there, or are you just happy to see me?'' I pointed to the unloaded pistol on his desk.

''Actually, I'm thinking of using it on you,'' he glumly responded. The bags beneath his eyes would have made a bloodhound proud. ''Chances are the brass in Washington would give me a medal, and I'd stand a better chance of getting out of this hole.''

''Rough weekend?'' I inquired, mustering up as much sympathy as I could.

''Nice of you to ask, especially since it's your actions that are screwing me over,'' Carlos retorted.

I didn't have to spend much time pondering exactly what that was; Cardenas quickly informed me.

''I got a call from Tony Carrera yesterday. He says he's suing your ass for all it's worth.''

Boy, was he in for a big disappointment. ''Just what is he suing me for?'' As far as I could tell, I'd saved Carrera's life.

Call me crazy, but I'd expected something more like a thank-you note. Maybe even a bottle of wine.

"Correct me if I'm wrong, Porter, but the paperwork on his shipment had already been cleared." Carlos opened his desk drawer, pulled out a container of aspirin and popped the lid, upending the contents into his mouth.

More than 14,000 annual wildlife shipments flow into Miami, forcing our six inspectors to pick and choose what they look at—Fish and Wildlife triage. That meant rubber-stamping was the general modus operandi. Tony Carrera used that to maximum advantage.

"I thought a surprise inspection might help keep Tony on the straight and narrow," I explained.

"That's beside the point, Porter. The paperwork was cleared, yet you forced him to open the crates. As a result the man was bitten by a venomous snake, which means he could very well have died. Does that sum it up?" Carlos had begun to slowly twirl the gun round and round in a tight circle. "To say nothing of the fact that inspections aren't even part of your damn job!"

"And what is? Sitting at a desk and shuffling a pile of papers?" Damn—yep, it was. Fastest mouth east of the Mississippi.

Carlos glared at me and pulled on his mustache, a sure sign that a black mood was kicking in. The bureaucratic demand for paperwork was a sore point with him, with good reason. Although smugglers focused on Miami, our territory also ran from Martin County, down through Broward, to Dade, to the tip of Key West, with manatee and sea-turtle problems topping the list. And that wasn't even counting the other thirty-eight endangered species that call Florida home. The state was considered the Mission Impossible of the critter world. With all this going on, the thought of planting my fanny in front of a stack of paperwork was absurd.

"Can Carrera really sue me?" I was counting on some moral support.

Carlos was back to sniffing his gun. "Sure. Why not?"

It was nice to know the Service was solidly behind me, as usual. I filled Carlos in on the Dominguez case, hoping that 250 disappearing parrots would interest the man.

Carlos sighed and fingered an unfinished report. "Local theft of wildlife isn't a federal problem. That belongs to Dade County and the state. Don't waste our time."

But I'd been trained under Charlie Hickock, the most ornery, infamous, and best agent to have ever passed through the Service. Besides learning the ropes, I'd learned to depend on my instincts and wiles when it came to a case, latching on tight and not letting go. I pressed my point with Carlos.

"This involves more than just theft; it could be the tip of a large smuggling operation. I caught Willy muling parrot eggs for Alberto just the other night."

Carlos's eyes narrowed to two thin slits as he timed his opening shot. "You wouldn't happen to have some of that evidence by any chance, would you?" He watched as his point hit its mark. "Don't tell me, Porter. It all flew away?"

I felt my face redden. "Willy flushed everything before I could reach him. But I kept his vest, which has some dried yolk on it as evidence," I said eagerly.

"Weed is just one of hundreds of two-bit smugglers here in Miami. We don't have the time to be chasing our tails, running after them for piss-ass crimes."

He pointed a finger past me, clearly aimed at my desk. "You've got more than enough right there to keep you busy. Unless you'd like some extra paperwork, that is."

I'd sooner have played with a crate full of tarantulas. It was time to throw down my trump card. "Willy may be a two-bit smuggler, but he has enough savvy to have lined up contacts that are providing him with a pipeline of hyacinth and Cuban Amazon birds straight out of the wild."

Carlos's head snapped up at the mention of endangered parrots. He'd once told me about his grandmother's love for such birds. And right now, Amazons were hot, hot, hot to own. Especially in the Cuban community, where the bird was a living link to their homeland.

All I had to do was reel him in. "Alberto was running some kind of illegal courier service that dropped off American goods in exchange for Cuban birds and cigars." I told him about the sack of birds.

Carlos beat his hands lightly on his desk as if it were a bongo, his brow scrunched into a canvas of wrinkles. "All right, Porter. It could be worth looking into—just on the slim chance that you're really onto something.''

I was about to pull out the hyacinth feather when Carlos added a footnote.

''But I'm assigning the case to Phil.'' He gave his hands one final hard slap on the desk, turning the bongo into a kettledrum.

''What!'' I felt incredibly tactful by not lunging for his gun.

''Listen, Porter: We're talking about dealing with the Hispanic community. They aren't going to respond well to a female agent going around and questioning them.''

I wasn't about to swallow that line. ''Don't you think that might be your own bias?''

''Number two. Phil's been based in Miami a lot longer than you and already has good informants in place,'' Carlos continued.

''If his informants are so good, why hasn't he come up with his own smuggling case involving endangered parrots?'' I challenged.

Carlos conveniently turned a deaf ear. ''And, number three, Phil speaks Spanish.''

Damn! If only I hadn't fallen for that line in school about French being the language of love!

I opened my mouth to protest, but Carlos cut me off at the pass. ''End of discussion, Porter. Finish that paperwork on your desk and we'll talk about sending you out on dove detail.'' He smirked.

I'd joined the Service to take on the bad guys and save the critters of the world. I'd already done my share of duck duty, sitting on my rear end in the swamps of Louisiana. I had no desire to spend my time in Florida playing nanny again to a group of hormonally challenged hunters with the hots to shoot birds.

''Write up a report on Dominguez and Weed, and the parrots that you saw in that sack. I'll look it over and pass it on to Phil,'' Carlos commanded.

I hadn't seen Phil voluntarily leave his desk for anything other than lunch in the entire six months that I'd been here. I was damned if I was about to hand my case over to him.

Maybe my fanny was the property of Uncle Sam, but it sure

didn't belong to Carlos. It was time to practice the fine art of backpedaling, no matter how stupid it made me sound.

"I don't really feel comfortable with putting anything down on paper," I began.

Carlos raised his head, beginning to sense trouble. "And just why is that?"

I demurely lowered my eyes, wondering how Lucy Ricardo would have gotten out of this one. "Well, to tell you the truth, it all happened so fast that I'm not really sure *what* it was I saw in that sack. I only had enough time to see there were some large blue and green birds." I topped it off with an apologetic shrug.

"I knew it!" Carlos exploded. He squeezed his head tightly between his hands, as if it were about to burst. "It's the sixty eggs, all over again! Forget it, Porter. Just do your damn paperwork!"

I headed to my desk, silently fuming even though I'd kept my case out of Phil's lackadaisical paws.

The infamous sixty eggs case took place one month after I'd arrived in Miami, gung ho to make my mark. I'd received a tip about a small-time smuggler flying in from Brazil with illegal goods, and had watched and waited, my adrenaline revved, as a customs inspector gave the smuggler a cursory one-two glance and passed him through. I'd immediately stopped the mule, explaining that I needed to do my own inspection. The customs inspector had shot me an unappreciative look as I tore the smuggler's luggage apart and triumphantly found a small wooden box, its lid tightly nailed closed as if it were a miniature coffin. Except for the tiny airholes that had been drilled in its top.

My pulse raced as I pried the crate open to discover a cobalt blue bird nestled as quiet as a corpse inside. Its beak and legs had been tightly taped and a thimble of tequila used to keep it tranquilized. Worst of all, the hyacinth's beautiful tail feathers had been crudely hacked off in order to fit the bird inside its cramped quarters.

I opened a second box, where sixty eggs had been packed as carefully as a treasure trove of pearls. My heart pounded, certain I'd discovered endangered hyacinth eggs.

The customs inspector hurriedly informed a U.S. Department of Agriculture agent about what I had found, fully aware that foreign eggs are routinely destroyed for fear of disease.

"But these are from an endangered species!" I'd argued, keeping tight hold of the box in a precious tug of war.

The fight escalated until I threatened to have the USDA agent thrown into jail for breaking the Endangered Species Act. Carlos was immediately called to the scene, with the expectation that he'd force me to hand over the tainted goods. Instead Carlos joined in the act, his Cuban dander riled to a tizzy as he yelled "death to anyone who would harm endangered birds!"

The fight took flight up the ranks all the way to Washington, D.C., where it was finally decided the parrots would be allowed to hatch, and then tested for disease. Carlos had gone to bat for me like a trooper, even managing to finagle an incubator out of USDA's hands. Then we'd waited with baited breath, anxious to savor the fruits of our victory. I should have been clued in on what to expect when it was my customs inspector who made the call.

"Hey, Porter. Looks like you finally got yourself a cock. Sixty of them, to be exact," he'd gloated triumphantly.

My hyacinth macaws had hatched into fighting cocks. For the next few months, Carlos and I were the butt of endless chicken jokes. My presence inside the terminal was still met with calls of "cock-a-doodle doo," and "how's it hanging?" But Carlos and his macho pride had taken the hardest hit. I was paying for it now.

I sat at my desk feeling comatose at the mere sight of so much paperwork, when my phone rang, allowing me a momentary reprieve. My savior turned out to be none other than Tony Carrera.

"Hi, Tony. I hear you're so overwhelmed at my saving your life that you're planning to sue me," I said, feeling unappreciated all the way around.

"Yeah. That's right. I almost died 'cause of you, Porter. All I need to do is make one call to my lawyer and your ass is grass," Tony answered in a cocksure tone.

I could almost hear him gnawing on the soggy nub of his cigar.

"But maybe there's something you can do for me instead."

"What are we playing, Tony? Let's Make a Deal?" I asked, curious as to what the favor would be.

"Yeah, that's it," Tony snickered. "You be nice to me and maybe I'll consider dropping the charges against you."

"You don't have a case, Tony," I said, calling his bluff.

"Don't screw with me, Porter," Carrera warned. "Your boss wasn't too happy when I told him about what you did. He gave a scream like he'd swallowed a hot tamale."

I sighed, knowing there was no sense trying to enlighten him that Mexicans ate tamales, not Cubans. "What's your problem, Tony?"

"I got this crazy neighbor who don't like my flamingos. Can ya imagine that?" Carrera sounded sincerely hurt.

I had heard about the flock of pink Chilean flamingos that Tony kept on his grounds. Supposedly they made the ones at Parrot Jungle look chintzy.

"You gotta see my birds—they're gorgeous. And very well behaved, too. I gotta great place for them here, ya know? I gotta pond and everything. Okay, so once in a while a couple of 'em get a little rowdy and wander next door. They're like kids. So what's the big deal, huh?" Tony paused, waiting for me to respond.

"I don't know, Tony. You tell me."

"The big goddamn deal is that they poop a little on this guy's lawn. That's what's giving him a heart attack! I told him, 'Schmuck! That stuff is what they call organic. It's good for your lawn, putz.' But he's one of these anal assholes," Carrera fumed.

"I'm sure you can work something out with him," I replied. "There's nothing official I can do."

"I ain't done yet, Porter!" Tony gave a dramatic pause. "This morning the bastard escalated the battle. He nailed one of my birds that innocently wandered over. Now the sick fuck's got it rigged to the grille of his Rover and is driving back and forth in front of my place beeping his horn and driving me nuts! The guy's a lunatic and I want his ass thrown in jail!"

There was the distinct sound of a car horn beeping in the background.

"Ya hear that? I'm supposed to be recuperating! I'm a sick

man, and I can tell you, this ain't helping things any!'' Tony wailed.

I found myself commiserating with him. ''I'd really like to help you, Tony, but this falls under the state's jurisdiction. You need to call the Game and Freshwater Fish Commission.''

''Bullshit. I need a fed showing up on the scene to scare the shit out of this guy. He ain't gonna listen to no state agent.''

''I can't get involved in this,'' I tried to explain.

Carrera interrupted, his voice rising above the sound of his neighbor's car horn. ''Let me ask you something, Porter. Just how much does that insurance company of yours cover your ass for?''

His point was well taken. ''I'll be right over,'' I replied.

Carlos had stepped out, allowing me to make a quick getaway. I left a note that an emergency call had come in and hopped into my Tempo, setting sail for the posh suburb of Coral Gables in search of Tony Carrera's domain.

''I'll be right there'' stretched into an hour as I fought my way down the Palmetto, turning off to land smack in the traffic of Miracle Mile. A four-block-long shopper's extravaganza, the miracle is that there are actually people who can afford to buy anything there. I crawled along, my dented slice of American sandwiched between a silver-blue Jaguar and a metallic gold Mercedes, both the exact color of their owner's hair.

I followed Tony's directions out to the burbs where the streets began to curve, winding and ending with no apparent rhyme or reason. Even more infuriating, all the addresses were painted in tiny black letters on obscure white stones that sat low to the ground. I was just about to give up, drive home, and start totaling up my meager net worth, when the god of insurance companies smiled down upon me. A life-sized street sign appeared and pointed me in the right direction.

Carrera's hideaway lay fortressed behind a high brick wall. It was immediately evident that the reptile biz had been very, very good to the man. The neighborhood was a hot zone for the rich, famous, and corrupt.

Tony met me at the gate in a pair of burgundy silk pajamas and white patent leather shoes, a flashy gold chain perfectly centered on his unruly jungle of chest hair. He'd forgotten to slap on his toupee, exposing a few limp strands that clung to his scalp for dear life.

"What the fuck took you so long?" he demanded. "I swear, my heart is palpitating like a goddamn squirrel trapped inside a paper bag. It's threatening to explode every time that miserable bastard drives by. I coulda been dead by now, standing out here waiting for you to show!"

He swiped at his forehead with a meaty paw, then motioned for me to follow. I dutifully treaded along toward the back of his house, only to come to a sudden stop when I saw a massive German shepherd before us, its teeth bared. The dog instantaneously transformed into a locomotive of flying fur and paws, eyeing my body like a large T-bone steak.

"Halt, Poopsie, halt!" Tony commanded, with a gesture that made the delicate charm bracelet dangling from his thick wrist flash in the sun. Poopsie froze in midair and crashed to the ground at my feet.

"Ya can't be too careful," he said. "There's a lot a scum out there, if ya know what I mean."

I exhaled in short, jagged bursts, still not trusting the dog, who licked his chops with his eyes locked on my throat. "Friendly pooch you've got there, Carrera. He must get his warm, cuddly personality from your side of the family."

"Just don't piss me off and you'll be fine," Tony snickered.

I walked by Carrera's side with Poopsie loping along, his snout noisily sniffing my fingers. Tony's house was a sprawling ranch, but it was the grounds in back that made his residence special. Gathered around a large pond were twenty-five flamingos, so seemingly perfect they could have been mistaken for lawn ornaments. They were deep coral in color, with the long, elegant necks of well-bred society matrons. They turned toward me in unison, shyly displaying a chorus line of hooked, Roman beaks. Then the birds leisurely moved away, their long, spindly legs stepping as gingerly as though in a minefield.

Carrera grunted, collapsing into one of the large pink lounge chairs that was sculpted in the shape of a sleeping flamingo. I joined him, with Poopsie attached to my side. Tony lifted a dark green pitcher and filled two brightly colored plastic glasses to the brim. I picked up my glass and took a sip, expecting it to be some sort of summer drink. Instead, a hot combo of Tabasco sauce and tomato juice bombarded my taste buds with a rousing snap, crackle, and pop.

"What the hell is this?" I sputtered with a gasp.

Poopsie let loose a low growl, apparently not pleased with my tone.

"Haven't you ever had a Bloody Mary before, Porter?" Tony reached down along the side of his chair and hoisted up a bottle of vodka, looking tickled at having taken me by surprise. He unscrewed the cap and gave his glass an extra hit. "Maybe you should consider bribing someone to take you out once in a while."

"You probably shouldn't be drinking. Aren't you on some sort of medication for that snake bite?" I wondered if there was any way I could be held responsible, should Tony be found floating face down in his pond. Even more to the point, I wondered if I could get away with the deed.

"Yeah. So what?" he snorted. "I only buy the good stuff—this vodka'll kill anything. Even the venom of a goddamn snake." He downed his drink and poured himself another. "Besides, it's a nice, healthy midmorning refresher. All that vitamin C and A."

I took another sip. Then I thought of how Carlos had been ready to turn my case and all my hard-earned information over to a male agent, and took a larger gulp. The Bloody Mary was beginning to taste better and better. Besides, it seemed to make Poopsie a happy dog. He wagged his tail as Carrera topped off my drink.

"So, tell me about your neighbor," I suggested.

Tony's eyes instantly filled with tears. "That sick sonuvabitch has been out to get my birds since Day One. I'm talking from the moment the bastard moved in. As far as I'm concerned, you can't trust someone who don't have a soft spot for dumb animals, ya know what I mean?"

I was sure the animal kingdom felt pretty much the same way about Tony.

"What's the guy's name?" I asked.

Carrera reached toward my glass again with the pitcher. I

waved it away, only to hear a low snarl at my feet. I was beginning to wonder if Poopsie had a drinking problem of his own.

"The bastard's name is Phil Langer. And the bird that he got was poor little Tallulah." Tony blew his nose between his fingers.

"You have names for your flamingos?" I asked, edging as far as I could from Carrera.

Tony wiped his fingers on his pajama pants, leaving a long squiggly streak. "Course they have names. Don't your pets have names?"

I didn't even want to guess how he could tell each bird apart. "What does Mr. Langer do for a living?"

"You're gonna love this." Tony gave a contemptuous snort. "He's the goddamn founder of the Electric Doggy Fence Company. You know, one of those places that buries a bunch of electric wires under your lawn, shoves some flags in the ground, sticks a collar on your dog, and then shocks 'em to hell if they try to get out. In fact, that's their slogan. 'You lock 'em. We shock 'em.' Real clever, huh?"

The name had a familiar ring. "I've heard of the company before. I'm just not sure why."

Carrera laughed. "It's 'cause a few of Langer's branch offices in Georgia and central Florida were recently blown up by some animal rights nuts. Shit—they should have gotten Langer while they were at it."

Tony's fingers fumbled with his pajama top, undoing one button after another until he sighed in relief, exposing a large girth of pink, flabby skin.

"I'm not so sure it's good for you to be lying out here in the sun. Maybe you should go inside and rest." I was beginning to feel woozy at the sight of so much soft, naked flesh.

"What are you, my mother?" Tony glared. "Just go nail that sucker, will ya?"

Poopsie bared his yellowed choppers and growled, seconding his master.

"That's whatcha gotta do, or I don't drop the charges against you." Tony smirked, displaying his own yellow dentures.

I picked up my glass and polished off the remaining Bloody Mary.

I headed over to Langer's hoping that the man would know virtually nothing about the law. I had no legal business sticking my nose in anywhere near their feud. Carrera's flamingos had been born and bred in captivity right here in south Florida. In addition, the birds weren't even an endangered species. That made this mess entirely a state wildlife affair. The most I could do was try to scare some sense into the man.

Langer's house was situated behind a towering stone wall, the entrance blocked by a locked iron gate. I pulled up to the intercom box and touched the buzzer. The voice that boomed out held all the warmth of a marine sergeant and the force of a jackhammer.

"State your name, your business, and your rank, if you have one."

Oh, brother. Carrera hadn't warned me that I'd be dealing with some crackpot military wanna-be.

"My name is Rachel Porter, and I'm a special agent with the U.S. Fish and Wildlife Service." The heat made me feel as if the Bloody Marys were performing a cancan in my head. "I'd like to speak with you, Mr. Langer."

The gate swung open, allowing me to pass through. I navigated up the long circular drive to the front of the house, where I discovered that Langer's vehicle was no mundane Land Rover, but an imposing Hummer—the four-wheel drive, all-terrain jeep used by the army during Desert Storm. These days, it was popular among drug dealers and macho men desiring a vehicle reeking with attitude.

I parked and walked around to check the front of the Hummer. Sure enough, there was Carrera's flamingo lashed to the vehicle's grille, its pink plumage stained with blood. Tallulah's long, lifeless neck hung low like a worn out rubber band, nearly touching the ground, and its skinny green legs were clumsily bent, crisscrossing at its pink, wrinkled feet. The flamingo's body was held in place with razor-sharp wire that cut through feathers and skin. From a distance, the flattened flamingo could have been that crazy cartoon character, the Roadrunner. Up close, it was simply a disgusting sight.

I was about to cut the bird down when the front door flew open. The stench of a cigar barreled through the door, down the steps, and across the gravel drive. Then Langer emerged like a phantom from behind a thick cloud of smoke.

His thin-rimmed sunglasses were darkly tinted, allowing him to see out while not allowing anyone to see in. The man's neck had the density of a tree stump, supporting a head of equally impressive size. His strong, square jaw jutted forward in an unspoken dare. I took the challenge and continued up to the thick black stogie held hostage between tightly clenched teeth, framed by lips which pulled back in a grimace. I moved on to Langer's aquiline nose, his thin nostrils pinched in a display of excessive distaste. I hurriedly passed over the sunglasses, unsettled to see my reflection trapped in their black lenses. Finally I reached the summit, where Langer's forehead loomed large and wide, the skin as rough and dry as sandpaper. This was topped by a thick flank of white hair, razor-cut into an abrupt, no-nonsense flattop.

Langer stood more than six feet tall, with arms and legs as massive as tree limbs. He continued to puff on his stogie, staring down at me through those annoyingly impenetrable sunglasses. I stared back with my best bad-ass, Bloody Mary-induced glare, wishing I had something other than Sophie's shocking-pink sunglasses slapped on my face.

He finally raised two fingers the size of derringer pistols and removed the cigar from his lips, breaking the silence. "Did I hear you say that you're from some sort of animal activist organization?"

His voice rumbled toward me in shock waves that could have logged in on the Richter scale.

"What I said was that I'm an agent with U.S. Fish and Wildlife," I answered, standing my ground.

If this had been the old West, we would have drawn our guns and shot it out right about now. Langer removed his sunglasses, which pretty much produced the same effect.

I had thought his dark glasses were scary, but Langer's eyes took the prize. The irises were densely black, with wafer-slim rings of yellow circling each pupil like a solar eclipse. Predator eyes.

Langer looked me up and down, his lips parting in a silent

laugh. "Fish and Wildlife, huh? Well, in my book that's pretty much the same thing. It's just a federally funded animal activist organization."

Langer's rough and tough act was beginning to wear on my nerves. "Well, *this* federally funded wildlife organization has laws which are illegal to break," I informed him.

Langer stuck his shades back on, once again blocking me out. "I suppose that means you want me to surrender the bird?"

He didn't bother to wait for my answer, but let loose a yawn. Then, grabbing both sides of his head, he casually cracked his neck. "Let me tell you about a little law we have here in this country, that has to do with something sacred called private property rights. It's *my* right not to have some long-necked bird flying onto my property and constantly taking a shit. But if that does happen, it's *also* my right to get in my vehicle and run the damn thing down!" Langer announced in a bellicose boom. "By the way, when did Fish and Wildlife decide to shoot themselves in the foot by hiring girls to do their dirty work?"

I didn't answer, but pulled out my pocket knife and flicked the blade open, allowing a stream of sun to glint off its keen steel edge.

"What you just said is 100 percent pure horseshit," I calmly replied. "When you ran that bird over, you broke the law."

Langer's face momentarily darkened before breaking into a Cheshire-cat grin. "I think we're both aware that it all depends on who you know."

"I'll be reporting this incident to the state wildlife office. Do you happen to know anyone there?" I didn't wait for his answer, but cut the flamingo down from the Hummer's grille.

"Damn. Now I need to go snag myself another good hood ornament," Langer replied with an indifferent shrug.

I finished cutting the wire, then looked up toward him. The sun's rays bounced off Langer's dark lenses with the concentrated strength of a laser, reflecting back into my eyes. I solved that by bounding up the steps, to put us on the same level. My presence was greeted by a hiss that instantly turned my legs to mush.

Something brushed against the back of Langer's pants leg and I looked down to see a pair of deep amber eyes locked onto mine, and quivering whiskers silhouetted against the bright noonday light. An unleashed cougar stood by Langer's side.

"That's my kitty cat." Langer's voice curled around my insides and gave a hard yank. "He's old, but he still earns his keep."

The cougar bared its teeth and flattened its ears, as if on cue. I stood mesmerized, half in awe, half in fear. It was the first time I'd stood this close to an uncaged critter that was truly a specialized killing machine.

"He's just part of my menagerie." Langer's tone was soft and low as a soothing lullaby, his hand gently lingering on the cougar's head. "Wait here and I'll show you the rest of my zoo."

I couldn't have moved if I'd wanted to. As Langer disappeared inside his house the cat stood guard, every rippling muscle beneath its sun-dappled fur tightly coiled and ready for instant response.

Langer returned almost immediately with a flimsy leash, attaching it to the shock collar that was buckled around the cougar's neck.

"Does that collar really work?" I asked.

Langer's eyes flickered over me, the wisp of a smile licking his lips. "You'd do well to hope so. I'd say that right now, your life depended on it."

A shiver softly murmured that I had more to fear from Langer than I ever would from any cat.

"Meet Fidel," he said. "I'd invite you to pet him, but you might lose your hand."

I suppressed the overwhelming urge to stroke the cat's tawny coat. "In that case, I'll pass."

As the cougar sniffed the air and looked over his realm, I noticed a scar in the shape of a teardrop under the cat's right eye. The animal's body suddenly tensed, then he turned toward me and snarled. I pulled back and glanced at Langer, who held a small radio transmitter in his hand.

"It's how I control the cat," he stated simply.

"Must be a pretty powerful zap that you use." Call me a

cynic, but I was beginning to wonder if the cat had been given a jolt in order to provoke it. Specifically at me.

"I don't call it a zap," Langer replied disdainfully. "I think of it as different levels of correction that I choose to administer."

Uh huh. That made it sound a whole lot better. "Whatever it's called, it must hurt like hell."

Langer's mouth curled down in an unpleasant smirk. "Not really. Nothing that you or I couldn't take."

"Have you ever stuck one of those around your own neck and given it a try?" I challenged.

Langer didn't respond, but led the way around to the back of his house.

"Why do you call him Fidel?" I asked, curious as to the unusual choice of name.

"Because he's old and declawed, pretty much like that crackpot, Castro. But he can still be a real pain in the ass."

Except for being declawed, Langer could have been describing himself. As we reached the backyard, I saw that Langer hadn't been joking when he offered to show me his private zoo. Steel-reinforced cages held clouded leopards, lions, black panthers, ocelots, bobcats, cougars, and African servals, along with Siberian tigers. A few of the large cats paced back and forth in boredom, their heads lolling from side to side in the heat. Others had given up completely and stared blankly out into space, their bodies almost comatose on their concrete floors.

"See. I'm an animal lover, too." Langer gave a sour smile.

"What's the obsession with cats?" I inquired, fighting the urge to run and fling open every cage door.

Langer studied the animals. "I like the control it gives me over carnivores who think they're stronger and smarter than I am," he replied.

I didn't doubt that the answer was honest. I counted twenty-seven large cats to be lodged and cared for. It had to cost Langer an astonishing amount of money to feed his harem every day.

"The Electric Doggy Fence Company must be doing a bang-up business to allow you to maintain this number of animals. To say nothing of what you must have paid to buy them all in the first place,'' I remarked.

Langer turned and looked at me. ''You've got it wrong, Agent Porter. I didn't buy these cats. I was given them all for free, compliments of the Game and Freshwater Fish Commission.''

I couldn't be certain whether I heard Langer laugh, or if it was my imagination. Either way, I got his point.

It's common practice for the Florida state wildlife office to confiscate illegally owned large cats and place them with licensed individuals who have the means to care for them. It's the only way to keep impounded exotics from being destroyed.

This told me exactly who might feel inclined to do Langer a favor, making it clear that the issue of Carrera's flamingo had probably been as dead from the get go as the bird itself.

I decided to remind Langer that while he might have powerful friends, he also had his share of enemies. ''I hear some of your branch offices have been bombed in the past few months.''

Langer didn't blink an eye.

''In fact, wasn't there an attack on your central Florida office just this past Saturday night? It would seem whoever is responsible is heading this way. You must be worried about that,'' I prodded.

Langer's hand hovered in magician-like fashion above his feline companion's head. ''Just let them come to Miami. Fidel here would love it.''

I was caught by surprise as an angry shriek tore from Fidel's throat. The cat lunged at me, getting within inches of my leg. The rest of Langer's menagerie instantly picked up on Fidel's cry, the air bristling with their angry roars. My own temper flew into overdrive, though there was no way for me to be sure that Langer's finger had actually hit the control button.

A smirk raced across the man's lips. ''It's always difficult to know if an animal is going to attack. Don't you find that to be the case with wild things, Agent Porter?''

Too bad those shock collars didn't come in *his* size. I turned and stalked to the front of the house, Langer watching in amusement as I loaded Carrera's flamingo inside the trunk of my car.

"You be sure and file that report with the Game and Freshwater Fish Commission as soon as you get back to the office, Agent Porter. After all, I wouldn't want to think you were slacking off on your job." Langer laughed, pleased with his joke.

"Oh, don't worry about me. It's *you* that I'm concerned about," I lightly replied.

"And just why is that?"

"Because someday, when you least expect it, Fidel is going to turn around and rip out your throat."

Langer's silent stare followed me out the gate and down the road, burning two holes in my back. I felt as if I'd just played a game of Russian roulette—except that in Langer's case, all the chambers were loaded.

Carrera stared at the lifeless flamingo that lay at his feet. "I thought you'd come back with that bastard in cuffs, Porter! I want his goddamn ass in jail!" His burgundy silk pajamas appeared to have come alive, vibrating on a body that shook in rage.

"Look, Tony, I did what I could. I gave Langer a warning and told him I'd be filing an official report with the state Game and Fish Commission. As far as any penalties go, that's up to them. The only thing I can do is try to push the case with one of their agents."

"Maybe that'll make *you* feel better, but we both know how much good it'll do," he fumed.

Carrera must have realized he'd been minus his toupee after I'd left for Langer's. He fiddled with it now, setting it askew on top of his head. "Nobody gives a damn about my birds. Who do I gotta know to get some kind of justice around here? The goddamn governor?"

After meeting Langer, I wasn't sure even that would do any good. "Just keep your birds off Langer's property," I advised. "That way, if he does anything else we'll have a strong case."

I had no doubt that a psychotic like Langer would be yanking Tony's chain with another gruesome prank in the not-too-distant future.

"If that sonuvabitch even thinks of hurting any more of my birds, I'm gonna kill him. I swear it!" Carrera poured himself another drink and downed it in one noisy gulp. The heat of the day had reached its zenith, infusing the air like a pot on slow boil. Anything with sense was lying low in a siesta, making me wonder where Carrera and I fit in.

Tony threw Poopsie a piece of ice but the dog refused to move from under the lounge, having discovered that Carrera's rear end supplied a good dose of shade.

"Okay, Tony. I did my part. Now I want a favor in return."

"Yeah, yeah," Tony murmured. His eyes fluttered closed, worn out from too many Bloody Marys, the morning's emotional upheaval, and the overbearing sun. "I'll think about dropping my lawsuit against you."

"That's a given, Carrera. We had an agreement. You don't honor it and you'll be sunning yourself tied to the grille of *my* car," I warned. "This has to do with something else."

Tony cocked open an eye, instantly suspicious. "Uh, uh. I don't owe you any favors, Porter. You want something, you go get yourself another patsy. I don't believe in this public service crap."

I plowed straight ahead. "Alberto Dominguez was murdered last night. I discovered his body right after I learned he was back to trafficking in illegal birds. Do you have any idea who he was tied in with?"

Tony rolled the waist of his pajama bottoms down, exposing enough hairy flesh to have driven a female gorilla wild. Dipping his fingers into the pitcher of Bloody Marys, he removed an ice cube and slowly slid it back and forth across his bare stomach, leaving a melted track of tomato juice and vodka in its wake.

"All you bring me back is a dead bird and you think I owe you? Get ouddah here." Tony popped the tainted remains of the cube into his mouth and noisily sucked on it.

"Come on, Tony; I saved your life," I reasoned. "You'd be dead now if it weren't for me."

"Who are you kidding, Porter?" Tony chewed on the cube like a frenzied beaver. "You said it yourself—you nearly gave me a heart attack. Remember? I heard ya."

"Listen up, Carrera: if you know who Alberto was involved with, I want the information right now. Otherwise, you know I can make your life difficult." I'd about had it with Tony's misplaced sense of self-righteousness. Evidently, Poopsie felt the same way. The dog popped up and ran off after a squirrel, knocking over Carrera's drink, which spilled on his chest.

Tony groaned in frustration. "How the hell should I know who Dominguez was involved with? The guy was a lowlife scam artist who'd do anything for a buck."

"Unlike your own legitimate dealings?" I sweetly inquired.

"Damned straight," Tony huffed. "I'm the fucking American Express Gold Card when it comes to wildlife dealers."

As far as I was concerned, his gold card was about to be revoked. "You know, it would be a shame if some of your paperwork were to accidentally be misplaced. I bet it would slow down your shipments for weeks. Who knows? Your clients might even end up taking their business elsewhere."

Carrera threw up his hands in horror. "Am I hearing you right, Porter? Is this blackmail you're threatening me with?"

I looked at him without saying a word.

"*This* is exactly why people hate the government, Porter. It's enough to make law-abiding citizens join militias. You'll have only yourself to blame when our system of free enterprise folds."

"I'll learn to live with it. Besides, I know you too well, Tony," I chuckled. "You'd rather become legit than wear camouflage."

Carrera played with the gold chain around his neck. "All right, Porter. But you don't know who you got this from, and you promise to leave me alone. Right?"

"You got it, Tony," I vowed, keeping my fingers crossed.

Carrera leaned in toward me. "Alberto was in tight with the neighbors I got on the other side of me, here." Tony motioned to the house on the right with his thumb. "Dominguez was over there all the time. It was almost like he was living with them, if ya know what I mean." Carrera gave me a wink.

"And who are those neighbors?"

Tony brought his voice down lower. "That's Elena Vallardes and her brother, Ramon. Two wacko Cubans, wouldn't ya know. I'm not sure what the brother does, but she's some kinda pretty boy photographer. I'm damned if those two aren't dealing a sideline in birds, though. I mean, I'll be sitting out here minding my own business, when a bunch of damn parrots start squawking it up to high hell over there, driving me crazy. Just when I think I've reached my limit, it'll become nice and quiet. Then after a coupla months, like clockwork, it starts all over again."

"Maybe you should be a little neighborly, especially if you're in the same line of business. Call and introduce yourself," I suggested.

"I've been neighborly enough!" Carrera sniffed. "I told 'em outright I didn't give a shit whether or not they had a license for their fucking birds. I just warned them they better do something about the damn noise."

Ever the diplomat. "How did they respond?" I asked.

Tony removed his pajama top and rubbed his hands back and forth over his stomach. "Hey, whadda ya think? Maybe this Bloody Mary stuff has some of that UV protection crap in it. Now *that* would be the way to market sunscreen. 'Buy Tony's Bloody Mary mix: The only drink that makes you feel good both inside and out!' I could become a millionaire and get outta the lousy animal trade." Carrera giggled. "Of course, then what would you do, huh, Porter? Without me, you'd be sitting on your ass all day, not having any fun."

"Yeah, Tony. You're my salvation," I replied.

He'd begun to resemble a human barbecue. The Bloody Mary mix had started cooking on his stomach, giving his skin a nicely baked orange glaze.

"You were telling me about your neighbors. How did the Vallardes react when you approached them about the noise?"

Tony spat on the ground. "That Cuban bitch told me it was a flock of Quaker parrots nesting in their trees that was causing the racket, and that I should mind my own damn business. Hell, she treated me like I was the one didn't belong here, instead of it being the other way around. I think Miss Elena Vallardes has gone and forgot that it was *her* ass that got off the damn boat!"

I waited until Tony calmed down. "So, what do you think is really going on over there?"

Tony poured himself another drink. "Personally, from the noise, I'd say they're making their money incubating eggs, hatching 'em, and selling the suckers."

So Carrera's next door neighbor was the very same Elena

tied in with Dominguez and Weed! Hanging around Coral Gables was beginning to change my view of the suburbs as a quiet and boring place.

"Just do your best to keep your flamingos from flying over that wall," I reminded Carrera as I got up to leave. "I can vouch for the fact that Langer has some nasty cats at his place."

Tony puffed out his well-done chest. "Just let the bastard try something and I'm telling ya, there'll be hell to pay."

Letting Langer and Tony have a go at each other could have its advantages. It would certainly lighten my workload, and help make the animal kingdom a safer place for its inhabitants.

I gave him a small nod. "By all means, knock yourself out."

Seven

The pungent smell of dead flamingo clung to the interior of my Ford as I drove to the Vallardes's palatial estate. My Tempo chug-chugged alongside a wall that encompassed a plot of land the size of Carrera's and Langer's combined. When I finally arrived at the entrance, I was faced with the standard locked gate. I'd already made up a story to slip inside, only to discover I could have saved myself the trouble. The wrought-iron entrance swung open without demanding my name, license plate number, or shoe size.

Hello Cinderella, I thought, catching a gander of the villa that lay sprawled before me. Ten thousand square feet of pure Mediterranean, high-falutin' fantasy was encircled by an army of palm trees of every species and size. The main residence was a two-storied white stucco affair topped with a fashionable red-tiled roof, and flanked by two massive wings snaking out on either side. The place appeared large enough to hold a small army.

I parked between two tasteful sports cars of Continental vintage. The burgundy Porsche Turbo and convertible hunter green Jaguar XJ made my poor Tempo look shabbier than ever, so I jumped back into my car and parked it farther away—knowing how I'd feel if someone stuck me between Cindy Crawford and Sharon Stone.

By the time I walked up to the front door, a South Beach stud was waiting to let me in. I did a double take at the hunk of beefcake dressed in minuscule bathing briefs that would have made a Speedo look large. His only other attire was a shiny gold Rolex, flashing the time on his wrist. He returned my once-over, tapping an impatient bare foot on the elegant marble floor.

"It's about time you decided to make an appearance. Elena's been waiting for you to show—although I can't believe you're what the agency sent. I can tell you, she's not going to be happy," snapped the resident doorman.

I was too focused on his pumped-up pecs and washboard abs to reply. Speedo responded by rolling his eyes, turning on his heels and sashaying inside. I followed the bouncing buns, figuring if he hadn't asked who I was, that wasn't my problem. Any way I got in was fine by me.

My entrance was greeted by two gigantic statues on either side of the hall, their ceramic pedestals sculpted into large, foamy waves on which a pair of happy dolphins cheerfully balanced on their tails. That was just the beginning of the Vallardes's ceramic animal kingdom. Giraffes, tigers, and zebras all stood captured in brightly glazed splendor as I made my way down the hall. Even a large red-and-green parrot had been caught midwing, as if ready to take flight, its Plexiglas base burping rose-colored Lawrence Welk bubbles.

My escort could have been a statue himself, so perfectly formed Michelangelo would have cried. I vowed to find more time to work out—even if it was in my next life. I glanced into room after room as we passed through the house, seeing a general theme to the decor. It was as if a troop of leopards had decided to commit mass suicide all over the place. Couches and chairs were covered in synthetic faux leopard, as were throw pillows, room carpets, and drapes. A bathroom even offered leopard-print towels.

But the crowning moment was when we tramped up to the second floor, passing a bedroom whose door was flung wide open. I stopped and stared in open-mouthed wonder as my attendant continued to sway down the hall.

An enormous bed lay nestled in a frame shaped like a huge pink conch shell, a leopard-skin fur tossed across its length. But even more bizarre was the lifelike leopard that sat guarding the room. The cat gazed dreamily off into space, its neck encased in a jewel-studded collar that Cartier would have killed for. But there was something odd about the feline. I moved in closer for a better look, only to realize the cat was no fake but the real thing, taxidermied into a lifeless figurine.

I felt a tug on my elbow and turned to find the Speedo stud by my side.

"Forget it, nature girl. You're definitely not Elena's type."

That was just fine with me. My guide led me toward a room with a hot salsa beat pumping out the door, into a photographic wonderland. Lights popped and flashed in a series of miniexplosions, the eruptions originating from silver umbrellas locked on stands that reached for the sky. The whir of an angry hornet turned into a camera, its click a succession of rapid-fire bursts.

"That's it, darling. Give me the bad-boy look this time, just the way I like!" purred a voice as smoky as a five-alarm fire.

Elena stood center stage in a clingy, one-piece leopard-print jumpsuit. Its plunging décolletage was capped by two heaving mounds of flesh, compliments of one industrial-strength bra. An electric mane of hair, bright as the yellow brick road, tumbled down her back. But her face was the main attraction. More precisely, a pair of full lips pursed in a perpetual pout that could easily have been X-rated. This entire package was precariously held up on a pair of fiery red, four-and-one-half-inch stiletto heels.

I was torn between paying homage to sensible Nikes, and taking a flying leap to tackle the woman for her shoes. There was no doubt that high heels did what no sneakers could. I watched Elena move with attitude, balanced on a pair of stilts which threw out her butt and emphasized her breasts, while giving her the calves of an Olympic sprinter. She was the kind of woman I'd always sworn I never wanted to be. At the moment, I would have given almost anything to look something like her.

"Ooh! That's so hot, Ricardo. Now give me a little more smolder," she growled. Elena emphasized the point with a slow gyration of her hips.

I shifted my attention to the muscled Adonis whose expression hadn't changed one iota since I'd walked in.

"Yes! That's it! Perfect!" exulted the crushed-velvet voice. "Now break loose, darling. Give me 100 percent undisguised lust." Elena wriggled and pouted like an unsatisfied lover.

Adonis remained 100 percent undisguised stone. A subtle

shift of the hips and tilt of the head was about as far as Ricardo seemed willing to go.

''That was wonderful!'' Elena raved. ''Take a two-minute break. You've earned it.''

Elena's expression instantly changed to one of annoyance as she turned and grabbed a look at me.

''You call this a model? What are you, cuckoo?'' she seethed. ''Get someone else out here and tell them they'd better make it fast!''

Speedo hopped to it, running out of the room on the double.

Elena's critique topped off an already prize-winning morning. I couldn't decide which was worse—dealing with a slug like Carrera, facing off against a military psychotic, or duking it out with a high-heeled, unmitigated bitch.

''I'm not a model,'' I said, my secret fantasy totally shot and my ego badly bruised.

''Good. At least we're both in agreement on that,'' she snapped.

Elena tossed her mane and began to swish away as my self-esteem clicked in. Checking my mental mirror to reaffirm that I looked damned good, I brought Elena's exit to a halt by stepping in front of her, pushing out my own chest, and giving my Nikes some bad-girl, kick-ass attitude.

''I'm a federal agent here on official business. I have some questions, and I'm going to need a few minutes of your time.'' I purposefully left out the key words, ''U.S. Fish and Wildlife Service.''

Elena's eyes narrowed, zooming in on me like a telescopic lens. ''Official business? What do you possibly want with me?''

I rolled the dice, hoping to hit a pair of sixes. ''I understand you were a friend of Alberto Dominguez.''

The phrase hung in the air like the crackle of fire. Adonis sauntered back onto the set, ready for more hard-core emoting. But Elena hadn't noticed, her brow furrowed as she contemplated her next move. I didn't want to allow her too much time to think.

''This is important, or I wouldn't be out here wasting my time,'' I said, pressing the point home.

Elena removed the camera from around her neck and thrust it into the hands of a waiting assistant.

"We're taking a fifteen-minute break. Then it's everyone back to work with no more screwing around," she barked at her coterie of workers.

Adonis checked out a series of subliminal poses in front of a full-length mirror as Elena stormed out of the room without another word. I followed hot on her sky-high heels down the steps, along the hall, and out the back door, into a tropical jungle showcasing the most ostentatious pool this side of Beverly Hills.

The pool floor was a multihued mosaic, its tiles portraying a nude Elena in all her toned glory. Equally impressive was the patio which boasted plaster replicas of Michelangelo's David and the Venus de Milo, along with other classical nudes of both persuasions. Scarlet bougainvillea teased the senses, as did large white and pink blossoms of angels trumpet. The jungle atmosphere was made complete by banana plants, their luxurious leaves looking like a runaway herd of giant, green elephant ears.

A cottage stood at the rear corner of the property, partially hidden by a flotilla of palms, with an old man sitting outside its door.

"That's Miguel, the caretaker for the grounds," Elena said airily. "He's been with my family ever since I was a little girl in Cuba. He can no longer keep up with all the work by himself, but we allow him to live on here."

Elena headed over to a wrought-iron table which held a delicate gold and black tin, along with a lighter. She flipped open the tin's lid, her fingers hesitating as they floated above a row of diminutive cigars, studying each as carefully as if she were choosing from an array of tiny torpedoes. Having made her decision, Elena plucked one out and placed it between pursed lips. A perfectly manicured red nail flicked the wheel of the lighter, and a spark of fire seared the air. The flame rose up and caressed the tiny smoke, which she enthusiastically sucked on with the abandon of a porn star.

I followed Elena to a group of lounge chairs. I had just begun to sit down when I caught sight of the leopard posed by her side. I jumped back up, wondering if everyone in the neighborhood was stark raving mad, only to realize this was yet another taxidermied cat. The feline was a near perfect twin to the one that guarded her bedroom, down to its collar of jewels.

Elena sniffed, as if able to smell the tail end of my fear. "This is Geraldo. He likes being kept out in the sun."

I was tempted to ask if his twin's name was "Rivera," and inquire as to why he preferred the shade, when a tickling sensation started between my shoulder blades.

I turned around and saw a man slowly walking toward us, his stride exuding power and feline grace that filled the very air with electricity. The man's jet black hair, pulled back into a ponytail, was the type I'd always dreamed of having. Long, silky, and perfectly straight. I'd gone through my formative years with frizzy red hair that had made me feel like a cousin to Bozo the clown. An elegant mustache brushed his upper lip, but it was the dark, smoldering eyes that were the clincher, their gaze capable of melting the steel lock on the strongest of chastity belts.

Elena's voice broke the high beam of tension that pinned me against the lounge with the force of a straitjacket. "This is my brother, Ramon. Sorry, but I seem to have forgotten your name."

"Rachel Porter," I managed to croak.

Ramon bent over and picked up my hand, never allowing his eyes to leave mine. I had to work hard to wrench my gaze away, focusing instead on the cigar lightly gripped between his teeth. Big mistake. I now found myself mesmerized as Ramon parted his lips, so that the cigar lay perfectly balanced, as if offering itself up in total surrender.

"It's a pleasure to meet you, Raquel." His voice rolled over me like a pool of warm caramel drenching my senses, and his lips grazed the back of my hand.

This guy was *soooo* good.

"My name's Rachel," I corrected him. My guess was that the man was practicing his own form of mind control, with me as the latest guinea pig.

"Raquel suits you better. You don't mind if I call you that, do you?" he murmured.

The warmth of his breath tangoed across my skin, his fingers seducing my hand with a slow, sensual release. He lightly stroked the length of my palm, my fingers, and finally my very fingertips, sending my entire body soaring into a radioactive tingle.

The guy was oozing charm like an oil slick, and I could feel myself heading for a full frontal fall. I made a supreme effort to gather my wits, and the sight of Elena rolling her eyes careened me back into hard-core reality. This guy was a master of the old hook, line, and sinker routine. I decided to get down to business before I forgot why I'd barged in here to begin with.

"I understand that Alberto Dominguez was a friend of yours," I began. "I'm sorry to have to tell you that he was found murdered on Sunday night."

"We've already heard," Ramon replied. He took a seat on the end of Elena's lounge chair and lifted her feet, placing them on his lap. Then he carefully removed each of her shoes and tossed them next to Geraldo. "Do you have any leads yet as to who the killer could be?" His hands slowly massaged her toes.

"Not yet. That's one of the reasons I wanted to talk to you," I said, beginning to feel uncomfortable.

"Feel free to ask us anything you need to know." Ramon's voice was as soothing as a scoop of soft ice cream on a hot summer's day. "We're both very upset over what has happened and will do whatever we can to help find whoever did such a horrible thing to Alberto."

Elena was silent as a sphinx.

"Why don't you start by telling me how you knew him," I suggested coolly.

Ramon's face glowed as if a match had been struck from inside. "The Cuban community is very tight here in Florida. We're all like one big family, with our weddings and births, baptisms and deaths. Even our feuds flow naturally, tying together our lives. But with Alberto it went even deeper than that. We'd known him since we were small children together in Cuba."

Elena's expression was a portrait of sadness.

"In 1960, a year after Castro took over, both our fathers fled the homeland together, taking their families with them."

Ramon's eyes burned as bright as twin shooting stars. "As children, we looked upon our escape as a game, an adventure in which we were the heroes who would one day return to set Cuba free. Though that hasn't yet happened, it creates a bond for all exiles that can never be broken. That's what we had with Alberto." He finished, giving Elena's foot a final slow rub.

The stillness was shattered by raucous bird cries. I looked up to see a pair of Quaker parrots perusing the scene from a nearby tree.

"Were you and Alberto involved in any kind of business together?" I asked.

Elena skewered me with her eyes. "Federal agents don't usually work with the local police. What agency did you say you were with?" she asked suspiciously.

I took a deep breath, aware that the jig was up. "I work with the U.S. Fish and Wildlife Service."

"What?" Elena exploded. She jumped to her feet, knocking Geraldo over in the process. "What the hell are we doing wasting our time talking to you?"

Ramon picked up the leopard and positioned him so that the cat now sat facing me. I could have almost sworn I heard the animal growl. Then he reached up and grabbed his sister's hand, gently pulling her back down to his side.

"Raquel, let me ask. If you're not with the police, why are you involved in this case?" All the while, he stroked his sister's hand.

"I knew Alberto because of the nature of his business," I carefully replied. "I went to his house on the night he was murdered to discuss something he was helping me with. When I walked inside, the first thing I saw was that all his birds were missing. After that, I found Alberto's body."

"So, you're the one." Ramon solemnly nodded, as though I'd just passed some sort of secret test.

Elena held tightly on to her brother, unwilling to let me into their club. "That still doesn't explain what right you have to come here and question us. If you're not with the police, then what happened is none of your business." Elena and Geraldo glared at me in perfect stereovision. "Or are animal officers after bigger game these days than chasing stray cats and dogs?''

I smiled, determined not to let a woman dressed like an overgrown feline get the better of me. ''You must have me confused with your local animal control. Alberto was involved with smuggling endangered birds into the country. Those birds are missing, along with his others, which leads me to believe that a business rival could be responsible. I'm investigating his death from that standpoint.'' I shot Elena a pointed look. ''And don't worry; I have every right to be here,'' I lied.

''As I said, we'll be glad to help in any way that we can,'' Ramon warmly reassured me.

Dressed in cream-colored linen pants, a loose, pale yellow shirt, and tasseled loafers made from the very softest leather on his sockless feet, he looked as casually confident as only someone with plenty of money could be.

''Are you a photographer, as well?'' I inquired.

Ramon gave a dazzling smile. ''Oh, no. There is only one great artist in this family. I'm merely a simple businessman.''

''That's not true at all,'' Elena intervened, her voice set on slow burn. ''My brother is every inch an artist. He's known throughout the world for producing the best cigars anywhere outside of Havana.''

I didn't mention the stash of Cuban Cohibas under Alberto's bed. The Vallardes probably already knew. One of Elena's fingernails followed the trail of her brother's cheekbone, gently coming to a stop as it reached his lips. Ramon lightly kissed her finger, his gaze firmly planted on mine.

''One more thing,'' I said, curious as to just how far their brother/sister act went. ''When was the last time that either of you saw Alberto?''

Ramon's eyes wandered off in one direction and Elena's went in the other, as each carefully considered the question.

''It must have been at least two years ago,'' Ramon finally offered.

Unless Tony Carerra was wrong, I'd just nabbed the duo in a very major lie.

Ramon tenderly slipped Elena's ruby-red slippers back onto her feet as she rose with a purr.

''Enough. I must get back to work.'' She cast a sidelong

glance in my direction, picked up Geraldo, and headed toward the house.

Ramon put his arm through mine as he walked me to my car. "I would very much like you to come and see my cigar store in Little Havana," he said, giving my arm a squeeze.

I planned to take him up on his offer. "What's it called?" I asked.

The right side of his body pressed tightly against mine. "The store's name is Puffin," he whispered. "Come visit me soon."

Two days seemed like plenty of time for Metro Dade's medical examiner to have come up with the details of how Alberto had died. I decided it was time to check in with Hal Cooper.

"Well, hello there, sexy. I like it when a woman makes the first move and gives the man a call." Coop nearly panted over the phone.

Oy vay, as my grandmother would have said. I pictured him twirling the tips of his mustache as he played with his bow tie. I didn't even want to think about what else he might be doing.

"Now, I'm not going to play hard to get," Coop warned, as if that were a major surprise. "So—yes. I am free tonight for dinner and dancing. We can take it from there, after that," he added with a growl.

"I'm calling to see if you've come up with anything further concerning Alberto Dominguez's death." I kept my voice disinterested.

"Well, I'd say that all depends on what you mean by 'further.' Such as, we could discuss this 'further' over a glass of wine. Or, what say we take this relationship of ours the next step 'further.' "

The man was doing a good job of driving me "further" away. "What *I* mean by 'further' is, do you have any more information regarding what exactly caused Dominguez's death?" I asked, gritting my teeth.

"In that case, I'd have to say it was murder." Coop barely bothered to contain the laughter in his voice. "Of course, I might be willing to help you out a little more if we were to get together in person."

Right: He'd help me keep in shape, by making me run a few laps around his desk. Coop had me, and he knew it. Officially, as a mere Fish and Wildlife agent, I had no right to demand access to forensic information on Dominguez. It all came down to being a matter of Hal Cooper's goodwill. Damn the man and his sexist games! But if those were the rules, then down and dirty was how we would play it.

"In that case, are we talking your place or mine?" I asked in throaty imitation of Elena. I could almost feel Hal Cooper's testosterone level screech into overdrive through the phone.

"Sweetheart, you're not playing games with old Coop now, are you?" he asked, all aflutter.

"Not unless there are certain games you really like to play." I fought off the overwhelming feeling of nausea.

I heard Coop begin to breathe heavily and decided to cut to the chase, not wanting to risk his having a heart attack. "But first, don't you think you could give me the teensiest bit of information? Just something to keep me going until we meet later on?"

It was hard to believe that men actually fell for this stuff, but Cooper did a double somersault, and then landed a triple flip.

"What is it that you want to know?" he nearly wheezed. Desire clearly had hold of one part of his body, completely cutting off the flow of blood to his brain.

"What was the murder weapon that was used?" I kept my fingers crossed that Cooper would remain anxious to please.

He took his time, weighing whether or not to hand over such information.

"I know this great little place for oysters," I added shamelessly, counting on his firm belief in the power of aphrodisiacs.

"All right! I'll tell you!" Coop raised the white flag of surrender. "The murder weapon was a serrated knife."

"Are you sure about that?" A nagging inner doubt made me question it.

"As sure as I need to be for my report," he retorted, making it clear that was all I was getting for now. "So then, what time shall I pick you up? Or should we skip dinner and just head straight for dessert?" His voice trembled with enough lust to send me screaming for a suit of armor.

"Oops! Sorry, I just remembered. I've already got plans for tonight."

"Goddammit, Porter!" Coop's shriek bellowed through the air as I quickly hung up the phone.

I felt fairly certain I could expect no further information out of Coop on any case in the foreseeable future. Picking up the phone, I dialed Vern.

"Reardon here," Vern drawled in his best John Wayne tone.

"Hey, Vern. It's Rachel."

"Hell. In that case, I can get back to drinking my coffee," Vern said, taking a slurp.

At least I always knew where the man's top priorities lay.

"So, what's up now, Porter?" he asked, beginning to munch on what I imagined to be a donut.

"I noticed that one of Alberto's file folders was gone when I was last out there. It had a complete inventory of Dominguez's birds. Do you think I could get a copy of the contents?"

My question was met by a long pause.

"What the hell are you talking about, gal?" he asked, sounding totally dumbfounded.

"You know: It's a record that gives the date of each bird's birth or purchase," I began to explain.

"Jesus Christ, Porter! I know what the hell an inventory is. I just never saw any such thing there!" Reardon exploded.

It was my turn to feel puzzled. "But I thought you took it."

"Well, if I had, don't you suppose I'd know what you're talking about?" Reardon observed.

"You're *sure* that you didn't see it?" I refused to believe the information had simply disappeared. "It was a thick folder filed in the bottom drawer of Alberto's desk, labeled BREEDS."

"You could tell me it was a pink elephant with purple ears, and I still wouldn't have it," Vern retorted. "Musta been those damn Santeria devil worshippers—cause I sure as hell can't think of what Skunk Ape would have wanted it for."

I got off the phone, cursing myself for not taking the folder when I'd had the chance, even though that would've been illegal. Then I made one more call.

"Dr. Samuels," the voice resonated in my ear.

"I think I need a favor and a drink," I morosely informed him.

"Porter?" Dr. Bob laughed. "Has anyone ever told you that you're a high-maintenance dame?"

"Yeah, me and Ivana Trump. I hear we both shop at the same place," I parried. "Do you have time to take a quick break?"

"Don't tell me: You've managed to injure a few more people on the job," he replied.

"Very funny. Meet you at the QT Diner in about a half hour?"

"My favorite place," Dr. Bob cheerfully agreed. "They never blink when I walk in with a body bag."

I hopped into my Ford and headed straight for the heart of Miami.

The city of Miami is a whole different animal from South Beach. It's a Wild West atmosphere, with a simmering stew of Cuban, Haitian, Nicaraguan, Colombian, Mexican, Dominican, Honduran, and Peruvian refugees. The local joke is that the only true Miamians to be found are the Miccosuke Indians, now relegated to running bingo games and wrestling gators on their Everglades reservation.

As far as I was concerned, if there was a center for wackos anywhere in the world, it had to be right here. After all, this is the place where an angry ex-lover spent a day driving around town, exhibiting his girlfriend's decomposing corpse to a gang of his buddies. It was also here that a drunken driver was discovered slumped down in his seat, with his pet iguana steering his car. And only in Miami would government employees express their job dissatisfaction by hanging voodoo dolls, with their necks in tiny nooses, all over city hall.

Dr. Bob was waiting at the counter of the QT when I arrived, ogling kool-pop waitresses decked out in fifties-style shirtwaist uniforms, their dresses unbuttoned to showcase low-cut, black lacy bras. Combat boots and body piercing added distinctive personal touches.

What *I* liked best about the QT was that it was a no-nonsense diner that had finagled itself a liquor license. I ordered a vodka tonic and waited for Dr. Bob's tongue to reel back inside his mouth.

He took a sip of his beer and then turned to me with a grin. "Okay—the doctor's now in. What can I do you for?"

I watched in metabolic envy as one of the waitresses slipped an extra-large piece of double fudge cake in front of Dr. Bob. A groan escaped my lips as the first bite disappeared into his mouth.

"For chrissakes, Porter. Why don't you just break down and order yourself a slice?" he suggested.

My attention was fixed on the second forkful of pure chocolate bliss that hovered in midair. "Can't. I'm on a diet," I explained, lost in a chocoholic haze.

"Oh, all right. Here—you win," he said, handing me a second fork.

I dug in.

"You want to explain to me why you can eat my dessert, but can't order your own?" Dr. Bob interrogated me.

"It's one of the unwritten laws of the universe. There are fewer calories this way," I explained between bites.

"That makes a lot of sense," he retorted, watching his slice of cake disappear. "Vodka and chocolate. You know what that says about you, don't you?"

"That I can blame my dietary lapse on fermented potatoes, I suppose." I took the last bite, feeling totally satisfied, and then ordered Dr. Bob his very own second slice. "I need help with a case that's come up."

"Animal, vegetable, mineral, or man?" Dr. Bob queried.

I filled him in on the gruesome remains that had once been Alberto Dominguez.

Dr. Bob gave me the once-over from behind his bottle-lens glasses, his finger idly stroking the few hairs on his chin. "Is there some reason you're not buying the serrated-blade scenario? Perhaps due to a personal dislike of a certain Metro Dade medical examiner?"

I looked at the good doctor with disdain. "Do you really think I would be so petty?" I countered, figuring there was a good chance he might be right.

"Listen, it's all a moot point, anyway. I can't barge in there and personally examine the body, so it's impossible for me to tell whether Cooper's autopsy conclusion is in any way wrong,'' Dr. Bob explained.

I slipped my hand inside my purse and whipped out a brown paper bag, containing the ragged patch of fabric that I'd found near Dominguez's body.

''I can't produce a corpse. But I did recover this,'' I smugly revealed.

Dr. Bob took a peek inside. ''Congratulations, Porter. I see that you managed to get yourself a real memento there.''

''This fabric was wet and slimy when I found it near the body. Is there any way to tell what caused that?'' I asked.

''What are you on the lookout for? A slobbering killer?'' Dr. Bob joked.

I continued to dangle the bag.

''Besides, why not just hand it over to Metro Dade and let them figure it out? They're the ones with all the pertinent information,'' he said.

''I suspect they might not appreciate my questioning Hal Cooper's work. Besides, I trust that you'll do a better job,'' I replied, appealing to his sense of vanity. ''And I'll get you a date with that waitress over there if you do this for me.'' I indicated the babe who'd delivered his cake.

Dr. Bob looked at me skeptically. ''You really believe you can do that?''

''One hundred percent guaranteed.'' I'd already caught her giving him the eye; just the whisper that he was a highly regarded doctor would undoubtedly clinch the deal.

Dr. Bob went for the bait, removing the paper bag from my hand. ''I have a friend who's a whiz with DNA analysis,'' he said with a grin. ''If I were you, I'd get busy setting up that date.''

Eight

The sun was set on late-afternoon mellow as I made my way home, the air temperature akin to a light sauté. I drove up to find that Sophie had been true to her word. Her house, which had been a deep periwinkle blue, was now painted magenta and lime. But it was the sound coming from inside which aroused my curiosity. Instead of two distinct laughs, there were now three—one of which washed over me as powerfully as a fifty-foot wave.

I dashed through the door and into the kitchen, where I found Sophie and Lucinda all dolled up to party in outrageous Carmen Miranda outfits. But it was the tall, slender figure angled away from me that I was interested in. I followed a pair of gorgeous gams, up past the Chinese-red kimono, to a headful of curls as blond and voluminous as one of Dolly Parton's wigs.

"Oh, my God. Terri?" I whispered, unable to believe it was my best friend from New Orleans.

Terri Tune whirled around and grabbed me in a long overdue hug, as we both screamed in excitement. Then I stepped away to take a good look at my former French Quarter landlord, whose smile created dimples the size of quarters in each cheek.

He shook his curls in dismay. "See? I let you move away and look what happens. Your complexion and makeup get all shot to hell. Now I'm going to have to start again from scratch," he scolded, a hand gracefully placed on each hip.

I couldn't say the same for Terri. He looked as if he'd just walked off the cover of *Cosmo* magazine, except that his baby blues were hidden behind a large pair of Sophie's sunglasses, replete with dancing dolphins.

Terri turned back to the kitchen counter to put the finishing touches on four highly potent piña coladas, each embellished with a brightly colored paper umbrella.

I looked at him in amazement as he handed me one. "How did you know I'd be home in time for this?"

Terri gave me a quick peck on the cheek. "Rach, the day you can't home in on my piña coladas from fifty miles away is the day I become straight."

I flashed him a grin.

"All right, already. If you're gonna fix her up, you can count on giving the two of us a complete overhaul while you're at it," Sophie chimed in. She held on to her turban, which was loaded down with fruit, while taking hold of her glass. "Here's to playing *Queen For a Day* for the rest of our lives."

"Sophie honey, I've been playing that number for years," Terri laughingly told her.

Lucinda leaned over and gently gave his cheek a pinch. "Yes, but now you get to play it Cuban style."

We raised our glasses and gave each one a clink. I took a sip and twirled the paper umbrella, feeling almost as if I were back home in New Orleans.

"Why didn't you call and let me know that you were coming? I would have picked you up at the airport. Hell, I even would have cleaned up my bungalow for you," I wailed.

"Save it, *bubeleh*. We've already compared notes," Sophie informed me.

"That's right. We found out that you never bothered to defrost your freezer back in New Orleans, either," Lucinda added with a sly grin.

I was trying to come up with a cast-iron defense when a ball of fur rubbed against my leg. I looked down to find it was Terri's cat.

"You even brought Rocky?" I asked in amazement. Obviously, something more than a quick visit was afoot. "I'm really glad that you're here, Terri. But why don't you let me in on what exactly is going on."

Terri slowly removed Sophie's shades to reveal a *muy* black eye that encompassed every color of the rainbow.

"Oh, my God! What happened to you?" My first guess was that he'd been through another episode of gay bashing. "Was there some sort of riot in town?"

Terri shook his curls. "No skinheads this time, Rach. Just old-fashioned boyfriend trouble." He sighed. "I have lousy taste in men. You know me—I'm just a sucker when it comes to black leather."

"It's not your taste that's bad, sweetheart." Sophie gave him a consoling pat. "It's just the male of the species in general. Lucinda and I gave up men years ago and we feel all the better for it. You're welcome to join the club anytime."

Terri sat down and picked up Rocky, who purred in contentment as he curled up in his lap. "I decided this was the perfect time to get out of town for a while: this look isn't exactly going to have them flocking in to see my act." He crossed his legs and a cherry-red mule, balancing a fuzzy pom pom the size of a hamster on hormones, dangled off his big toe.

Terri had a running gig in the Quarter as one of the best female impersonators in the business, performing at a nightspot known as the Boy Toy. I'd seen him do a better job portraying Madonna than she did herself.

A screech drew my attention to Bonkers, who was dangling from a brand new avian Evel Knievel jungle gym in a corner of Sophie's kitchen. The gym touted a climbing rope, a perma-play ring, a hanging pogo stick, a parrot mobile, plus ladders and bells, putting the simple swing I'd bought him to shame. This could only mean one thing: we were in a showdown for the bird's affection. I caught Sophie's eye.

She looked at me and shrugged. "It's the closest thing I've got to a grandkid. So, what are you going to do? Sue me if I spoil him?"

Rocky noticed the bird as well but wisely stayed put, as Bonkers dug into a piece of mango that Lucinda hand-fed him.

Terri whirled his finger around the lip of his glass, collecting the excess foam. "Personally, I think it's time to start shopping around for a good plastic surgeon. What do you say, girls? I hear there are some terrific ones here in Miami. Maybe we can get ourselves a group rate."

I sat down next to him and gave his arm a squeeze. "Why not? I've got a few things that could use touching up."

Lucinda leaned over and slid the sunglasses down Terri's nose, closely examining his eye. "Before we all resort to plastic surgery, I think I'm going to teach you how to fight." She clucked her tongue. "I hope you at least gave that guy a good shot in the *cojones*."

Terri sipped at his drink. "Actually, Bruno knocked me out cold. He's one of those men who take breakups rather badly." His finger wandered up to touch the swollen skin. "That's why I've decided to try celibacy for a while. I was going to check into a convent, but I look lousy in black. So instead I decided to come and visit you, Rach." He added his paper umbrella to my drink.

I looked at Terri sitting there with his perfectly shaved legs, manicured nails, and golden blond curls, and was grateful that he wasn't a girl. The competition would have been impossible.

"You're welcome to stay as long as you like." I just wished I had something better for guests than my worn-out, second-hand couch.

"We've already discussed it, and he'll be bunking here in our spare room," Sophie stated.

I wasn't all that crazy about the idea. It was one thing to have Sophie vying for Bonkers' attention—but Terri was my closest friend, and I found myself feeling the tiniest bit possessive.

"It's okay, Rach, I'll be right next door. Besides, you'll be off at work all day—so we'll have fun after you get home at night."

He was right. "Sophie, Lucinda, he's all yours," I agreed with a smile.

"Good; that's settled," Sophie rasped. "You two go catch up on old times. Lucinda and I are going to the Warsaw Ballroom tonight."

Both women wore floor-length, red and black, form-fitting gowns, so that they resembled a cross between oversized ladybugs and psychotic flamenco dancers. Each dress had a wide cummerbund. While Lucinda's sash emphasized the shapeliness of her hips, Sophie resembled a tiny cigar whose band had fallen partially down.

A split surrounded by an explosion of ruffles ran up the middle of each skirt to their thighs. But the finishing touches were the real whoppers: They not only balanced enormous baskets of fruit on their heads, but had their feet strapped into mile-high platform shoes.

I couldn't have dreamed up a better way of growing old. I gave each of them a kiss goodnight, then Terri and I headed out the door.

We followed a group of powder-puff clouds toward Ocean Drive. Though evening was just kicking in, the South Beach carnival scene was already working up a full head of steam. We stopped in at a cafe for a drink, settling into ringside seats to watch the endless parade go by.

Terri sighed contentedly as an oversized mai tai appeared before him. "This is perfect, Rach. Just what the doctor ordered."

Two bleached-blonde beach boys sporting golden tans strolled past, followed by surfer dudes, a bodybuilder, and a Gucci-attired senior citizen with the skin of a lizard.

Terri followed the procession with his eyes. "I could definitely get used to this."

The sun began to set, launching the nightly meat market into gear with its array of young model wanna-bes. Their bodies squeezed into vivid spandex dresses, each looked beautiful and bored as they trolled the chi-chi strip, their radar fine-tuned to catch *Miami Vice* clones wafting the distinctive bouquet of freshly laundered money.

"All right. I've told you what's been going on with me. Now it's time to catch up on your life." Terri popped a slice of rum-soaked pineapple into his mouth. "Since I'm living vicariously these days, fill me in on the juicy details. How's that ragin' Cajun of yours doing?"

I speared the olive in my martini like Ahab going after Moby-Dick. "I'm afraid that chapter in my life is over. In fact, I plan on joining you in taking celibacy vows," I dourly noted.

Terri looked at me in surprise. "What are you talking about? The last thing I heard, the two of you were contemplating marriage."

I flashed him a sidelong glance.

"Or at least Santou was," he amended.

"What happened was that the man I fell in love with turned into Archie Bunker before my eyes!" I drowned my sorrow in my martini.

"Santou as a homophobic, pot-bellied bigot? You've lost me, Rach."

My drink took on a saltwater kick as tears skidded down my cheeks and plopped into my glass. "His biological clock is ticking faster than mine. Not only does he want to immediately start producing a flock of kids, but he's looking for a twenty-four-hour maid, cook, and bottle washer as well."

Terri gave me a quizzical look.

"Jake insisted that I quit my job and devote my energies to being a full-time wife and mother. And I don't even know if I want kids!"

Terri remained silent for a moment and then flagged down the waiter, motioning for two more drinks. "Well if that's his attitude, then to hell with the man! I don't care *how* hot he is. Tell him to hit-the-road-Jack, take-the-bus-Gus, don't-pass-go-Moe." Terri put an arm around my shoulder and kissed my cheek. "Cheer up, Rach. Life is a series of never-ending adventures. The next one is just around the corner waiting to take place."

"It's just that it happened so fast, Ter. One minute, everything seemed to be fine. The next, I was being handed an ultimatum to choose between Jake or my job." I polished off my martini. "You can guess how I felt about that. My temper kicked in and made the decision for me."

The waiter placed our drinks before us and Terri lifted his mai tai in salute. "Sophie and Lucinda are right. To no more men in our lives!" We sipped our drinks, and I wondered if Terri's fingers were crossed as tightly as mine.

The throbbing beat of salsa sizzled on the street, luring us out to a crowd that had gathered round a musician hawking tapes of his band. The infectious rhythm prompted one Cuban *mamacita* to throw her inhibitions to the sky. Though her once-voluptuous body had given way to the gravity of years, that didn't stop the woman from cutting loose. The music wriggled through her, spilling out in a torrid dance.

But competition is tough on the street. A young, leaner version moved in, grabbing the spotlight away. Denim hip-hugger shorts came alive on a body that gyrated in a sensual grind. Taut stomach muscles glistened, leading up to a pair of full breasts, barely covered by thin strips of peek-a-boo crocheted fabric. The girl's hands twisted and curled like two writhing snakes, running up and down her figure in a steamy show of self-gratification. Pulsating neon made the strip a voyeuristic wet dream.

We moved on toward another young girl reeking of sensual heat, swaying to the beat. Her skimpy outfit was demurely hidden behind a cigar-filled vendor's tray that hung from her neck.

"I have Montecristos, Romeo y Julietas, Cohibas, and Upmanns, straight from Havana," she called out in a singsong voice.

"It's just that it happened so fast, Ter. One minute, everything seemed to be fine. The next, I was being handed an ultimatum to choose between Jake or my job." I polished off my martini. "You can guess how I felt about that. My temper kicked in and made the decision for me."

"Are those genuine Cuban cigars?" Terri asked, acting like a wide-eyed tourist.

The girl gave a mock pout at having her honesty questioned. "I sell to Demi, Bruce, Arnold, and Madonna." She gave Terri a closer look. "In fact, has anyone ever told you that you look a little bit like Madonna?"

Terri struck a pose. "No way. People always say I'm much better looking." He bought a cigar and slipped it into the shirt pocket of the first man who caught his fancy as we wended our way home.

I wasn't surprised to find the Two Musketeers were still out when we arrived. In South Beach, the night stayed young until dawn. I retrieved Bonkers from Sophie's house, having decided there was no way she was going to keep both Terri *and* my bird.

Bonkers's crown of feathers stood up in excitement as he watched me drag his new jungle gym into my small cottage.

"Wheee!!!" the bird screeched in delight. He dangled by one daredevil foot, hanging upside down from his ring.

As I headed for the bedroom, Bonkers's angry squawk

brought my exit to a halt. I held out my arm and he hopped on, running up to give me a nip on the ear in reprimand for leaving without him. At least I could count on one male who planned on permanently hanging around.

Nine

The next morning I awoke before the sun had come up. Even Bonkers wasn't awake as I tiptoed out the door.

This was my favorite time to walk around South Beach—when the insanity of the night had dispersed. I strolled down empty Washington Street, with its run-down buildings the color of candy Valentine hearts. My sneakers whispered against the pavement as I passed the darkened windows of the Art Deco Market and Larry's Kosher Meats. It wasn't until I hit the block containing a transient hotel that I saw any other people.

"*Hola, señorita*," muttered a man sitting on the building's steps. He slouched against the railing, his thin white shirt unbuttoned to his waist to display a chest covered with damp, curly hair. His eyes conveyed a "come-hither" look through half-closed lids.

Feeling cocky and young, I headed for the Pepto-pink storefront of Max's Place. Max's is open twenty-four hours a day, with a take-out window offering the greasiest food south of New York City. The middle-aged woman behind the counter wore a midriff top the size of an Ace bandage which threatened to burst apart.

"*Buenos días*," I chirped. "I'll take two hits."

She silently nodded, having given up hope I'd ever speak more than two words of Spanish. The espresso machine hummed, spitting out a double order of black liquid, into which nearly as much sugar was mixed. The woman handed me the concoction, and I headed off for my morning ritual.

Sea grape trees lined the boardwalk, their rubbery leaves an explosion of miniature fans, their fallen grapes squishing beneath my feet, turning the pavement purple.

"You haven't seen anything yet, girl. Wait till the grapes are ripe," Tommy had once told me over a cup of his homemade brew. "The crows love to eat them, but the grapes make 'em drunk. Pretty soon the birds are flying upside down."

A lazy strip of clouds hovered over the horizon, as if still trying to rouse themselves into action for the day, the lick of a red glow along their edge threatening to ignite at any moment. I walked through a hula-skirt patch of pampas grass to the beach, removing my sneakers to luxuriate in the feel of warm sand between my toes, inhaling the air drenched in the scent of salt water as I listened to the surf.

Along with the first rays of the sun came a group of senior citizens decked out for their morning swim, the women wearing shower caps over their beauty-parlor curls. They slowly walked into the water in a tightly knit group. The waves lapped at their ankles, then nibbled on their varicose veins, and before long the waves were up past their waists, with the women bobbing like colorful corks in the surf.

One older man faithfully did his morning exercises before taking a dip. Baggy trunks hung low on his hips, and a chartreuse elastic band held back his remaining hair. Raising his hands high above his head, he slowly bent his knees and touched his toes.

Others took their daily exercise walking up and down the beach with metal detectors in hand, their excitement building with each swing of the needle, their pockets bulging with loose change.

Eventually Bird Man approached, scattering bags of bread crumbs. He nodded as he passed, followed by a conga line of seagulls.

I downed the last of my inky elixir, and made my way home. Walking into my kitchen, I heard the insistent ring of the telephone, accompanied by Bonkers shrieking at the top of his lungs, "*To hell with the commander!*"

I raced into the bedroom wondering if it might be Santou calling to apologize; his excuse, a temporary bout of insanity. But the ringing stopped as I reached for the receiver.

"Down with Castro!" The bird screeched in delight at my

breakneck entrance. His crown of feathers stood up as he clambered onto my shoulder, and rubbed his head against my ear.

I tried to bury all thoughts of Santou by heading back out to the kitchen, where I prepared a colorful mix of mango, grapes, strawberries, papaya, carrots, green pepper, zucchini, and sunflower seeds. Then, spooning some of the mixture into Bonkers's bowl, I set it on the table and watched him go to work, picking out one piece of fruit at a time.

"It's nice to know one of us eats well," I observed.

Bonkers answered by giving a lunatic giggle and hurling a piece of papaya high in the air.

After breakfast I put Bonkers on his jungle gym, where he broke into a wild chorus of wolf whistles while hanging upside down from his swing. Furiously beating his wings, he launched himself round and round, his body spinning like an orbiting rocket.

I took a quick shower and then left a message on Carlos's voice mail that I wouldn't be in the office until later that afternoon. Bonkers tried to tempt me to stay, breaking into a Spanish serenade as I headed for the door. But my dance card was filled for the morning: I planned to pay Willie Weed another visit. If he really was making weekly trips out of town, I was going to find out exactly where he was going.

The heat had climbed to the temperature of a rotisserie grill, with my body subbing as the chicken on a skewer, by the time I turned into the dirt road that doubled as Weed's driveway. Fallen pine needles crackled like tiny bones under my tires as I drove around the bend and entered Willy's "Scamalot."

Weed's hulking Dodge pickup sat in its accustomed place like a foreboding gatekeeper. I stood and listened for a moment, but there was no pounding of heavy metal music.

I kicked a rusty motor-oil can out of the way, the echo shattering the sinister silence. The sudden noise awakened a few gaunt vultures that were stiffly standing on the ground; their scrawny, bald heads turned and glared menacingly at me.

I pushed Weed's door open and the stench raced out, sending me backward. Taking a few deep breaths, I steeled myself and stuck my head inside, where I was prepared to find Willy lying dead on the floor, his body an Everglades version of Limburger cheese.

The beer bottles and cardboard boxes had multiplied. The once-fossilized remains of pizza were now alive with transparent squiggles of maggots, squirming like animated shredded cheese. There was nothing resembling a mutation of Willy. Only Big Mama lay curled in the corner, kept company by a growing swarm of giant black bugs.

I stepped outside and shut the door, not in the mood to battle the army of Florida roaches. Instead I stopped in front of a cage, where a cougar pulled back its lips and hissed, causing shivers to Rollerblade down my spine. I studied the cat's fangs, which were ready and waiting to tear me apart, and decided that Hal Cooper had been right. Upper and lower canines like these would have ripped Alberto's throat clear out of his body.

The rest of Weed's menagerie stared idly off into space, all with the same glazed look in their eyes. Even the vultures had begun to succumb, their heads drooping like wilted flowers onto their feathered chests. I glanced around at the broken-down trailers, knowing Weed would never invite me to inspect what they held inside—which meant this was the perfect time for me to explore.

I marched over to the closest door, found it was locked, and shoved my shoulder against it, but the damn thing wouldn't budge. Having little choice, I moved on to the next four-wheeled treasure chest down the line.

This trailer stood out because of the layers of plywood piled precariously on its roof. I grabbed on to a sticky handle, which turned under my touch. The interior was bathed in darkness. I felt along the wall until I found the toggle switch and flicked it up, flooding the trailer with light.

A scream lodged tight as a fist in my throat. Wall-to-wall aquariums came alive with hundreds of pissed-off snakes, hissing and spitting, tails rattling and tongues flicking, all determined to get out and nail me. I'd heard of "hot rooms" filled with venomous snakes, but I'd never seen one before now. I waited until my pulse stopped ricocheting before I examined Weed's deadly collection.

Gaboon vipers with two-inch fangs lay camouflaged, their

patterned bodies of buff, russet, and black perfectly blending in with their bed of leaves. Eyelash vipers stood out like splashy harlequins, brazenly flaunting brilliant hues of bright green, terra-cotta, and gold. A five-foot puff adder huffed and puffed, inflating its body in warning. The turquoise skins of a pair of African boomslangs barely masked the fangs which lay slyly situated below their eyes.

I passed by rattlesnakes, Australian taipans, and South American bushmasters, then sixteen-foot king cobras that slammed against their glass walls in repeated attempts at a jail break.

But the black mamba made my blood run cold. The snake stared out at me, its fourteen feet of pure muscle solid as a piece of coiled steel, with a mouth curved up in a humorless grin on a head appropriately shaped like a coffin. Legend had it that mambas were fast enough to tag a bird in flight or overtake a man on horseback, while slim enough to slither under doors, and agile enough to glide up trees. The mamba has even been said to drop down chimneys and wipe out entire families.

What I knew for a fact was that mambas were extremely aggressive, biting their prey not once, but over and over again. The snake was cold-blooded death incarnate. It continued to stare at me, knowing there was no hurry.

I was unaware of how much time had passed, when something began to slither up my leg. I didn't dare move. All I could hope was that whatever it was, would go away. My pounding heart told me to run as fast as I could, but my attacker gathered speed, zooming up my thigh and onto my back, my shoulder, and then my neck, quickly nicking me on the ear. I screamed in terror, whipped around, and slugged Willy Weed smack in the kisser.

"Goddammit, bitch! What the hell are you tryin' to do? Send me back to the friggin' hospital?" Willy squealed, his hand held tightly over his nose.

"Don't ever sneak up on me like that again!" I snarled. I was tempted to toss him to the mamba, saving myself and the reptile world any number of headaches.

"Sneak up on you? Sheeet, Porter; you're the one that just broke into my goddamn trailer!" Willy shot back. "Your problem is that you got no sense of humor, you know that? Hell, you don't find me whalin' on you just cause I got a bum foot which is partly your fault."

The lower portion of Willy's right leg was encased in a dingy white cast, covered with pen-and-ink drawings that a horny high school boy might have made. Disembodied women's breasts, topped with perky nipples, floated like airborne Dixie cups, intermingling with a crude assortment of flying penises. The theme tied in nicely with the grimy yellow T-shirt that begged, JUST DO ME. No one could ever accuse Weed of being subtle.

"I didn't think a fed like you'd get all riled up and scared over some lil 'ol snake. Why, a bite from a mamba like that one won't kill ya; it'll just make you feel warm and tingly all over."

"Is that before or after they nail you inside the coffin?" I wasn't in the mood for jokes.

"You don't trust what I'm telling you, Porter? Or don't you think I've ever been bit?" Willy snorted, his manhood on the line. "How else would I have gotten into the Cobra Club? Huh? You tell me that, why doncha?"

The Cobra Club had been formed by a group of local yokels whose members had mucho machismo and the combined IQ of a road-killed squirrel. In order to become a member, you first had to endure the bite of a cobra. Next, you had to survive.

"Hell! I seen a guy didn't even go to a doctor afterwards. His buddies fixed him up just fine. They dragged him over to a pickup, hooked up some battery cables, and gave him a coupla electroshock jolts," Willy bragged.

"Uh, that didn't exactly work too well, Willy. Timmy Tom's arm blew up so bad, it looked like it was inflated by an air pump," said a voice from behind Weed. "I thought it would explode for sure before we got him to the hospital."

Weed's compatriot was grinning like a hyena. I estimated him to be about five feet two, until I glanced down and saw that he wore a pair of elevated boots. His hair was shorn into a buzz cut, and he wore a white T-shirt stating, JESUS LOVES ME. I wondered what a born-again was doing hanging around with Weed, until I caught sight of his tattooed bicep. Porky the Pig was a hellacious red, carried a pitchfork, and had sprouted a pair of pointy horns. The logo beneath it declared, I'M A LITTLE DEVIL!

Willy's diminutive friend punched Weed hard in the arm. "Hey! Aren't you gonna introduce me to this bodacious-looking woman here?" He flashed a smile, boasting a set of canines that Dracula would have loved.

"Yeah, yeah. This crazy redheaded mama is Rachel Porter, one of those nasty Fish and Wildlife employees." Willy threw an arm around his friend's shoulders. "And this here is Buzz Tregler, a real good bud of mine."

Buzz reached up and tousled Willy's greasy mop of hair. Weed reciprocated by knuckle balling the top of Tregler's head.

"Hey, Porter! You're here just in time to witness one of those real, live nature phenomenas I bet you're so fond of," Weed said with a leer.

"Don't tell me. You're going to shed your cocoon and transform into a human being?" Buzz and Willy made the extras from *Deliverance* look like MIT graduates.

Buzz doubled over in laughter, and slapped a thigh. "That's a good one, mama. Hey, she got you there, Willy!"

Weed flashed his friend an unamused glare and then reached into a sack, producing a small gray mouse that he held upside down by the tail. The rodent clawed the air in a vain attempt to break loose as Willy brought it toward my face and swung the critter from side to side like a hypnotist's watch.

"Keep your eye on the mousie!" he said in a singsong voice.

The mouse's whiskers twitched nervously, trying to figure out what I already knew was coming next.

Willy half-limped, half-clunked over to a glass terrarium housing a juvenile diamondback rattler, and held the mouse so that it could view its fate.

"See that big old snake in there? That's gonna be your new roommate!" Weed removed the lid and dropped the small rodent inside.

The mouse hit the ground running. It frantically darted back and forth, searching for any means of escape as it stood on its short hind legs and desperately tried to scale the glass walls.

I could all but smell the rodent's fear, its tiny heart beating almost straight through its chest, the pounding of its panic loud in my ears.

Eventually the mouse rolled itself up into a tight ball and cowered in a corner, too exhausted to do anything but emit small squeals of fear. But the snake barely paid the tiny creature any mind.

Willy snickered and directed my attention to a different aquarium, where I spotted a mouse that dozed snuggled up against a pygmy rattler's side.

"This is my own form of psychological warfare, Porter. The trick is to put a mouse in with a snake that's already been fed. That's how the fun begins."

One of Willy's hands edged toward my thigh, and I gave the offending paw a hard smack.

"Ouch!" he yelped.

"You were saying?" I asked with an icy stare.

He broke into a shit-eating grin. "Well, the kicker is that after a few days, that rodent will start feeling all safe and cozy. Then, just when mousie's pretty damn sure nothing bad is ever going to happen, WHAP! The snake gets hungry and moves in for the kill."

Willy jiggled in place as if his bladder were about to burst. "It's great, I'm telling ya! The snake is slowly swallowing the little bastard, while the sucker's itsy-bitsy brain is working overtime, trying to figure out just what in the hell went wrong.

"But that's the way life is, Porter. You let your guard down for just one little ol' minute, and KERPOWEE! The next thing you know, you're nothing but a hunk of dead, smelly, old meat."

I looked at him in disgust. "Thanks for the lesson on what makes scum like you tick, Willy."

"Hey, Porter—you're the one snooping in here. What am I supposed to think, except maybe you've got yourself an itch for one of my great big ol' snakes." Willy swiveled his hips and giggled.

"The only thing I've got an itch for, Willy, is to take a look at your passport," I informed him coldly, hoping he wouldn't question my authority.

"What the hell you wanna go and do that for?" Weed bristled, suspicion edging into his voice.

"I hear you're out of town at least once a week. I'm curious to see if you're going to Club Med."

"Goddamn! It was that bitch Bambi told you that, wasn't it? What the hell else does that woman want from me? She's taken almost every lousy thing I own!"

Oh, I don't know. "Lousy" seemed to describe his entire estate. "Listen, Willy. If you've got nothing to hide, you shouldn't have any problem showing me where you've been going. Or would you prefer I place a call to a friend of mine with the IRS, and fill him in on the true nature of your non-profit foundation?"

Willy stood defiantly in front of me, his hands opening and closing in tight fists. Taking a deep breath, he shook his head, the shiver traveling down his body as he flicked out his wrists. If I hadn't known better, I would have sworn I was viewing an exorcism.

"Getting rid of all the evil spirits, Willy?" I inquired.

"Yeah. I'm studying with Swami Gottagetmesomebootie," Weed smartly replied. "You wait here and I'll go get my passport." He turned to Tregler. "You watch her for me, Buzz. Make sure she don't do nothing funny."

After Willy left the trailer, I asked Tregler, "Do you mind if I step outside and join you?"

Buzz looked pleased at the suggestion. "Heck, I think that'd be just fine," he said, giving his shirt an extra tuck inside his jeans. "Don't get put off by old Willy. He's really not such a bad guy."

"I guess that all depends on your definition of 'bad,' " I replied.

Buzz leaned in toward me, his chin only the height of my chest. "Truth be told, the problem is he's got little-pee-pee syndrome," Tregler confided.

"Little-pee-pee syndrome?" I repeated.

"Yeah, you know—he's got some kinda complex cause his weenie is so small." Buzz hitched his thumbs in his pants. "Hey! I bet you didn't know that I work for the government, just like you," he divulged with a wink.

I doubted that, unless there was a branch for the seriously demented.

"That means we got a lot in common. Maybe you and me ought to plan on getting together."

Only if I was looking to do some serious research on sex deviation. "I'm all booked up for the next couple of months," I informed him.

Tregler wasn't about to be put off that easily. He sidled up to me and grinned. "You don't have to be afraid of *my* stinger, mama. Cause this Buzz is for you."

I was considering squashing him then and there, when Weed limped back into view. I knew it was a bad day if I looked upon Willy as my salvation.

"Here you go, Porter." Willy threw me his passport. "Have yourself a blast."

I thumbed through the document. Except for an excursion to Puerto Rico, it appeared to have been barely used at all. I tossed the passport back to Willy, disappointed. Still, having the inside track on Weed's little-pee-pee syndrome made me feel ever so much better.

"So tell me, Willy. Just where is it that you're disappearing to every week?"

"Not that it's any of your business, Porter, but I got a sick mama that I go visit in Macon, Georgia."

"Yeah. And then he comes and sees me," Buzz genially added.

I suddenly clicked in to Tregler's identity, certain he must be the old air force buddy that Bambi had mentioned. Turning on my best one-hundred-fifty-watt smile, I aimed it at Tregler. "You said you work for the government? Why, you must be a military man."

Buzz broke into a surprised grin. "Wow! That's pretty good! How'd you figure that out?"

"You've just got that air of authority about you. So, you're stationed somewhere in Georgia?"

"Sure am. Robins Air Force Base, right outside of Macon. I'm in charge of the surplus division," Tregler bragged.

"Like hell you are," Willy sniped, jealous at Buzz receiving so much attention.

"Well, I'm second in command!" Buzz responded defensively. "That's close enough. Shit, I've even got a desk right next to a window. It's considered to be status of sorts, when you get a window. That way you get extra light." Tregler sniffed, his pride having been hurt.

"A window with extra light!" Willie snorted contemptuously. "That's a good one. Maybe you just finally got around to popping your head out of your ass."

With friends like Willy, who needed enemies? "What kind of surplus do you deal in?" I asked.

Buzz brightened back up. "Lots of stuff. If you like, I can get you a Swatch watch, or even a strand of pearls. They'd look real pretty on you."

Willy dug the heel of his cast into the ground. "For chrissakes! The man deals in surplus Spam! Is there anything else that you're itching to know, Porter?"

I nailed Willy with a shot between the eyes. "How about filling me in on that Cuban Amazon you gave Bambi?"

Willy snickered, more than happy to share the joke. "That bird is one mean sonofabitch, ain't it? There was no way in hell I was ever going to be able to sell the damn thing, so I pawned it off on her."

"And where did *you* get the bird from?"

Willy smirked, enjoying the game. "Somebody gave it to me as payment."

"Payment for what?" I pressed.

"For services rendered," Willy sneered.

"There's no band on that bird's leg, which means it wasn't captive bred. That leads me to believe it must have been smuggled into Miami."

Buzz looked at me with a blank stare.

"It's a hot bird," I interpreted for him.

Willy slapped his palm to his forehead. "Hot damn! You mean I was suckered? Well, don't that just beat all!" He grinned. "Course ya gotta prove it, first. But be my guest!" he graciously offered. "Confiscate the damn thing, why doncha? You can send it to that Fish and Wildlife animal lab you got out West, for all I care."

Carlos would wring my neck before he'd allow me to do any such thing. The time and money it would cost to prove one measly parrot had been caught in the wild wasn't high on Fish and Wildlife's agenda.

"From what I hear, Elena Vallardes gave it to you," I told him.

Willy hocked a lugie, spitting the wad of phlegm on the ground. "That bitch don't give away nothing. Hell, that's the problem with those damn Cubans."

"And you do?" I asked. "In that case, how about giving me some information I want."

"You know damn well what I'm talking about. It's the way they come salsa-ing their asses over here, acting like this is Havana and *we're* their goddamn slaves," Willy answered peevishly.

"Oh, I get it. Instead of realizing they're *our* slaves, you mean," I responded.

"Fuck you, Porter!" he glowered. "Those people need to be taught a lesson. Well, just you wait—before too long, there's gonna be a reckoning."

I wondered if Elena had any idea of how unpopular she was with both Willy and the former Mrs. Weed. "I hope you don't plan on being the one to carry it out," I warned him.

Willy blew me a kiss. "Why, mama! I didn't know you cared."

"I just don't want any innocent Cubans having to get rabies shots because Willy the Weed is on a rampage," I shot back.

Weed punched Buzz in the arm. "Hear that, dickbrain? That's why I tell you never to get married. You meet a babe who promises to cook and screw you forever. Then you get hitched and the next thing you know, they wind up talking to you like this bitch."

Buzz smiled, not paying Willy any mind. "Uh huh. But this one's lookin' real gooood!"

"Yeah. That's generally how they work it," Willy muttered. "That's all the fun and games I got time for today, Porter. Buzz and me've got an appointment we gotta get to."

Buzz climbed behind the wheel of Willy's Dodge, and Weed crawled in the passenger seat beside him. I noticed that a tarp covered the cargo bed of the pickup. It hadn't been there when I arrived.

"That means you gotta go, too, Porter," Willy called out,

interrupting my train of thought. He waited until I started my Ford. "Ladies first," he said with a smirk.

I drove out, curious as to what lay beneath the tarp, since Buzz and Weed had clearly been on the grounds at the time of my arrival. My mind also drifted back to the trailer with the locked door, my gut instinct whispering that there could be a connection.

Ten

I pointed my Tempo for Tommy's.

Since it was early in the day, the fishermen hadn't gathered yet. I saw Tommy perched on a stool, dressed in his usual *Gilligan's Island* garb, gutting a pile of red snapper between extra-long sips of beer. By the time I sat down next to him, a beer was ready and waiting for me.

Tommy grunted his hello and reached behind the bar's makeshift counter to produce a bowl of seviche, which we picked at in silence. Tommy's homemade brew slid easily down my throat, cooling the spicy marinated fish.

I leaned back and let the place work its magic. Biscayne Bay lay blue and smooth, daring any clouds to cast a blemish on its surface. An egret lazily drifted by, its wings slowly beating the heavy air like two giant white feathery fans. The remnants of Willy that had clung to me began to let go, melting beneath the sun.

It wasn't until I was working on my second beer and feasting on grilled red snapper that I broached what was bothering me. "You told me that Cuban Amazons are usually smuggled by cigar boat into the Keys."

Tommy removed a small cigar from his pocket, bit off the end and lit up. "That's right."

"There's someone that I'm certain is smuggling in Amazons. But there's no way this guy is a sailor." I grinned as I visualized Willy tossing around on the high seas.

"Then he's probably flying the birds in by plane straight from Cuba," Tommy said.

"Exactly," I agreed. "The only thing is, I took a look at

his passport this morning. There were no Cuban entry or exit stamps there.''

Tommy picked up a well-worn toothpick and dug at his gums, producing a fibrous string of snapper.

''Cuba doesn't stamp American passports. Neither does Mexico, for that matter,'' Tommy informed me.

A gull flew past, passing judgment with a raucous snicker. Willy must be having a good laugh over my stupidity, too.

''What does Mexico have to do with anything?'' I asked, my mind feeling dense from the heat.

''Well, you certainly don't think your friend is flying in and out of Cuba from Miami, do you?'' Tommy's question slapped me awake. ''There's still a boycott going on, remember? If I were going to fly, I'd hop a plane to Mexico and from there connect to Cuba—leaving plenty of time for a few margaritas and *señoritas*, of course. No muss, no fuss—but best of all, no paper trail.''

Tommy slid off the stool and disappeared. When he returned he had a bottle of scotch in his hand, formally announcing that morning was over and his afternoon had begun.

''Tell me something, Tommy. How is it that you seem to know so much about Cuba?''

Tommy poured himself a shot. ''Can you guarantee that whatever I tell you will go no farther than here?'' he asked.

''As long as it has nothing to do with illegal wildlife, your activities don't concern me,'' I answered honestly.

''This is a great life. I make the rules. People don't like 'em, they go somewhere else. It's that simple.'' Tommy turned his head and stared out at the water, his gaze so intent that my eyes were drawn to follow. But whatever he saw remained hidden from my view.

''It doesn't take much to see that I can't make a living just running this dive.'' He waved to a couple of fishermen who lurched in, done with their day's work before noon.

''What do you do to keep going?'' I gently prodded.

Tommy's blue eyes carried me along on their own inner wave. ''When I need to, I hire myself out and make hauls running merchandise back and forth between here and Cuba.''

My heart beat the slightest bit faster, secretly wishing that

I could go along. "What kind of merchandise are we talking about?"

Tommy shrugged. "Almost anything you can think of. Computers, TVs, radios, any kind of electronic equipment. Those people have next to nothing."

"And what do you bring back in return?" I asked.

Tommy blew a series of carefully constructed smoke rings and then smiled. "Mostly, I bring back Cuban cigars."

"Where do they go?" I asked, genuinely curious.

Tommy took another sip of his scotch. "I was only in charge of hauling the stuff. The guy I delivered them to did the actual selling. In fact, it was someone you knew."

I barely dared ask, fearing my suspicions would fall into the realm of conspiracy theory. "Alberto Dominguez?"

Tommy gave a slight nod.

My stomach tightened at the next logical question which sprang to mind. "Did you haul Cuban Amazons for him, as well?"

"Now you're getting into one of those gray areas that I can't talk about," Tommy replied noncommittally.

I gave myself a mental slap. No wonder he knew so much about the ways in which Cuban Amazons were smuggled!

Tommy must have noticed the invisible foot that kicked me in the rear end. "For chrissakes, Porter, stop beating yourself up," he groused. "There was no way for you to know. Besides, with Alberto knocked off, I won't be doing those hauls anymore." Tommy peeled off his flip-flops and buried his toes in the sand. "It got to the point where it was turning my stomach, anyway," he grudgingly admitted. "I saw too many of the damn things die. I'd already made up my mind not to haul any more birds."

"Do you know if Alberto had any business partners?" I was hoping a few more familiar names would pop up.

Tommy shook his head. "I was an employee; I wasn't his goddamn confidant."

"You must have been privy to some information," I pressed.

Tommy got up and served a round of beer and snapper to the fishermen who had begun to appear and sat swapping tales at the bar. But if he thought that was my cue to leave, he was in for a surprise. I liked it here well enough. I didn't care if it took all night for me to get the information I wanted. I stretched back and created flying angels in the sand.

When Tommy returned, he had a couple of rolls that he tore into chunks and threw in the air. A swarm of hungry gulls appeared from out of nowhere, swooping down to catch the pieces.

"Alberto was tight with the Cuban community," he continued as though having never left off. "If he had a partner, it was probably one of his own kind."

"So, it was a Cuban cigar ring all round," I replied, smiling at my cleverness.

"Wrong," Tommy countered. "I'm talking about the birds. No other Cuban would've touched those cigars with a ten-foot pole. In fact, if the Cuban community had gotten wind of what Alberto was doing, the guy would have found himself totally ostracized."

There was something I wasn't quite getting here. "You want to explain this to me a little better? I thought it was only *our* government that had a problem with bringing in Cuban cigars."

"What the hell were they teaching when you went to school, Porter?" Tommy asked. "How to set a dinner table and catch a wealthy man?"

"Yeah. That's why I'm sitting here next to you," I shot back. "Don't get sand on my debutante gown."

"Alright," Tommy said gruffly. "Ninety-nine percent of Cubans don't approve of smuggling in Cuban cigars, because they feel it helps to financially support the Castro regime. The Cuban community here in the States has one focus and one focus only: to get the hell rid of Fidel Castro. Which is why no Cuban with a conscience is going to deal in cigars made in Havana."

"Does that mean Alberto was a secret supporter of Castro?" I asked.

"Nah." Tommy brushed off the thought. "It just means he was a greedy bastard. I figure he shipped 'em all up to cigar stores in New York."

"Okay. Then let me ask you something about his illegal bird dealings." I raised a finger, cutting off Tommy before he could protest. "I'm not asking about *your* role in it. What I want to know is, who else was involved?"

Tommy picked up a fistful of sand. "You really think Alberto would have told me something like that?"

"You're a smart guy. I'm sure you picked things up along the way," I countered.

Tommy released the sand. "I don't know who they were, other than Cubans. What I *will* tell you is that I wasn't the only one making trips. Dominguez liked to cover his bases. He had one pigeon that always flew. From Miami, to Mexico, to Cuba, and back."

"Does the name Willy Weed sound familiar?" I asked.

"Like I said, names were never mentioned," Tommy answered.

I popped one last question to confirm something that had made little sense until now. "What are green coins?"

Tommy's head jerked up. "Where did you pick up that phrase?"

"It was in a letter I found at Alberto's from a woman in Cuba. She promised to have ten green coins ready for him," I replied. "What are coins, Tommy?"

He stared at me, as if questioning just how dumb I really was, and how much I already knew. "It was Alberto's code word for parrots. Green stands for Cuban Amazons."

"So blue coins would be hyacinth macaws."

A sudden whoosh of wings caught me by surprise as a flock of snowy-white egrets lifted off from their roosts in nearby trees, their long, slender bodies silhouetted like ribbons against the sky.

Tommy nodded and followed the birds with his eyes as they winged out to sea. "I bet you didn't know that there are more escaped parrots flying around here in south Florida, than there are flying free in the entire Amazon rain forest." He stared again at me. "Did you know that, Porter?"

I didn't answer, intrigued by the feverish look which had sneaked into his eyes.

Tommy cocked an ear. "You wanna know why I really stopped bringing in birds? I began to hear their calls in the wind. When I listened closer, I realized I was hearing their cries for help." His eyes held me captive. "You know what they call the few that are left in the wild? They're known as the living dead, because odds are that they'll never survive."

A shiver passed through me. Tommy reached into his shirt pocket and pulled out a business card.

"This is a place for you to check out. The guy's no longer involved in smuggling, but he knows the trade here in Florida better than anyone else."

All I knew about Hialeah was that the racetrack was there. Also, that the track's resident flock of pink flamingos had starred in the opening montage of *Miami Vice*, without ever earning a dime in royalties. It appeared I was about to learn more. Hialeah was where Wickee Wackee Bird World and its owner, Saul Greenberg, were located.

Wickie Wackee Bird World stood on a strip filled with rundown stores that had seen better days. The place was just as charming inside. Grimy windows kept out most of the sun, while ancient fluorescent lights provided a sick, yellowish glow. The man behind the counter fit in perfectly with the general motif. His pasty white complexion made Bonkers look tan, and the large glasses that covered his eyes gave him the visage of an owl. You'd have been hard pressed to guess this was a man who lived in the sun capital of the world.

What the store did have was plenty of birds, screeching louder than a roomful of senior citizens playing a high-stakes game of canasta. One bird barked like a dog, another was a dead ringer for a fire alarm, while a third scatted to jazz.

A quick look around revealed some yellow-crowned Amazons. Natives of Mexico, the birds are closed to the trade. But Saul's collection got even better. Perched in a corner were rare black palm cockatoos, with a going price of $50,000 a pair. After seeing that, it came as no surprise to spot two hyacinths, along with a Cuban Amazon. The only strange thing was that Saul kept one hell of an inventory in such a crummy little store.

I walked over to the cage containing the hyacinths, their violet-blue plumage iridescent even in the dim light. The yellow feathers that circled their eyes looked like circus clown makeup, and a golden racing stripe ran along either side of their tongues. I brought a finger up toward the cage, tempted to pet them.

"You really don't want to do that."

I turned around, where Saul held up his hand for me to view. It was missing the tips of two fingers. "If you're not careful, those huge hooked beaks of theirs will chop your finger right off." He produced two Brazil nuts, and fed one to each of the birds. "I've learned to be careful." He smiled.

One of the hyacinths flipped the Brazil nut in the air and caught it, smashing the hard shell as easily as a grape.

"They can crush two thousand pounds per square inch in those beaks," Greenberg revealed with pride.

I gazed at the pair, remembering the tranquilized hyacinths I'd glimpsed at Alberto's.

"How long have you had these birds?" I asked.

Greenberg blinked at me from behind his oversized lenses. "You're a fed, aren't you?"

I laughed and added a dash of bewilderment. "What makes you say that?"

"Let's just say I used to dabble in the trade. I can smell an agent almost before I spot him." He raised his chin and sniffed at the air like a well-trained hound dog. "I'd say you're definitely Fish and Wildlife."

I was going to have to try a different brand of soap. I stretched my hand out toward him. "My name is Rachel Porter."

A flicker of a smile crossed his lips as he shook my hand. "I'd give you my name, but I'm sure you already know it. I'll tell you straight off that I'm not involved in that side of the business anymore."

"A change of heart?" I asked.

Saul stretched a finger out to an African grey parrot that sat on a branch. "No. I've just reached the age where I don't want to take chances anymore."

The bird stepped onto the human perch and Saul raised the bird up to his face, where he planted a kiss on its beak.

"You see this parrot? He's got a better vocabulary than most people I know." The bird kissed Saul's nose in return. "Parrots are the chimps of the bird world in terms of intelligence."

"It's the feds! It's the feds! Run for cover!" screeched the elegant red-tailed parrot.

"I told you he was smart," Saul grinned.

"You might feel too old for smuggling these days; the question is whether you still deal in hot birds?"

"Absolutely not." Saul crossed his heart and then crossed the bird's chest with his fingertip. "I guarantee you that, on the life of Megabite here."

Hmm. I hoped the bird would be around to see a ripe old age. "Then where did the palms, the yellow-napes, the hyacinths, and the Cuban come from?" I asked.

Megabite tackled the rim of Saul's glasses. "They're from my former days. And by the way—those particular birds aren't for sale. Neither is this one here."

I gave Saul a dubious look. "That's a good way to run your business into the ground."

Greenberg shrugged. "I've already made my money. This is more of a way to keep me out of the house. My wife tells me that the birds and I drive her crazy. I look at this shop as our sanctuary. But then, I bet you didn't come here to buy a bird."

It was apparent the guy knew his customers. "Actually, I'm looking into a bird-theft ring."

Saul swayed back and forth on the balls of his feet. "I've heard about what's going on. If you're trying to track down those birds, you're wasting your time."

"Why is that?" I inquired. I thought about checking Saul's birds for any telltale markings, but the man was too smart to take in parrots that were traceable.

"Let me explain how a ring like this works." Greenberg took a seat behind his counter and offered me a stool. "You ever have a car stolen?"

I shook my head.

"That's probably because you've had nothing but secondhand cars, and cheap ones at that," he surmised.

I shot him a look. "What do you do for a sideline? Work as an FBI profiler?"

"Funny." Greenberg pushed his glasses up with his index finger, and placed Megabite on a stationary perch. "A car-theft ring doesn't steal just any car. They go out and hunt around till they find a white BMW sports model, or the latest Toyota Camry in hunter green. Particular cars are stolen to fill specific orders. It's the same thing with these birds. They're already sold before the theft has even taken place.''

It was nice to know there was an upside to driving around in a junk heap.

''That's a great theory, but I've already got a case that disproves it,'' I told him. ''A few days ago, a bird dealer was knocked off and all two hundred and fifty of his birds were stolen. You can't tell me that every one of those parrots was already sold.''

Saul raised his palms. ''You're right. What you're describing is something different. That was a revenge burglary.''

Now I knew the guy was nuts. ''You want to explain that one?''

''Look—you and I both know that the rings working this area have never murdered anyone, and that they always take the most valuable birds. The robbery you're telling me about is something completely different. That theft was personal. The guy was whacked because he pissed somebody off.''

''He was bringing in lots of Cuban Amazons,'' I revealed. ''Have you heard about any pipeline dealing in a large number of those birds?''

Saul thought for a moment and then shook his head. ''Nah. All I know of is the occasional small-time hustler bringing in a few parrots here and there. What was the dead guy's name?''

I figured there was no harm in telling. ''Alberto Dominguez.''

Saul rolled his eyes. ''Oh, a Cuban guy. Yeah, they deal with their own.''

Tommy had sent me on a wild-goose chase. This guy was racking up nothing but zeros.

''What you gotta do is figure this thing out like a puzzle until all the pieces fit. That dead guy of yours could have been smuggling for his own personal gain. Or the murder could have been for something else, too.''

I had the feeling that Saul didn't get much in the way of human company these days. ''Like what?'' I asked, working my way out from behind the counter.

''Well, the case involves smuggling Amazons out of Cuba,

right? And the guy doing it, Alberto, was a Cuban. So, take a look around,'' Saul suggested.

I had no idea what the man was talking about. I cleared the counter and edged toward the door.

''Ask yourself, what have you got here in Miami?'' Saul answered his own question. ''You've got a community of exiled Cubans who are stirring the pot, plotting their brains out to overthrow Castro. If I were you, I'd be checking out what else this Alberto was into. You might even be looking for a political angle to this thing. Speaking of which, have you seen this morning's paper?''

Greenberg handed me a copy of the *Miami Herald*, which I hadn't had the chance to read. Right on the front page was a story about a bomb attack on a hotel and well-known restaurant in the middle of Havana. The bombing had taken the life of an Italian tourist. The Cuban foreign minister laid the blame on a Miami-based Cuban exile group, referring to it as a CIA-backed, terrorist mafia. This was the third recent attack aimed at the country's booming tourist industry. Any connection to Dominguez seemed totally farfetched. I rolled up the paper and stuck it under my arm as I headed out the door.

''By the way,'' Saul called out. ''My sense of smell isn't really all that good. Tommy called and told me that you'd be coming.''

Eleven

Little Havana is three and a half square miles of pure Cuban heart and soul located west of downtown and south of the Miami River. It got its name from the Cuban exiles who settled there in the late sixties and immediately set about recreating the Cuban capital. I headed there now. The news article had reminded me of Ramon's story about his family's flight from the island, and this seemed to be as good a time as any to visit his shop. Maybe I could pry something out of him without that sister of his around.

I navigated through the traffic fumes, where the beep of horns intermingled with the strains of Cuban Muzak, the sound pulsating out of shop doors. It was easy to take in the sights this way, patiently crawling along in a game of bumper cars as I searched for a parking space. I finally bit the dust and swerved into a pay garage, after losing a showdown over four precious yards of asphalt to a determined *mamacita.*

The staccato sounds of Spanish rat-a-tat-tatted like a machine gun around me. Even the street signs were in Spanish, making me the stranger in an exotic, strange land as I hit the pavement. Cafeterias tempted me with their aroma of roast pork sandwiches and white bean soup. But since I'd already had lunch with Tommy, I couldn't come up with a decent excuse to bolt another one down.

I enviously eyed the women who glided past smartly shaded by brightly blooming umbrellas the colors of cool tropical drinks. They eyed me as well, wondering why a gringa would be dumb enough to walk unprotected beneath the blazing sun.

I continued on past a fenced-in park where a group of old

men smoked cigars and sipped their coffee, intently concentrating on a mean game of dominoes. The *clack, clack, clack* of the black-and-white tiles transmuted into the sympathetic clucking of tongues, the consoling sound of men kibitzing about when Castro would die and they could finally go home.

I didn't have to look in order to know that the humidity had caused my hair to revert to its natural state of frizz. I was so worried about my appearance that I nearly walked past the window with its colorful painting of a puffin, a cigar jauntily stuck in the side of its tangerine beak, giving it an uncanny resemblance to Groucho Marx. The image was set in a circle with the puffin's wings popping out to point at the words 100% HAND ROLLED, 100% NATURAL. There was no question that this was Ramon's store, PUFFIN CIGARS.

As I was on my way in, I collided with a human freight train barreling out. The locomotive was none other than Phil Langer, who leaned his hulking frame against the door.

I took a step back, and gave him the once-over. "Sorry. I almost didn't recognize you without the dead bird."

His mouth twitched into the sliver of a smile. "Why, Agent Porter. I would never have taken you for a cigar aficionado."

"You're right about that," I replied.

"That's too bad. And you were just about to rise a notch in my estimation."

I sighed. "I'll just have to learn to live with that."

"So what brings you here? Rumors that tobacco leaves are being tortured in the back room?" Langer mocked.

Since it was an innocent question, I filled in the answer. "I'm just here to visit the owner."

Langer's eyes blinked behind their Polaroid shades. "How is it that you know my neighbor, Ramon? Nothing personal, but you're not his usual type."

I found it hard to believe that was the best the man could come up with. I'd received better jabs from my own grandmother.

"He's developing better taste these days."

Langer let the remark float by. "Too bad you haven't developed an appreciation for cigars. Ramon makes the best in the business. But you still haven't told me how the two of you met."

"Through a mutual acquaintance." Alberto's mangled form flashed in my mind. "Someone with a fondness for Cuban cigars."

His lips pulled back tightly. "Then you're obviously referring to a person with a complete lack of moral character. Some people are just too weak to resist temptation. Then there are those who love to flaunt their disdain for the law—there *are* deviants in our society who take pleasure in breaking the rules. The next thing you know, the press picks up on this issue and blows it out of all proportion, making the public believe there's actually a demand for the damn cigars."

Jeez—who put a nickel in his slot and got him going? I couldn't resist a dig. "Do you honestly expect me to believe that a connoisseur like you has never tried a Cuban cigar?"

Langer's features hardened. "I guarantee that one has never passed my lips. We're at war with Cuba, Porter. In case you don't know, there's something called the Trading with the Enemy Act. That makes the purchase of Cuban cigars tantamount to treason."

I couldn't help but laugh. "Treason? You've got to be joking."

Langer bridled. "You work for the government, Porter; you, of all people, should know better than that. Or do you consider our laws to be some sort of joke?"

Langer was turning out to be even crazier than I had imagined. "Oh, come on. It's not as if smuggling Cuban cigars is the same as giving away military secrets."

"As far as I'm concerned, it's nearly as bad," Langer snapped. "That kind of attitude is what supports a dictatorship, Porter. You're helping prop up Castro's regime anytime one of his cigars is sold."

"If the Bay of Pigs, numerous assassination attempts, and an embargo of nearly forty years haven't dislodged Castro, do you really think boycotting cigars is going to hurt him?" I scoffed.

Langer glared at me like an angry bulldog.

"There are more important things to spend our manpower on—beside the fact that it's nearly impossible to keep people from bringing in cigars."

"You want to know how you stop people?" Langer's eyes

warned against any wise-ass response. "You set an example. The punishment should be death. Fry a few of the bastards, and you'll see the market in Cuban cigars dry up fast enough."

Any impulse I had to laugh had vanished. "You can't be serious."

The look Langer gave me could have frozen the sun. "There's much more at stake here than cigars, Porter. If you don't know that by now, you'd better learn fast."

I watched as he stiffly walked away. Now I knew who the guy reminded me of—Schwarzenegger, in the first *Terminator* movie.

I walked into Ramon's shop, where a pretty Cuban girl stood behind a display counter showcasing a wide variety of cigars. A scoop-necked, skintight dress highlighted her wares. A small gold crucifix dangled, nearly lost, between two mounds of flesh.

She smiled at me, though her heart wasn't in it. "May I help you?"

I'd felt like something out of a Sears store before walking in. Now it was down to Kmart. "I'd like to see Ramon. You can tell him Rachel Porter is here."

The girl flashed me a sympathetic glance, kindly letting me know that I didn't stand a chance, then sashayed into the back room to get him.

I gazed down at the glass counter to catch my reflection, and a familiar titillation nipped at the nerve endings under my skin. I knew Ramon couldn't be far away. I didn't move, but silently waited until his image hovered over me in the display case, like a Cuban missile coming in to land.

"Raquel! I'm so happy that you took me up on my offer!"

His voice poured over me like hot fudge on an ice-cream sundae. He paused, letting me melt, before dropping the proverbial cherry. "I can't tell you how much I was hoping that you would come."

He took hold of my hand and raised it to his lips, where his mustache softly brushed against my skin, the ensuing tickle his very own personal art form. His eyes locked onto mine as they drew me into a tango, his gaze slowly bending me back in a visual dip. Then his breath sensuously stroked my palm, followed by what I could have sworn was the faintest touch of the tip of his tongue. I couldn't believe the hot moves on this guy. I would have decked him if I hadn't been enjoying it so much.

"Let me show you my cigars." Ramon's fingers were as hot as five embers where they rested on the crook of my elbow, the rustle of his linen pants a confidential murmur as he guided the way.

"Creating a premium cigar is much like producing a fine wine. It's all in the soil and seeds." Ramon's voice was as soothing as a bedtime story. "I'll tell you the real secret though," he whispered in my ear. "It's that each leaf is hand-chosen personally by me."

He opened a door to display a room that was lined with red cedar. The fragrance cocooned me as Ramon softly closed the door behind us.

"This is what I call the marriage room." The words were said like a reverent prayer. "It is here that the various flavors in each cigar marry and age. This is the room where I put them to bed."

I shot a suspicious glance his way, but he appeared to be totally serious. The room contained bundles of cigars, each labeled with a person's name.

"What do the names stand for?" I questioned.

Ramon smiled, pleased with my interest. "That tells me which of my six rollers made those particular cigars, along with the types of tobacco used, and the brand. Here, I'll show you."

He picked one of the cigars up and held it lovingly in his hand. "This one I call the Churchill. See how long and thick it is?" His fingers danced along its length. "Yet it burns mild with a full-bodied taste." Ramon held it out toward me.

I didn't know whether to touch it, or slap him.

He smiled and moved on. "This is the Torpedo. True, it is wide at one end. But look how nicely it tapers where it fits in your mouth." He brought it up to his nose and took a deep whiff.

Though my face burned, I didn't say anything, playing it cool, deaf, and dumb.

Ramon picked up a cigar that could have passed for a miniature dachshund. "This one is called the Old Style, because at seven and a half inches, it is the biggest of them all. Though not everyone can handle it, this is the cigar that is desired by the true . . . aficionado.''

Okay—it was time to put the brakes on, before the innuendos skidded out of control. ''Thanks, Ramon. But I've learned more than I'll ever need to know.'' I turned to leave the room.

Ramon's hand shot out, pulling me close. ''Raquel, wait! Just one more.'' He picked up the last cigar. ''This one is called Passion. It's slimmer than the Churchill, and not as long as Old Style. But when it burns, it ignites a craving that very few others can fully satisfy. Its smoke is deep and long and smooth. This is the cigar for someone like you. Here. I want you to have it.''

As he placed the roll of tobacco in my hand, it took every ounce of control I had not to throw the thing away. I left the room feeling as if I'd been seduced and bedded without even knowing it.

''That was very educational, Ramon. But I don't want to take up your time, and I do have some questions,'' I said.

''Raquel, please be patient.'' Ramon held up a long, tapered finger and slowly brought it to rest on my lips. ''You will truly hurt me if you will not allow me to show you how my cigars are made.'' His eyes smoldered through me, searing my T-shirt to my skin.

My feet moved as if under his control, as my libido put a stranglehold on what little was left of my reasoning. Who was this guy, Svengali?

We entered a room where six elderly Cuban men sat on long wooden planks, hunched over their work.

''These are my master rollers,'' Ramon said with pride. ''What you are watching is a dying art.''

One old man folded three different types of long leaf tobacco together, placing the finished product inside a large wooden mold.

We walked over to another elderly man, who gave me a wink.

''This is Armando. He takes each cigar that has been pressed and nestles it inside still another leaf of tobacco, which is called a wrapper,'' Ramon explained.

Armando's fingers were as brown and wrinkled as the tobacco. He sealed the final leaf closed with a touch of vegetable glue, laid the tight roll on a guillotine-like contraption, and released the blade, chopping off the cigar's end.

''Do you sell any cigars other than those that are made here on your premises?'' I asked with wide-eyed innocence.

Ramon smiled at the question. ''Now, why would I do something like that when we make the best cigars in the world?''

''Even better than Cubans?'' I questioned, opening my eyes a little wider.

''No. Cuba is the only place that can produce a cigar which is better,'' Ramon solemnly admitted.

I brought my voice down a notch lower. ''You wouldn't by any chance happen to have a small stash of Cuban cigars here, would you? Believe me, I have no official interest when I ask about this. I'm only inquiring for a friend who's desperate to get hold of some. He would be willing to pay top dollar.''

Ramon's expression turned from seductive to horrified. ''But that's absolute treason! It's against the law,'' he sputtered.

Gee, where had I heard those same words only a few minutes ago?

''I'm sorry; I have no intention of getting you into any trouble. But if you don't carry them, perhaps you might know of someone who does?'' I urged.

A fine layer of perspiration lightly moistened his brow. For a moment, I thought he might ask me to leave. Instead he pressed my hand to his heart.

''Raquel, I can only imagine that you don't truly understand the implications of what you are asking,'' he said.

He gently stroked my fingers. It was enough to make me almost feel guilty for trying to trap him.

''No decent Cuban would ever allow himself to be involved in the sale of such cigars. It would be the same as taking blood money from our people,'' he explained. ''Cubans have died attempting to escape Castro. That's what everyone in this country forgets. Cuban cigars that are sold in America only help support a ruthless and despicable dictator.''

He and Langer were clearly reading from the same script.

He kissed my hand, then placed his own squarely on my chest. I started to feel much less guilty.

"Haven't there been many attempts to overthrow Castro's regime?" I firmly removed Ramon's hand.

"Yes, and, unfortunately, each one has failed." A note of sorrow hung in his voice like a teardrop. "However, we continue to work toward trying to get rid of him."

"I've heard there are Cubans here in Miami training for an invasion," I ventured.

Armando now looked up at me with a pair of sad, rheumy eyes.

Ramon gave an impassive shrug. "That sort of thing took place back when Kennedy was president, but the Bay of Pigs put an end to all that. Since then, we try to do what we can, which is really very little."

"But aren't there groups of Cubans still hoping to mount an invasion?" I persisted. "There's been a rash of recent bombings in Havana, all aimed at the island's tourist industry. One took place just last night that's being blamed on paramilitary groups based right here in Miami."

Ramon shook his head and smiled, conveying that I still had much to learn. "The CIA stopped helping those groups long ago. What you're hearing about is nothing more than a bunch of old men holding on to their dreams."

The old men beside us never stopped rolling.

"Those bombings are most likely the work of an anti-Castro faction within Cuba itself. I know little about them—only that they are brave men fighting to gain our country's freedom." Ramon broke into a smile, his ivories gleaming as bright as tiny suns in a tropical sky. "One day soon, the dream of a free Cuba will become a reality." Ramon placed a hand on one of the old men's backs. "Isn't that so, Roberto?"

Roberto gazed up at him with a near toothless grin. "*Sí, señor Ramón.*"

"My master rollers did this very same work in Cuba for years. I've promised them that they'll do it again back home before they die. Isn't that true, my friends?" Ramon asked, with a magnanimous wave of his arm.

The men continued to roll without saying a word.

I moved back to the last row, where one of the workers was

rummaging through a drawer. A flash of silver caught my eye, its shape resembling the small silver leg band breeders placed on hatchling parrots to mark their birds as captive bred. I walked over, but the drawer was quickly closed. As the man reached for a mold, his short sleeve rode up to reveal the tattoo of a parrot clutching an automatic rifle in its talons.

The old man stared up at me with a deadly cold glare as he slowly pulled his sleeve back down.

I finally headed for the office, where Carlos was nowhere to be found. Even the receptionist had turned on the answering machine and gone home.

I sat at my desk and looked at the pile of papers that covered its surface. It had grown larger than it was two days ago. Either the paperwork was mutating on its own, or Carlos had had a hand in it.

Just shuffling the papers around wore me out, the thought of actually slogging through them had me verging on the edge of a coma. I knew that fairly soon, Carlos would ask what I'd been up to. I scribbled a note, taped it to his computer, and took off for home.

I pulled up to the cottage, parking close behind Sophie's ancient Volvo. It was amazing that it still had any life left in it: it had 150,000 miles on its odometer, the vinyl seats were ripped apart, both taillights were out, and its pale turquoise exterior was rusted and badly peeling. I'd once asked her why she didn't just buy a new one.

"What the hell for?" she'd replied. "It's still running. Besides, I've got a contest going to see which of us is going to outlast the other. Kinda like a couple of old Energizer batteries."

I walked into the garden, expecting to hear Sophie's cottage brimming with chatter, but there was only silence. The quiet was oddly depressing. I'd become used to walking in to the hustle and bustle of Sophie and Lucinda. Even better, that now included Terri. The three comprised my nearest and dearest family, and I'd quickly grown spoiled, anticipating that they'd be there whenever I arrived home. I continued on and entered my bungalow, where the silence was shattered by the ring of the telephone, followed by an earpiercing shriek from Bonkers.

"Hola! Hola!" the bird screeched.

"Hello?" I yelled into the phone. There was no reply and I was about to hang up, figuring it was a wrong number, when Santou's voice stopped me cold.

"Hey, *chère.* Remember me?"

My legs felt weak and I sat down on the bed. "How's New Orleans these days?" I asked, really meaning, Are you sorry you left me? Do you regret your demands?

"It could be better," he answered tentatively. "You could be here."

I imagined Jake flashing one of his lopsided grins that always flip-flopped my heart and turned my brain to Silly Putty. For once, I was glad of the distance between us. "Yeah. Well, I have this little thing that keeps me busy. It's known as a job."

"A job? I think what you're talking about is your life's obsession." His laugh was short and strained.

Bonkers filled the awkward silence with a perfect imitation of Sophie. *"Oy vay!"*

"Listen, *chère.* I've been thinking things over and maybe I was wrong." His voice smoothly wound around my heart. "It's not Fish and Wildlife I object to so much."

My pulse fluttered, and I wondered if Jake had really begun to understand how important my job was to me.

"I want to work this out, so maybe we can compromise. You could continue with the Service but just do something safer, like a part-time desk job."

Santou was lucky he was in New Orleans. Had he been any closer, I might have been tempted to get in my car, hunt him down and take a few well-aimed potshots. "Actually Jake, I was going to suggest the same thing to you," I countered, working to keep my cool. "I've decided I'm not all that crazy about what you do, either. In fact, I'm in the market for a house husband these days. Sound appealing?"

"If you're not going to be reasonable about this Rachel, we're never going to get anywhere," Jake answered shortly.

I always hate when men throw a term like "reasonable" around, as if that's supposed to make a woman sit up and behave. "That's something we agree on, Jake. I'm waiting for you to come to your senses, as well."

Santou slowly exhaled, as if blowing out a candle. "I love you with all my heart, *chère*. But I can see we're not going to make any progress on this," he paused. The silence sat like a wall between us. "Goodbye, Rachel."

I quickly hung up, not wanting the phone to click dead in my ear, and jumped into the shower where the water disguised my tears. Then I started on a bag of Snickers bars, until I saw Sophie and Terri coming up the walk. I ran out, relieved that the troops had finally arrived home.

Sophie was draped in one of her original caftans, its pattern of electric tangerine and green circles making her look like a walking orange grove. Terri's well-toned physique was displayed in a tight fuschia Speedo, demurely covered by a transparent pink top that looked suspiciously like a baby-doll nightie. Both wore gold sandals, large floppy hats, and sunscreen on their nose. Terri's skin had a golden glow, making me totally envious. Put me in the sun and I come out the shade of a well-boiled lobster.

"You look terrific," I said, taking another bite of the Snickers bar.

"You'll look great, too, once you go cold turkey off all that junk food." Terri pulled the candy bar out of my hand. "That's it, Rach. I didn't put all that hard work into you in New Orleans just to watch it go down the drain. As of today, you're eating healthy." He lowered his sunglasses, the skin around his eye now psychedelic shades of yellow and purple. "Something else is going on with you. What is it?"

"I just got off the phone with Santou," I confessed.

Terri shook his blonde curls and tapped his foot on the ground. "I love the man, but why do I get the feeling he's being a stubborn ass?"

I couldn't help but smile. "Because he is."

Terri slipped his arm through mine and walked me to my door. "I'm taking you out for dinner tonight. You can use the diversion and I've got some special news. I'll be ready in ten minutes."

"So, what's this news that you have?" I asked curiously as we strolled down South Beach.

"I think Sophie and I came up with something really big today," Terri said, and then paused dramatically. "We're launching a line of designer yarmulkes for pets of the Jewish persuasion!"

If my teeth had been false, they'd have dropped right out. "You're kidding."

"It's a great idea, Rach. With my costume experience and Sophie's contacts in the garment industry, it's a natural," Terri enthused. "We're going to call it 'Yarmulke Schlemmer.' "

While it was true that Terri designed drop-dead costumes for his drag show, Sophie's fashion taste ran to the left of eccentric, to put it mildly. Still, when it came to yarmulkes, I figured they'd all have to come out looking pretty much the same.

"We're planning to do a whole line in different fabrics and colors," Terri explained. "Miami is loaded with old geezers who dote on their pets. And if we start now, we'll be up and running in time for the Jewish holidays. We're expecting a big rush for Rosh Hashanah and Yom Kippur, which means we have to get cracking. We've decided to make Lucinda our sales rep."

I wondered how Lucinda was going to take the news. But my musing was put on hold as Terri dragged me into a macrobiotic cafe, where we ate steamed veggies and brown rice that tasted healthy no matter how hard I tried to imagine otherwise.

After dinner we walked along Lummus Park, to catch a volleyball game where hot boys with washboard abs showed off their prowess. While Terri took in the scene, I focused on the other end of the age spectrum.

Twilight was when the Geritol generation turned out for their evening constitutional. The women were gussied up in their best dresses and jewelry. Let the temperature dip below seventy degrees, and the accessories included mink coats. The men took a more casual approach to their evening apparel, turning out in a uniform of Bermuda shorts and ankle socks up to their knees, the height presumably ordained by city regulation.

"What's this obsession that Sophie and Lucinda have with miniature flags?" Terri's voice broke my focus.

"What are you talking about?" I asked.

"They have this strange little collection of flags in all different colors and shapes in their house."

"You mean like a mini-UN?"

"No, they definitely aren't flags of countries," Terri informed me.

I leaned back and stretched, working to make my stomach as taut as it would get. When you're in a town of exhibitionists, you do what you can. "The flags are probably tied in with all the protest rallies they attend. You know, different colors for different causes," I suggested.

Terri wrinkled up his nose.

"Okay, then. Maybe they're hanging out at amusement parks. Or robbing concession stands," I responded. "Better yet, they're probably little drink accessories, like your paper umbrellas."

"You're showing a lack of imagination, Rach. Personally, I think they're into some form of corporate espionage," Terri remarked. His attention had become focused on a guy in a thong and bandana who kickboxed nearby.

Mr. Kung Fu continued to practice, unaware of the runaway laundry cart that jerked its way toward him, seemingly under its own power. A whiff of strong perfume and a mound of peroxided fluff revealed its driver to be a tiny elderly woman, who peered over the handle as she tottered in a pair of high heels. I called out and Mr. Kung Fu raised his leg, allowing her to pass underneath and proceed down the concrete walk.

Terri and I headed home by way of the beach, where the only moving vehicles were sandpipers playing tag with the tide. Above us, lingering hues of deep purple and pink strafed the sky like renegade bullets.

"You're still thinking about Jake, aren't you?" he asked, as we followed a trail of tiny bird tracks.

I nodded and leaned my head against his shoulder, where I breathed in the lingering scent of sun, sand, and coconut oil. "I'm finding it hard to get him out of my mind."

Terri's fingers braided themselves between mine. "Listen, Rach. Ultimately, the person you have to be true to is yourself. Otherwise you'll never be happy." Bending down, he picked up a conch shell and placed it against my ear. ''If you don't believe me, listen to the sea.''

I held my breath, but all I heard was my name tossed about on the echo of waves.

Bonkers greeted me with a loud tirade when I walked in, angry that I had left but happy that I was now home.

The red message light on my answering machine blinked in eager anticipation, and I wondered if it was Santou calling back with an actual compromise.

''Porter? Goddammit! Where the hell are you? I just had a gun barrel shoved in my mouth, thanks to you!'' Bambi's voice hurtled toward me with the force of an exploding grenade. ''Willy was just here, and he didn't appreciate all the blabbing I've been doing to you. He said he's gonna whack me, and he told me just how he's gonna do it! You better do something about this, Porter, before I decide to!''

I played the message over to be sure I'd heard it correctly. There was no mistake. The call had come in at nine o'clock and it was midnight now, so I'd drive over to see her first thing in the morning. I wasn't surprised that Willy was out of control; only that he hadn't killed someone already.

Twelve

The smell of red clay and mangoes filled the air as I headed for Homestead to see Bambi early the next morning. I stopped at a local farmers' market for a freshly baked cinnamon bun, washing it down with a Key lime shake, and arrived at Bambi's shack fully armed and ready for combat.

As Bambi's emaciated dog approached, I opened the car door and dumped some kibble on the ground before it could ravage me, then dragged the bag of dog food with me to the front door.

On the alert for two prepubescent maniacs, I was prepared for the ambush when it came. Bambi's sons approached from two separate directions, decorated with angry stripes of war paint on their faces and bare chests, and thin strings of snot hanging from their noses. Both boys gripped hatchets in lieu of tomahawks, their Indian war cries straight out of a Hollywood production. I dropped the kibble and produced bags of licorice and candy to hold them off until the door was opened.

Bambi met me in a dainty ensemble straight out of a Frederick's of Hollywood catalogue. A sheer black nightie provided the overlay for a fluorescent red G-string and a bra three sizes too small. Sequined bull's-eyes decorated the nipple of each cup, and a rhinestone *X* marked the spot on her thong.

It was evident she wasn't an early riser. Her makeup was still smudged from the night before. Two large black rings circled her eyes, giving her the countenance of a drowsy raccoon, and her platinum spikes stood straight up in a field of exclamation points.

"I take it you got my message," she barked. "Let me fill

you in on the gory details. Then you can tell me just what the hell you plan to do about it.''

I followed her into the kitchen, where a bottle of cheap tequila sat on the counter. She poured herself a shot, threw back her head, and downed the contents. Then she poured herself another.

''That lunatic bastard ex-husband of mine came barging in here last night. He was drunk as a skunk, high on bad dope, and waving a goddamn M-16 in my face. Just what kind of an impression do you think that makes on my kids? Huh?''

I glanced out the kitchen window, where her impressionable darlings were chasing after the dog with their hatchets.

''What did he threaten to do?'' Willy must have come up with something especially atrocious to have her drinking so early in the morning. Either that, or Bambi just liked to start her day with a hefty tequila punch.

''You mean besides threatening to permanently shut my mouth for me?'' Bambi snapped.

''She's a slut! She's a slut!'' squawked the Cuban Amazon sitting in the corner of the room.

Bambi threw her empty glass at the bird's cage as the parrot deliriously flapped its wings.

''You're a bitch! You're a bitch!'' the bird screeched. It hooked its beak around the bars and pulled, trying to get out.

''I swear, I'm gonna sic that thing on Willy some day.'' Bambi pointed a midnight-blue fingernail in the bird's direction and then brought it up to her neck, sliding the rapier slowly across her throat.

I didn't blame the bird for trying to escape. In his position, I'd have been sawing away at the bars by now. I knew I was going to have to rescue the parrot, even if it meant staging a break-in myself. ''What exactly did he say he was going to do?'' I asked once again.

Bambi licked the top of the tequila bottle, and then screwed the cap back on. ''He said first he's gonna shoot me. After that, he plans on getting in one last screw for old time's sake. Except it'll be better than ever, he said, 'cause for once my mouth won't be flapping.''

I was about to respond when the sound of hatchets at work made us run to the kitchen window. Willy's young progeny were chopping away at the house like so much firewood.

"Stop that, you little bastards!" Bambi shrieked.

She opened the door, picked up a broom, and flung it at them. But aim wasn't one of her strong points. The boys screeched in delight as the broom hit the dog. They immediately followed suit, pouncing on top of the mangy mutt, who managed to squirm out from beneath the two flailing bodies and hightail it around to the front of the house. Both boys took their frustration out on the broom. They swung their hatchets like mini-serial killers, hacking the wooden handle into scores of tiny pieces.

Bambi picked up the thread of her story as if there had been no interruption. "Then, he said he plans to saw my body up into itty-bitty chunks. After which he's gonna dump the parts in a trough, throw on some lime, set the whole thing on fire, and have himself a Bambi-que."

"It's time that you call the police, Bambi. You've got to file a complaint. That way, you can get the court to issue a restraining order against him."

"Yeah, right. All you're talking about is a temporary stay of execution. What I need is to get rid of the bastard somehow." She ran her fingers up along the rows of her platinum spikes, as if testing their use as potential weapons.

"All that's going to accomplish is to land you in jail. You really need to let the police handle this," I pressed.

Bambi swung the tequila bottle menacingly in her hand. "You know, Porter, you're the one who got me in this mess to begin with. If it hadn't been for you shooting your big mouth off to Willy, all I'd be worrying about is getting my boobs lifted and landing a good job at a club."

The sequined bull's-eyes on her bra glittered in agreement. I watched out the window, where the boys picked up sharpened pieces of the chopped broom and went after each other with their newly made spears. Call me crazy, but it seemed she had bigger problems to contend with than booking a plastic surgeon.

"Listen, Bambi. The last thing I ever meant to do was to bring you any more trouble, and I plan to take care of it. But you've got to call the police, to be safe. They need to know what Willy is threatening to do."

Bambi stubbornly shook her head. ''Bullshit, Porter. The cops are useless, and you know it. By the time they show up, I'll be dead and Willy will have gotten rid of all the evidence.''

She unscrewed the tequila cap with her teeth, took one last swig, and stuck the bottle inside the freezer. ''I ain't done hard time in this place, with those kids, and that bird, to end up looking like an overdone rump roast.''

''Maybe you should consider going away for a while,'' I suggested. ''Let things with Willy cool down.''

''Uh, uh. I'm not going nowhere. I hear he's been sleeping with the girls from the club where I used to work—and that's where I draw the line. He's running around making a fool out of me.'' Bambi's voice trembled, and her eyes began to brim with tears. She raised the hem of her nightie and swiped at her makeup. But the darkened shadows had already spread, like a layer of soot washing away in a downpour.

''Hell, that man would screw a maple tree if the sap was running high,'' she said, wiping her nose.

I could easily imagine Willy having more luck with a maple than with most women. ''I'll go and talk to him, Bambi,'' I promised. ''But do me a favor and keep your doors locked.''

The sequined bull's-eyes glittered. ''You just tell that bastard to lay off the girls I know. Otherwise, he'll be holding his pecker in his hand and singing soprano,'' Bambi vowed.

I headed for Willy's as visions of chain saws, troughs, and barbecues ran through my head. I felt sure that, given the time, I could come up with the horror flick he'd stolen that imaginative scenario from. The continuing mystery to me was how Bambi could be in love with such a man.

As I turned down the dirt road that led to Willy's, I had to slam on the brakes. Writhing on the ground lay a five-foot-long Eastern diamondback rattler. It had been run over and left to suffer and slowly die, pecked alive by vultures.

I got out of the Tempo and walked to where the reptile was trying to slither away from my oncoming tires, its body jerking spasmodically in tortuous contractions. Then I slowly knelt down.

Willy couldn't have been responsible for the deed. Not due

to any compassion for a critter's pain, but because he would have finished the snake off, taken its skin, and left the bloody carcass to rot.

The snake struggled to raise its head, rattling halfheartedly to ward me away.

Pulling out my 9mm revolver, I shot the rattler clean through the head. It was the second time I'd had to kill a critter; the second time I'd broken my vow. I picked the lifeless snake up, and moved it out of the path of any more cars.

Then I continued down the dirt road, the normally sun-dappled pines and palmettos now holding dark, ominous shadows. Though I tried to brush away the feeling of impending doom, ghostly whispers sprang up in the still air, their cries eerily reminiscent of Willy's neglected cats.

I pulled up to where Weed's Dodge Ram normally sat. My guess was that after threatening Bambi, he'd sobered up, got in his truck, and hightailed it north to visit Mama Weed and Buzz in Georgia.

I parked and got out of the car.

Willy's menagerie lay pathetically on the floors of their cages with their usual hopeless stares. I decided to poke around until I discovered where Willy kept his stash of raw meat. If the animals had to be locked up, I could at least make sure they had plenty of fresh food and water.

The door to Willy's trailer was locked, but easy to jimmy. I'd come prepared for the stench this time by bringing a bandana. I tied it bandito-style over my mouth and nose, then pulled open the aluminum door.

There was just something about Willy's trailer that reminded me of a spider's lair. Maybe it was the innate sense of evil that hung over the place.

I flicked on the light switch and looked over to where Big Mama usually lay, but the eighteen-foot python wasn't there. I remembered Willy telling me how cranky she got when she couldn't be with him, which bolstered my theory that Willy had decided to vamoose for a while. I wondered if she insisted on sitting in the front seat of his Dodge Ram next to him.

I stepped over Willy's mushrooming pile of laundry and headed for his poor excuse for a desk: a piece of plywood resting on two empty plastic garbage pails. The desktop contained a hefty assortment of bills, spanning everything from overdue child support to his latest visit to the emergency clinic. A grocery receipt attested that Weed still had enough moolah to stock up on his favorite beer.

On the floor between the two pails sat a cardboard box. I pulled it out as carefully as if it were the remains of a contagiously diseased animal.

Dear Lord, just don't let there be any spiders, centipedes, roaches, or other multilegged things inside.

Wishing I had gloves, I slowly lowered two fingers into the box. Out came dried snakeskins, then Guns N' Roses, and Aerosmith cassette tapes. I dove back down to pull out cougar teeth and claws, which I assumed were from Weed's unhappy menagerie. Handfuls of yellowed newspaper articles touted the grand opening of his sanctuary. One had a photo of Willy looking even more malnourished than usual. A small black leopard was slung around his shoulders, and a 9mm Beretta was stuck in his belt. The accompanying caption read, "a protector of God's endangered critters." The perfect image for the local youth to aspire to.

I reached farther down and brushed against the pebble-textured cover of a photo album. A quick flip through its pages left me feeling as if I was bearing witness to the downfall of civilization. There were the obligatory photos of Bambi as star in a variety of *"Oh my God, I can't believe my legs can actually bend this way"* poses. These were followed by shots of Willy in flagrante with an assortment of "models," most of whom looked like they belonged in a smack-shooting gallery. My stomach took a dive as the album deteriorated into the even more perverse.

The next few pages had photos of a waifish young girl who looked to be about eleven, dressed in high heels, a micro-miniskirt, lots of makeup, and little else. I realized that Willy was playing with a smaller deck than I had even imagined. Then I turned the pages and landed smack dab in Willy's real wonderland. Stomach-churning magazine photos displayed bloated, dead bodies being munched on by hungry dogs, while other corpses provided a quick pick-me-up for bands of roving coyotes.

The walls of the room began to beat like a quickening pulse

around me, and the taste of bile rushed up on an express elevator straight into my mouth. I threw Willy's obscene trash back into the cardboard box.

The only place left to examine was in the back of the trailer. Just the thought of entering Willy's bedroom made my skin crawl. There are spiders' webs, and then there are things far worse: dank and frightening places where even creepy crawlers won't go. I headed for his dungeon, which I'd heard referred to as "Willy's weenie-whacking boudoir." Stepping over the pile of laundry, my shoe landed in something oozing and sticky. I looked down to discover the decomposing remains of a tiny gray mouse.

I tore off the bandana and screamed with all the pent-up tension, rage, and nausea that had built up within me. In response, a chorus of fierce roars from outside shook the tin walls. I swore to myself then and there that I'd call every city, state, and federal agency until I got Weed's cats removed immediately and placed in decent homes. The fact that Weed had gone away and left them alone should make the job that much easier. And if that didn't work, then, damn it, I'd pry the cage doors open myself and let them wreak their own havoc on Willy Weed's body and soul.

I lifted my foot and moved on, refusing to faint in this hellhole. But I was going to burn every article of clothing I had on as soon as I got home.

Willy's bedroom held even less charm than the rest of his abode. A far nastier pile of laundry was heaped in the corner of this room. Posters of screaming, nude women fleeing dementos armed with chain saws, axes, and Freddy Krueger nails lined the dingy walls. Other than that, the bedroom was decorated with a filthy, stained mattress that lay on the floor. A stack of magazines was piled near the bed. A quick glance proved his choice of reading material to be almost as good as his photo album—*Bra Busters, Open Legs,* and *Barely Sixteen.*

Next to the magazines was a shopping bag. I peered inside to make sure that nothing was dead or moving before rummaging through the contents, then pulled out his-and-her handcuffs, a black leather hood with zippered mouth, a leather whip, a large can of shaving cream, and a couple of razors.

All that appeared to be missing was a vibrator. But then, I suppose Willy wasn't looking for any competition.

I hated to touch Weed's mattress, but it was the last possible place to look. I lifted the worn-out bedding, leaning it against the wall. Bingo! Willy and Alberto had something else in common besides smuggling birds. What was it with these guys and hiding things under their beds?

Three separate passports lay like large, squashed bugs on the floor. All three contained Willy's photo, but each passport bore a different identity. There was Hank Hefner, Bo Guccione, and Lyle Flynt. It made twisted sense that he'd taken the last names of his "why-the-hell-couldn't-I have-their-life" porn-king idols.

Hank, Bo, and Lyle had all been pretty busy traveling in and out of Brazil over the past few years. The fictitious trio had doubtless smuggled a fortune in hyacinth parrots and their eggs into the U.S.

Tap, tap, tap came a flurry of sound above me. I froze. The tinny vibration started up again a moment later. *Tap, tap, tap, tap, tap!* The noise was louder and longer this time, as if dozens of tiny demons in tap shoes were prancing on the metal roof directly over my head. Then a shadowy form caught my eye.

I moved toward the grimy bedroom window. Ever so slowly, the dark shadow flickered into view a second time—a foreboding grim reaper hovering in lascivious anticipation, waiting for the right moment to grab me.

My fingertips brushed against the poster of a screaming babe for support as an icy shiver shook my body. The shadow emerged again and my heart stopped—until I saw that it was the silhouette of a large pair of wings, and realized what was terrorizing me. Dozens of black vultures had congregated on the roof of Willy's trailer. They must have sensed that Weed was one of their own.

My heartbeat returned to normal, and I glanced quickly around the room one last time, eager to leave. Weed's telephone and answering machine sat nearly hidden alongside the heap of malodorous laundry. A bottle of half-finished tequila lay on the floor nearby with a pickled worm floating inside, having died in a drunken reverie. It was a no-brainer as to where Willy had picked up this souvenir. The label on the bottle read, MADE AND BOTTLED IN MEXICO.

I hit the rewind button on Willy's answering machine. With any luck, he wouldn't have bothered to erase his last few messages. I thanked the god of dumb psychos, as what distinctly sounded like a mechanically distorted voice boomed out over Weed's machine.

"This is the Commander, you insolent fuck-up. I want your ass over here right now."

The caller had Willy's character nailed to a tee. Maybe there was a pecking order in the Cobra Club, complete with titles and ranks. Then a second message began to play.

"Tell the Commander that he can place his grocery list whenever he wants. All's clear to fill another order from the candy store."

Okay. Now I really *was* curious. I played the messages back one more time, listening carefully. But there were no secret clues to be gathered. I wondered who the Commander was, and why he'd be calling a lowlife like Weed. And just what was this candy store the second message had spoken of? It had to be some sort of code.

I stuffed Willy's three passports into my back pocket, figuring that should put a stop to his trips for awhile. If nothing else, it might give some birds a reprieve. Then I lowered the mattress to the floor and returned to the front of the trailer, satisfied that I'd discovered whatever was to be found in Weed's squalid abode. My entire body felt like it needed to be steamcleaned and dried—maybe even given a flea bath—but there was another trailer to explore first.

I opened the flimsy door to leave and walked smack into Willy. The cast had been cut off his leg, revealing a foot that was swollen the size of a football, its color a nasty mix of purple and green. He'd nestled his tootsies in the bottom half of a sneaker, whose top and sides had been cut out. Filthy strips of adhesive tape anchored the sneaker's raggedy sole to his foot. Otherwise, he looked the same as I'd last seen him, down to his yellow JUST DO ME T-shirt.

Willy looked nearly as startled as I was. Then he smiled a slow molasses of a grin, his eyes looking me up and down as if I were one of his mice and he was the big, bad snake. The ruby in his tooth caught a ray of sun, causing me to imagine Bambi knocking it out of his mouth, and wondering how much she would get for it. My train of thought was rudely interrupted as Willy reached up and shoved me back inside, his hands cupped over my breasts.

"Hey there, darlin'. You been waiting here all by your lonesome for big Willy?" His breath was as rancid as his laundry.

I knocked his hands off my chest, only to have Willy grin wider and enter the trailer. Before today, I had thought of him as just one more easily handled slimeball. Now that I'd caught an eyeful of his photo album, I was afraid he was far tougher than I had imagined. To make matters worse, I'd left my revolver in the glove compartment of my car.

"I just got here a minute ago," I bluffed. "The door was unlocked, so I assumed you'd be in. There are a few things I want to talk to you about."

The corners of Willy's mouth pulled down. "Now that's stranger than a coon's tail, Agent Porter." His voice curled around my name as constrictingly as a snake, and his fingers wound themselves in my curls. " 'Cause I just ran my hand along the hood of your engine, and it's nice and cool. Not hot, like you'd expect it to be."

Willy closed the door of the trailer behind him. "Besides, I distinctly remember locking this door. But I see that couldn't keep you out. Must be that you're wanting me real bad, Porter—so let me help you get your engine started."

Weed walked toward me slowly, grinding his groin in a poor imitation of a Chippendales dancer. I pushed him away as hard as I could and moved back, nearly stumbling into the pile of laundry.

"Cut the crap, Willy," I warned.

Weed licked his lips and rubbed his crotch. "You know, if you're nice to me, I might be able to get you some publicity. I'm talking real good, glossy photos. I got connections, big time. Hell, we could have you pose with some of my cats out there." Willy's eyes glittered. "I'm not talking some piece of crap, but a *Playboy* or a *Penthouse* spread. One of those high-class magazines."

"I've heard all about your connections in the porn world, Willy. They're very impressive," I said sarcastically. "But all

I really want is to have your rear end keeping a jail cell warm.''

He limped forward, aware that there wasn't much more space into which I could retreat.

''You must have done some miraculous healing for the hospital to have removed your cast so quickly,'' I observed, trying to divert the conversation. The way his foot looked, it was probably infected, and well on its way to a whopping case of gangrene.

He gave a broad leer, taking the comment as flattery. ''The Swamp Cowboy has lotsa magic powers you're just beginning to learn about. Besides, it wasn't the hospital that done it. The damn thing got to be too hot and itchy, so I decided to hell with it and cut it off myself. When you're a real man, you can do that kinda thing,'' he said with a wink.

I wondered if Willy also knew that real men didn't need to hurt eleven-year-old girls, or look at bloated, dead bodies to get aroused. I wisely kept those questions to myself.

His hand began to climb up my leg like a large, crafty spider. I locked onto his eyes and swatted his fingers away with all the concern I'd have for a bug, damned if I'd give him the upper hand by showing any fear.

''I came by to tell you to stay away from Bambi. She's called the police, and the court is in the process of issuing a restraining order against you. So unless you're looking for a few hot meals courtesy of the county, I suggest that you cool it with the threats and behave.''

Willy came closer, forcing me to step into the pile of laundry.

''Ouch!'' Willy giggled. ''You got me there, Porter. Why, I'm just gonna have to put my big old tail between my legs and scamper away lickety-split, like a good little boy. Is that what you wanna hear me say?'' he asked, his voice turning deep and raspy.

His breath covered me like a layer of grime. ''I swear to God, Willy—you come any closer, and a jail cell will be the least of your concerns.'' If nothing else, I could smother him to death with his own clothes.

''That's what I like about you, Porter—you're feisty.'' Willy began to pick at his chest, as if he were removing scabs.

"As for Bambi? I got my plans for her; don't you worry. But right now, it's you that I'm thinking about. And that's beginning to make me feel prickly all over."

Weeds hand slunk down to his jeans. His fingers loosened the button on his pants, then moved for the zipper.

"I do believe you're just gonna have to do the right thing and scratch this big ol' itch for me," he smirked. "Besides, I did promise to show you my cockatoo."

Willy's free hand slithered up along the inside of my thigh. I quickly raised my knee, aiming for his groin, but Weed was prepared for the move. Apparently he'd had plenty of practice. He caught my leg in both his hands and laughed harder.

"Come on, Porter, I got your tune. You're the kind who finds dancing on the edge fun. Well, I'm about to take you right over. I like women who try and fight. It just makes it all that much better. Besides, I've been hankering to find out if you're really a redhead."

I grabbed hold of the cougar's tooth that hung from his ear and gave it a sharp jerk, while my other palm shoved his jaw upward. Weed's mouth snapped shut, and he bit down hard on his tongue.

He screamed in pain, dropping my leg. "Goddamn you, bitch! Now you've gone and done it!" Weed spat out a thin stream of blood. "You just sealed your fate, Porter. I was gonna do you nice—now I'll do you any way I want."

"Gee, Willy, and all this time I thought you were a gentleman." I feinted to the left, then veered right, hoping to get around him.

But Weed was surprisingly quick. He blocked my exit and roughly shoved me out of the laundry, backing me up until I was pinned in Big Mama's corner. I was caught off-balance as one of his hands grasped me firmly between the legs, while the other wrapped tightly around my throat.

Willy brought his mouth close to my ear. "I think what you need is a lesson. You gotta learn who's the boss around here, just like those boat-lovin' Cubans."

I tried to move, but that only caused Weed to tighten his grip on my body.

Willy's voice attacked me, his tone low and surly. "You gotta remember that, badge or no badge, you're still nothing but a woman, and that means you should know your place. And you know what that place is, Porter?'' Willy's fingers crab-walked up my crotch and began to undo my zipper.

''Yeah, Willy. I've got a pretty good idea,'' I told him, my eyes narrowing.

I waited until his fingers were lodged tight in my pants. Then I raised my leg and rammed my shoe down as hard as I could on top of his bare, broken foot. I dug my heel in, grinding it back and forth.

Willy's hand flew out of the top of my pants as an unearthly cry ripped from his throat. I slammed my elbow hard into his solar plexus, then pushed past him and tore out of the trailer. A dozen vultures blocked the path to my car, looking like a gang of schoolyard bullies. But they must have seen who'd be the victor in this showdown, because they lowered their bald heads and quickly split up, parting like the Red Sea.

I got into the Tempo and retrieved my gun, then revved the engine and turned the car around. I took off, my eyes glued to the rearview mirror, where I saw Willy standing outside screeching at the top of his lungs.

''You're a dead woman, Porter!''

Thirteen

What I needed more than anything was a shower. My skin felt as if thousands of lice had set up camp on every part of my body. I scratched my arms, my legs, my torso, even behind my ears, intent on finding mites, bedbugs, fleas, or ticks. Finally satisfied that nothing had claimed squatter's rights, I pulled out my cell phone and placed a call to Metro Dade.

''Reardon here,'' Vern drawled in a bored-out-of-his-gourd, can't- wait-to-retire monotone.

Going from Willy to Vern was almost surreal. ''Officer Reardon, please hurry! Skunk Ape's just hit your concession stand and taken off with all your official I SAW THE SKUNK APE T-shirts!''

''What?!'' Vern's voice rose a couple octaves, kick-starting to life.

''It's okay, Vern. Rachel Porter here. I just wanted to wake you up,'' I chuckled.

Vern's chair creaked as he collapsed back into it. ''Goddamn you, Porter,'' he panted, sounding short of breath. ''Anybody ever tell you that your sense of humor stinks?'' He gave a little grunt, followed by silence.

I waited for a moment, beginning to wonder if maybe he was right. Oh, my God, I worried, as the silence continued, thinking of Carrera. What if I'd given the man a heart attack?

''Vern, are you okay?'' I asked, trying my best to remain calm.

But there was no snappy retort to my question.

''Reardon?'' I couldn't stop the note of panic from creeping into my voice. ''Speak to me, Vern! Please, answer me!''

The morning's cinnamon bun churned in my stomach like heavy, wet cement.

"Hold on, Vern!" I urged, my heart beating like a hummingbird's wings. "I'm going to call and alert your desk sergeant, and have him ring an ambulance." I was about to hang up when Vern's snigger stopped me.

"Thanks, Porter. But I'm suddenly feeling a whole lot better."

My temper went into countdown and was about to blast off, when I reminded myself just who had started the sneak attack.

"Next time you try and pull off a joke, Porter, remember to carry it all the way through. That's what separates the girls from us men. So, are you calling about anything in particular? Or just looking to learn some pointers from a pro?" he smugly questioned.

I allowed Vern to savor his moment of victory, fully aware of how fragile the male ego could be. Besides, I was hoping I could turn it to my advantage.

"Weed's at it again," I reported. "This time he's threatening Bambi with torture and murder. Can we get some kind of injunction against him?"

Vern sighed. "Is Madam Stripper coming in to press charges?"

I'd encountered the same attitude before. It was the us-versus-them mentality, in the never-ending war between the sexes.

"No," I conceded. "But Weed's serious this time, Vern. I was just there to see him and the guy is out of control. This is going to have a bad ending unless you do something about it."

"Come on, Porter. You know that we can't do a thing unless Bambi asks us to arrest him." Vern let loose a loud yawn. "And I haven't heard shit from that dainty damsel. In fact, the last time we were out there, I believe it was Madam herself who was poised to slice off Weed's willy." Vern chuckled at his play on words.

"Why do I get the feeling you're not taking this seriously? Can't you at least haul him in and scare him a bit?" I suggested.

"You wanna convince the broad to come in and file a complaint? Great.'' Vern's voice held all the concern of a snail on Prozac. ''Otherwise, have her give me a call the next time he's around and physically threatening her. Then we'll have something to go on.''

''Right. A dead body,'' I responded brusquely. ''Which reminds me, what's happening with the Dominguez case? Have there been any further developments?''

''Yeah. A little birdie keeps calling in and leaving messages. We're working day and night trying to break the code. As soon as we do, I'll let you know what he's been telling us. Anything else I can help you with today, Porter?''

''No. As usual, you've met all my expectations.'' I hung up.

Then I dialed again, this time calling the state Game and Fresh Water Fish Commission.

''Officer Stevens,'' answered the wildlife agent on desk duty.

''I've got a violation to report over at Willy Weed's residence. A bunch of his cats are malnourished and neglected,'' I said, not bothering to identify myself.

There was a pause while I sat and contemplated what I could eat next without gaining another five pounds.

''Is this you again, Porter?'' Stevens responded. ''I already told you last week, there isn't enough evidence against him to warrant removing those cats.''

''You mean the fact that they're kept in minuscule cages and fed rotten food doesn't hold any weight?'' I was beginning to reach my limit with bureaucracy.

Stevens sighed impatiently. ''If it's filth you're complaining about this time, we'll send someone out there again the next chance we get. After that we'll file our decision,'' he informed me in a get-at-the-end-of-the-line-and-don't-hold-your-breath tone.

''Just so you know, I plan on calling tomorrow, and the day after, and the day after that until something is done. Those cats are pathetic, Stevens. How about just contacting some decent sanctuaries and offering the animals to them?''

''For chrissakes, Porter. Don't you have better things to do with your time?'' Stevens snapped. ''Like maybe focusing on your own work, for starters? You don't see us jumping all over you feds. How about getting off the rag and giving us a break?''

I hung up without responding. At this point, I was ready to scan the Yellow Pages and see if there might be a group more willing to take the necessary action. Something like Dial-A-Vigilante.

I stopped at a local health food store and, after careful consideration, picked up a pack of whole-wheat, organic fig newton bars. It took only one tasteless bite to understand why they'd never made it to the shelves of my local grocery store. Faced with the dilemma of chucking them or chewing 'em, I polished off the fruit bars and made one last call.

''Get the hell off my leg, dammit!'' yelled the voice in my ear.

Bambi could have been dealing with the dog, her kids, or any other bizarre entity in her life.

''Bambi? It's Rachel. The police want you to come in and file a formal complaint against Willy,'' I lied.

''Bullshit, they do,'' Bambi responded without hesitation. ''Don't screw with me, Porter. They care about what happens to me about as much as they care whether you ever nab your parrot burglar.''

''Then how about at least hightailing it out of town for a week or two? Go visit a friend or some relatives. Think of it as a vacation,'' I suggested.

''Vacation, my ass,'' Bambi spat back. ''A vacation is planting my behind in a lounge chair on some tropical isle with a drink in my hand, and a rich old man dying at my feet with a pen and a will in his paw. Otherwise, I'm not dragging my sorry butt around with two screaming kids, one horny dog, and a deranged bird. You wanna do something worthwhile? Tell Willy it's time he starts watching his own ass.''

The phone clicked dead in my ear. I figured at this point, I might as well top off my day by going into the office and facing Carlos's wrath.

I found my boss sitting back in his chair with his legs stretched out and a gun in his lap, watching the hallway as if he somehow knew I was about to show. He picked up the gun and took a deep whiff, sniffing along the end of its barrel as he caught sight of my head poking through the door.

"Agent Porter. So nice to know you still work here. I wasn't sure you planned on coming back," Carlos purred. "By the way, let me express my deepest sympathy."

"For what?" I cautiously asked, aware I was stepping into a trap.

"For the fact that someone in your family must have unexpectedly died. Otherwise, I can't think of any possible reason why you haven't been working at your desk since I last saw you," he snarled.

I knew there were only two choices. Come clean with Carlos and fill him in on what I'd discovered, or spend the rest of my career chained in paperwork purgatory.

"There's a good reason why I haven't been here," I began.

"There always is," Carlos answered, his accent heavily saturated with irony.

I pulled Willy's three passports out of my back pocket, dug the hyacinth feather out of my purse, and placed the evidence on his desktop.

"Willy has been muling both hyacinths and Cuban Amazons for years. He was working for Dominguez."

"You already filled me in on something like that a few days ago," Carlos reminded me. "Remember? Right before you took it all back and told me you weren't really sure exactly what you'd seen in that sack?"

He held my gaze, reducing me to a pupil caught in a lie by her teacher. Then he picked up the passports and examined them.

"I've got another flash for you, Porter. Dominguez is dead—which makes all this old news. You've been running around wasting your time and mine, along with the government's, for nothing," he informed me.

An internal bonfire made my cheeks burn bright red. "But the fake passports!"

Carlos cut me off, adding fuel to the fire. "Those illegal passports fall under Customs' jurisdiction. Or do you want to do their job for them, too?"

He picked up the feather and thrust its shaft into the barrel of his gun, creating an in-your-face vase. I was going to have to give up all the information I'd been holding, and hope I could convince Carlos to let me handle the case.

"I'm certain the smuggling's still going on," I reluctantly revealed.

Carlos sat up straight in his chair and placed his palms on the desk, all business now. "Why is that?"

"One of my informants was hauling cigars in for Dominguez. He's led me to believe that Alberto had other Cuban partners involved in the bird trafficking. They're being brought in by boat, as well as by plane."

Carlos remained silent, contemplating the handle of his gun. When he finally spoke, his tone was subdued resignation. "Did he say if these Cuban partners were also involved in Dominguez's cigar dealings?"

"I was told absolutely not. Evidently, if anyone in the Cuban community had known about it, Alberto would have been ostracized."'

"Your informant is correct," Carlos conceded. "All right. I'll believe you on this one, Porter."

"There's something else that's been bothering me," I admitted.

Carlos cocked an eyebrow and stopped playing with his gun.

"There was a tattoo on Alberto's left bicep." I paused, wondering if I was beginning to get conspiracy crazy.

Carlos impatiently interrupted my thoughts. "Well, was there something about this particular tattoo? Or do you just have a distaste for body decorations?"

His abruptness made me wonder what Carlos had hidden beneath his own shirt. "The tattoo was of a parrot with a rifle clutched in its talons. I didn't think much about it, until I saw someone else with the same tattoo on his arm the other day."

"Do you know who the man was?" Carlos casually asked.

I hesitated, still not ready to give everything away. "Just someone I saw working in the back room of a cigar store in Little Havana."

Carlos got up, pointed for me to sit down, and closed the door. Then he walked back to his desk and pulled out a cigar.

Being that he was such a stickler on rules, I filled him in on one. "You do know it's illegal to smoke in this building, don't you?"

Carlos propped his feet up on his desk and blew a smoke

ring my way. "That's what closed doors are for," he responded.

I waited for about thirty seconds, which is generally the amount of time it takes before my patience meter runs out. "Okay, you didn't have me sit down just to watch you smoke a cigar. What's up?"

Carlos squinted at me through his man-made cloud of smoke. "That tattoo you saw? It's the emblem of Omega-12," he announced.

My pulse picked up speed. Maybe it's the hidden gossip columnist lurking within me, but give me a secret and I go to town. As a child, I sniffed out my Christmas presents way before the holidays, no matter where my mother hid them. It had escalated from there into full-blown, collar-grabbing, "if you don't tell me I'll find out anyway" proportions. Okay—so it wasn't my most attractive quality.

I pinched the skin between my thumb and index finger to keep from jumping out of my chair. "What exactly is Omega-12?"

Carlos took his time, fully aware that I considered that torture. "It's a right-wing, Cuban paramilitary group. I've heard rumors they're still active. You must have stumbled upon two of their members."

"This is the group that trains out in the Glades?" I asked.

Carlos gave a silent nod, his way of letting me know I was going to have to work for any information.

"What kind of weapons do they have?"

Carlos gave a self-satisfied smile. "The sky's the limit."

"Where do they get their supplies from?" I wondered how much information he really had, and what he might not be disclosing.

"That's something that nobody seems to know," Carlos responded.

I threw down my last card.

"Have you ever heard of Elena and Ramon Vallardes?" I asked.

Carlos studied me unblinkingly as he took a deep puff on his cigar and blew a smoke ring in the shape of a noose.

Long pauses laden with silence drive me round-the-bend crazy. Forget water torture. Just put me in a room with someone who won't talk, and I'll do almost anything to fill the void. Usually it consists of a gibbering song-and-dance routine, before drowning them in my life story.

Okay, I'd start it and get the ball rolling. "They were close friends of Alberto Dominguez." I paused for a moment. "They all grew up together as children," was the next tidbit I threw out. "Alberto was over at their place all the time." I stopped and waited. Still no response. "For god sakes! They're very prominent in the Cuban community. How could you not know who they are?"

Carlos threw me the band off his cigar. "Of course I know of the Vallardes: Puffin is where I buy my cigars. Remind me never to send you into enemy territory. You'd give them our attack plans in no time, and then probably cook them dinner."

I silently acknowledged the lesson: I'd handed him all my information without receiving anything in return. "How naive do you think I am? I haven't told you the best part yet," I bluffed.

Carlos obviously felt confident enough to go for the bait. "Which is?"

I smiled. "I've given you plenty. How about giving me something in return as a show of good faith?"

Carlos clasped his hands behind his head and smiled, amused at the game. "All right. Here's something I bet you don't know. Their father, Tito Vallardes, was one of the original founders of Omega-12, along with Alberto's father, Jorge Dominguez."

The information hit me like a one-two punch. I scurried to keep my wits before Carlos decided to pull the plug on Information Central. "Are they still active with the group?"

Carlos hesitated, and I jumped in with both feet. "Come on. Fair is fair. I've given you plenty so far."

He munched on the end of his cigar, attacking the spongy shreds of tobacco as if he were noshing on a hot pastrami sandwich. I could almost hear the wheels of his brain grinding, carefully weighing what information to hand me.

"What I've got is reeeally good," I added temptingly.

Carlos sighed in admission that I'd won him over. "Jorge died in Miami from too much of the good life a few years back,'' he disclosed. ''As for Tito? He's a prisoner of Castro's hospitality.''

I kept a damper on any outward sign of excitement. ''How long has he been there?''

''Let's see . . .'' Carlos closed his eyes, pondering. ''I'd say it's been about eighteen years now. The son of a bitch was caught hauling rockets over to anti-Castro groups that still exist within Cuba.''

''Rockets!'' Oops—it was too late to cover up my astonishment.

Carlos grinned, as if he'd known it was just a matter of time before I tripped over my own enthusiasm. ''That's right. In fact, Omega-12 claims Tito was doing it undercover at the request of the U.S. government.''

''Is that possible?'' I asked in amazement.

Carlos gave a small shrug. ''The U.S. government tried its best to overthrow Castro for thirty years. I don't see why Omega-12 wouldn't be telling the truth. But there's something much more interesting about Omega-12's background.'' He chuckled.

I bit my tongue, curling my toes and fingers into tight little knots in a show of overwhelming patience.

Carlos took several quick puffs on his cigar. ''You've heard of the Cuban-American United Stand Foundation?''

I nodded. ''They're a lobbying organization.''

''Not just *any* lobbying organization,'' Carlos corrected. ''One of *the* most powerful lobbying organizations in the U.S. They've raised more than one million dollars for both Republicans and Democrats.''

Carlos removed the cigar from his mouth and held it reverently. His fingers firmly tapped its burning end, sending smoldering ashes to the ground in a flurry of fairy dust. ''CAUSF likes to spread their money around. That means they wield enormous political power, no matter which party holds the reins at any given time. It's due to the influence of CAUSF that there's been no loosening of the economic embargo against Cuba.''

Carlos gave a dramatic pause, allowing just enough time for my pinpricks of anticipation to spread until my whole body tingled deliciously.

"Now that I've told you all that, do you have any idea who the founder of CAUSF is?" Carlos's eyes twinkled and his mustache twitched.

I shook my head, barely daring to breathe.

"It's Frederico Vallardes. Tito's brother," he revealed.

"Elena and Ramon's uncle?" I marveled, beginning to wonder where this was all leading. "But CAUSF advocates only a nonviolent approach to bringing about Castro's downfall."

"That's right," Carlos agreed. "Publicly, that's exactly what CAUSF espouses." He played with the end of his mustache, letting the information sink in. "But, privately, just how do you think Omega-12 got started? Both Frederico and Tito Vallardes, as well as Jorge Dominguez, fought in the Bay of Pigs together. Bonds like that are never broken."

"So CAUSF is the nonviolent, political front, and Omega-12 is their underground paramilitary offshoot?" I ventured.

Carlos barely arched an eyebrow. "I suppose some would say that's possible. After all, not many people know of their connection." He pulled his chair forward and leaned in toward me. "Okay. I've given you plenty. Now tell me the rest of what you've got."

"Huh?" I was caught off-guard, too busy absorbing all I'd been told to have any idea what he was talking about.

"We had a deal," he reminded me. "Now it's time for you to put the rest of your cards on the table."

Uh, oh. I'd forgotten about that part. Then it hit me.

"Hey, wait a minute. That was a great history lesson on Cuban-American politics, but what does it have to do with my case on birds?" I challenged.

Carlos gave a sly smile, letting me know who was still master when it came to the art of game playing. "I never said it did. You asked what I knew about Elena and Ramon, and that's exactly what I told you." He gave a satisfied chomp on his cigar, and cracked his knuckles one by one. "You may not be a rookie, Porter, but you're still not a seasoned agent. You forgot all about your real objective here. Wasn't it to learn more about the illegal bird trade in Miami?" He pointed his cigar at me. "Don't let perps steer you off course so easily, or your curiosity and enthusiasm will be your downfall. Now I'll hear the rest of your information.''

My stomach churned. I was pretty well full-up when it came to receiving lessons. But one good turn deserved another.

''I think Bambi Weed has hold of an illegal Cuban Amazon,'' I blithely announced.

We both knew what that information amounted to. It was about as helpful as knowing there was a group of fanatics target-practicing out in the Everglades.

Carlos looked disdainfully at Willy's three passports, and the hyacinth feather. ''So, that's it then? This is all you've managed to get on this big case of yours so far?'' He waved a dismissive hand across the meager evidence, scornful of the space it was taking up.

''It's more than enough to start with,'' I jumped to my defense.

''Sure, if I want to let you lead us on a wild-goose chase again,'' Carlos shot back.

It was at times like this that I commiserated with fed-up postal workers who bypassed Hallmark Cards when expressing their feelings. ''But you said yourself that you believed me about this one!'' There was no way in hell I would let Carlos compare this to the sixty-egg fiasco.

Carlos matched my glare. ''Listen, Porter. There's nothing earth-shattering about what you've told me so far. Let me sum it up for you.'' He picked up the passport closest to him and stood it on the table. ''Dominguez was pipelining in hyacinths and Cuban Amazons.'' He scooped up the second passport, waved it at me, and set it upright next to the first. ''Dominguez was killed.'' Carlos reached for the final passport and placed it next to its two companions. ''But you think some of his Cuban partners might still be carrying on the trade.''

His index finger pushed lightly against the first passport in a game of all-fall-down.

''That's what you've got, Porter. Nothing but a worthless house of cards. You think I don't know things like that are going on? Here in Miami, they're a dime a dozen. So what?''

Maybe I was wrong, but I seemed to be missing something here. ''Does that mean you simply ignore them?''

''What that means is that without rock-solid proof to go on, all we're doing is running around looking like a bunch of imbeciles,'' Carlos lashed out. ''This is the last time I'll say this: I came to Miami to clean up this office, and I'll be dammed if I'm going to let you make me the laughingstock of this agency. And while we're on the subject, don't let me hear about you poking around in the activities of Cuban exiles, either.''

Carlos pointed a finger in my direction, giving me fair warning that his temper was alive and kicking. I took a deep breath, counted to ten, and turned on what charm I could.

''I'm certain there's a case here, Carlos. And if we make it, you're the one who's going to come out the hero. Just let me have a little more time to nose around. That's all I'm asking.''

That ought to do it—humble, yet determined, with Carlos cast as the victor.

''And if you don't make the case, *I'm* the one who comes out looking like an idiot for letting you run rampant.'' The ends of his mustache jerked in a skittish dance. ''I'm touched by your concern for my career, but if you don't mind, I'll make the decisions around here, Porter.''

Carlos raised his arm like a glowering Moses, with a cigar in his hand instead of a staff. ''You see that pile of paperwork in there on your desk? I suggest you get to work on it, because another batch is on its way. Translated into English, that means I don't care if you have to live here twenty-four hours a day. I want every one of those documents entered into the computer. After that, you can set up a filing system and post past documents in it, as well.''

The way I translated it, Carlos was doing his damnedest to turn my job into that of a glorified secretary. ''Then should I assume you don't plan on looking into the case?'' I asked in a parting shot.

Carlos mashed his cigar butt out on the sole of his shoe. ''You want to play? Fine. But do it on your own time. Not on mine.'' He leaned in closer. ''We work for the government here. Like it or not, we're part of the bureaucracy. And if I have to tie you to your desk with red tape in order to control you, believe me, I will. I don't need some female running amok in the Hispanic community, causing me nothing but trouble."

There—that was it. Silly me. The missing piece of the puzzle.

I lined up my twin baby-blue barrels. "This is all because I'm a woman, isn't it? That's the bottom line." I waited for a response, but there was none. "If Phil made the request, you'd have your badge and your gun strapped on, more than happy to work on the case."

Carlos busied himself at his desk, refusing to meet my gaze. I turned and began to walk out.

"El mejor lugar de una mujer es en la casa."

I hadn't let Carlos know that for the past six months, I'd been learning Spanish. This seemed the perfect moment to demonstrate my progress. "So, the best place for the woman is in the house, huh?"

Carlos's eyes met mine, startled by my response.

"I did get that right, didn't I?" I asked, flinging daggers of sarcasm straight for his heart.

Carlos held my eyes without flinching as he stood up and grabbed his badge and his gun. I was sure that this was it: he'd finally come round to accept me.

"Real women get married and have children, Porter. Why is it that you never have?"

That bastard! "Does the term 'gender discrimination' mean anything to you, Carlos?" I hollered as he stormed out of the office, grumbling about females playing at being agents.

I spent the remainder of the afternoon behind my desk using every curse word I could think of, and placing them in sentences that included the name Carlos. Then I came up with a few more.

My fingers slogged through the papers, entering each dreary detail into the computer. Four cups of badly brewed *café Cubano* from the local Quik Pik had my nerves doing somersaults. Unfortunately, the caffeine did little for my eyes, which were glazed over from sheer boredom. I'd just begun to make a dent in the paperwork when my fingers slipped and hit a wrong key. I watched helplessly as a black hole swallowed all my newly entered data.

That was it! I didn't care if Carlos chose to hogtie, quarter, or fire me. I was out of here. I was damned if I'd been assigned to the most notorious port in the country just to sit back and cool my heels.

I peeked into the cubicle that doubled as Phil's office. He lay with his head on his arms, snoozing away. It being common knowledge that Phil would rather do anything than go out in the field, I filled my arms up with papers, and left them in a nice, neat pile sitting next to him.

Then I split.

Fourteen

"What a putz!" Bonkers screeched as I walked in the door. He hopped onto my shoulder and pulled my ear for good measure. There was no doubt about it, the bird was hanging around with Sophie too much. I was even beginning to detect a slight New York accent.

"I'm a horny boy!" Bonkers squawked, as he ran up and down my arm.

"Great. A lot of good that does me," I muttered.

I pulled out a spray bottle and misted him lightly with water, and Bonkers trilled with delight, hitting operatic high notes. He spread his wings and bobbed his head up and down in rhythm to whatever music was jiving in his brain, his stubby legs teetering back and forth like a pigeon-toed tightrope artist.

From there, our games became progressively more raucous. Bored with being pushed around on the floor, Bonkers insisted on more creative levels of entertainment. We'd lately struck on a game where he'd steal away to sneak under the sheets of my bed, and I'd pretend to search for him. I'd call his name, drawing closer and closer. Then, lifting the sheet, I'd let out a roar. *There you are, Bonkers! You crazy bird!*

Bonkers would rush out giggling like a lunatic, to grab at my hair and dash back beneath the covers.

But his favorite game these days was "Old MacDonald." I'd sing the song, complete with moos, neighs, quacks, and baas, and Bonkers would join in, shrieking his head off. We had just launched into the chorus of "with a quack, quack here" when Terri walked in. He was clad in his favorite red kimono, and the pompommed slippers that resembled Pekingese dogs with a bad dye job. Bonkers immediately charged Terri's feet. Terri tried to shake him off, but the bird was intent on his mission.

"For God sake! Call your attack bird off before he plucks Liz and Dick clean!" Terri commanded.

I scooped Bonkers up, pulled a few red feathers out of his beak, and placed him on his perch with a slice of papaya.

"Bad bird!" I said, knowing if I were him, I would have done the same thing.

Terri gave me a peck on the cheek. "Taylor and Burton thank you immensely." He looked over at Bonkers and shook his stylish curls. "I love you, Rach, but trust me on this one: you've really got to get yourself a more rewarding life."

"I thought I already had one," I said defensively.

"Well, tonight it's going to get even better: Sophie's taking us all out to celebrate the start of our yarmulke business. So dress yourself in something hot and spicy, my dear. We're going to the Havana Club for drinks, dinner, and dancing. Just pop on over whenever you're ready. You've got plenty of time." Terri snapped his fingers, his feet tapping to the silent strains of a flamenco beat. "I'm going to be busy working on Sophie and Lucinda's makeup for a while."

He clip-clopped back down the path.

I showered, lathering every inch of my hair and body until any sneaky, lingering germs that might have hitched a ride from Willy's place had been thoroughly scrubbed off. Between my recent blowups with both Santou and Carlos, a cloud of gloom had been hovering over me. Well, that was about to change. I was determined to let loose and have nothing but pure fun tonight. I took extra pains with my makeup, and gathered my curls into a saucy arrangement on top of my head. Then I pulled out the slinky little blue dress I'd been brave enough to buy but too cowardly to wear, along with a pair of breakneck stilettos. When I checked out my reflection in the mirror, I was pleasantly surprised. My, my . . . not bad at all!

Then, I held on to every bush and twig I could as I minced over to Sophie's. Was it possible that the feet of all the chichi South Beach babes I'd envied actually hurt this much?

"Well, you sure as hell aren't gonna be the wallflower of our group tonight," Sophie declared as I wobbled through the door. ''Is it really you? Or has some alien with a flare for how to dress taken over your body?''

I didn't say a word as I took in the vision that was Sophie. A gold-lamé dress, capable of lighting up New York during a blackout, clung to her frame. She drank in the attention as if I were a film crew for the eleven o'clock news, slowly twirling around and then extending her left leg to display the thigh-high slit.

Chunky rhinestone bracelets and dangling earrings added to the sparkle. Then I caught sight of her footwear. She was sporting a pair of sneakers that had been spray painted gold and covered with sequins.

''What's with the shoes?'' I asked.

''You've gotta be crazy to try and walk in those things you're wearing,'' she declared. ''Don't you know you could end up with bunions, hammertoes, and tendinitis, not to mention a charley horse or shooting pains in your lower back, from prancing around in those heels?''

Yeah. But the bottom line was that they made me look really terrific. I'd seen my silhouette in the mirror. What these heels did for the line of my butt and my breasts was nearly as good as having plastic surgery.

''They're perfectly fine.'' I smiled as I headed for the nearest chair. I suspected that by the end of the evening, though, I'd be wrestling Sophie to the ground for her sneakers.

She watched as I lowered myself with a sigh. ''Good idea. Rest your tootsies while I check on how Lucinda and Terri are doing.''

I resisted the temptation to kick my shoes off, knowing I'd never be able to get them back on, and I focused my attention on my surroundings as a distraction.

I'd always known both women were major collectors, with the number of kitschy tchotchkes cluttering their place. There were the usual last minute souvenirs from airports, interspersed with rescued treasures from flea markets and garage sales. They even had a glass menagerie of critters. But I'd never taken notice of the flags that Terri had spoken of. Nearly hidden in the mix, they now seemed to pop up like bouquets of colorful flowers.

''So, what do you think?'' asked a lilting Cuban voice.

Lucinda stood in the doorway looking like a twenty-five-year-old model. She was elegantly attired in a white, off-the-shoulder slip of a dress that accentuated her shape and played up her tan. I noticed that she had been smart enough to put on a pair of stylish yet comfortable sandals.

"You look amazing," I said, and wholeheartedly meant it. Terri had done a bang-up job on both women's makeup. They'd never looked better.

I got up and hobbled over to their collection of souvenirs. "So, where did you get all these flags?"

"Aren't they unique?" Lucinda bubbled. "No one else that we know collects them."

I plucked one out that bore the initials ED and gave it a swirl.

"I'm especially fond of that one," Sophie commented, slipping her arm through Lucinda's.

"What's the ED stand for?" I asked.

Sophie gave me a wink. "Eccentric dyke," she wisecracked.

Lying next to the flags was a pair of round-trip bus ticket stubs to Tallahassee, from one of their weekend jaunts out of town. Lucinda and Sophie caught me eyeballing them.

"Pro-abortion rally," Lucinda explained.

"Gay rights march," Sophie chirped at the same time.

I gave them a quizzical look. "So, which one was it?"

"It was one of those blowout, hit-em-where-it-hurts weekends," Sophie replied.

"One rally was on Saturday and the other on Sunday," Lucinda added.

Terri breezed into the room in a pair of flowing apricot pants and a matching billowy shirt. A tasteful pair of sunglasses covered his black-and-blue eye. "My God, Rach—so there really is a body under all those *shmattes* you usually wear. Congratulations!"

I arched an eyebrow. "Since when did you begin speaking Yiddish?"

Terri flashed me a mega-watt smile. "Sophie's been broadening my vocabulary. You're going to be impressed with the other words I've learned."

I could hardly wait.

* * *

I'd heard the Havana Club was the hottest spot in town, evidenced by the velvet rope guarded by an impenetrable wall of solid Latin muscle. Oh no! It was the fashion police!

"Don't worry," Lucinda purred in a low, sexy whisper. "I'll take care of this."

A swish of hips, a flexed bicep, a palmed tenspot, and we were through the rope and in the door, hobnobbing with a crowd of the most beautiful people on the planet.

"Have you ever seen so many fake boob jobs all in one place in your life?" Sophie observed.

She was right. Even worse was the fact that I was envious. Not only was almost every ounce of female skin in the room tightly pulled back and standing at attention, but most of it was garbed in thong-flashing microminiskirts and the teensiest tightest of braless T-shirts. Suddenly my little blue dress didn't seem quite so daring.

The dance floor resembled a Roman bacchanalia, Miami style, replete with flashing laser lights and gleaming flesh. Salsa undulated through the air like a maddening temptress, whipping the dancers into a frenzy of swinging hips and gyrating pelvises, making it hard to tell where bodies began and ended. The insistent throb of the music seeped into my skin and my stiletto heels insisted on dancing to our table, where I sank down into the softest of red leather banquettes. Even the seats in this place were hedonistic.

"This makes the Kit Kat Club look tame," Terri remarked, eyeing a couple of barely dressed babes. "God, I'd love to know who did their plastic surgery," he sighed longingly.

"Yeah. Isn't this place great?" Sophie rasped. "I swear that couple over there looks like they're *shtupping* right on the dance floor."

"Mojitos all around!" Lucinda placed the order with a hunky waiter who was "shoulda been a model/coulda been an actor" gorgeous.

"I think it's love at first sight," Terri whispered to me, catching his eye. "It's that hot Latin blood, Rach. It drives me absolutely crazy."

But our waiter wasn't playing favorites tonight. He gave me

a wink as he squeezed Lucinda's arm, and wiggled his fanny at Sophie.

"Should I break the news to him that shaking his booty won't influence his tip? Or are the two of you enjoying it?" Sophie asked us.

"Don't you dare say a word!" Terri warned her.

The mojitos arrived with neon pink flamingo stirrers. I took a sip and felt certain I had landed in heaven.

"What is this stuff?" I asked, wondering how I'd survived up to now without it.

Lucinda laughed. "It's Cuban white rum, mint, soda, lemon, and sugar."

In no time flat, a second round magically appeared at our table. All around us, people puffed up a storm on their cigars while gorging themselves on thick slabs of rare steak. Men knocked back scotches served neat; the women sipped gin martinis straight up with olives. The atmosphere was pure, pleasure-loving decadence.

I decided to skip a full meal, and picked at an order of tapas instead. I hadn't squeezed into this dress just to risk unsightly bulges. Sophie and Lucinda took a different approach. Jumping up on their feet, they danced off their dinner. My feet tapped along with them as they laughed and swirled away, swallowed up in the infectious music and the heady mosaic of other happy cha-cha-chaing couples.

"Why do I feel like I've died and surfaced in Ricky Ricardo's Copacabana Club?" Terri asked.

"Oh, I don't know—I suppose it might have something to do with the music, and the fact that there are so many great looking guys here."

A *Miami Vice* wanna-be clad in a pastel linen suit, sans socks, seductively wiggled a ring-laden finger at me, followed by a roll of his hips. I shook my head and waved him away, not wishing to tempt fate by trying to dance in my stilettos. His reaction was blocked when a bronzed Antonio Banderas lookalike rhumbaed past, and smiled at Terri.

"I'd say Mr. Wonderful there is interested in making your acquaintance."

Terri's blonde curls shook as he slid his sunglasses down his nose. "Look at me, Rach. When it comes to sane, normal relationships, I don't seem to have much of a knack, do I?"

The blotchy colors beneath his eyes had settled into a muddy reservoir of bad memories and pain. When it came to failed romantic involvements, I'd felt the same way myself too many times.

"Like hell you'll sit back," I scolded him. "You remember the old adage about falling off a horse, don't you?"

The ghost of a smile flitted across his lips. "If you're referring to my last *amore* as a horse's ass, I'd have to say you were correct."

"More to the point, we've all gone through our fair share of louses. But you know what?" I wiped a trace of Sophie's lipstick off his cheek. "I also don't think we really have much choice in the matter. Not unless we're willing to bow out of life—and neither one of us is ready for that yet."

A couple that were clenched lip-to-lip danced by, prompting a sigh from the two of us.

I looked at Terri and laughed. "That proves we're still in the race. Besides, Ter—it's just a dance. Get a grip!"

"All right, already. Enough." Terri struck an elegant pose. "I'll be brave and see what happens."

"That's the spirit. Have a good time—just take it nice and slow."

Terri gave me an affectionate hug. "Thanks, Mom. I'll try to remember that."

I watched as he headed in Antonio's direction. Then I turned my attention back to the couples burning up the dance floor.

I enjoy playing the role of observer and being swallowed up by the crowd. That's the best time to discover secrets. That's when people relax and let down their guard. I motioned to the waiter, determined to work on my own relaxation with yet another mojito.

But all thoughts of mojitos drifted right out of my head, replaced by a sizzling sensation, as ten beguiling fingers began to massage their way down my back, where they burned through my dress and set my skin on fire.

"Raquel. What a pleasure it is to see you." Ramon hovered tantalizingly above me, his hips swaying hypnotically to the sensual beat. "Come, you must dance with me!" He pulled me out of my chair and onto the floor, holding me tightly against him.

"I don't know how to salsa," I gasped, trying to remember how to breathe, let alone dance. My head swam to the music, and my feet tapped out the rhythm.

"It doesn't matter. A woman like you shouldn't be sitting. Just stay close to me, and soon your body will be making love to the music."

I hoped that was all I'd be making love to, by dancing this close. I felt fairly sure the throbbing heat coming from Ramon was due to more than the music.

"Just relax and let me lead. I'll do the rest," he murmured.

He was doing plenty already.

"Your dancing is absolutely perrrrfect," he purred. "But there's something else I've been wanting to teach you—the fine art of cigars."

Uh oh. I thought I'd already had that lesson, learning everything there was about taste, shape, and size. "You did a great job of covering that topic the other day," I reminded him.

He initiated a heated round of eye-lock foreplay. "But now I must teach you how to smoke them. After tonight, you'll no longer be a virgin."

My reply was placed on hold as my senses shifted into high gear. Ooh . . . what was *that*? The titillated nerve endings in my ear reeled with joy. Tiny electrical sparks of blissful pleasure sped through every vein, every cell. My better judgment ordered an immediate APB as Ramon continued to nibble away on my ear. I could feel myself going down for the count, and I was thoroughly enjoying it. This guy should have been running a school for seduction.

"Don't be afraid, Raquel. I promise the cigar will be most gentle." The words spilled from lips that beguilingly beckoned me to him. "Are you ready for your lesson?" Ramon's voice teased. He placed his hands on my hips, matching the sensuous rhythm.

"Why not?" I managed to gasp.

"Good. We'll start by learning some basic anatomy." He slid his fingers up my spine, nearly melting my lingerie off me. "The first thing to remember is that the open end of the cigar is referred to as the foot."

Oh, God. Was that the tip of his tongue barely touching the nape of my neck?

"It is the cigar's head which you clip with the utmost tender precision." Ramon's voice was muffled, due to his lips exploring my throat.

God, the guy smelled terrific. I took another whiff. "I've got it," I said breathily. "First you clip the cigar, then you smoke it."

The beat quickened, and colors pulsated to highlight legs wrapped around thighs in a hot, sensual lambada. Ramon slid his hand to my tush.

"But you mustn't be too anxious. It's all a matter of . . . timing." Ramon brushed his hand along the curve of my hip. "Next, you must learn how to light it."

He pressed his hips so tightly against mine that I nearly leaped out of my stilettos.

"First you turn the cigar's foot above a long, hot, burning flame." Ramon's voice caressed each separate word, as he slowly licked all ten of my fingers. "Only then, when the end of the cigar is brightly glowing, do you place it between your lips . . . pull in gently with your cheeks . . . and wet the head—as you suck it."

The very room seemed to vibrate with white-hot stogie lust around me. Macanudo-clutching babes intently eyed the guys at every table, gauging which men held the biggest cigars. Even I was beginning to be curious. Ramon bent me back in a low, steamy dip, where I found myself gazing upside down at a guy talking into a cell phone while smoking a cigar the size of a big-ass Caddy.

Ramon leaned over me, his mustache tickling my throat, his voice low and husky. "This is when you surrender yourself to the cigar, Raquel, allowing its essence to overtake you. You pull on the tip, as you swirl the smoke lusciously in your mouth. Then you pucker your lips . . . and exhale."

I looked up as Ramon descended toward me with teeth bared, like a cigar-chomping Dracula.

His teeth skillfully grabbed the pin which held up my hair, and one swift jerk sent my curls tumbling down. I struggled to catch my breath, ready to explode. If this was the lambada, I planned on signing up for nightly sessions.

Ramon's voice was heavy with passion as he pulled me close, and the fire in his eyes consumed me. "Once your cigar is properly lit it will burn evenly all the way down, with its ash staying long . . . to give enjoyment for hours. Since the objective is to experience as much sensual pleasure as possible, it's wise to choose one that's firm—and resilient. Don't you agree?" he whispered into my ear.

It took all my strength just to nod.

Ramon moved in for the kill. "After all, if you're going to put something in your mouth—you want to make sure to enjoy it."

My body went limp as I tried to decide whether to slap the man or jump on him.

"I think we'd better sit down," I moaned.

"Of course, Raquel," Ramon graciously murmured.

We arrived at the table to find Elena perched in my seat. She was rhapsodizing to Sophie and Lucinda, who watched her with gazes that were utterly transfixed. My eyes were drawn to her Cinderella knockoff glass slippers, complete with five-inch stiletto heels. The rest of her spilled out of a tight leopard-print bodice, with a matching feline skirt that couldn't have been larger than a napkin. Gone was her usual tiny cigar; tonight her lips were wrapped around an eight-inch Cohiba. If Freud were alive, he'd have had a field day in this place.

"How come you never introduced us to your friends before?" Sophie asked. Her hand furiously rummaged inside her purse and she whipped out a cigar, stuck it in her mouth, bit off the end, and set the thing on fire.

"I only recently met them," I informed her.

"That's right," Elena purred, in a voice thick as cigar smoke. "She led me to believe she was with the police. I could have had her arrested."

I would have come up with a good retort if I'd been able to think above the fiery pounding of my feet. Ramon slipped a chair behind my legs as a waitress with a body the width of a toothpick appeared. In her hand was a tray with a bottle of Cristal champagne and five glasses.

"We must toast to the evening," Ramon announced.

He popped the cork, filled the glass flutes, and pulled two cigars from his pocket.

"First you sip the champagne. Then you smoke a cigar," he said, angling one in my direction.

And all this time, I'd thought his spiel was merely a ruse to seduce me. "I think I'll pass."

"Don't be such a wuss," Sophie bit down on her stogie as if it were a piece of beef jerky. "Live it up—women smoking cigars are very sexy." She gazed at Catwoman with open admiration.

Elena handed Sophie her stogie, and reached inside her bodice. "Absolutely! Men come and go, but a woman never forgets her first cigar," she remarked, adjusting her breasts to exhibit as much cleavage as possible.

"You gotta learn to relax," Sophie continued. "That's your biggest problem." She shook her head in resignation.

Elena's pouty red lips parted in an amused smile. "She must not be involved with a man who knows how to lambada. Otherwise she'd be more relaxed and satisfied. In cases like that, a cigar can be a good substitute."

"Judging from the size of the one you're smoking, I'd say you had a rough day yourself," I replied smartly.

"Not at all—my taste in cigars matches my taste in men. I like them to be big and potent." She balanced her cigar wantonly between her teeth.

"It would give me great pleasure if you would try one of mine, Raquel," Ramon softly murmured in my ear.

I glanced at the man and decided two could play the game of seduction. "In that case, how can I refuse?" I let my hand wander to the neck of my dress and discreetly readjusted my own chest for maximum cleavage.

Ramon smiled as he held out a cigar. "Then this is the one you must smoke. I make it only for our most special customers."

Elena flashed me a look to kill, and gave Ramon a slow, lingering kiss. "As usual, my brother is overly generous."

Hmm. Just how close-knit was this family? I reached for the proffered stogie, letting my fingers run seductively along its length as I tried to recall each step of his highly charged lesson. Ramon played tug of war, and I felt the sting of a stiletto heel nip my leg. Elena carefully kept her eyes averted, chatting with Sophie. Damn the woman! I was determined to smoke this cigar perfectly, even if it killed me.

I was about to light up when Lucinda caught my eye, and mimed biting down. Now I remembered! I first had to clip it. I shot her a grateful glance and performed the circumcision. Then I lit it, making sure to hold the match against the foot at a perfect forty-five-degree angle. Next came the part I'd been dreading the most. I pulled in, swirled, and blew out. The cigar stayed lit, the ash nicely firm. Ramon beamed proudly, while my mouth felt as if it had been out picnicking all night in a garbage dump. It amazed me that people actually paid to smoke this stuff.

I leaned in close to Ramon and leisurely held the cigar near my mouth, aware his eyes were glued to my lips. "So Elena, I hear you know Willy Weed." My fingers lightly rested on Ramon's shoulder as I caught Catwoman's eye.

Elena sucked her cigar to a slow burn. "Sorry, I've never heard of the man." She blew a puff of smoke in my direction.

"That's funny. He claims you gave him a Cuban Amazon." My foot teasingly brushed up against Ramon's pant leg as I drew a breath and took the plunge again, pulling, swirling, then puffing.

Elena's heavily mascaraed lashes resembled two battling tarantulas. "I've never heard of anything so ridiculous. You know those birds are expensive. If I had one, I doubt I would easily give it away."

Ramon's hand fluttered over to Elena and languidly caressed her cheek as his other hand stroked my arm.

"You must have had contact with Weed at one time," I persisted. "It was his wife who gave me your address."

Elena's free hand stroked Ramon's chest, working inside his shirt. "I'm well known around Miami for my photography. There are even those who consider me to be a minor celebrity."

"Never minor." Ramon removed her hand from his chest and kissed it. "Elena is a major talent. That makes people jealous."

"It makes no difference," Elena continued. "Either way, you become a target. Who knows? Maybe this Weed and his wife planned to blackmail me."

Ramon's fingers began to play along my back. I shamelessly

sighed and stretched. "That feels absolutely wonderful," I purred. "By the way, you never told me if you and Alberto were in business together, Ramon."

His lips zeroed in on my neck. "Of course not, Raquel. We were like brothers, nothing more."

"Still, you both dealt in cigars," I said softly, turning so that my lips were only inches away from his. "You did know that Alberto smuggled Cuban cigars into Miami, didn't you?"

Ramon licked his lips and hesitated. I moved a millimeter closer.

"Yes. I was one of the few who knew about it. Alberto approached me at one point, and asked if I'd be willing to sell them through my store. Of course, I refused."

He moved in for the kiss, but I quickly placed a finger against his lips. "Your neighbor, Phil Langer, believes that those who smuggle cigars, including Cubans like Alberto, should be sentenced to death as their punishment. How do you feel about that?"

Ramon lightly nipped my fingertip. "We appreciate Mr. Langer's support. But he is not judge and jury over our fellow Cubans. We take care of our own problems in our own way."

Elena rose swiftly from her chair. "People like Langer would do best to learn that lesson. I'm going to lambada."

Between the mojitos and the cigar, all I wanted to do now was go home and crawl into bed. I leaned back and looked around for Terri, but he was nowhere in sight.

"Sophie, Lucinda, Ramon, it's been a lovely evening, but I'm exhausted and it's way past my bedtime," I said, standing up to take my leave. "Please say goodnight to Terri for me."

Ramon rose up next to me. "Raquel! You must stay. The night is only beginning," he implored. "Besides, I cannot go with you just yet. It would not do to leave my sister unchaperoned."

The guy had to be joking. Elena needed about as much protection as a vampire on a moonless night. As for going home with me, Ramon was taking a hell of a lot for granted.

"That's all right. I planned on going home by myself anyway," I gently informed him.

"Then perhaps I'll see you again soon," he sadly murmured. ''You never know when you might want a brush-up lesson.''

''You'll be all right getting home by yourself?'' Sophie used the tip of her cigar to swat a fly off the table.

''I'll be fine,'' I assured her.

''If you have any problem, just use that killer karate move I showed you,'' Lucinda suggested.

''I'll do that,'' I promised.

I skirted the edge of the dance floor, passing through the ebb and flow of bodies where Elena still managed to stand out from the crowd. It was partially her electric-gold hair and her leopard-print outfit. But it was also because she danced with a sense of abandon I wouldn't have dreamed of. Elena raised her arms above her head, her napkin-sized skirt lifting up to reveal a thong—and even that was faux leopard! For a split second, I caught sight of a tattoo on one of her rear cheeks. Ha!—she and Bambi were apparently soul sisters, after all.

I stepped out of the club and into a rainstorm that blurred South Beach's hot pink, blue, and green neon lights into a colorful swirl. Heavy drops hit the hot asphalt, where they sizzled back up in long, ghostly fingers of steam, creating a diaphanous mist. In an effort to save what little was left of my feet, I took off my stilettos.

The crowd and the music faded as fallen dates from overhead palms squished beneath my bare heels, their densely rich aroma intoxicating the night air. I walked onto the beach and wriggled my toes down deep into the sand, the grains massaging my grateful feet.

By the time I stepped back onto the street, the rain had stopped, taking with it all remnants of clouds, revealing a full moon. I continued home, my clothes dripping a trail of water.

I unlocked the door, dropped my keys in my purse and walked inside the darkened house.

The only noise was the soft pat, pat, pat of my bare feet on the floor. In the bedroom, the full moon provided all the illumination that was needed. I hung my purse on the chair by the door, and discovered where Terri had disappeared to: he was passed out cold on my bed. I was even more surprised to see Bonkers sitting motionless on his perch in the corner, his eyes open wide, not making a peep.

Any further thoughts were put on hold when I caught sight of a movement in the moonlight. I stared in disbelief, not quite certain what it was that I saw, until my stomach clenched, the muscles twisting tight as a rubber band, my blood turning deathly cold.

Slowly slithering between Terri's legs was a deadly black mamba, its skin gleaming luminescent in the lunar light. Now I understood why Bonkers was quietly cowering on his perch.

When a mamba bites, all you have left is the choice between having your last drink or your last cigarette.

I took a deep breath, trying to get my nerves back under control, as a wave of sheer terror gripped me. As long as Terri didn't wake, I knew he'd be safe. The problem was that sooner or later, he was bound to move.

The snake stopped, sensing another presence had entered the room. It twisted its javelin-shaped head to the side, regarding me with eyes like two flecks of steel, its upcurved smile growing ever more grim. Then it flicked out its tongue in warning. I stood perfectly still. The snake leisurely turned back to face Terri, convinced that I posed no threat.

I kept my eyes riveted on the reptile, my hand drifting toward my purse hanging off the chair. The snake immediately stopped again, instinctively suspicious. I paused, motionless as a mannequin. Reassured, the serpent turned its attention back to the body at hand, winding farther up along the bed. I reached toward my bag once more, working to keep my movement a slow, steady flow instead of a frantic jerk.

My hand touched the leather purse and I slowly bent my knees, squatting down until my fingers could nearly reach inside—only to be brought to a halt by the closed zipper.

Drops of perspiration trickled in my eyes, stinging as sharp as a scorpion's kiss. I blinked them back away, wanting to scream in frustration. Placing my index finger against the zipper's foot, I gently began to push. Then, stealthy as a spider, my fingers crawled down inside to wrap around the butt of my gun. I quickly reeled my hand back up—only to have the barrel catch on my keys with a heart-wrenching jangle.

The snake's upper body immediately rose to sway high in the air and it turned toward me, its nape flared wide in cobralike fashion. It was about to strike, the only question was who would be its victim. Tales of its legendary speed replayed in my mind as I gripped the gun in my hands, the key ring merrily jingling from the end of the barrel, when Terri opened his eyes and began to stir.

I didn't have time to think, only to follow the mesmerizing sway of the serpent's head as I pulled the trigger.

"No!!" came the shout, though I couldn't be certain which of us had shrieked it.

The scream vibrated off the walls of the room with the roar of the bullet as Terri bolted upright in bed, wide-eyed.

"Jesus, Rach! If you've got some kind of problem with me crashing in your bed, just say so!"

I dropped the gun and picked up the inert form of the mamba from between Terri's legs, careful not to scratch my fingers on its fangs in a last fatal nick.

"I'm pretty sure this doesn't belong to you," I said.

Terri took a deep breath and slowly exhaled, the sound as jagged as a ripsaw. "Holy shit," he whispered. "A simple thank-you doesn't seem quite enough. Give me a minute and I'll try to come up with something more appropriate."

I nodded, unable to speak. My body began to tremble in relief, and I collapsed onto the bed beside Terri. He wrapped an arm around my shoulders and continued to stare at the snake. Finally, he stretched a tentative finger toward it.

"I hear snakeskin is going to be very big in the fashion industry this year—and this thing would make some fabulous yarmulkes!" He glanced over at me. "I *do* get to keep it, don't I?"

Fifteen

The next morning, the phone rang while Terri and I were eating breakfast, with the mamba wrapped in plastic at his feet.

"Hey, Porter. I've got the damnedest news for you," Dr. Bob's voice greeted me. "By any chance, did your corpse have some kind of pet?"

It was way too early to play Twenty Questions, after last night's episode. "Yeah, about two hundred and fifty parrots. Does that count?" I asked tiredly.

"Not unless one of them was big, had lots of hair, and purred," Dr. Bob retorted.

My interest was immediately pricked. Maybe Vern was right after all—maybe there really was a Skunk Ape.

"I just got the DNA test results back. That piece of cloth you gave me was drenched with saliva from a cougar," Dr. Bob revealed.

"But Dominguez didn't have the wounds of a cougar attack," I responded, repeating what Hal Cooper had told me. "There were no claw marks, and the body didn't show the distinctive gashes there would have been from a cat's upper and lower canines ripping into flesh."

"It's not as if the police let me waltz in and examine the body," Dr. Bob retorted. "The conclusion is based on DNA analysis, which in my book is even better. Who knows? Maybe some big pussycat found its way inside this guy's house and drooled on him after he was already dead."

I snorted. "Yeah. I can just see an endangered Florida panther wandering around the Redlands, killing someone in their bedroom, and then making a quick getaway."

Terri rolled his eyes in agreement.

"Whatever—I still expect you to set me up on that date," Dr. Bob reminded me.

I'd forgotten all about the kool-pop waitress at the QT. "I'll get you her phone number," I assured him.

"Hey! You promised to do more than that. You said you'd absolutely be able to get me a date, no problemo. If you can't produce, you're subbing in her place." He chuckled. "And I'm not sure how you'll look in combat boots, a shirtwaist dress, and a lacy black bra."

"Actually, I'd look terrific," I informed him. There was just no way in hell I'd ever show my face in such a getup. "Plan on picking her up at the QT at eight-thirty on Saturday night."

Now all I had to do was convince the waitress.

Terri took Bonkers and his fruit bowl over to Sophie's for the day, and I set off to check out a growing hunch. I was determined to even the score for the unexpected visit by that snake—and I badly needed an outlet for my anger.

I knew of only one herp freak who dealt in black mambas, and that was Willy Weed. Throw in his menagerie of mangy cougars, along with Dr. Bob's information, and the plot grew thicker by the moment. There was still the hitch about the gashes on Alberto's body, but I'd deal with that later. Willy had said that Dominguez owed him money; maybe he'd decided he wanted to be paid sooner rather than later. Or felt he deserved an extra-large bonus. Weed had plenty of contacts who could have helped him dispose of Alberto's parrots. And if that wasn't enough, Willy's words from my last visit still rang in my ears. *"You're a dead woman, Porter!"*

I knew it was crazy to go back out to his place alone, but today I just didn't care. I pressed the pedal to the metal on my clunker and broke every speed limit, kissing the taillights of vehicles as I wove in and out of traffic. When I reached the edge of Willy's driveway I sped past the row of palm trees and pines, their canopy hovering above me like the lid of a coffin waiting to be closed.

Weed's Dodge Ram wasn't the only vehicle in residence today. Parked next to it was a dark blue utility van, conveniently missing its license plates—probably Buzz Tregler's mode of transportation. With Willy, two was a crowd; three was a swarm. I popped open the trunk and pulled out my pump shotgun. I might have been crazy, but I was damned if I'd be stupid.

A tarp once again covered the cargo bed of Weed's pickup and I walked over to see what goodies Willy had lying inside. I lifted one corner and nearly fell flat on my butt, barely able to believe what I saw. Quickly wrenching the rest of the tarp off, I grabbed a better look. Now I knew Willy had totally lost his marbles.

Lying on top of a packing blanket was everything from M-15 and M-16 rifles to M-79 grenade launchers, .50 caliber machine guns, 9mm Glock semiautomatic pistols, and night-vision scopes and gear. There was even a flamethrower, along with an assortment of .38 and .45 revolvers. Willy was ready to take out half of Dade County. Apparently, I could add gun-running to his list of activities.

"Willy! I know you're here!" I shouted. "We need to talk."

There was no reply.

I pushed the safety off my shotgun and pumped a round into the chamber.

Cha-chiiiing!

The sound reverberated with a bone-chilling clarity that boldly stated its purpose. I placed my finger lightly against the trigger and headed for Weed's trailer. Raising the shotgun, I kicked in the door.

Nothing had changed. The stench and the garbage were the same as ever; so was the platoon of road-warrior roaches that scattered as I made my way in, avoiding the unidentifiable food items that littered the floor.

"I advise you to come out, Willy!" I warned.

The trailer mocked me with its silence. Even Big Mama still wasn't around. I headed toward Weed's bedroom, stepping over his putrid laundry. The mound was nearly generating toxic fumes by now.

The sweet smell of a recently lit joint filled the air. Lying near the stained mattress was a partially packed suitcase. I placed my gun down and began to rifle through its contents, gingerly picking up soiled T-shirts and underwear emanating a distinct odor that even the smell of pot couldn't disguise. I dumped the articles one by one on the floor.

Beneath the clothes was a pile of small muslin sacks that were neatly folded, waiting to be used. Nearly identical to the bag in Dominguez's living room, except these sacks were smaller. I removed the miniature shrouds and dug a little deeper.

I hit pay dirt in the form of an airline ticket. Whadda ya know—Willy had managed to cook up a new passport. Wally Wang was booked to migrate south, all the way to Brazil. Along with the ticket was a wad of crisp green bills, most of them bearing the likeness of Ulysses S. Grant and Benjamin Franklin. Willy had either won lotto, or was being paid extremely well for his illegal talents. It seemed entirely possible that Willy had knocked Alberto off to go into business for himself. Without Dominguez working as middleman, Willy could now deal directly with the next level up in the pipeline and make double the money he had before.

The bottom of the suitcase was lined with choice reading material, including those all-time favorites, *Shaved Orient Tails*, *Big Ones*, and *Black and Blue*. It was nice to know that even when Willy traveled, he managed to stay current.

A jarring creak outside abruptly split the air. I grabbed my shotgun and stood up, Willy's underwear jumbled around my feet. The blood pounded in my head with the steady beat of a conductor's baton as I tiptoed out of the bedroom, my ears trained to pick up the slightest sound.

Craaaack!

I jerked the shotgun up, ready to transform Willy's home into an air-conditioned canister. Then I saw that my foot had landed squarely on one of the dozen empty Budweiser cans. So much for sneaking up on my quarry.

I opened the door of the trailer and stepped outside. No one was there. Holding the shotgun in front of me like a high-powered shield, I headed for the remaining trailers.

A gang of bad-boy vultures sat like leather-clad thugs, eyeing my shotgun with as little respect as if it were a toy. Even the lions lazily dismissed me, turning their backs and rolling onto their sides. I readjusted my grip on the stock and boosted my confidence by picturing myself as Sigourney Weaver. The image came in handy when I spotted one of the trailer doors standing ajar. It was the entrance to the "hot" room.

A wave of queasiness broke over me. I nudged the pump's barrel against the door, pushing it open a little further.

"Willy? I know you're in there. So why don't you stop with the games and come out," I called.

Again, there was no answer. Damn! Damn! Damn! I hated this part.

"All right, Willy. That's it—I'm coming in," I warned. "Just don't make any sudden moves. I've got a pump, and I swear to God, I'll use it."

I waited for Weed to surrender, but there still wasn't a sound. Taking a deep breath, I screwed up my courage by rehashing my encounter with the black mamba. If you can't be brave, sometimes anger works.

The metal steps creaked beneath my feet as I walked through the door into the dark den, as airless and hot as a sauna. I was prepared for the hundreds of hostile snakes as I flicked on the switch—but something additional was lying in wait.

A huge cocoa-colored mountain of flesh, Big Mama was curled up on the floor, her muscles undulating as she drew her girth in tighter and tighter. I caught a flash of something deep within her coils and daringly edged closer. Big Mama paid little attention, consumed by whatever was hidden within her rings of shiny skin. I crept forward inch by inch, determined to see what the big attraction was.

The crown of a beat-up, brown leather cowboy hat bobbed into view. The next moment, I caught sight of the head that was attached to it. Willy had described himself and his python as being like one; it looked as if Big Mama had taken the next step in the progression of their relationship. Willy Weed stared out at me with dead, unseeing eyes.

I stared back as Big Mama proceeded to give Willy one last love squeeze, making his mouth fly open and his tongue slide out. Then the room went pitch-black, followed by the thud of the door slamming closed.

I stood stock-still with cold, gut-wrenching fear, tempted to use my shotgun to blow a hole straight through the ceiling—

until I remembered the stack of plywood piled on the trailer's roof. I'd end up creating an instant skylight, only to knock myself unconscious and uncage a few nasty critters.

As I wavered between finding the light switch and screaming my lungs out, I could almost feel Big Mama slither in my direction, making it ''two for the price of one'' day. That was all the impetus I needed.

I stretched out my hand, my fingers break dancing along the wall in a desperate race for the light switch, praying the power line outside hadn't been cut. A hard, plastic nub bit into my skin and I flicked it up, bathing the room in bright light.

I quickly grabbed the door handle, more than willing to face whatever lowdown, nasty creature was waiting on the other side. But the metal arm refused to budge: I'd been deliberately locked inside.

I peered back over my shoulder, where Willy's corpse now wore a maniacal grin, the blood-red ruby gleaming in his front tooth. Then Big Mama turned her head toward me and flicked out her tongue. The next moment, a car's engine roared to life and a vehicle screeched away.

That did it. I took a few steps back, wedged the butt of the shotgun up against my shoulder, aimed at the door, and pulled the trigger. The blast nearly rocked the trailer over, and the pump's recoil flung me back, knocking me right off my feet.

My fall was buffered by something soft, and I turned to find myself face-to-face with Big Mama and her boy toy. I was on my feet and flying through what was left of the trailer door faster than the speeding bullets.

Willy's pickup still sat in its place. It was the unmarked utility vehicle that had vamoosed, taking Weed's mother lode of weapons with it. I ran back inside Willy's trailer and tore straight for the bedroom. His suitcase was gone, as were his fake passport, the ticket to Brazil, the muslin sacks, and the thick wad of moolah.

The lid of Willy's answering machine was flipped up in salute, its interior as bare as Mother Hubbard's cupboard. Even the message tape was missing. There was nothing left to tie Willy to any of the things I had discovered. Damn!

Then I remembered the third trailer that Weed kept locked. I grabbed my shotgun and headed out. But there was no need to resort to violence; this time the door easily swung open.

I was relieved to find it contained no creepy crawlies, but disappointed to discover it held nothing at all. I kicked around some scattered remnants of rubble, and my foot hit something beneath a piece of discarded cardboard. I slowly lifted its edge with my toe. Lo and behold: a box of ammo sat on the floor. Inside were 9mm hollow point bullets, announcing loud and clear that this had been where Willy kept his stash of arms. Beneath the box lay a crumpled receipt from a Quik Pik convenience store, with an address that leapt up and grabbed me. The store was located in Macon, Georgia.

I headed back to my car, pulled out my cell phone, and punched in a number.

"Reardon here," Vern said in a just-let-me-fish-and-leave-me-alone drawl.

"I'm at Willy Weed's place. You're going to want to head over this way with a body bag," I informed him.

"Shit! That sucker didn't actually kill Bambi, did he?" Vern asked, with a tremor in his voice.

I was genuinely touched, until I realized Vern was probably scrambling to cover his ass.

"No. The bag is for Willy," I replied.

"What happened? You didn't kill the bastard, did you?"

"Nothing like that. But when you come, bring a herp expert with you. Willy's death involved a large snake."

"A case of kinky sex, huh?"

"More like an embrace that just wouldn't stop. Did you ever meet Big Mama?" I inquired.

"Who the hell is that?" Vern sputtered. "Some female wrestler, or something?"

"Yeah. Something like that."

My next call was one that I was looking forward to. I dialed the office of the state Game and Fresh Water Fish Commission.

"Hey, Stevens!" I greeted the wildlife desk duty agent. "Guess what? You're not going to be needing that warrant for Weed, after all. In fact, you can even skip filing the violation report."

"What's this?" Stevens asked suspiciously. "Some new kind of approach you've come up with? Well, it won't work.

I don't care how many times you call. Everything is being done by the book.''

I snickered. ''That's why I'm calling. You're going to have to make arrangements for someone to feed Weed's cats until you get them placed in a sanctuary.''

''What's with you, Porter?'' Stevens griped. ''Haven't you heard one word I've been saying?''

''Of course,'' I politely responded. ''But situations change, Stevens. And that's when adjustments have to be made.''

''Oh yeah? Like what, for instance?'' Stevens shot back.

''Like the fact that Willy Weed was just murdered, placing his cats in the abandoned category. I'd hate to think what would happen if the local newspaper got wind that these animals were left to starve due to bureaucratic red tape. It might sell a lot of newspapers, but it wouldn't win any of us a popularity contest,'' I observed.

There was a moment of silence before Stevens finally answered. ''You've made your point, Porter. I'll get on it right away.''

''I'm sure the cats would appreciate that,'' I replied.

I had told Reardon that Willy had been murdered. I believed that was true. Not that I didn't put it past Big Mama to grab a meal where she could get one, but it didn't make sense that Willy wouldn't have been able to get away. Not unless he'd been knocked out cold or killed first.

Buzz Tregler was the first to pop to mind, but I couldn't see a motive on his part. Not only did Buzz not strike me as the violent type, but I couldn't believe he would have locked me in the trailer to await such a gruesome fate. Bambi was the only other connection I had, and it was entirely possible she'd made good on her threats. I decided to find out by breaking the news to her.

Bambi answered the door in an outfit that the postman, the milkman, the handyman, or almost any other red-blooded male would have given a day's pay for just to catch her in. Her 38 Ds were covered by a pair of pasties from which protruded two miniature American flags. The flags stood at a forty-five-degree angle, mounted on tiny plastic sticks. Her red, white, and blue G-string continued the theme with a gold sequined star in its center. The finishing touch was the foam rubber Statue of Liberty crown embedded on her platinum spikes.

"I'm practicing for my new act," Bambi explained as she opened the door. "I'm going for a patriotic theme."

"You got a job, then?" I asked.

Bambi led the way into the kitchen, the two flags gaily waving with each bounce. "Did I have a choice? Besides, I need to get out of this damn house. How the hell else am I ever going to meet anyone?"

The tattooed heart bearing Willy's name winked at me from her right cheek as I followed behind.

"You won't believe what I've got planned to do with a sparkler," Bambi confided. "As far as I know, it's never been done before."

I could only imagine. Before I informed Bambi of Willy's untimely demise, though, I wanted to see what information I could get. "Can you tell me a little about Buzz Tregler?"

Bambi's eyes narrowed to two rings of heavy liner, forming parallel black holes where her peepers should have been.

"Whaddaya wanna know?" she asked suspiciously.

"For instance, do you have any idea what kind of surplus Buzz deals in at Robins Air Force Base?" I asked, going for an off-the-cuff tone.

But Bambi wasn't about to be suckered. "How the hell should I know?" She pulled her lips back in a sarcastic smile. "Probably Spam."

Cute—especially since Willy had used those exact words before.

She poured two cups of coffee and joined me at the kitchen table.

"Willy's a shit!" squawked a high-pitched voice.

Bambi grabbed a ripe peach, picked up a kitchen knife and cut it into slices, one of which she stuck between her teeth. Walking over to the cage, she slipped the fruit halfway through the bars. The Amazon hopped over and gently took the slice from her lips.

"I see the two of you are getting along better," I commented.

Bambi sat down and picked up the sugar bowl, dumping some into her coffee. Then she lowered her finger into the cup and stirred. When she was done, she popped her fingertip into her mouth and sucked off the liquid.

"He's my bird now," she replied.

I took a sip of the coffee. Even sugar wouldn't have helped. "Do you know if Buzz's job involves dealing with weapons in any way?"

Bambi leaned forward, resting her 38 Ds on the table. "Listen, Porter. The guy filched me a watch, and once Willy even had him snatch a pearl necklace. Other than that, I don't know shit."

This wasn't getting me anywhere. It was time to hand her the news.

"Somebody planted a black mamba in my bungalow last night. I'm pretty sure it was Willy," I told her.

Bambi adjusted her flags so that they lay neatly on the Formica surface. "He's a sick fuck. He coulda done that—except for the fact that he's outta town again. Must be somebody else out there who hates your guts, Porter."

"He never left town," I told her.

Bambi glared at me, running all ten of her sharpened nails across the table. "Are you trying to tell me that he's out at his place shacked up, doing it with a couple of broads?" she asked.

"Willy's a shit!" screeched the Amazon.

"Shut up!" Bambi yowled.

"He's not shacking up with anyone anymore. I went over to his place this morning. He was dead when I got there."

Bambi's expression didn't change. Only her mouth fell open. She quickly shut it. "What are you talking about? He flew to Brazil first thing this morning."

I couldn't believe what I'd just heard. "You mean you've known about those trips to Brazil all along?"

"How the hell else am I supposed to take care of these kids?" Tears started to run down her face. "For chrissakes! We're only talking about birds!"

It irritates the hell out of me when people say something stupid like that. "Yeah? Well, now we're also talking about guns. Whoever killed Willy made off with a pile of weapons from the cargo bed of his pickup."

Black mascara ran down Bambi's cheeks. A few drops

plopped into her coffee; the rest streaked onto her neck before settling on her breasts. "Buzz would never do something like that," she said in a whisper.

I jumped on the nugget of information. "Why not?"

Bambi turned her tear-stained face toward me. "Because they were partners, dammit! Buzz was the source, but Willy was the brains behind the plan. You tell me why Buzz would go and screw himself on a sweet deal, huh? I'm telling you, there's no way he'd do that!"

The phone rang and Bambi jumped up to get it. She listened for a moment, and then cupped her hand around the mouthpiece.

"Willy's dead. Porter's here and she's looking for you. Don't go back," she warned. I grabbed the phone out of her hand.

"Listen to me, Buzz. This is important," I began. But the phone was already dead. I turned toward Bambi. "All right. Where can I find him?" I pressed. "Is he back at the base?"

Bambi wiped her eyes, spreading mascara and eyeliner across her face. "Not anymore, he's not."

"Bambi, you're going to have to talk to me, as well as to the police."

Bambi stood up and placed a hand on each of her bare hips, her flags waving in indignation. "I'm not saying another damn word without talking to my lawyer."

Naturally, she meant the killer shark in a suit that I'd gotten for her. Great.

There was only one person who knew something about the military I could talk to, and that was Tommy. Not that I expected much, but it seemed the logical place to go next.

The lunch crowd must have been pretty light at his place today. Most people were already gone, and Tommy was well on his way to being half soused. His sailor cap was pulled down low, and he'd lost his trademark luau shirt, giving me full view of a gallery of faded tattoos. A forties pinup girl sat coyly poised on his left bicep, flaunting her chest with each twitch of his muscle. On his right arm was a tattoo of a heart inscribed with the word MOTHER. Another tattoo of a heart had a dagger stuck through it, a drop of blood hanging from the tip of its blade. Maybe it was his answer to a love affair gone wrong.

He threw ball after misguided ball across a small patch of Astroturf in a one-man game of bocci. So far, he'd managed to work up a sweat without hitting a thing. He removed his cap, exposing a bald, shiny head, and used it to wipe the perspiration off his face.

"You gonna let me stand here and die of thirst? Why don't ya get us a coupla cold ones?"

I walked behind the bar, opened up the cooler, and ladled the brew into two clean but dented tin cups. When I returned Tommy was parked on the Astroturf, having knocked the bocci pins onto the ground.

He slapped a section of the turf beside him. "This stuff is great. Sorta like a pillow for your butt."

I handed him one of the cups and sat down.

He took a gulp of the beer, and wiped his mouth off with the back of his hand. "You here to drink or to talk?"

"Today I'm here to talk," I regretfully replied.

Tommy slapped his cap back on his head. "In that case, we need some food."

He got a container of homemade smoked fish dip and a box of Saltine crackers from the bar. My stomach gurgled as I caught a whiff, and I dug in.

"So, what's the next piece you're looking to fit into the puzzle?" Tommy asked.

I looked at him, a cracker stuffed in my mouth.

"That's why you're here, isn't it?"

I nodded, swallowed, and took a sip of beer. "You remember my telling you about the person who I thought was bringing Cuban Amazons and hyacinth macaws into Miami for Alberto?"

"Yeah. The guy who had a passport without any entry or exit stamps from Cuba." Tommy snickered.

I blushed. "I discovered he's been involved in something else besides smuggling birds."

"Aren't they all?" Tommy remarked. He piled a mound of fish dip onto a cracker and popped it into his mouth.

"This guy, Willy, has also been running guns," I said.

Tommy flipped the brim of his cap off his eyes. "Nothing unusual about that," he replied.

I took a deep breath. "Let me re-word it. What I caught a gander of were M-15s and M-16s, along with grenade launchers, 9mm Glocks, machine guns, night-vision gear, and flame-throwers. And that's just what I saw in the back of his pickup truck. God knows what else he's been selling."

Tommy raised an eyebrow. "Sounds like he's got quite the source for supplies."

"That's exactly what I wanted to talk to you about. His best friend is stationed at an air force base in Georgia, where he works in the surplus division. When I was out at Willy's, I heard a message on his answering machine that said the Commander could place his grocery list to be filled at the candy store whenever he wants." I glanced over at Tommy, who had his head tilted back and his eyes closed. "You were in the military; does any of this make sense to you? Or have I just managed to put you to sleep?"

A smile stole across Tommy's face, followed by a low chuckle. "What a scam. Hell, you can't help but admire that kind of ingenuity. Especially coming from two crackerbarrel numbskulls."

I hate it when I'm left out of the loop. "Do you want to tell me what you're talking about?"

Tommy got up, walked over to the bar again, and dragged back the entire cooler. He opened the lid and refilled both our cups.

"You know what I like about you, Porter?" He took a long swig of beer.

"No, what's that, Tommy?" I was sure there was a punch line.

"It's all the shit you get yourself involved in. It amuses the hell out of me," Tommy replied with a laugh.

"Glad I keep you entertained," I answered, irritation creeping into my voice.

Tommy gave me a sidelong glance. "Hey, cool down, Porter. If you weren't out there putting your butt on the line, you'd never find out about any of this. I'm giving you credit for going out there and doing it."

I took a sip of beer and unruffled my feathers. "Great. Then tell me what this scam is that you're talking about."

Tommy leaned back on his elbows, sinking into the Astroturf. "You ever hear of Defense Reutilization and Marketing Offices?"

He could have been speaking a foreign language. "No. What are those?"

"Those, my girl, are where the U.S. sells its military surplus. Think of it as sort of a designer's outlet. Except instead of sweaters and pantyhose, these outlets offer helicopters, rocket launchers, missiles—things like that."

"You've got to be joking," was all I could think of to say.

"Absolutely not," Tommy retorted. "In fact, it's one of the few programs the Pentagon has that's actually capable of paying for itself. Hell! Last year, they made $302 million selling stuff."

Maybe I was tired, but none of this was making a whole lot of sense to me. "Don't play games by leaving things out, Tommy. How about just explaining the setup to me, and how it works?"

"Alright. Basically, DRMOs are a network of sales offices at different military bases. The idea is simple: When the military has a surplus of stuff, instead of just junking it, the material is trucked to a warehouse and offered to buyers who submit sealed bids. Anything that's a weapon is supposed to be rendered harmless before being sold. Of course, a lot of times that isn't the case."

"Why not? What's the problem?" I took another sip of beer and began to relax.

"What? You want just one problem? Forget it!" he snorted. "This program is loaded with them." Tommy picked up a flat stone and sent it skimming over the water. "The main objective of DRMOs is profit, which means just about everything else tends to get overlooked. Stuff is supposed to be coded so that high-level weapons are destroyed and key weapon parts are prevented from reaching foreign buyers—that kind of thing. However, this is the military we're dealing with, which means there are nothing *but* fuck-ups. Military surplus is presumed to be stuff that's been used. Not in this program! I'd say more than half of what's sold is brand new. Hell, I've known guys who've nearly built their own army from what they've bought out of DRMOs.''

Educational as this was, I still wasn't sure how it tied in with Weed. ''This guy I'm talking about wouldn't have been involved in auctions with a bunch of hot shots. He was a lowlife, two-bit wanna-be.''

Tommy held up a hand. ''Hey. I'm laying it out, giving you the background here. I'm not finished yet.''

He ladled out another cup of beer. ''Okay, now where was I? My guess is that this friend of Willy's—what's his name?''

''Buzz,'' I replied.

Tommy snickered. ''Buzz—I love it. Anyway, Buzz is probably stationed at Robins Air Force Base. Am I right?''

I nodded my head in surprise. ''How did you come up with that?''

''Piece of cake,'' he grinned. ''You already told me that he's stationed in Georgia. And if Buzz is doing what I think, Robins is the perfect place. He's probably stealing them blind and they don't even know it.''

It was my turn to hold up a hand. ''Whoa! This Buzz is no brain surgeon, either.''

Tommy polished off his beer, and ladled himself another. ''It doesn't matter. We're talking about a program that's an absolute disaster. The Pentagon's tracking system for surplus is lame as hell, which makes it easy pickings. Not only that, but their sales system is so overloaded that the computers at a number of DRMOs have actually broken down.'' Tommy burped and flexed a bicep, giving the forties pinup girl a free ride. ''It just so happens that Robins was one of those places. So much property came into their DRMO three years ago that their system collapsed. By the time they got it back up and running, close to $40 million in surplus had disappeared. The base lost track of it, pure and simple. To this day, no one knows where the stuff went.''

''And you think Buzz could have had something to do with that?'' I asked dubiously.

Tommy picked up the container of dip and ran his finger inside, digging out whatever was left. ''I'm not saying he knocked out the system. But once it was down? Yeah, he could have taken advantage of it. Hell, he can probably even tap into other DRMOs around the country and order whatever he wants, from .38 revolvers to parts for Stealth airplanes. You don't need a lot of brains. All you need are the right connections to sell the stuff on the outside.''

That's where Willy came in. But something about this still didn't sound quite right.

''I have a problem believing the military would sell working grenade launchers,'' I told him. ''It makes these places sound like grocery stores for terrorists.''

Tommy tipped his cap in my direction. ''Don't it, though? Or like candy stores for your military-minded, entrepreneurial civilian Rambos.'' He gave me a wink.

I looked at him. ''Just like the message on Willy's machine.''

He nodded. ''You got it. Except that I can't tell you who the Commander is.'' Tommy sipped his beer, getting more and more soused. ''Remember I told you everything is supposed to be coded, so that weapons are permanently disabled before any sale? Well, fuck-ups generally happen on purpose—to hide whatever crap is going on. The guy in charge of coding will give intact rocket launchers the same code as an ordinary table, since launchers in working order get more money on the black market. A Pentagon investigation even confirmed that DRMOs are a big source of supplies for arms traffickers.''

Tommy hiccuped, rolled down onto his back, and closed his eyes. Though I wanted to believe him, I was still skeptical. For all I knew, Tommy was drunk to the gills and making this up.

He turned his head in my direction and opened his eyes, as if he'd heard my thoughts. ''You want proof of this, Porter?''

''That would be good for a start,'' I replied.

Tommy's eyes floated in their sockets, like two castaways out at sea on a raft.

''Set your fanny behind that computer in your office, log onto the Internet, and type in the letters DRMO. Then, list whatever kind of weapons your little heart desires.'' Tommy turned his head back up to the sky, and began to snore.

I figured that was my cue to leave—story time was clearly over.

Sixteen

Since I had to face Carlos at some point anyway, I headed to the office, hoping Phil hadn't reported me for dumping all my paperwork on him.

I walked into my cubicle, where my desk sat sparkling clean, without one file on it. Oh, God—I'd probably been fired, and hadn't been told yet. I had no choice but to play wait-and-see until Carlos returned to the office. I logged on to the computer to make good use of my time.

"Hey, Porter."

I jumped. My finger hit a key and deleted whatever had been on the computer screen. The place was so quiet I'd figured no one else was around, but Phil was leaning against the doorway. Creeping into his late forties, he was attired in a pair of navy polyester pants and a white shirt, making him look more like an accountant than a wildlife agent. Even his sleeves were rolled up, as if he'd been hard at work crunching numbers.

A hot flush rose up into my cheeks, and I instantly regretted my actions of the other day. I'd had no reason to dump my paperwork punishment on him.

"Listen, Phil. I'm really sorry about sneaking all those files over to your desk. All I can say is, it was done in a moment of anger." I started to get up. "Let me haul them back here right now."

"No need to, Porter. It's already been taken care of. In fact, I came over to see if we could work something out." He folded his arms and smiled.

I was instantly suspicious. "What are you thinking about?"

"You know that I hate fieldwork, right?" He sauntered over to my desk, and sat on the edge.

It couldn't have been more obvious: not only was the man wearing a pocket protector, but he even had ink marks on his hands.

"Right," I agreed.

"So, what say you take on the footwork for me when you can. In return, I'll do all the paperwork," he suggested. "And by the way, Carlos thinks you've been in here at night catching up on all those folders he slapped on you. You haven't gotten around to setting up a new filing system yet, or posting past documents, but you're working on it," he grinned.

That clinched the deal. "Just give me a list of the calls you're supposed to be following up on."

Phil had it ready and waiting. He placed the list on my desk and I quickly perused it, with the promise that I'd start cracking on it in the next few days. As he left, I turned my attention back to the computer.

Besides hating paperwork, I'm also no whiz when it comes to dealing with things high-tech. I immediately discovered that Tommy had been wrong: it wasn't as easy as typing in the letters, DRMO, and magically having a list of military weapons appear. I made a few discouraging stabs at trying to figure out what the web address for the Defense and Reutilization Marketing Offices would be, with little luck. Finally at my wit's end, I typed in the simplest and most stupid thing I could think of—the Department of Defense web page—and hoped it would connect me.

I love technology when it works. A quick peck and search immediately led me to what I'd been tearing my hair out about only a minute before: the home page for DRMOs, in living color. Tommy had been right, after all—this was almost better than the Home Shopping Network. From boots, to office furniture, to computer equipment, to missiles and bombs—it was *Tool Time* meets the Unabomber.

I typed in grenade launchers and learned that yes, there were some lovely M-79s for sale through an outlet in Crane, Indiana. I even discovered I could pick up three complete TOW antitank missile systems at a DRMO outlet at Fort Benning, Georgia. I was about to add machine guns to my shopping list when Carlos came in, catching me by surprise.

"*Buenos tardes,* Porter. *¿Como está?*"

Phil must have done one bang-up job on that paperwork. Carlos had never inquired how I was before.

"*Buenos tardes,* Carlos. *Bien, grácias.*" I figured he'd appreciate the attempt, even if my accent could use a little work.

"I think we should talk about what happened the other day." He sat down in a chair next to my desk.

"All right," I agreed, my fingers itching to get back to the keyboard.

"I deal with a lot of pressure, being in charge of this port," he said.

"Everyone knows this is the toughest port in the country," I assured him.

"This place is a black hole that eats agents and their careers alive," Carlos drove his point home.

"But you're doing everything you can with the shoestring budget Washington's given you to work with." Even though I meant what I said, I was hoping to rack up some points.

"I've also found this position very frustrating. I'm not someone who does well sitting behind a desk doing paperwork," he added.

Tell me about it.

"Which is one reason why maybe I've been too hard on you," Carlos conceded.

"Why is that? Because women should do the paperwork?" Me and my big mouth—I just couldn't stop myself.

"That could be part of it." His fingers twitched, lost without the revolver they normally held on to. "That bird case we discussed may be worth your looking into after all. Since you're able to handle the paperwork as well as carry out an investigation, you have my permission to proceed."

Well, knock me over with a bocci ball. I silently said a prayer of thanks to Phil.

"That's great—especially since there's been a new development," I began in a rush. "I went over to Weed's place this morning, where I discovered he had been preparing to head out again for Brazil. He'd procured another fake passport, along with an airline ticket to Brasília, a bunch of muslin sacks, and a chunk of cash."

"What do you mean by 'he had been' preparing?" Carlos asked, kind enough to overlook the fact that I'd gone to Weed's on company time, after having been instructed not to.

"Weed was murdered. I discovered the body," I informed him.

"You seem to have the magic touch," Carlos noted dryly. "How was he murdered?"

I knew I was setting myself up to be shot down. "Constriction," I muttered.

Carlos's mustache twitched in surprise. "Did I hear you correctly? Did you say constriction?"

I nodded, figuring that was the safest reply.

Carlos sat back, stretched his legs, and laced his fingers behind his head. "Would you care to elaborate on that, Agent Porter?" he inquired, in a voice oozing with sarcasm.

Just when we were beginning to get along so well. "At first glance, it would appear his Burmese python squeezed him to death."

"You call that murder?" Carlos asked. "It sounds to me like a crazy herp dealer got himself into some trouble he couldn't get out of."

I started to laugh. "I suppose that's one way of looking at it."

Carlos wasn't amused. I tried to put a lid on my case of the giggles, but between too little sleep, and having been locked in with a bunch of lethal snakes and a squished dead man, I must have needed the release.

Carlos's lips stretched into a thin smile. "I'm glad to see you're laughing, Agent Porter. Because that's about how seriously I'm taking everything you told me."

That sobered me up quickly. "I haven't fully explained the situation. Someone else was at Willy's while I was there. Whoever it was took the necessary steps not to be discovered, by locking me inside the trailer that contained Willy and his snake."

"I take it you have no idea who locked you in?" Carlos inquired, methodically laying the groundwork to ensnare me.

"No." I moved a step closer to his trap. "They had the foresight to turn out the lights right before the door was closed and locked. By the time I got out, they were gone."

"Still, I'm sure you were smart enough to pick up the plane ticket, the passport, and the money when you found them," Carlos said, handing me the rope with which to hang myself.

"By the time I went back to retrieve them, those items were missing, as well," I explained, compliantly sticking my head in the noose.

Carlos slapped his hands on my desk and stood up. His expression told me I'd performed exactly as he had expected. "In that case, you seem to be running around in circles, with nothing but two dead bodies to show for your trouble."

Then Carlos's eyes fell on my computer screen, where he took in my shopping list. He brought his face down close to mine.

"Do you want to tell me what's really going on here, Porter?" he asked, in a tone that chilled the air.

What I didn't want was to hand him any more ammunition; at least, not until I had a better handle on exactly what I had stumbled upon.

"I was just computer surfing," I lightly replied.

"M-79s? Antitank missile systems?" Carlos's eyes were glued onto mine. "This investigation wouldn't have anything to do with gun running, would it? Because, if it does, this case goes well beyond Fish and Wildlife's authority."

Great. Decoded, that meant I could expect to spend the rest of my days seated next to Phil, bogged down in paperwork for eternity.

"Call me crazy," I figured a plea of insanity might do the trick, "but I've been tossing around some conspiracy theories."

Carlos looked pleased at my admission toward lunacy. "Such as?"

"You remember our talk on how Cuban paramilitary groups are armed to the teeth with weapons?" I asked.

"That's right."

"Well, it's possible that our government might still be secretly supplying them with arms," I proposed.

A patronizing smile flitted across his face. "Of course they're not, Porter. Those days are long over."

"Are you absolutely certain of that?" I felt like the female version of Oliver Stone.

"Listen, Porter: the failure of Operation Mongoose put an end to all U.S. covert activities in Cuba," Carlos stated.

"Operation Mongoose?" I repeated. Carlos had to be making some of this stuff up as he went along.

"How can you not know about Operation Mongoose?" He sighed.

What I knew was that Carlos got a kick out of stumping me. "Is there any reason I should have heard of it?" I snapped.

"That information was declassified in 1993," he condescendingly informed me, his male pride fully sated. "It was a covert program cooked up after the Bay of Pigs to get native Cubans to rebel and oust Castro. The CIA targeted Cuban industries and transport ships for sabotage, and contaminated Cuban sugar shipments on their way to other countries. The plan even considered convincing Cubans that Castro was the anti-Christ and then staging Jesus' return from heaven."

"No wonder it failed." I was amazed at some of the loony-tune things that had been concocted.

"Exactly. Which is why the U.S. has done nothing but maintain sanctions against Cuba for the past thirty-eight years. Now it's just a waiting game."

What continued to nag at me was Saul Greenberg's hint of a political tie-in with the parrot smuggling. That, along with the recent bombings aimed at the tourist industry in Cuba, left too many questions unanswered.

"But what about the Cuban-American United Stand Foundation?" I probed. "You said yourself that they exercise enormous power: Maybe they've worked out a deal where the government supplies Omega-12 with arms, but doesn't get involved in any other way."

Carlos waved his hand as if I were an annoying fly not worthy of being swatted. "You're getting carried away with your conspiracy theory, Porter. Even CAUSF isn't *that* powerful."

"Maybe not. But isn't it possible that Omega-12 still has some sort of tenuous ties to the CIA?" I challenged.

Carlos shrugged. "I suppose there could be a lone renegade who's never given up on the fight against Castro, some wild-card fanatic who might be working with them. But it doesn't seem very likely. Without government backing, he'd just be spinning his wheels.''

I remained silent, my attention back on the on-line DRMO candy stores.

''If there's something else you want to tell me, this is your chance,'' Carlos warned, almost as if he knew I was withholding information.

''I found a piece of fabric that had been torn off Alberto's shirt lying near the body, the night of the murder,'' I revealed. ''The material was wet with some substance other than blood. I removed it from the scene and sent it to a doctor I know over at Jackson Memorial, where he passed it on to a forensic scientist for DNA analysis. Apparently this guy maintains a collection of DNA samples from an assortment of wildlife. I got the report this morning.'' I waited, expecting Carlos to blast me for having removed evidence from the scene of a crime.

''And what did it conclude?'' was all he asked.

''The fabric was soaked with cougar saliva.'' One look at Carlos's face was all it took to make me feel uncomfortably foolish.

''You know, Porter, I've tried to give you the benefit of the doubt, precisely because you *are* a woman. But at times like this, I wonder why. Do you honestly expect me to believe that someone's escaped pet killed Dominguez, nabbed the birds, and made a clean getaway?'' His fingers drummed on my desk in a subtle form of torture. ''My guess is that your 'scientist' is a rank amateur who shouldn't be allowed anywhere near crime-scene evidence.''

I could have told Carlos that I'd felt pretty much the same way when Dr. Bob had first given me the news. But I didn't think it would make much difference in his opinion of me.

Carlos took off his cap. I considered that a bad sign, knowing how sensitive he was about losing his hair. He rhythmically slapped the hat against the palm of his hand.

''Why do I get the feeling that you're intent on making this job more exciting than it really is? Maybe *you* should consider applying for work with the CIA.''

''And I think the problem is that you're too limited in your scope. There's more to this case than you seem to want to deal with,'' I shot back.

Carlos lunged at the opening I'd unwittingly given him.

''I knew it! You're holding something back. I can feel it!'' Carlos crowed. ''Here's the deal, Porter. You want to follow up the bird-smuggling angle? Go ahead. But, if this case involves gun running, I advise you to tell me now or you'll find yourself out of a job.''

''I found a bunch of arms stashed in the cargo bed of Weed's pickup,'' I admitted.

''That still doesn't explain why you're sitting here ogling the web page for DRMOs,'' he sniped, turning the screws.

It was clear that I couldn't hold out any longer. All I could hope was that Carlos would remain true to his word, and still let me follow the bird smuggling angle.

''All right. You win,'' I conceded. ''The arms included M-15 and M-16 rifles, along with M-79 grenade launchers.''

Carlos nodded, silently acknowledging that he knew those to be military weapons.

''I've also learned that Weed's best friend works in the surplus division at Robins Air Force Base,'' I added.

Carlos erupted as predictably as Old Faithful.

''What are you, loco? How could you even *think* of keeping this kind of information from me? Two homeboys are possibly running guns from out of a military base, and you imagine you can take this on?'' he sputtered in disbelief.

''I just found out about it myself,'' I offered as my sole, lame defense.

Carlos glared. ''Where are the guns now?'' he demanded.

''They were also gone by the time I managed to get out of the trailer,'' I admitted.

Carlos's face glowered, as incandescent as a setting sun. ''That's it, Porter. You're officially off the case. There will be no more digging around. Do you understand me? Whatever you're on to has *nada* to do with birds, and *mucho* to do with illegal arms,'' he declared. ''Unless, of course, you're on another one of your wild-goose chases.''

Carlos was never going to let me forget the chicken eggs. I kept my mouth closed, knowing anything I said could only make matters worse.

"I don't need to have you running around playing Chicken Little, screaming that the sky is falling. That won't do any good, even if there really is something going on." He leaned in toward me, his voice icy cold. "Stay the hell out of this, Porter. I intend to look into the situation myself, and decide if there's any merit to what you've been telling me. As of now, all your work will be done sitting behind this desk. If you have a problem with that, you can write a letter of resignation right this minute, and hand it to me."

He turned around and stormed off.

I headed home feeling more confused and dejected than ever. As much as it killed me to admit it, Carlos was right on one point. Even if Tregler and Willy had been running weapons from Robins, I hadn't yet linked it to Weed's parrot-smuggling gig. I felt as if I'd been banging my head against a brick wall with nothing but a battered ego to show for it, and a job that was threatening to slip away from me.

I headed for the most calorie-riddled Cuban dive that I knew of. The best thing about Latin food is that it's quick, cheap, and good. The restaurant was the size of the tiny apartment I'd had back in New York. A few creaking fans spun slowly overhead, panting like exhausted old men as they circulated the same hot, stale air around the room. If I was going to punish myself, I was determined to do it right. I took a seat in a red booth, the hot vinyl plastering itself against my skin.

Ordering *arroz con pollo*, I added a side of heavy fried plantains just to top off the calorie count, and washed it all down with a couple of Hatuey beers. Then I went for broke by requesting the flan.

I was waiting for dessert when I finally dragged myself back from the depths of despair, and took the time to gaze around. Behind me hung a dartboard with an unusual feature: Castro's face had been used as the backdrop. Looking at the cluster of patrons, I realized I was the only Caucasian in the room. I studied each person's face, wondering how many secretly bore the tattoo of a parrot clutching a gun.

By the time my dessert arrived, I'd decided that I'd punished myself quite enough. I left my flan untouched and headed for home.

The late daylight turned the pastel condos lining the shore into a row of tempting gumdrops. I took a spin down Ocean Drive, losing myself among the traffic that swarmed as thick as mosquitoes after a rainstorm. I crept past Lummus Park, where a little girl dressed in virginal white, with a long mane of glossy black hair, touched the sky with the tips of her shoes as she rose higher and higher on the seat of a soaring swing, patiently pushed by a Cuban woman in a brightly colored housedress.

Off in the distance, the steamy beat of Latin music was just beginning to gear up for the night, its rhythm in direct competition with the resident crickets.

Sophie and Terri must have made a late afternoon run to the beach to bake, since Bonkers was ensconced in his cage in my kitchen. A loud shriek greeted me as I walked in the door, followed by one of the best wolf whistles I'd heard in a while.

I laughed in spite of myself. ''Typical guy—you'll do whatever it takes to get your way.''

I opened the cage door and the cockatoo scampered up my arm, settling himself on my shoulder, where his thick, rubbery tongue nibbled at my ear. I turned my head and lightly planted a kiss on his beak. Bonkers responded by crawling down the front of my shirt and nestling in my arms.

I headed over to the fridge and pulled out a head of lettuce, then deposited both bird and lettuce on the kitchen counter. Turning on the tap, I tore off the large leaves and ran them under cold water, spreading them out on the counter top. Bonkers raised his comb and bobbed his head in an imitation of kool-kat jive, as he spread his wings and sank down into the leaves to luxuriate in an avian beauty bath.

I walked back to the fridge and bent to drag out a smorgasbord of fruit and veggies for his evening snack, only to curse as my jeans cut into my skin. Damn! My body couldn't have expanded that much in just an hour. Relief flooded over me as I realized the extra couple of inches were due to the .38 I'd tucked inside the waistband of my pants. I pulled out the gun and laid it on the kitchen table, then turned back to the fridge.

''Fuck the commander! Fuck the commander! Candy store!

Candy store!'' Bonkers suddenly started to squawk, his head jerking frantically toward the gun.

Cold chills crept up my neck.

''Puffin! Puffin! Candy store! Candy store!''

He continued to screech until I put the gun in the drawer, out of his sight. Then he settled down to continue his bird bath, while my stomach clenched in a sickening mixture of fried plantains, grilled chicken, and fear.

For the first time, I understood what Bonkers had been saying since the first day I got him. He hadn't been commending Sophie for not inhaling, or jabbering senseless words: he'd been my one key crime witness. Bonkers had held the pieces to the puzzle all along. I had no doubt that the ''Puffin'' he was talking about was Ramon Vallardes's cigar store.

Did that mean Ramon was the person referred to as the ''Commander''? I thought again of the tattoo that was Omega-12's emblem, and a few more pieces fell into place.

I was caught up in trying to make my theory fit as perfectly as a completed jigsaw puzzle when Terri walked in. It was clear that Sophie's influence had started to go too far. He was sporting an aquamarine turban, along with sunglasses decorated with chimpanzees dressed in bathing suits.

''*Oy!* I'm *verklempt!* Yarmulke Schlemmer just received its first big order, and we haven't even finished designing our fall line yet.'' Terri collapsed into a chair, his transparent beach cover falling open to expose a pair of bathing trunks that carried out the theme of his shades.

''It all happened so fast. One minute, I'm sitting on the beach talking to some *shlub* from New York. The next minute, the guy turns out to be a buyer for Pampered Pets Galore!'' Terri exclaimed.

''What's that?'' I idly asked, my mind elsewhere.

''You're kidding. Right, Rach?'' Terri tried crossing his legs only to have them slide apart, his skin loaded down with sunscreen.

I had the sneaky suspicion that before this afternoon, Terri had never heard of Pampered Pets Galore, either. ''Sorry, Ter. I'm afraid I haven't kept up with fashion lately—either for humans or pets.''

Terri got up and grabbed a few paper towels. He sat back

down, layered them on his left thigh, and crossed his legs once again. "Well, it so happens that Pampered Pets Galore is the largest chain of pet stores in the world. And this guy, Harold Klein, swears our yarmulkes are going to become the biggest thing since holiday bandana collars." Terri removed his sunglasses and batted his baby blues. "Do you know what this means, Rach?"

I shook my head no, trying to fit that last puzzle piece into place.

"Liposuction and face lifts whenever we want them! But first, I'm setting up maid service for both of us. I've had it with cleaning. Sophie isn't exactly June Cleaver, and God knows, you must have experienced a trauma with dust bunnies as a child." Terri took a look around the place and sighed.

"For the birds! For the birds!" Bonkers interjected, tearing the lettuce into long, thin strips.

"If that's a comment on my business, just keep it to yourself," Terri responded over his shoulder.

I stopped cutting up fruit and stared in amazement at the cockatoo, as the last puzzle piece snapped into place.

"That's it!" I whispered. "It's so simple! My God! Why didn't I figure this out before?" I gave Bonkers a grape, along with a spritz of water from the plant mister.

"That's great, Rach—I'm happy for you. Almost as happy as I am for me." Terri popped a few of Bonkers's grapes into his own mouth. "Just what is it, exactly, that you've figured out?"

My head felt like a pinwheel spinning faster and faster, the information thrown together through the magical power of centrifugal force. "I can't believe it, Terri! You know this case I've been working on? The one with the bird breeder that was murdered? It suddenly all makes sense!"

"Does this have anything to do with that redneck cowboy you were telling me about?" Terri inquired.

"Willy Weed? Yes! Absolutely!"

I cut up a kiwi and handed Bonkers a slice. The bird immediately tossed it into the air, like a child throwing a tantrum. It didn't matter—at this moment, he could do no wrong.

"What a smart boy you are," I praised the cockatoo,

scratching his neck. "I swear, Bonkers just helped me put this whole thing together."

Terri gave me a wary glance. "Maybe you want to explain this to me a little bit better?"

I took a deep breath, my mind racing as I tried to figure out how I'd ever prove my theory. "I've been convinced that a steady supply of endangered parrots is being smuggled into Miami. Well, listening to what Bonkers has been saying just made me realize they're being brought in by a Cuban paramilitary group called Omega-12."

Terri rose from his seat and wet a paper towel. Guiding me back to the table, he pulled out a chair and sat me down, placing the wet soak against the back of my neck.

"There's something I've been meaning to tell you, Rach. You've been looking a little peaked and flushed lately. At what age did your mother first begin to get hot flashes?"

I glared at him. He knew age was a sore point with me, and that I was nowhere near menopause. "I'm not having hot flashes, and what I'm saying isn't as far-fetched as it sounds."

Terri sat down and paid attention. "Okay. So this right-wing group of Cubans is running around smuggling birds. For what? As some sort of political statement?"

"No, they're selling these parrots for big bucks! They've been using the money to buy arms from Willy Weed and a friend of his, who have been running a scam out of a military base!"

"Whoa! Slow down, Rach. What are you talking about? What are the weapons for?" Terri asked. "And what does this group want to do, anyway? Take over Miami?"

I shook my head, anxious to get the words out. "Cuba, Terri. They want to take back the mainland. It's been their dream for close to forty years," I explained. "But a new twist has just been added: Willy Weed was murdered today. I found his body when I stopped by his place this morning." I quickly glanced down at my feet, imagining the steely coils of a snake begin to wrap around me. "I figure whoever was responsible is also involved with Omega-12."

Terri stood up and got another cold compress, this time for himself. "You know, Rach, this job of yours is going to make me old before my time." He carefully patted the skin around his eyes. ''But if any of what you're saying is true, it's lucky that you know Ramon and Elena. You're going to need people who are well connected in the Cuban community.'' He reached over to grab a plum out of a bowl. ''Besides, if nothing else, it gives you a good reason to contact Ramon again. Who knows? Maybe you'll even get another dance lesson.''

I hesitated for a second, knowing what I was about to say would sound like total lunacy. ''That's the other thing: I believe Elena and Ramon are involved in this. So was Alberto Dominguez. He was the conduit for bringing in the parrots.'' Just saying it out loud made me feel as if I was actually making progress on the case. I went for broke and took the next leap. ''I'm also beginning to think that Ramon might have been involved in Alberto's murder.''

Terri's expression was pure disbelief. ''Let me get this straight. Now—you believe all this because—that crazy bird over there told you so?''

When he put it that way, my reasoning did sound a bit birdbrained.

''Stop, thief! Stop!'' Bonkers screeched on cue.

''Need I say more?'' Terri bit into the plum. ''I think you've got a bird that's been watching way too many adventure flicks on TV. I'm telling you, Lucinda and Sophie live on that stuff.''

His fingers idly played with a curl that had escaped from his turban. ''I can't believe you'd seriously think Elena and Ramon are part of a right-wing group of maniacs plotting to overthrow Castro, and killing anyone who gets in their way. How many right-wingers do you know of who hang out at clubs and dance the lambada?''

His reasoning was beginning to jostle my carefully constructed jigsaw puzzle. ''Elena and Ramon's father was one of the founders of Omega-12. In fact, he's sitting in a Cuban prison right now for hauling rockets over there to further the cause.''

Bonkers screeched, letting me know he was done with his bath. I placed him on top of his jungle gym, where he attacked a mobile filled with tiny bells.

''So in other words, Elena and Ramon are just carrying on a family tradition? There's only one thing you're forgetting.''

Terri didn't immediately tell me what that was. Instead, he went to work with my blender, some fruit, and a bottle of seltzer. Kitchen drawers flew open and shut until he located my stash of paper parasols.

"What is it that I'm forgetting?" I asked, trying to remain patient as he placed two glasses filled with his mystery concoction on the table.

Terri removed the purple parasol from his drink and licked the end of the stick. "Wouldn't it be pretty silly for Elena and Ramon to kill your Everglades cowboy? From what you say, they'd be cutting off their main source for weapons. That doesn't make any sense to me."

Terri was right. I'd overlooked a huge, gaping hole in my own logic.

"Besides, this whole business about Dominguez being attacked by some rampaging cougar sounds crazy to me," Terri continued. "Do Elena and Ramon even own one of those cats?"

Elena's taxidermied pets, Geraldo and Rivera, didn't seem to pose much of a threat. "No," I had to admit.

"There, you see? Also, why would they kill a close friend of theirs? They all grew up together; they even came over to Miami on the same boat as children."

Terri had efficiently decimated my entire theory into a pile of shreds in less than five minutes. I looked at Bonkers, who was dangling by a single toe while chewing a wooden stick to pieces.

"You're right. It doesn't make much sense," I conceded. "Damn!" What kind of an agent was I, anyway? I'd sunk to depending on a bird to solve the case for me.

"Think of it this way: You may have lost a couple of suspects, but you've managed to retain one incredibly hot lambada partner," Terri said consolingly. "Here—sip your drink." He pushed the glass toward me. "After that, I have a little activity planned for this evening."

I took a sip, feeling despondent. "Have Sophie and Lucinda gone away?"

"They're around, but they're being very mysterious about what they've got planned this weekend. Knowing those two, they're probably rallying Miami's senior citizens for a protest demanding a female version of Viagra.'' Terri emptied the contents of the blender into his glass. ''In any case, you and I are going to have a wonderful weekend filled with nothing but R & R. And that doesn't stand for rest and relaxation; we're talking reggae and rhumbas.''

My world might be crumbling around me, but I thanked my lucky stars for Terri. ''What would I do without you?'' I tried to keep my tone light, but a slight quiver snuck in.

Terri covered my hand with his. ''That's one thing you'll never have to worry about. Don't you know by now that we're soul mates?''

''Yeah, I guess I do,'' I acknowledged. ''You truly are the best friend I could ever have.''

Terri wiped a tear from beneath my eye. ''Now, perk up, Rach. You've been under way too much strain with everything that's been going on. So what say we go dance our rear ends off? God knows, my butt could use the exercise. My only workout since coming to Miami has been planting my rump down on warm sand.''

Terri was right. I was at the point where gravity was beginning to kick in; loud music and an aerobic workout might be just what I needed.

''You're on.'' I blew my nose into a napkin as the phone rang, sending Bonkers into a tizzy at the commingling of sounds.

''Fuck the commander! Make the call! Make the call!'' the bird shrieked.

I cupped one hand over my ear while I pressed the other tightly against the receiver.

''Hello?'' I bellowed over Bonkers's surround-sound screech.

''For chrissakes, Porter, what the hell are you running over there? Some kinda illegal zoo?''

I recognized the voice. ''How are you feeling, Tony? Back to business as usual?'' I asked, aware that a phone call from him could bode nothing but trouble.

''I feel like shit, Porter! That's how I feel. That putz next door is at it again!'' Carrera exploded.

''Exactly who are you talking about?'' I inquired, figuring

either neighbor stood a fifty-fifty shot of landing on Carrera's shit list.

"Langer! Who the hell else do you think? I'm not calling about the Cuban Donny and Marie, even though they've got a damn party going on that's giving me a splitting headache. Unless you're doing double duty these days, and can handle a complaint for noise while you're out here," he groused.

Ramon was having a party and I hadn't been invited.

For God's sake! Stop acting like a schoolgirl whose feelings are hurt because you've been left out.

The scolding did little good. I still wondered why Ramon hadn't mentioned it to me the other night.

"Hello? Anybody home? You still there, Porter? Or are you bailing out on me? Just remember—I can still press that lawsuit against you whenever I want, ya know," Carrera threatened.

I brought my focus back to Mr. Charm. "What do you want, Tony?" I wasn't in the mood for chitchat when I could be brooding about being left off the Vallardes's party list.

"I'm calling because Langer's messing with my birds again, and you promised to help," he reminded me.

"I told you before, Tony, this is something that needs to be handled by a state wildlife agent."

"And I told you before that I don't give a damn. So I suggest you get over here right away—otherwise, I swear I'm gonna blow that bastard's brains out!"

The only thing that kept me from telling Tony to go right ahead was my curiosity about Ramon's party. While it wasn't a very noble motive, it did provide the proper dash of incentive.

"All right, Tony. I'll be right over," I told him. "Just don't do anything crazy before I get there."

"Make it snappy! Otherwise, I can't make any promises," Carrera warned.

I turned around, and Terri homed in on me with a questioning expression. So much for his planned diversion. "Sorry, Ter. I'm afraid dancing is out for me tonight. That was a call I have to go on."

"So where are we headed?" he asked. "And what's the appropriate apparel?"

I looked at Terri in his beach cover and turban. Carlos would consign me to paperwork hell for the rest of my days if he ever got wind that I'd taken a civilian along on an official call. "It's work related. Believe me, it won't be any fun."

"Of course it will be!" he insisted. "I'll keep you company. What could be more fun than that? And we'll find someplace to go afterward." Terri pulled another curl out from under his turban. "You'd better get used to the idea, Rach. Like it or not, I'm your sidekick this weekend—like Batman and Robin, Miami style."

The image was good enough to give me a warm chortle. Besides, Carrera's call wasn't really all that official. And I had to face facts: Carlos had made it clear that my life was to be relegated to a desk anyway.

"Well, this guy does live near Ramon and Elena," I teased Terri. "And he did mention that they're having a party tonight."

He was instantly on his feet. "What? And you weren't going to take me along?"

"I'm not planning on going myself," I informed him. "We weren't invited."

"Of course we were. You know the postal service; nothing ever arrives on time," Terri reasoned blithely.

"Neither of them mentioned it the other night at the Havana Club."

"It skipped their minds."

Once Terri decided upon a course of action, there was no talking him out of it. "You're determined to crash this party, aren't you?"

"Damned straight," Terri replied. "I just have to figure out what I should wear."

"Whatever it is, you'd better hurry. I'm leaving in fifteen minutes," I warned him. That would give me just enough time to slip into something myself.

"Make it twenty!" Terri shot back, making a beeline out the door.

It was a real brainteaser: What to wear while on duty and at the same time look like a put-together, sexy kind of gal? I pulled out the tightest pair of pants I could squeeze into. Shirts were another matter. I couldn't prance around in a camisole top while trying to get someone like Langer to take me seriously.

The best shirt I had was the one I'd worn the night of Alberto's murder, and I hadn't done any laundry since then. I took a whiff at the important spots. Not too bad; it would pass. My twenty minutes were quickly winding down. I threw on the shirt and slipped into a pair of knockoff designer sandals.

"Be a good boy, Bonkers. I'll be back later, and let you out of your cage," I promised.

He tipped his bowl of veggies onto the floor of his cage.

"That's it, young man. We'll talk about your manners when I get home," I said sternly. Grabbing my purse, I headed out the door.

"Candy store! Candy store!" Bonkers called after me.

Maybe he hadn't been referring to DRMOs after all, but just wanted a chocolate bar all along. I could understand that; it ran in the family.

Seventeen

I headed down the path toward Sophie's cottage and was pleased to find Terri waiting.

"What do you think, Rach?" he asked, twirling around.

Terri wore an elegant, understated outfit à la Audrey Hepburn. "You look great," I told him, envious that I hadn't put myself together half as well.

"Let's get rolling, then."

He headed down the walk and pulled on the passenger door of the Tempo. It grudgingly creaked open, sounding like a cat in heat. Terri watched me perform my usual free-form dance as I squeezed into the driver's side, then turned the key in the ignition. The Ford wheezed to life, the engine finally turning over.

"Remind me to include a new car on that list, when Sophie and I hit it big time," he said.

We flew over the causeway, being one of the few vehicles to leave South Beach on a Friday night. This was Terri's first journey into Miami's burbs, or the "hinterlands" as he called them. Traffic was fine until we hit Miracle Mile where, even at this hour, people were determined to shop till they dropped. Mercedes, Jaguars, and Ferraris clogged the street.

"This neighborhood isn't half bad," he observed. "In fact, it could be the perfect spot for our Yarmulke Schlemmer flagship store."

"You're thinking of making it a chain now?"

"Of course," he replied. "Like I've always said, if all you do is plan to meet Prince Charming, you're going to find yourself parked out on a corner with a sign and an empty tin cup in your hand.''

Terri flipped down the visor to check his image in the vanity mirror and dislodged a strawberry seed from between his front teeth, being careful not to smudge his lipstick. ''I'm going to need something to fall back on in my old age. Sure, I can do Madonna and Marilyn and Barbra right now. But who am I going to impersonate in few years? Sophie Tucker?''

He had a good point. If I ended up getting sacked, maybe I could get a job at Terri's store. Especially if they had a retirement plan.

I was grateful that I'd first gone to Tony's house during daylight hours. At night, finding it would have been mission impossible. I followed the curves, trying to remember where to turn and managing to avoid most of the unmarked dead ends. Terri took in the sights as we drove past one mansion after another, safely ensconced behind metal gates and imposing stone walls. There was no denying that the neighborhood put on the ritz, even in the dark.

''This guy sells pet reptiles and he lives *here?*'' Terri asked incredulously.

''He imports them for the pet trade. That is, when he's not busy trying to smuggle in something illegal.''

Terri's wig gleamed in the moonlight, surrounding his head like a halo of gold. ''I hate to break the news to you, Rach, but you're obviously on the wrong side of the wildlife trade. Start sneaking in a few primo items here and there, and in no time at all you'll have a solid nest egg.''

I was shocked. ''In case you haven't noticed, I'm trying to save species—not give them an additional shove toward extinction.''

Terri pulled one of my unruly curls. ''Lighten up, Rach; I'm only teasing. I just hope all those furry little four-legged creatures out there appreciate your idealism.''

I gave him a grin. ''They don't have to, Ter. If I can just shake up the bad guys a bit, it helps make my day.''

''Hmm. Very Clint Eastwood. You might want to try softening that with a dash of Julia Roberts,'' he suggested.

Carrera's white brick wall came into view. He was obviously expecting me; the gate was unlocked and stood open a fraction. I drove through, expecting to be greeted by Poopsie, but the dog was nowhere in sight.

The loud pulse of salsa from next door rattled the night, reminding me that we hadn't made the A-list. I headed to Carrera's front door and rang the bell, but Tony had either turned hard of hearing or he wasn't bothering to answer.

I walked back to the car and grabbed a flashlight. "I'm going to head around to the rear of the house and see if I can find Carrera. Why don't you wait here?" I suggested.

"Absolutely not!" Terri asserted. "I'm your sidekick this weekend, remember?"

"Okay. But be prepared for a large dog to suddenly come zooming toward you," I warned.

"What's the dog's name?" he asked. "They usually like to hear me scream it just once, before sinking their teeth into me."

"Poopsie," I replied.

Terri gave me a "you've-got-to-be-kidding" look. "I always consider it a personal affront when someone who's gay has such schmaltzy taste."

I was about to tell him that as far as I knew, Carrera was straight, but then thought better of it. I'd let Terri decide that for himself.

We were nearly at the back of the house when I heard a noise behind us. I whirled around to catch a dark figure separate from the shadow of night, like a ghoul rising from beneath the earth. I stood transfixed as Terri's fingers bit into my skin with a grip as fierce as ten scorpions, transmitting his terror through me. The specter clutched a piece of hardware capable of ejecting enough fire power to disintegrate half the neighborhood, pointed straight at our chests.

I abruptly raised the flashlight and leveled it into the demon's eyes, attempting to blind him to ruin his aim. But there were no eyes—only a large, black protrusion with lenses that jutted out toward me. The terrifying phantom sprang at us in a rage.

"Don't shoot!" I screamed, hoping it could hear me above the throbbing beat of Gloria Estefan.

The ghoul instantly stopped and lowered his Terminator-sized gun. "For chrissake, will you get that damn thing out of my eyes? Your flashlight is killing me!"

Tony Carrera stood before us dressed in a black wetsuit, skull cap, and night-vision goggles, holding an assassin's wet dream. I looked in disbelief at the M-16 rifle, fitted with an M-203 grenade launcher, as well as a silencer to tone down what would have been a call-out-the-National-Guard, earshattering blast.

"Holy shit, Porter! What the hell's the matter with you? Do you know how close I just came to blowing away you and your friend there? Next time, call out and let me know where you are. You could get yourself killed skulking around my backyard at night!"

I didn't plan on there ever being a "next" time. It was evident that Tony was capable of handling his problems all on his own.

"What are you planning to do with that thing?" I asked, grateful the dark gave me cover to corral my nerves. "Invade a small country?"

"Hey, listen. If that bastard is gonna come into my yard, he's gonna have to deal with the consequences," Carrera fumed.

"Actually, Rach, we could use one of those things in South Beach," Terri piped up. "You wouldn't happen to know of any discount outlets that carry them, would you?"

"Who are you?" Carrera pulled off the goggles and closely eyed Terri.

"I'm her sidekick. The name's Robin," Terri answered, enjoying the charade now that all danger was past.

I flashed Terri a warning glance and turned my attention back to Carrera. "Do you mean to tell me that Langer actually came over here and took one of your birds this time?"

"All I know is that another of my flamingos is gone, and I got a good idea who's responsible." Carrera stormed off toward his pond.

"He's definitely into some heavy S and M," Terri murmured as we followed. "Very butch."

We stopped at the edge of the water. On the opposite bank were twenty-four sleeping flamingos, each standing on one leg, the other leg tucked beneath a fan of ghostly pink feathers.

''My God! That's how I want to look in my next life. Tall, thin, and elegant. Sort of like a living question mark with feathers,'' Terri whispered.

Tony gave him a lingering once-over. ''You kinda look that way already.''

Terri lifted his chin, his fingers traveling the length of his neck as his lips softly curved up into a smile. ''They're absolutely gorgeous.''

Tony nodded appreciatively. ''I can tell you got a real eye for the finer things in life.''

''And how can you tell that?'' Terri gave his baby blues a slow bat.

Tony stood up straight and made an obvious effort to pull in his immense stomach. ''Well for one thing, you like my birds. And then there's how you dress. Real classy-like.'' Carrera nervously cleared his throat. ''By the way, I think it's Lula Belle that's missing this time.''

''Why would someone kill anything as beautiful as a flamingo?'' Terri asked, turning back to gaze at the peaceful scene before him.

''You must not be from around here. Let me warn you; this place is loaded with loonies,'' Carrera responded.

''Doesn't matter where you live. It's all the same loonies, just different addresses,'' Terri said philosophically.

Carrera nodded in agreement. I was starting to wonder where the slimy wildlife smuggler I knew had vanished to, when he reappeared.

''So, are you gonna go over and arrest the bastard, or what?'' Carrera demanded.

''Tony, you don't even know if it was Langer who took your flamingo.''

''He did it before. You damn well better believe it was him that did it again.'' Tony jabbed a black-gloved finger at me. ''You're the one that's so damned hot about protecting wildlife. How come you don't seem to care what Langer does? Huh? Don't you like flamingos? Or is there something else going on here I should know about?''

''Who is this Langer, anyway?'' Terri inquired.

''He's the goddamn certified lunatic that lives next door,'' Tony retorted.

"Langer owns the Electric Doggy Fence Company," I replied.

"Ooh. That's big bucks," Terri remarked. "There's even one of those in New Orleans."

"That's right. Kinda makes you wonder if the feds have been bought off, don't it?" Carrera snorted.

"All right! I'll go over and talk to him. But unless he's got your flamingo lashed to his grille again, or is willing to admit to taking it, there's nothing I can do."

"Well, you better figure out something to stop him or I swear I'll take care of it myself. Even if I have to lure him over here and shoot him for trespassing," Tony threatened.

I turned to Terri. "Why don't you stay here? I'll only be a minute."

"Yeah. Stay. We can watch the flamingos together," Carrera shyly offered, once more Mr. Sensitive Nice Guy.

"So, these reptiles that you sell to pet stores—have you ever considered offering an attractive line of accessories to go with them?" I heard Terri ask as I headed for the car.

I parked in front of Langer's iron gate, which was securely locked, and hit the buzzer, prepared for his booming voice to jump out at me from the intercom. But all was quiet on the western front. If Langer was home, he wasn't in the mood for company. There was nothing more I could do about Tony's missing flamingo tonight.

I drove back to Carrera's to collect Terri and hit the road.

"Whadda ya mean, Langer isn't there? I saw a van pull into his place less than an hour ago," Carrera argued.

"Then you must have missed it when it pulled back out," I informed him. "I looked through the gate, and there's not a vehicle anywhere in sight."

"I'm telling ya, he's in there!" Tony stubbornly insisted. "You shoulda just gone inside and confronted him."

"And how would you suggest I do that, Tony? The entrance gate is locked, and I'm afraid I left my handy-dandy burglar kit at home," I snapped.

"Hell! That gate's nothing but a joke. Follow me."

We traipsed across his lawn to a far corner of the wall that separated his property from Langer's.

"If a flamingo can get over this thing, so can you," Carrera declared.

I looked up at the eight-foot wall, and wondered what combination of drugs Carrera was ingesting these days. "That bird *flew* over the wall, Tony."

"Well, these arms of mine are just like a big pair of wings. I can hoist you up and over that thing real easy."

I stared at the pot-bellied imitation of a Navy SEAL standing before me. "What are you, crazy? You said yourself that the man's a certified lunatic. He's got a zoo full of angry critters over there! For all I know, Langer could have one of his cats loose prowling the grounds at night."

A vision of Fidel, Langer's guard cat, flashed through my mind. The cougar's amber eyes had sized me up as if I were walking steak tartare. Granted, the cat was declawed. But he still had very sharp teeth I preferred not to come into contact with.

"Don't be such a wuss, Porter. I thought wildlife agents were supposed to be brave—or is that just the men?" he baited me.

If it had been anyone else, I might have accepted the challenge. But there was no way I was going to take an overweight guy dressed in a rubber suit seriously.

"You're the one with night goggles and an assault rifle. Why don't you breach the wall and have a look-see?" I shot back.

" 'Cause that's not my job—it's yours. I'm a taxpayer and I figure this is part of the services I'm paying for," Carrera huffily replied.

This was a novel approach. "As far as I know, becoming a mountain lion's chew toy isn't part of my job description. If you've got a problem with that, feel free to file a complaint. Otherwise, I'll come back first thing in the morning and talk to Langer." I looked for Terri, but he was nowhere in sight.

"If you're looking for your friend, he followed the music over to the Bobbsey Twins' place next door," Carrera glumly informed me.

It figured. Terri knew that this way, I wouldn't be able to chicken out and refuse to go over.

"Is Robin working with you full-time now?" Tony asked.

I had no idea who Carrera was talking about at first.

"You know. The guy that was just here with you," Tony prompted.

"Oh—no. He only comes out on special assignments. But I believe he'll be retiring after tonight," I firmly replied.

"Too bad," Carrera said wistfully. "Maybe you could tell him that he can stop by whenever he wants, to see the birds."

"Sure, I'll pass it along—as long as you promise not to mistake him for a trespasser and shoot him."

"Very funny, Porter. Just do your job, and I won't have to be out here doing it for you."

I planned on doing just that—with each and every one of Carrera's shipments receiving a full and thorough inspection.

I've never been one to crash parties. I'd sooner track a poacher into an alligator-infested swamp, or take on a rough-and-tough cowboy who calls you "ma'am" and then threatens to hang you. So, I very reluctantly pulled up to Ramon's open gate.

The long, circular driveway was filled with a mini-UN of cars that included every pretentious model imaginable. It was enough to make any made-in-the-U.S.A. girl feel dowdy in her second-hand, straight-out-of-Detroit tin can. I parked my heap just outside the gate.

Lights burned bright in every window of the 10,000-square-foot Mediterranean mansion, creating the appearance of a house in midblaze. It was a toss-up whether to call the fire department, or to think of the villa as a giant birthday cake. If there was a blackout in the area tonight, I'd know why.

People spilled out of the front door like froth gushing from a newly uncorked bottle of champagne. Some gathered in groups, while others headed around to the back of the house. I joined those on the move, hoping to be invisible amidst the crowd, in which I stood out like a daisy among a bouquet of exotic flowers. Surrounded by drop-dead-gorgeous models, I wondered what penance I could pay to come back looking like them in my next life.

My ego took another dive as the Vallardes's patio came into view. Festive lights had been slung around the poolside replicas of the Venus de Milo, Michelangelo's David, and the remaining chorus line of life-size plaster nudes. But it was the other nudes, sans lights, that drew my attention. A number of them moved in and out of the pool, boasting hard bodies that had been sculpted by the most highly skilled professional hands. Terri was right: when gravity hits, forget the gym. Go immediately under the knife.

A perfectly built waiter passed by dressed only in a slim gold thong, a tray of champagne flutes delicately balanced on his hand. I took one and silently toasted the glory of tight buns.

Neither Elena nor Ramon were in sight, and I hoped I could quickly find Terri and vamoose. If we weren't thrown out for gate-crashing, it would be for wearing too much clothing.

A tempting aroma snuck up from behind and I turned to see a tray of food passing by. Figuring I needed to keep up my energy, I grabbed a crab puff that tasted so good, I latched on to another. I was considering just following the tray, when a couple of wildly flamboyant dresses off in the distance caught my eye. The outfits were a rainbow swirl of colors decorated with layers of flounces, ribbons, and lace. The dancing duo was either a couple of cross-dressing peacocks, or else Sophie and Lucinda had been invited to the party.

I stood on my tiptoes, trying to see over the sea of heads, when a Tito Puente song swept everyone up into a wild dance, blocking the two women from my view. I worked my way through the crowd with a New York shuffle: an elbow here, a hip thrust out there—then slide, slide, slide. I was nearly halfway through the mob when I bumped into Terri.

"Rach! You made it!" He gaily flagged down a waiter, who produced two glasses of freshly poured champagne.

"Did I have any other choice?" I handed the nearly nude beefcake my first partially drained glass.

"Not really." Terri clinked his champagne flute against mine, and raised his face to the night sky. A slight breeze ruffled his blonde hair, which curled gracefully about his face. "Pinch me, Rach. I think I've died and gone to heaven!"

"You said the same thing at the Havana Club," I reminded him.

Terri beamed at a muscled Adonis who returned his smile. It was Ricardo, the model Elena had been photographing the first time I'd stopped by. Flaunting his torso in a shrunken muscle T-shirt, Ricardo flexed a bicep at Terri, followed up by a wink of his pec.

"You're right, I did." Terri gave a satisfied sigh. "Isn't life wonderful?"

"Have you seen Lucinda and Sophie?" I asked, looking around.

"Why would they be here?" Terri shrugged off my question. "After all, we weren't invited. What makes you think they were?"

I didn't put it past my landladies to crash a party. Still, I supposed there could be two other women who dressed as wild-and-wackily as Lucinda and Sophie.

"Listen, Ter. I really think we ought to get out of here before either Ramon or Elena catches us."

"I'm afraid it's too late for that," Terri remarked under his breath.

A hand intimately wound around my waist, giving me an electrical volt of sheer, unadulterated pleasure.

"Raquel. I was hoping you would come." Ramon's breath seductively tickled my ear. "I have so much yet to teach you."

Ramon was draped in a pair of charcoal linen pants and a gray silk shirt, pale as a puff of smoke. The soft fabric was unbuttoned to reveal a chest as deliciously smooth and brown as rich cocoa butter. His jet black hair, pulled back in its signature ponytail, hung damp against his head. I realized he must have been one of the nudes swimming in the pool. Droplets of water still clung to his face as he leaned in toward me and lifted my hand to his lips, so that moisture sizzled against my skin.

My brain reined in my hormones. Who did this guy think he was trying to kid? He hadn't even invited me to his damn party!

But Ramon gave my champagne to Terri and pulled me in tight as the music turned into a beguiling tango.

No way! my head yelled. My body didn't care.

Ramon's voice seared passionately through me as his hips swayed suggestively against mine. "Your progress has been wonderful so far, Raquel. Let us celebrate by vowing to make this evening special—I promise that tonight will be like no other. Everything you've learned has helped to prepare you for this moment. I believe you're now ready to take on the Grand Master.'' Ramon swept me back into a deep dip, his lips zeroing in to burn between my breasts.

I was up and out of the dip faster than you could say ''giddyap,'' Ramon's lips still plastered against my chest.

''What are you celebrating this evening?'' I asked breathlessly.

''Nothing special; it's only a party.'' Ramon's fingers slowly massaged my back, seductively moving down from my neck, past my shoulder blades, until they were well on their way toward uninvited territory.

It was time for me to turn on the charm. ''Everything you do is special, Ramon. Though I must admit when I saw the festivities, I was hoping your father might have been released from prison.'' My fingers gently did their own dance along the nape of his neck. ''What was he doing inside Cuba, anyway? I thought he came to Miami with you and your sister.''

Ramon's fingers came to a dead halt. ''He did,'' he tersely replied. ''However, my father was lured back to the homeland only to be jailed in a government conspiracy.''

I softly brushed my lips against his ear, keeping my voice soothingly low. ''How terrible for you! Though I'm sure you know rumor says your father was caught hauling rockets into Cuba. In fact, there are those who say he was the founder of the terrorist group, Omega-12.''

Ramon snorted contemptuously. ''That is totally ridiculous; it is Castro who is the terrorist. Don't you find it interesting that no one ever bothers to mention that little detail?''

I wanted to play out a hunch that was growing nearly as hot as Ramon's hands. ''Absolutely,'' I whispered seductively. ''But what's even more interesting, is that there are those who claim you've stepped in and taken over as Omega-12's leader, filling your father's place.''

Ramon's skin paled to a light shade of beige. ''There are people who will say almost anything to have something to gossip about. What you've heard is totally false. I suggest you not believe what everyone tells you.''

Ramon glanced around, and I followed his gaze to Elena, playing queen bee to a fawning circle of male models. Tonight's attire consisted of a teensy-weensy leopard-print bikini that was barely covered by a white, see-through dress. Stiletto-heeled mules stabbed the ground where she walked. Elena's phosphorescent hair glowed nearly as brightly as the Japanese lanterns that littered the trees, her tresses teased into a glorious lion's mane, so that I expected her to throw back her head and let out a roar.

"Please forgive me for a moment. There is something I must see to," Ramon courteously excused himself.

He turned on his heel and glided away toward Elena. Ramon whispered in her ear, and I guessed that I was about to be approached by a couple of burly hunks and quietly escorted out of the party. But Elena just pivoted and sinuously wrapped her arms around her brother, as the two melted into a slow and torrid dance.

Apparently, I'd had a stay of execution. I wandered deeper through the crowd and soon I stood at the fringe of partygoers, near the rear of the estate. A thick grove of banana trees cast shadows on the caretaker's cottage, beckoning from beneath its haven of palms.

I'd noticed Miguel, the caretaker, on the far side of the lawn, drinking beer and playing cards with a group of elderly Cuban men who were well on their way to being soused.

I melted among the shadows and was soon standing in front of the cottage door.

I don't know what I expected to find inside—an illegal stash of firearms; grizzled old men plotting an overthrow; maybe just Miguel's memories of the home he'd left far behind. But as I turned the knob and slipped inside, the awakening shrieks of at least fifty young birds greeted my entrance. I quickly closed the door and pressed my back against it, hoping the sound had been covered by the blasting salsa.

Sitting on two long tables were fifty small metal cages, stacked five high. I stood mesmerized at the sight of a hundred wings fluttering in the air, keeping pace with the pounding of fifty tiny beating hearts, all wrapped in an explosion of electrically charged colors. Each tiny green bundle of feathers had a throat that was dabbed with a touch of red: Cuban Amazons.

Then a glimmer of cobalt blue caught my eye. I glanced up at the higher cages, where pale yellow rings surrounding starry black irises hungrily glared down at me. Either Ramon was secretly subbing as Dr. Dolittle, or these flashy, exotic creatures were extremely valuable, critically endangered, and highly illegal baby hyacinth macaws. I had stumbled upon a mini–Fort Knox of endangered birds. And this was only the first room.

The sane thing would be to leave before I was found, and get hold of a search warrant. But Carlos had kicked me off the case, and I'd be damned if I'd see all my hard work handed to somebody else.

I opened the next door and entered a temperate room, soothingly quiet after the racket of the nursery. A Formica counter ran along its length, where plastic buckets sat neatly lined up like pretty maids, all in a row. I tiptoed over, not daring to make a sound as I peeked inside, and found exactly what I had suspected. Each tub served as a nesting box, its bottom thickly lined with soft cotton towels, its occupants scrawny balls of fluff that lay curled up together. Dozens of week-old nestlings slept peacefully. I wondered if these babies ever dreamed of having been snatched from their jungle home.

Above a stainless-steel sink a hand-lettered sign read, A DIRTY BIRD IS A SICK BIRD. In the basin were a number of small plastic syringes without needles, and a bowl filled with a semiliquid mixture. All the chicks, the nestlings as well as those in the nursery, had to be hand fed every two hours. Suddenly, Miguel's title of caretaker took on a whole new meaning. The old man clearly had his work cut out for him.

There was one more closed door. I walked into a small, dark room that was considerably warmer than either of the other two. Flicking on the light, I saw two high-tech incubators, fully loaded and set to bake and hatch.

I leaned down and counted forty-five eggs in all, each glossy surface about two inches long and an inch and a half in diameter: endangered hyacinths. After my earlier airport egg fiasco, I'd trained myself to recognize a hyacinth egg on sight. The rest of the room was bare, except for empty plastic bird carriers that stood like a sixties pop-art monument in the corner, ready and waiting to be used.

The incubators were set at ninety-nine degrees. Besides feeding the birds, Miguel would have to frequently give the eggs a quarter turn. I definitely needed to get out of here fast.

Suddenly the chorus from the nursery rose sharply in volume, their shrill shrieks piercing my nerves. I didn't dare move a muscle, straining to hear above the sound of my blood's Morse-code warning.

Then the door to the nestlings' room opened, followed by the sound of someone rattling around in the stainless-steel sink. I quickly flicked off the light, hoping Miguel hadn't looked at the crack under the door, then squeezed behind the stack of carriers and rolled myself up into a tight, compact ball. After Miguel finished feeding the birds, he'd be in to check on the eggs.

I passed the time imagining parrots in flight, their wings hiding me beneath their colorful canopy. With plenty of time to think, it finally dawned on me that there were no breeding cages here. Female hyacinths tend to lay only two eggs to a clutch, which meant that whoever had gathered the eggs must have ripped off at least twenty-two nests. Talk about the rape of the forest.

Having still more time to think, I added up what kind of money the uninterrupted sale of hyacinths and Cuban Amazons must produce. *¡Aiiee caramba*! The amount was more than enough to purchase M-16s, grenade launchers, and all the rockets Omega-12's heart could desire. I was ready to run out and call in the armed forces, when Terri's words echoed in my brain.

Elena hoisting an automatic rifle in stilettos was more than even I could imagine. It wasn't any easier picturing Ramon in cammo, swiveling his hips and smoking a cigar. But it was clear that the high-flying gravy train of birds kept the siblings rolling in their sumptuous lifestyle. At least I now knew who Alberto's partners in the bird business had been.

The door abruptly flew open, and Miguel marched in and turned on the light. I lowered my head to my knees and closed my eyes like one more sleeping nestling. But some tiny feathers floating around chose this moment to lodge themselves up my nose, bringing back memories of the night I'd walked into Alberto's, when feathers had rained down through the air. The struggle to hold back the sneeze became sheer torture. I was on the verge of raising my hands in surrender, when Miguel finished jiggling the last egg and left the room. I dug my nails into my palms until the volume in the nursery rose, announcing that Miguel had passed through. After that, I counted to sixty for good measure.

Then, I darted out from behind the carriers and hightailed it past the eggs, the nestlings, and the rambunctious babies. I peeked around the cottage door to make sure the coast was clear, then slunk back into the cover of the palm trees' shadows.

I was surprised to find the world outside still going on as before. Grinning lanterns winked at me as though they were in on my secret. All I wanted to do was find Terri and leave; then I'd be able to figure out how to handle the situation. The trick was going to be convincing Carlos that the owner of his favorite cigar store was heading up an illegal bird operation.

My search for Terri came to a halt when I spotted Phil Langer, still wearing those damn impenetrable glasses, and smoking a stogie the size of a Buick, among a mixture of hot gay boys, nearly nude women, and assorted pillars of the Cuban community. Well, wasn't this neighborly?

Ramon suddenly materialized by Langer's side and I pulled back, planting myself behind a hefty Cuban *mamacita* who turned and looked at me curiously.

"A jealous boyfriend," I whispered.

She nodded her head and smiled understandingly.

I peered around her, furtively observing Ramon, who leaned in close to whisper something in Langer's ear. This was getting curiouser and curiouser. Ramon stayed only a moment before slipping away. I followed his silky gray shirt as he weaved in and out of the crowd to disappear inside the house. My eyes flickered back to Langer in time to catch him give an imperceptible nod. It was almost as if a whistle had been blown that could only be heard by males of Cuban descent, as one after another broke away from the party to follow in Ramon's trail.

Finally, Langer glanced nonchalantly around. Satisfied with whatever he saw, he turned on his heel and also strode to the door. Yet another party to which I hadn't been invited. I took my cue from Terri: Instead of allowing my feelings to be hurt, I'd simply go inside and join them.

"Good luck with your boyfriend," my *mamacita* offered as I left her side.

I thanked her and moved on.

Inside, couples kissed and groped on the faux-leopard chairs and couch. This was not the party I was looking for.

I passed the kitchen, where a small army of caterers filled trays with scrumptious hors d'oeuvres. A large roast pig sat patiently on a butcher block waiting to be carved, and cooked lobsters were whisked out of a massive Sub-Zero. The ring of crystal glasses danced through the air as waiters scurried about filling drink requests.

A man in a white jacket and tall chef's hat noticed me and walked over with one of the trays to press a flute of champagne into my hand.

"It's Dom Perignon," he urged.

Of course—only the best. I left, unable to drink it, thinking of all the birds I'd just seen and how the party was being paid for.

I took my search up to the second floor, where I poked my head into Elena's photo studio. Though the room was empty, in my mind I heard the ghost-whirr of the camera and the popping of strobe lights. My imagination added the rat-tat-tat of Elena's stilettos. The tapping grew louder and closer—and I realized that she was actually coming up the stairs.

I ducked into the darkened studio as the rap, rap, rap of her stilettos raced closer. Elena flashed into my sight, then the sound of her heels receded down the hall. A door squeaked open. Then it slammed closed.

So far, this party was turning out to be one big game of hide-and-seek. I pulled off my sandals and quietly headed down the hall. Elena's bedroom door stood ajar, and I couldn't help but peek in. There was Geraldo, regally stuffed for all time, his jeweled collar twinkling like a galaxy of stars around his neck. Next to him sat Rivera, looking equally aristocratic. I wondered how many parrots had gone into the purchase of their neckbands. The pair silently stood guard over Elena's pink conch-shell bed, its contents tossed around like some disemboweled creature from the sea. Even the leopard-skin fur was thrown carelessly on the floor. I looked back at the taxidermied cats, who steadily stared at me. I hurried on.

Figuring out which room Ramon's private party was being held in was a no-brainer. I simply followed the smell of cigars. I tiptoed up to the door, wondering what excuse to use if it should suddenly be flung open. Wildlife agent in search of a lambada lesson sounded pretty far off the mark.

I heard the distinct murmur of voices, but couldn't make out any of the words. Damn! Then I looked at the champagne glass I held in my hand. I quickly dumped the pricey Dom Perignon inside a vase of flowers, crept back, and held the rim of the glass up against the door. Next time I'd plan ahead, and ask for my champagne to be poured into a tumbler. Working with what I had, I pressed my ear tightly against the flute's crystal base. The jumble turned into words, though I could still only hear a few clearly. Nearly all the voices had Cuban accents, except for one heavy bass. There wasn't much doubt as to whom that belonged.

From what I picked up, the conversation focused mainly on coins and the weather. Remembering where I'd heard the term "coins" before, I pressed the flute harder against the door.

The talk had turned to hotels in Havana, and Willy Weed's name was mentioned. But my nerves didn't stand up in salute until I heard Elena use the term "Commander." Ramon responded instantly. My fingers began to shake uncontrollably, and the flute slipped from my hand.

My heart contracted in horror as the glass somersaulted into a 360-degree spin, producing a flurry of rainbows that flew up into the air, splattered against the walls, and were locked forever in my eyes. I fell to my knees as I followed the descending glass and my left hand flew out, still tightly clutching my sandals.

Plop!

The champagne flute landed in the cushioned valley where the shoes met, delicately balancing for one crystal-clear second, before it slid off and headed again for the floor. This time, I neatly caught the stem in my right hand just before it hit the ground.

I didn't wait to see if anyone came to investigate the thump of my fall; I jumped up and ran down the hall, dodging into the first open space I found. Geraldo and Rivera gave me a ghostly growl.

"Oh, shut up!" I hissed.

I waited a few moments and then took a peek into the hall, but there wasn't a sound. After a full minute passed, I quickly descended the stairs, past the scrutinizing eyes of Elena's ceramic zoo, beyond the bustling kitchen, and out the back door into mambo land.

A waiter stopped to offer a glass of champagne. I must have looked as if I needed it. I not only accepted; I drank it all down.

Langer was clearly involved with whatever was going on—I just hadn't figured out what that was, yet. Since smuggled parrots were being hidden here, though, I wondered if something else might be cached at Langer's house. With Langer occupied upstairs, this was the best opportunity I'd ever have to scope it out.

I quickly hunted down Terri, who was easy to find: all I had to do was look for the hottest male model.

"Hey, I remember you. Aren't you that model Elena fired?" Ricardo ran a hand lovingly over his washboard abs.

"Yeah, that's me," I replied, and turned my attention to Terri. "I have to run next door. That's where I'll be, if you need me."

"A model, huh?" Terri grinned. "That's what I love about this woman. She's always doing something that surprises me." He gave me a peck on the cheek. "I'll be fine here. Just check back later, and don't leave without me."

I promised not to.

Eighteen

I pulled up to find Carrera's gate locked for the night. Since this was the man who'd said I shouldn't let a secured entrance stop me, I took him up on his advice and played a rousing one-fingered rendition of the "Star Spangled Banner" on his intercom buzzer.

Tony was right; persistence did pay off. I was only halfway through the anthem when he finally responded.

"Who the hell is this? And what's the matter with you, anyway? Stop that goddamn buzzing! Otherwise, I got a gun and I gotta tell ya I enjoy using it!"

"Right now I'm feeling the same way. Open the gate, Tony. I need to come in."

"That you, Porter? It figures," he grumbled.

The gate swung open with a grouchy squeak and I pulled up to the front door. Tony had transformed into the human version of a cockatoo, wearing a ruffled hot-pink shirt, white pants and shoes that matched. His synthetic toupee even looked as if it had a slight pinkish tinge.

"Planning a big night out on the town?" I asked, wondering what had prompted the sudden change.

A blush crept up Tony's face, turning his skin a shade darker than his shirt. "I thought I might stop by and pay my regards to the two Cuban plantains next door. You know. Since they're having a party and all. Your friend's still over there, isn't he?"

I'd never have taken Carrera for such an ardent suitor. "He's still there. But I need you to help me before you go anywhere.'' I popped open the trunk of my car, and pulled out my pump shotgun and flashlight.

Tony's eyes grew to the size of two Florida grapefruits. ''What the hell's going on here? I ain't done nothing wrong, Porter.''

I closed the trunk and walked toward him in silence.

A drop of sweat rolled out from under Carrera's toupee. ''All right! You win! I swear to God, I never planned to file that lawsuit against you.''

Tony was turning out to be a pretty okay guy, after all.

''I've changed my mind. I want to go over your wall,'' I explained.

It could have been the moonlight, but Carrera's eyes appeared to glisten with tears. ''You're really gonna do this for me, Porter? That's terrific. As far as I'm concerned, this squares us on that snakebite business.''

What a gem.

I followed the reflection of Carrera's white patent leather shoes as they beat a path to the far corner of the wall.

''Good luck over there. If anything happens, just scream and I'll call the police,'' he offered cheerfully.

Knowing Tony, he'd probably be partying at the Vallardes's before I even hit the other side. I waited for some assistance, only to have Carrera stare blankly at me.

''I'm not one of your flamingos, Tony. I can't fly over this thing. You're going to have to give me some help here.''

''But I got white pants on!'' Tony whined. ''You know how hard it is to get grass stains out of these?''

''If you want me to check on your bird, I need a boost over the wall,'' I said impatiently. ''Or maybe Lula Belle isn't that important to you, after all?'' If I didn't move fast, Langer's meeting would be over before I even got started.

Carrera cursed under his breath, weighing the pros and cons of the situation.

''Either we do it now, or you're on your own with Langer,'' I warned him.

I drummed my fingers against the side of the concrete wall. Time was slipping by, as well as my patience. I decided to escalate the pace by picking up my shotgun. Tony immediately bent his knees and interlaced his fingers. I jacked the pump's slide back, removed the round, and placed the slug in my pant's pocket, before settling my heel in the center of Tony's palms and reaching up along the wall. That's where I remained, standing on one leg like Carrera's birds, ready, waiting, and in position.

"Come on! Let's get going," I urgently commanded.

Carrera broke into a series of grunts and groans while he made a halfhearted attempt to hoist me. "Jesus, Porter. How the hell much do you weigh?"

"Not that much," I snarled. "Maybe it's time you considered taking up weight lifting."

"What do you think I'm doing right now?" he retorted snidely.

I ended up half-scrambling, half-climbing under my own head of steam, until I finally reached the top of the wall. Tony finished his part of the job by tossing me the flashlight, and then the gun. I turned around and shone the flashlight around Langer's lawn.

"Everything okay over there?" Tony asked, champing at the bit to be on his way.

I checked out the pens of large cats below. All the cages were full. "It doesn't look as if anything's planning to eat me at the moment, if that's what you mean."

"Great. In that case, I'll catch ya later!" Carrera said, and scurried away.

I double-checked to make sure the shotgun's red safety button was secured, and then threw down the pump. The faint clunk sounded like the fall of the Berlin Wall to my ears, even with the strains of salsa quivering in the background. I waited to see if any attack cats would come running, but all remained silent. Besides the music, the only sound was the pounding of my pulse, which beat with the intensity of a ticking time bomb. I waited another moment, then drew a deep breath and took the plunge.

I landed with a hard thud and rolled along the ground, and my shoulder smacked into the sharp corner of a cage. A jolt of pain raced down my arm, only to be replaced by the cold, clammy sweat of pure fear as a high-pitched, otherworldly screech erupted nearby. To make matters worse, a warm breath slithered along the side of my face, followed by a deep, guttural hiss in my ear.

I rolled fast in the opposite direction. If Langer's menagerie hadn't known I was here before, they did now, thanks to my new perfume—eau de terror.

I grabbed the 12-gauge cartridge in my pant's pocket, my fingers rushing to catch up with my brain. I swiftly slid open the pump and jacked the round into the chamber.

So far, so good. The bright side was that I hadn't yet turned into cat food. The downside was that I had to keep doing my damnedest not to. I flicked on my flashlight and discovered that the cage I'd bumped into held Fidel, his eyes as hot and bright as twin bonfires as he watched my every move, silently sending the message that he'd been expecting me. His body glistened sleek and smooth, every muscle tautly poised beneath his skin, to pounce at the slightest provocation. I was glad to know Fidel spent his nights safely locked inside that enclosure.

I surveyed his pen, surprised to see a bowl of untouched food on the floor. The clump of spoiled ground meat was as gray as a corpse.

I glanced back at Fidel. He silently stared at me, the shock collar pulled tightly around his neck, the teardrop scar beneath his right eye hanging as daintily as an ornament. It seemed strange that he didn't have a hunk of raw meat. Perhaps he was too old, and his teeth were giving him trouble. Or maybe he was on a food strike, rebelling against Langer and his collar.

But time was running out, and I had yet to get started. I darted across the lawn and headed toward the house.

An imposing structure, Langer's home was more fortress than residence, which meant the place was probably wired with a state-of-the-art security system. When it comes to electronics, I'm one of those rank amateurs who can barely program a VCR. I peeked inside all the windows, trying to spot the components of an alarm system. I made a full sweep until I ended up exactly where I'd begun, facing the back door to the house. There were no miniature cameras, no electric eyes with invisible beams waiting to be broken by hit-and-run burglars. All I'd seen was one measly alarm-system touch pad.

Its green light tempted me on with its promise that it was safe to enter. Well, there was only one way to find out.

I walked over to a window and tried to pull it up, not surprised to find it was locked. Next, I went to the door and pulled out my all-purpose, start a fire—clip your nails—build a bomb—pick a safe—pocket-tool to jimmy the door. But I gave the knob an experimental twist first.

My, my—wasn't this quaint? A man with enough faith in humanity not to have locked his door. Was this guy nuts? Langer's macho pride probably led him to believe no one would be brash enough to attempt a break-in of his house. Most likely, he didn't plan to be gone long. Beside, his front gate was locked. I braced myself for the angry howl of an alarm as I opened the door, but no siren went off. I entered and closed the door behind me.

I found myself in a spotless kitchen which tattled that Langer never cooked a meal. Not one dirty dish or utensil lay in the sink. The countertops, the cabinets, even the floors were spick-and-span, shining with military spit and polish. No wonder I didn't care for the guy.

The living room was decorated in Danish contemporary, the atmosphere stiff and spare. There were no pictures, no tchotchkes, no decorations—fewer signs of life than on the planet Mars. If Langer had something that was hidden, it wasn't in here.

Next was Langer's study. A photograph of an F-117A Stealth was taken against a setting sun, while another captured an A-6 Intruder in midflight. Then a photo of a Cobra attack helicopter, with Langer as the pilot. When he'd asked for my name, rank, and serial number, he hadn't been kidding. This was becoming more and more interesting.

Langer's desk held a few more photos. One showed Langer in the full military dress of an army colonel. I hadn't realized I'd been dealing with such an important person. I examined the shot more closely, only to find that the name tag on his uniform read HUGHES. Either Langer had a twin brother with a different last name, or this guy had a split personality. In the next photo, Langer had morphed into a captain in the air force whose name was now Morgan. Talk about *The Three Faces of Eve*!

The last photo appeared to have been shot somewhere south of the border. Decked out in military fatigues, Langer stood next to a camouflage-clad man with a pockmarked face. I did a double-take. Could that be ousted Panamanian dictator Manuel Noriega?

This definitely cried out for further investigation. I tried to open one of the drawers, but it was locked up tight. No problem; I used the screwdriver blade of my pocket-tool and jimmied the desk open.

In the top drawer, pencils and pens were lined up in strict military precision. Like tiny toy soldiers, they'd also been arranged according to color and length.

The next compartment revealed a pile of bills placed in perfect alphabetical order. I was beginning to think Langer had the organized mind of a top-notch serial killer.

The last drawer contained files. Eureka! In the section marked C was a manila folder boldly marked THE CANDY STORE.

I pulled it out and scanned list after list of orders, all dated, with each item catalogued and then methodically checked off. This guy had quite the sweet tooth! Langer's requests ran from radar systems to rocket tubes to gun pods and missile launchers. There was even a request for the computer memory of the Tomahawk cruise missile. Either his Electric Doggy fences were packing a mighty powerful punch, or Langer was set to wage his own war.

I thumbed through pages until I hit upon the most recent grocery list. In place of caramels, M&Ms, and dark chocolate, Langer had a hankering for M-15 and M-16 rifles, M-79 grenade launchers, .50 caliber machine guns, and 9mm Glock semiautomatic rifles. And don't forget the night-vision scopes and gear, if you please. If memory served correctly, this "little piggy went to market" list matched the items I'd found hidden in Willy Weed's pickup.

Talk about your strange bedfellows! Langer must have been ordering his weapons directly from Weed. All I had to do now was figure out where the arms were kept. I no longer had any doubt that the birds and the arms were somehow linked together.

I exited the study and headed down the hall, stopping at the first closed door. But upon opening it, I found myself staring into his garage, instead of a munitions treasure trove. I switched on the light. Parked next to Langer's Hummer was the same dark blue utility van I'd spotted the day Big Mama had permanently wrapped herself around Willy.

A rush of excitement pulsed through my veins. I dashed to the back of the van and wrenched open its door, only to find the floor as spotless and clean as Langer's kitchen. If arms had ever been stashed inside, their trail was long cold.

I returned to the hall and opened closed-door number two. My astonishment couldn't have been greater if a tiger had leapt out and bitten me on the nose. Instead of the standard concrete-slab foundation, this house had been designed with a built-in basement, its stairs leading down into darkness before me.

I've never been partial to dark, dank places. Call it a fear of spiders, the whisper of ghosts, a lurking premonition of death. Perhaps I'd read too many fairy tales growing up as a child. But to me, things that are underground tend to be evil. I hesitated at the top of the steps as the pull string of a light fixture dangled in front of my eyes, as tempting as any snake in the Garden of Eden.

You're going to have to search harder. Come down if you dare.

I turned on the dim light, and slowly descended. The steps creaked an ominous warning as I was drawn deeper down into the cave. I'd finally found the one area that Langer didn't keep spotless. Dust, bugs, and cobwebs reigned supreme in this subterranean den. Its concrete walls and floor hinted of an underground bunker. The odor screamed of rot and of hell. I held my pump tightly clutched in both hands and continued down to the bottom of the stairs.

There were no boxes, no covered piles, no secret hideaways in sight. Only a mop, a pail, and a fire extinguisher sat in one corner. Then my eyes fell on a mound near the opposite wall, and I knew where the odor was coming from. Long green legs were strewn akimbo, bent at angles that would have defied a master contortionist, and wings sprawled in a lackluster droop. The sullied pink feathers looked like a heap of discarded refuse. Carrera needed to do a recount of his birds: Lula Belle and three other flamingos lay decomposing on the cold concrete floor.

Then I spotted the final closed door, in the very dimmest section of the basement. A pair of invisible hands thrust me across the floor, as a large palmetto bug scuttled in front of my path. It was all I could do not to scream. I did my best to ignore the fact that the walls had started to pulsate and the ceiling was beginning to lower. I knew it was my demons up to their old tricks. Cautiously opening the door, I stepped into the second half of Langer's basement.

The room was black as night. But it was the sound that caused my heart to lurch to a stop with a sickening thud. From somewhere within the darkened confines came a dull banging against metal bars. My hand automatically felt around in search of a switch; the other held the shotgun up and ready for action. Every nerve in my body was focused on the unidentified noise, my imagination a runaway train with me as its only passenger.

Fluorescent tubes sprang to life. Their stark illumination bounced off the concrete walls to reveal a cougar's pen which was being used as a jail cell.

I stared, unable to believe my eyes. Two bodies sat bound and gagged, struggling to free themselves from their bonds. Their outlandish outfits immediately told me who they were: none other than Lucinda and Sophie.

My mind raced with a million questions. "What are the two of you doing in there? What's going on?" was all that I could gasp.

I got two gagged mouthfuls of hysterical gibberish in reply. My stomach turned as I spotted the bruises that blossomed on each of them. Sophie's arms were black and blue. Her hands, bound in front, were scraped and bloody. But Lucinda had received the real beating. A purplish lump the size of a small eggplant sprouted on her temple, and her eyes were red and swollen.

"Don't try to talk," I told them. "Just nod to let me know if you're all right."

Both women eagerly signaled and then went back to kicking at the bars.

"Don't worry! I'll get you out pronto," I reassured them.

I could try to blow off the padlock with my pump, but it

hung too loose for a bullet to rip it clean off its hinge, and fragments could ricochet off the metal and hit me, which wouldn't do any of us much good. I pulled out my pocket-tool and furiously went to work.

My fingers felt clumsy and stiff as I tried every tool in my kit. Still, the padlock refused to budge. What was holding this thing together, an entire tube of Krazy Glue? Sophie's and Lucinda's expressions had shifted from relief to concern. At my wit's end, I remembered the fire extinguisher in the first basement: I'd use brute force and *knock* the damn thing off.

The extinguisher proved to be heavier than I had imagined, requiring two hands to lift it. Leaning my gun against the wall, I grabbed the extinguisher and ran back to the other room.

I wiped my hands on my pants, then raised the extinguisher above my head, directly over the lock. The two women picked that moment to break into noisy chatter.

"I'm moving as fast as I can!" I said in exasperation.

Sophie's garbled rant rose another two notches, and her eyebrows furiously fluttered up and down.

"I'll have you out in a minute," I replied, my voice rising to match their own.

I brought the canister down with a grunt, giving the lock a hard whack. The next instant the lights were doused, and the room was bathed in deathly black. Worse, the door abruptly slammed shut, its echo reverberating loudly.

I tried to breathe, but my body was running on 100 percent adrenaline in place of oxygen.

You're not alone.

A low cough issued from somewhere near the basement door. Déjà vu reared its head, taking me to the night I'd stumbled upon Alberto's slashed and bloodied body.

My hand inched into my pants pocket, grabbed hold of the flashlight, and flicked it on. A pair of amber eyes shone in my direction, their glare clearly warning of danger. My hand shook and the light dipped a few inches, revealing a teardrop-shaped patch of white fur. My opponent was 140 pounds of pure, solid muscle with a hair-trigger temper.

As Fidel growled, I remembered that I'd left my pump leaning against the wall in the first basement. I was facing the cougar in the dark, unarmed.

I had no place to run, no place to hide. I couldn't even join Lucinda and Sophie in the safety of their cage. Fidel had every advantage over me, including the fact that he could see better in the dark. He opened his jaws wide in a petrifying howl, revealing viciously sharp upper incisors—but no bottom canines. Terror roared through me like a hurricane. In a horrifying flash, I realized *Fidel* had killed Alberto! The odd punctures on his throat, the savage gashes on his chest—they were the marks of a cougar whose only weapon was a pair of deadly upper incisors. And I was to be his next victim.

Fidel slunk toward me, forcing me back against the cage until there was no farther I could go. I quickly grabbed the fire extinguisher, aimed it at the cat, and sharply pressed down on the handle.

Whooosssh! A blast of CO_2 spurted out of the can, its thick foam billowing across the floor. Fidel jumped back and the women gave a muffled cheer. Then he stalked slowly to the side, aiming to circle behind me, and their cheers turned to unhappy groans. Fidel was already back in action, and this time he was p.o.'d.

Cougars are notorious for lunging from behind, sinking their canines into a prey's skull or grabbing their victims by the neck. A sharp jerking motion would break their quarry's spine; a suffocating clench on the throat would quickly bring death.

I nervously pressed down on the extinguisher's handle before it was necessary, sending another wave jettisoning through the air. Again, the cougar became spooked and pulled back.

My heart hammered like a death march as Fidel impatiently paced back and forth, his brain methodically tackling the problem. A second later, my heart sank to the floor. The cougar warily lifted his front paw, sniffed at the air, and gingerly lowered his foot into the marshmallow fluff.

A moment later, Fidel's glowering headlights focused accusingly on me, slashing straight into my heart. He'd unmasked my trick. He was ready to call my bluff.

My right hand headed up for the comfort of my Saint Christopher medal. All I could do now was pray.

As my fingers brushed against my shirt pocket, I felt something hard in it. My pulse doubled its beat and I reached inside.

Fidel laid his ears back along his head and snarled, his long tail flicking back and forth. Then he lowered his chin and tucked his body into a crouch—a green light that he was ready to attack.

I pulled out the small can of pepper spray Santou had given me. The next instant, Fidel raced through the foam and sprang up into the air, his body heading straight for me.

It's amazing how long a second can last. Everything stopped. Time, space, the very movement of the planets. All but that long, lean figure suspended in flight with jaws open, paws thrust forward, nothing on its mind but death. As I tracked his leap in the beam of my light I aimed the container dead-on for his face, and pressed down hard to release a steady, debilitating plume of invisible vapor.

The cougar screamed in anger and pain as the juice worked its way down his throat and into his eyes. One of his clawless paws furiously thrashed in midair, knocking me back hard against the cage. I'd breathed in enough of the pepper spray that my lungs felt on fire. But not as much as Fidel, who fell to the ground in a helpless rage. The cougar rolled around, trying to rid himself of the blistering red pepper juice, howling wildly.

With Lucinda and Sophie safe in the cage, now I could get to a phone and get help.

Then the door flew open and the lights flashed back on, to reveal Langer with a .40mm Beretta grasped in his hand. A chuckle worked its way around the cigar in his mouth.

"Well, what do you know? Three birds with one stone." He glanced down to where Fidel was madly rolling, his paws frantically working to clear the spray from his eyes, his coat matted with white streaks of foam. Langer leaned down and swiftly looped a leash around the animal's neck, lashing Fidel to the basement door.

"Pepper spray, huh? Very clever, Porter—if you were Cuban, I'd have recruited you by now. But you and your friends have become annoyances that need to be done away with."

"What do Sophie and Lucinda have to do with all of this? You didn't need to lock up two old women just to lure me over here," I told him. "All you had to do was call."

The muffled screams from behind told me Lucinda and Sophie would never forgive me for that remark.

Langer gazed at me in amazement before removing the cigar from his mouth, his chuckle turning into a belly laugh. "My God! You really are unaware of what's been going on under your own nose, aren't you?"

"What the hell are you talking about, Langer?" If the man was going to insult me, he should at least have the decency to explain himself.

"For chrissakes, Porter. These two crazy old broads have been amusing themselves by blowing up branches of my Electric Doggy Fence Company all over the South," he retorted. "I finally tracked them down right before they were about to hit my warehouse in Miami. *They're* the ones that I lured here. You're just an added bonus."

I turned and stared at Lucinda and Sophie, stupefied. But I should have known that Columbia, South Carolina, and Tallahassee, Florida, were unlikely spots for lesbian rallies.

"*That's* where those little flags are from?" I asked, remembering the ED on one of the cloth triangles.

"You mean they even stole my property markers while they were at it?" Langer boomed.

I still couldn't see Sophie and Lucinda as mad bombers.

The container of pepper spray lay like a lethal bullet in my hand. Langer had yet to ask me for it, probably figuring he could shoot me faster than I'd be able to mist him. He was right. I stepped forward and pressed against the cage, keeping my back to Langer.

"I thought the two of you were against violence!" I blurted at the trussed-up women.

Sophie managed a shrug as I dropped the tiny spray can into her cupped hands. I had no idea what I intended to do, but sometimes strategy works best that way. I turned to face Langer and his gun.

"Then *you* were the one who killed Alberto," I said, my mind racing to formulate a plan.

"No. Fidel did the killing," Langer snickered. "I just set the events in motion."

"But why? Dominguez was your linchpin. Wasn't it the bird smuggling that was giving you the money to buy arms?"

''Congratulations,'' Langer said condescendingly. ''So you actually had begun to figure it out.''

''That doesn't answer why you killed him,'' I retorted.

Langer studied me. ''You don't have any idea what this is really all about, do you?''

''I'll go for murder and dealing in contraband,'' I countered.

Langer bristled. ''What I'm involved in is a moral mission. We've been at war with Cuba for over thirty years. I'm doing what our government doesn't have the guts for any longer, which is to help freedom fighters win back their homeland.'' Langer's lip curled up in distaste. ''Alberto Dominguez went against the rules when he started smuggling cigars in along with birds. That was helping the enemy. Besides, it's against the law. What he did was morally perverse.''

I just stared. This lunatic actually considered himself a genuine, all-American, gung-ho patriot. ''Didn't anybody ever tell you that smuggling endangered birds is as much against the law as bringing in Cuban cigars?'' I asked.

Langer dismissed my remark with a half laugh, half bark. ''That's a crock. That 'save the animals' law was cooked up by a bunch of left-wing, feeble-minded, pro-Castro commies.''

''Gee, thanks for reminding me,'' I snapped. ''I almost forgot that the Endangered Species Act was created and passed during the Nixon administration.''

Langer cocked his Beretta. Someday I'd learn to keep my mouth shut.

''Then there's Willy Weed. You were responsible for his death as well, weren't you?'' I needed to stall Langer until I came up with a plan.

A toxic smirk spread across his face. ''There you go, blaming me again.''

''But Weed was the one supplying you with the arms. I don't get it.'' I hoped the opportunity to show off just how smart he was would buy me time.

''I suppose there's no harm in telling you, since you won't be around to do anything about it.'' Langer removed an offending shred of tobacco from his tongue. ''Weed had a line into DRMOs, which is how we get our arms. Everything went just fine until he caught the greed bug like Dominguez.'' Langer shook his massive head. ''Weed got out of control, selling military weapons to anyone and everyone who flashed him a wad of bills. He was even selling to your two friends over there in the cage.''

''What!''

Langer nodded in commiseration. ''That's right. C-4. Plastic explosives. Nasty stuff for two batty old women to have.''

Low roars emanated from the cage behind me.

''You were there the morning that Willy died. I saw your van,'' I quietly said.

Langer's eyes turned as hard as granite. ''Weed was getting sloppy. He eventually would've been caught. Tregler will be sure not to make the same mistake his buddy did. I won't have Omega-12's mission blown over carelessness and greed.''

''And just what do you get out of all this, Langer?'' I asked. ''Why's a gringo like you working for a Cuban paramilitary group, anyway?''

Langer chomped down hard on his cigar before handing me the last piece of the puzzle. ''I go back to the days when Tito Vallardes was Omega's leader. I was with the CIA at the time.'' Langer's voice was flat and hard. ''My job was to train Vallardes and his recruits for an all-out attack on Castro. Then came the Bay of Pigs disaster. The U.S. officially pulled the plug on Omega-12, and I was yanked out of Miami and assigned to the Washington office. Later I landed in Central America, where I worked with the Contras. When I retired a few years ago, I decided there was nothing better I could do than help out my old friends here in Miami.''

I opted for a tactic my first boss had taught me—when in doubt, go for the jugular. ''Don't tell me: you were available for hire, and they were offering to pay big time.''

Bingo! Langer's eyes flinched as I hit my mark. Funny, how greed has a way of spreading. For all his spouting of high morals, Langer was nothing more than your average paid mercenary.

''Tell me, what do Ramon and Elena think of the fact that you murdered Alberto to appease your ethics? Surely you reported that to Ramon. After all, he is the commander of Omega-12, isn't he?''

Langer's mouth twisted in contempt as he lifted the gun and

aimed it at my head. "Actually, I'm the commander. Elena and Ramon Vallardes do as they're told."

There was no more time for a plan. I held my breath and closed my eyes. But in place of the searing pain of a bullet, a pair of feet shot out from between the bars of the cell, smashing into the back of my legs. The force sent me flying down to the floor.

At the same time, a smoky voice thundered from the door, "Wrong, Langer. *I'm* the commander of Omega-12, and your job has just been terminated."

The deafening blast of a gun roared through the room. I looked over to where Langer lay dead, his blood mingling with the dingy suds on the floor. Then I raised my eyes. The feline-clad form of Elena Vallardes stood defiantly over his body, my pump shotgun fiercely clenched in her hands.

Epilogue

The sound of Sophie's paint brush was as soothing as a lullaby, its long, smooth strokes as steady as the beat of the sun. She stood back and let loose a dissatisfied "harrumph" as she examined her handiwork.

"Whadda you think? I'm not sure it's colorful enough."

I took a break from playing tug-of-war with Bonkers to look. The walls pulsated an iridescent purple, and she'd highlighted the shutters with a retina-burning tangerine.

"There's no worry of that," I reported.

Bonkers made a beeline for my fingers with a saucy squawk, his body tottering back and forth. Then he screeched, *"Yo! Adrienne!"*

I gave Sophie a questioning glance.

"He thinks he's Stallone. It must be all those *Rocky* reruns he's been watching lately," she explained with a shrug.

A trickle of laughter drifted toward us from the walkway. Lucinda and Terri had returned from the beach. Lucinda's gold-lamé bikini blended in with her tan. Terri followed behind, kvetching with each step. Lucinda now had us on a regimen of lifting weights and learning self-protection. I had to admit that her master-sergeant tactics were working. I could finally button a pair of pants I'd never worn.

Lucinda strode over to Sophie's side and wrapped an arm around her waist. "You've done it again. The colors look great."

"You really think so?" Sophie lowered her neon-pink sunglasses sporting dancing birds. She'd worn the same pair for a couple of months now. It was her way of mourning the deaths of Tallulah, Lula Belle, and Carrera's three other flamingos.

"I'm going inside to make power shakes for everyone. Why don't you take a break from painting and come help me?" Lucinda suggested.

"Do I have a choice? It's the only way I can keep you from overdosing us all on protein powder." Sophie abandoned her brush and accompanied Lucinda inside.

Terri plopped down on the bench, taking a seat beside me.

"So, how was the beach?" I asked, extricating my earring from Bonkers's beak.

"The usual," Terri responded. He dipped a hand inside his beach bag and displayed a turquoise yarmulke, decorated with sequins sewn in the shape of dog biscuits. "I've been checking the orders and so far this is our biggest seller. Definitely a must among poodles."

Then he took out a plain fuschia yarmulke, a needle and thread, and a container of bugle beads, and started to work on his next creation. "So, tell me. What's the latest news on Elena these days? Any idea how long she'll actually be in jail?"

Elena had been sentenced to seven years in Miami Correctional Center for Langer's murder. She'd told me the gunrunning charge would never stick, and had proved to be right. The paper trail had led to Langer and stopped there. As for Buzz Tregler, he was officially listed as AWOL, having run for his life after Willy Weed was found dead.

I was still awaiting the DNA results to prove bird-smuggling charges. Without having nabbed Ramon or Elena in the actual act, DNA tests were the only way to prove their birds had been caught in the wild. Not that it really mattered. In a city battling skyrocketing rates of homicide, heroin, and theft, parrot smuggling was a penny-ante crime. Add to that the Vallardes's political connections, and nothing would ever come of the charge, no matter what the tests proved. Still, at least the pipeline had been shut down for now. And word was out on the street: smugglers knew that Fish and Wildlife meant business.

"Elena will serve four years with good behavior. Maybe less," I told him.

''It doesn't really seem fair, does it?'' Terri remarked. ''If she hadn't shown up when she did, the three of you would be dead.''

That's exactly why we had all appeared as character witnesses. Funny, the twists and turns that our justice system takes.

''Have you heard from Ramon?'' Terri ventured.

I shook my head. If Ramon was doing the lambada these days, it was with someone else.

The brightest spot in all this was that Carlos had gained his share of glory, with his reputation restored and shining brighter than ever. After Langer had been shot, my first call had been to my boss. The second had been to the police. With no arms to be found at Langer's house, I had a pretty good hunch where they were stored. I also knew that the only way I'd hang on to my job was if I turned the information over to Carlos. Shortly after my phone call, Carlos broke into Langer's warehouse and uncovered a large cache of arms that had been ripped off from Robins Air Force Base.

Then there was Sophie and Lucinda. Their secret life remained locked away, buried in that deep, dark cage. The only demand I'd made was that their career as pet-containment bombers come to a halt. They had promised to retire.

Equally good was that Weed and Langer's critters, including Fidel, had been placed in reputable sanctuaries. That left only the parrots inside the Vallardes's cottage. Ramon had donated them to a number of reputable bird breeders, claiming that without his sister around, he no longer had the time to care for the birds.

I watched Terri fashion the bugle beads into a pattern of puppy-dogs' tails. ''How was your trip to New Orleans?'' It was the first time I'd dared ask since his return a few days ago.

Terri didn't stop sewing. ''What you're really asking is, did I see Santou and was he filled with remorse?''

That was the downside to being best friends. Terri knew me too well to be fooled by my question. ''I admit it, Ter. I'm curious.''

Terri stopped sewing, put the yarmulke down, and took hold of my hand. ''Are you saying that you regret your decision?''

I slowly shook my head. ''No. There was no other choice to be made. If Santou can't accept me for who I am, we have no future together.'' I paused. ''Maybe that's the way it's meant to be. But that doesn't mean I don't miss him. I thought for sure he was the man I'd grow old-and-gray with.''

''Bite your tongue! That's what hair color and plastic surgery are for,'' Terri chided. ''Listen, Rach. We're all looking for that special someone to connect with. But believe me, make the wrong choice and your shining knight can quickly turn into your jailer.'' Terri patted my hand. ''Besides, I wouldn't write Santou off just yet. You never know. He might wise up and come around.''

I shot Terri a dubious glance.

''In any case, I'm certain that you won't be spending your golden years alone. In fact, I'd bet my last G-string on it.''

''And what makes you so sure of that?'' I asked, a smile slipping across my face.

''Because you've got me,'' Terri said, planting a kiss on my cheek.

The sound of flapping wings made me raise my eyes upward. Above us flew a flock of beautifully free birds, their backdrop the seamless blue of a perfect Miami sky. Their wings enveloped my heart and I closed my eyes and wished them well on their flight, a feeling of peace stealing over me.

The Joanna Brady Mysteries by National Bestselling Author

An assassin's bullet shattered Joanna Brady's world, leaving her policeman husband to die in the Arizona desert. But the young widow fought back the only way she knew how: by bringing the killers to justice . . . and winning herself a job as Cochise County Sheriff.

DESERT HEAT
0-380-76545-4/$6.99 US/$9.99 Can

TOMBSTONE COURAGE
0-380-76546-2/$6.99 US/$9.99 Can

SHOOT/DON'T SHOOT
0-380-76548-9/$6.50 US/$8.50 Can

DEAD TO RIGHTS
0-380-72432-4/$6.99 US/$8.99 Can

SKELETON CANYON
0-380-72433-2/$6.99 US/$8.99 Can

RATTLESNAKE CROSSING
0-380-79247-8/$6.99 US/$8.99 Can

OUTLAW MOUNTAIN
0-380-79248-6/$6.99 US/$9.99 Can

And in Hardcover

DEVIL'S CLAW
0-380-97501-7/$24.00 US/$36.50 Can

Available wherever books are sold or please call 1-800-331-3761 to order.

JB 1000